SETTING
SAIL

SETTING SAIL

a novel

Grace Elliot

Covenant Communications, Inc.

Cover images: *Flag of the United Kingdom* © Ayzek, courtesy istockphoto. *Storm Tossed Ship* © Wallace, C, courtesy Hope Gallery.

Cover design copyrighted 2010 by Covenant Communications, Inc.

Published by Covenant Communications, Inc.
American Fork, Utah

Printed in Canada
First Printing: January 2010

16 15 14 13 12 11 10   10 9 8 7 6 5 4 3 2 1

ISBN: 978-1-59811-815-5

To my eternal companion, Paul,
To our children and grandchildren who inspire and delight me,
And to our ancestors who had the courage to embrace a new life in a
foreign land so that we might prosper.

Acknowledgments

First and foremost I would like to thank my husband, Paul, an amazing man, who encourages and supports me, often at personal sacrifice, so that I might pursue my need to write the stories that "simply won't go away." Thanks also to our children and children-in-law, Jarom, Carrie, Carly, Kris, Dionne, Joshua, Lincoln, Desiree, and Jordan, who have always believed in me and who have also provided me with a continuing source of inspiration and delight; and to our grandchildren: Olivia, Harrison, Evelyn, Ashton-Paul, Delta, Anika, Ellie, and Brooklyn.

A special thanks to Mark and Jacquie Palmer, whose kindness enabled me to step back in time, and to write this novel in the beautiful sanctuary of historic Annandale.

I express my continuing appreciation to the staff at Covenant, especially Kathryn Jenkins, for her confidence in me, and Kirk Shaw, for his editorial insight, inspiration, and unfailing encouragement.

V. Ben Bloxham, James R. Moss, Larry C. Porter, and David M. W. Pickup must be thanked for their diligence in writing and compiling their histories of the Latter-day Saints in the United Kingdom, all of which have given me the temporal and spiritual insight I needed for this novel. I acknowledge the diligence of President Wilford Woodruff in his faithful recording of sermons and events which I have endeavored to portray as authentically as possible.

I thank Rangi Parker, who has been a friend and mentor and whose relentless passion to preserve the history of The Church of Jesus Christ of Latter-day Saints in New Zealand through the Kia Ngawiri Trust has provided invaluable resources and inspiration.

And finally to Gerald Lund, whose historical novels have been a source of inspiration and who, in a few personal words, gave me the motivation to write my own story of The Church of Jesus Christ of Latter-day Saints in New Zealand.

Historical Preface

THE MID-NINETEENTH CENTURY HAS ALWAYS been a source of fascination for me, especially as I have studied my own family history. The time marked a period of dramatic change in England, Scotland, and Ireland. Industrialization brought progress and wealth for some while the masses dwelt in poverty and famine. It also brought an increasing spiritual dissatisfaction for the poor, who desired to worship God but were constrained by the religious practices of the day.

I have read many historical accounts, both personal and reported, of the lives of groups and individuals and been both fascinated and frustrated by the social and religious contrasts portrayed. I have been inspired by the courage and determination of those men and women who undertook a lengthy, and usually dangerous, ocean journey in order to begin a new life in the colonies on the other side of the world so that they and their children might attain that social and religious freedom.

Having grandchildren has made me appreciate, even more, the contribution my ancestors and other pioneers have made to my life. Without their courage and willingness to travel to the other side of the world, in extreme conditions, I would never have had the life I love so much now. My writing enables me to share those thoughts and feelings with my posterity so that they might appreciate what they have been given.

This novel is the beginning of my attempt to interpret those stories, and I have chosen to use a fictional basis for the story so that I might place my characters into relevant social situations that combine to present a bigger picture. When I first contemplated writing this story, I felt to prepare myself with more study, resulting in a master's thesis on how a minority culture expresses itself through its literature. I chose the early members of The Church of Jesus Christ of Latter-day Saints as being representative of those men and women who felt their own spiritual worth but whose desire to worship God and Jesus Christ was contrary to the norms of the day. Their determination to adhere to their beliefs often brought great suffering despite their joy at attaining religious freedom.

In the great surge of colonization, families became divided physically and spiritually, but their desire was always that they might be reunited—somehow, sometime.

Edward Morgan, Lauryn Kelly, and Ewen and Bess McAllister and their families became very real to me as their personalities and situations increasingly reflected what I had learned from others and what I desired for my own family.

Their journey has become my journey, and I hope that it becomes yours as well.

Prologue

Liverpool, England, 1849
The New Zealand Company

THERE WAS BARELY ANY MOVEMENT at all in the bottom-floor office of the New Zealand Company offices as Mr. Noel Thornton let himself in through the front door. Not even the squeak of protest from the hinges on the heavy oak door drew any response from the room's sole occupant, an elderly man whose balding head was bent over a sheaf of papers while he wrote laboriously on the top page.

"Ah . . . hem!" Thornton cleared his throat loudly so that his whiskers trembled on his double chin, but when that didn't get a response either, he stamped the end of his cane several times on the uneven wood floor.

"What?" The elderly man looked up over the tip of narrow glasses then scrambled to his feet as he recognized the visitor. "Mr. Thornton! I'm sorry . . . I didn't . . ."

"Hear anything?" Thornton set his cane aside to remove his gloves then strolled over to the man's desk. "You could have been burgled and never known what happened, Miller. What is keeping you so occupied?"

"Umm . . . the latest passenger list, sir." Miller pointed at the papers then shook his head. "It's a big one . . . for such a little ship."

"When your opinion is needed, it will be asked for." Thornton leaned across the desk and picked up the top sheet of paper. The bottom lines of ink were still wet, so he held it carefully away from his brocade vest. He took only a few seconds to peruse it before one eyebrow arched on his forehead and he almost nodded. He placed the paper back on the pile. Without further comment, he walked back to the front of the office and stood before the paned glass window, his hands behind his back as he rocked thoughtfully on his heels.

Outside, he had an uninterrupted view of Union Passage, which already, at eight o'clock in the morning, was teeming with life. Horses and wagons full of goods jostled for space while their drivers yelled at all in their path, and a growing crowd of people was working its way to the markets. In the last five years, Birmingham had become so cluttered with people that Thornton had become reluctant to walk the streets at all. Fending off small children begging was distasteful, but it was when their mothers were there with them, begging as well, that he found it most unbearable. So much for industrialization and the promise of jobs for the masses.

Thornton drew a deep breath then called over his shoulder to Miller. "I don't suppose Captain Bayliss or Dr. Appleby have been in yet."

"Uh . . . no, sir." Miller shook his head. "I mean. Not today. The doctor dropped by. Yesterday afternoon." He spoke in short, clipped sentences as if he were still filling in the half-line entries on the shipping list. "He wanted the list . . . immediately." Miller gestured at the paper on the table as if asking permission to resume his work, and when Thornton nodded, he slipped quickly back onto his high stool, his back automatically arching over into its perennial roundedness as he raised the pen, dipped it into the inkwell, and resumed writing.

With no other sound except the rhythmic scratching of the pen on paper, Thornton felt compelled to even breathe quietly as he walked around the office, reluctant to sit down although he knew he had the right to the finely upholstered leather chair that sat behind a large desk at the back of the office. Filling in for Mr. Joseph Phipson as the New Zealand Company agent while the gentleman visited that country on the other side of the world was proving more arduous than he had anticipated, and he was finding himself reluctant to move into the role he had coveted for so long.

He hesitated in front of a poster that had been pinned to the wall for as long as he had been coming into the office.

IMMIGRATION
TO
NEW ZEALAND

———————

The Directors of the New Zealand
Company do hereby give notice that
they are ready to receive Applications
for a FREE PASSAGE to the
TOWN OF WELLINGTON,
AT LAMBTON HARBOUR,

PORT NICHOLSON, COOK'S STRAITS,
NEW ZEALAND,
From Agricultural Labourers, Shepherds, Miners,
Gardeners, Brickmakers, Mechanics, Handi-
craftsmen, and Domestic Servants, BEING
MARRIED, and not exceeding Forty years of
Age; also from SINGLE FEMALES, under the
care of near relatives, and SINGLE MEN, accompanied
by one or more ADULT SISTERS,
not exceeding, in either, the age of Thirty
years. Strict inquiry will be made as to
qualifications and character.
Apply on Mondays, Thursdays, and Saturdays,
to Mr. JOSEPH PHIPSON, 11, Union
Passage, Birmingham,
AGENT TO THE COMPANY.

TOWN and COUNTRY SECTIONS of
LAND on sale, full particulars of which may be
had on application as above.

"Town and country sections on sale . . . if there happen to be any left," he muttered under his breath. "For anybody who is prepared to work till they drop till the end of their days in a primitive wasteland . . . a free passage to hell."

He stopped as he recognized the figures of two men hesitating at the front door as each bid the other to enter first. The older man finally opened the door and walked in, his barrel-chested figure made larger by the short, dark jacket he wore above heavy woolen trousers. A black-banded hat sat tilted sideways on curling gray hair that rolled above his collar. His stolid appearance was a total contrast to the tall, slender figure of the younger man behind him.

"Ah, Appleby . . . Bayliss. Good you could make it. Awful out there, isn't it?" Thornton assumed the role of genial host as he gestured the men toward two hardback chairs beside the desk. "Take a seat, and we'll get straight into this new list. Miller is just finishing it."

Miller suddenly seemed to acquire better hearing as he glanced up at his employer with a woeful expression then began writing faster.

"Morning, Thornton." Captain Bayliss made his way to the chair but stopped to glance meaningfully at a large glass decanter of whisky sitting at the edge of the desk. "I think I could do with a wee reviver after getting through that crowd. Give me a wide open sea any day to this rat race."

Thornton took a quick breath as he obligingly poured a small amount of whisky into a glass that was obviously not clean. Eight o'clock in the morning, and the man was already tippling. It was no wonder his ships were often late into port. He handed the glass to the captain, who raised it slightly to look at the level of contents then sat down shaking his head. Almost as an afterthought, Thornton briefly lifted the decanter toward Dr. Appleby, who held up one hand and shook his head.

Relieved that the pleasantries were over, Thornton walked around the desk and flicked his coattails behind him as he sat down. The chair seemed to shrink each time he sat in it, and he had to adjust himself to sit comfortably.

"Well, then . . . are we ready to send the next lot out?" He placed both hands on the desk. "Captain?"

"Ship's ready, Mr. Thornton. Had to replace a few crew this trip, but we've nearly a full load now." Bayliss took a sip that became a gulp, and he coughed slightly as he lowered the glass. "We'll be right to sail on the fourteenth."

"And I'll be ready to do the health checks from the twelfth onwards." The doctor shook his head. "I'm a bit concerned about some of the Scots arriving. There's that blasted cholera wiping out everything north of the border, and some of them are trying to get away . . . I fear they'll be bringing it with them."

"If you suspect anything, you get rid of them," Thornton said briskly.

"But if they've paid already . . ." Appleby frowned. "That would mean the end of them. All of their money gone."

"That's not our fault." Thornton made his hands into fists. "We cannot afford to have a ship riddled with cholera."

"Never." Bayliss lifted the glass as if in a toast. "I pride myself on a clean ship."

There was a long silence as the other two men stared at him. Of all the captains utilized by the New Zealand Company, Bayliss was probably their most disreputable, but he at least had the reputation of getting his ship to port at all costs, and that was what was needed. From the time the company had been started by Edward Wakefield in 1840, there had been a constant stream of migrants, not only from England but from Scotland and Ireland, often entire families wanting to brave the ocean voyage and start a new life far across the sea. Hundreds of thousands had already gone to America, and now the Pacific Ocean countries like New Zealand and Australia were proving equally attractive.

"So . . ." Thornton cleared his throat, "assuming everybody is clear, the only issues we have are the numbers of single men and women. It seems there's a growing demand for more young ladies to work as maidservants."

"More likely as wives." Bayliss chuckled. "Or nearly wives."

"Whatever." Thornton frowned at the captain's insinuation. "The condition is that they should travel only with near relatives or employers, but I believe that all are not as honest as we might require in declaring who they travel with."

"Does it matter?" Bayliss waved his glass. "From what I've seen, some of the near relatives are a lot less caring than they should be, anyway. They all just want to get away from this place, so why should we stop them just because they're short a relative or two?" He burped slightly. "My ships used to have everybody in together, and it worked well, but now we have to keep the women away from the men . . . just uses up more space and everybody's unhappy."

Dr. Appleby finally spoke up, his voice expressing his discomfort with the captain's attitude. "The voyage is difficult enough without us giving these people some common courtesies."

"Courtesies are not my prime concern," Bayliss grumbled. "I'd be better off taking livestock or cargo with me. They're a lot less trouble."

Appleby frowned again. "Yes, I believe they often are treated little better than livestock," he responded briefly, stopping as he caught Thornton's look. "But it's their decision, of course. We're simply there to facilitate their desire to migrate."

"Perhaps we would be well-advised to remember Mr. Wakefield's thoughts on the matter." Thornton used one finger to tap a small book on the side of his desk and raised his voice as if to deliver a speech. "The New Zealand Company has been set up to help build the strength of the British Empire. By colonizing these far-flung outposts with good English stock, we create little Englands all over the world. The aboriginal people in these places need the civilizing influence of the more refined English society, and the more refined need the working class to help them set the standard. The more workers we can send, the more successful we're likely to be."

He finished and tapped the book once more as if to reinforce his words, then he closed his eyes briefly as Appleby spoke quietly.

"Mr. Wakefield is also an advocate of social reform. He wants the working class who are living in poverty to have a better chance than they have in this country. They do have some rights."

"They can have rights when they've earned them." Thornton's voice was a low growl. "Our job is merely to get them to that point." He stood up and began to pace behind his desk. It was some time before he spoke, and Bayliss and Appleby sat quietly waiting. Even Miller raised his head as if disturbed by the silence. Finally, Thornton gestured out toward the front of the office.

Through the grid of small, dusty panes of glass that started at waist height, they could see a small group of people gathered around a poster fixed to one of the panes. It was a copy of the same poster that Thornton had studied just minutes before.

"Look at them, gentlemen. Men, women, and children . . ." Thornton made a swift account of the group. "And by the look of them, all workers, with hardly a penny to their name. They are all looking at that poster because it gives them hope for something they will never, ever have here." He began to rub the heavy gold ring on his finger with his other hand. "They may be all one family, or they may never have set eyes on one another before. They don't care if they travel together and, gentlemen . . . neither do we. We merely have to get them to their destination as quickly and cheaply as possible, and then they will have the work they need from our cabin-class passengers who have the means to pay for our services." He took a deep breath. "Am I understood?"

"Perfectly." Bayliss raised his glass to suck on the single drop left then placed the glass on the desk with a slight thump. "Load 'em on and I'll deliver 'em. Send them to me on the fourteenth. Good mornin', gentlemen."

He was already walking toward the door, but the doctor hesitated, waiting until the captain had left, pausing only to glance briefly at the group still gathered around the poster and then turning to walk away as well, shaking his head.

"Appleby?" Thornton asked as soon as the front door closed. He had had enough conferences with the young doctor to recognize when he had questions. Despite the annoyance of the young medic's desire to cure people's social as well as physical ills, Thornton had developed a grudging respect for him.

"Um . . . yes." Dr. Appleby gave his customary frown then raised one finger. "I'd like to clarify a small point, if I may . . . with regard to the availability of land, etcetera . . . in the colonies."

"Mmm?" Thornton answered cautiously.

"Well, I've had some correspondence with a fellow who migrated a while ago." Appleby cleared his throat. "It appears that the promise of land being available for these people doesn't seem to be actually . . . happening." He held up one hand. "It appears that the land is only readily available to those who are . . . well-heeled, shall we say. Those who are not so fortunate are required to work for a very long time, sometimes years, in order to be able to afford any land at all."

"Well, surely that's the way it should be," Thornton interrupted immediately. "Give too much to those who aren't used to it straightaway, and they won't use it well. Mr. Wakefield recognizes that they need to watch their superiors use the land first and learn from them, then when they can afford their own . . . they'll do much better." Thornton finished his explanation with a satisfied nod. "My word, yes. Excellent idea."

"But not what the people are expecting, surely?" Appleby persisted. "My friend is more than capable of running his own land but is quite unable to afford it even now, and it's been nearly three years." He shrugged. "Is the company, in effect, operating under false pretences?"

"There's no false pretence about a free passage to the other side of the world." Thornton leaned back in his chair and rested his hands across his belly while he studied the doctor. "There's land, all right. The company bought up a mass of it when it was started. The trouble is with the Maoris, the natives down there in New Zealand, and the blasted government that England has installed. That Governor Hobson organized for them all to sign a treaty where the Maoris can only sell their land to the government—which cuts our company out of the deal. Now, we are only able to get land as the government decides, and that ups the price. Someone has to pay for it, and only the paying passengers can afford it." He grunted. "They can always go to Australia if New Zealand doesn't suit them. There's more land there than they know what to do with."

"Mmm, I've heard that it's a lot more unruly there." Appleby raised one eyebrow. "There must be a reason the British government has sent all its unwanted convicts there over the years."

"Which is precisely why the company has concentrated on New Zealand." Thornton nodded happily, as if the conversation were on safe territory at last. "Such a small country and so much easier to colonize and organize." He pointed at a framed map on the wall that showed two small, slender islands lying in an almost vertical line. "What we are part of, Appleby, is a surging tide of colonization that is going to see the foundation of a small England at the bottom of the Pacific, and our job is to get people there . . . at all costs and as soon as possible."

PART ONE

Chapter One

Liverpool, England, 1837
The Isles of the Sea

IT WAS THE CURIOUS BLEND of pungent smells that fascinated Edward Morgan as he watched the activities unfold on the Liverpool dockside. A rich mix of ocean salt, tar, and sea-soaked wood and rope overlaid with the stench of humans and their food and cargo. The smell could be nauseating and overwhelming, but Edward drew a deep breath and felt a thrill of excitement at the thought of all it represented. For the last eight years he had begged to accompany his father on his trips to Liverpool to pick up raw cotton, and these were the smells of ships and adventure and of the unknown that he had come to love.

He twisted his head as a sudden, raucous shout sounded ahead to his left. Looking up, he could see a man virtually hanging out of a second-floor window with his arm extended, pointing toward the harbor.

"It's comin'! The *Garrick's* got it. She be coming in foirst!"

There was an instant response to his cry as people began milling around the horse and cart that Edward's father drove and pushing their way toward the dockside. The world seemed to swarm around them as the horse began to pull sideways.

"Wait up, wait up." Jacob Morgan clenched his fists around the well-worn reins and pulled them sharply so that the horse stumbled slightly, its hooves slipping on the wet cobblestone paving. The cart lurched, and Jacob impatiently snapped the reins, whipping them against the horse's wet rump. The horse obediently lurched forward while at the same time Jacob pulled on the reins again.

"Da, don't!" Edward steadied himself on the narrow wooden cart seat with one hand and put out the other hand to still the reins but only earned a sour glare from his father. He frowned as Jacob belched and the air between them became saturated with the stale smell of ale.

"The *Garrick*'s in the harbor, but t'other is roight behind!"

The yell seemed to incense the crowd, and even more people joined the mass pressing along the cobbled sidewalk. Edward briefly forgot his father as he held onto the seat with both hands and craned his neck toward the harbor. He could vaguely see tall wooden masts moving in the distance beyond the mass of ships' spires and rope riggings that bobbed alongside the three-sided dock. His father had told him on the way to Liverpool that some twenty ships were expected to dock that day, but he could not have imagined the confusion that was seething around him.

He glanced down at the heads and faces of the people pressing past the cart. They were all looking forward, intent on the scene unfolding on the murky waters of the Liverpool harbor. Again, his father rattled the reins and forced the horse to move as the crowd seemed to ebb and flow like a tide around them until they were out of the main pedestrian pathway.

"Stupid fools!" Jacob muttered as he pulled the horse to a halt and roughly wrapped the reins around a wooden peg at the front of the cart. "Wait here, Edward. I'll be but a minute." He quickly examined a handful of money that he pulled from his trouser pocket.

Edward's eyes grew wide as his father took a couple of coins and slipped them into the top pocket of his shirt. "Da . . . you can't use that money. It's not yours! You haven't paid for the cotton yet!"

"Of course it's mine." Jacob scowled at his son as he rubbed at the dark stubble on his chin. "I have wages due to me for this trip." He burped slightly and nodded briefly toward the building behind him. "You be here when I return. I don't want to be late getting back."

Edward watched as his father jumped down from the cart, stumbling slightly as he landed then clenching a calloused hand onto the wooden side-board until he got his balance. A quick shake of his head, then he covered the few steps to the sturdy redbrick building behind him and opened a heavy wooden door with solid iron hinges. As he wrenched on the handle, the door swung wide, and Edward heard a burst of loud laughter from inside the public house.

"I'll be but a minute," Edward muttered to himself then shook his head as he leaned forward and rested his elbows on his knees. "Like the last minute that took an hour, which means that this minute will probably take two hours." He couldn't exactly remember which trip it was over the last few years that his father had first gone into the ale house. He did remember the first time his father had cuffed him hard across the ear for complaining about waiting. That had marked the beginning of the first of many long silences on their journeys together. It was also the first time that his younger brother William hadn't been with them, because William had been ill for weeks with the same fever that had taken Edward's two younger sisters to their graves.

Edward breathed deeply as he clasped his hands together. That had been the time when he watched the kind, hard-working father that he'd always known slowly change into a sullen, uncommunicative man who spent more time down at the Arms Alehouse spending the few precious coins they earned on ale. It was also when his mother began to work harder than ever, bent over the cotton handloom in the house, silently crying when she stopped long enough to think about her precious babies lying in the ground a few yards down the road.

"There's no excuse, Da," Edward muttered to himself. "*We're* still here."

As usual, when he thought about his father's actions, Edward felt his jaw tighten. So many times of late he'd had to fight the impulse to hit his own father, especially as he'd grown to his eye level and then well past. At seventeen years of age Edward was already some three inches taller than his father, with broad shoulders and long arms and legs. Even the shapeless heavy cotton shirt and baggy work trousers he wore seemed to emphasize his stature. These days, few people looking at Jacob and Edward Morgan together would have taken them for father and son. Where Jacob had a slender, wiry build with a noticeable hunch to his shoulders, Edward had developed a strong, muscular frame from hours of working on the farm estate where they lived. He also took after his mother in looks, with high cheekbones and thick eyebrows that indicated some Nordic ancestry. The most startling difference people noted, however, was in the eyes. Where Jacob had hazel eyes, offset by red-veined whites and an increasingly pale, florid complexion, Edward had again inherited his mother's intensely blue-green eyes, whose lightness created a startling contrast to his tanned skin. And unlike his father's eyes, which seemed to mirror his every thought, Edward's seemed to reflect others' reactions more than his own. Despite his youth, not many people could look Edward Morgan in the eye, especially if they had wronged him.

Edward shook his head as if to rid his mind of these wanderings, then he slowly stood up to get a better view of the scene before him. He braced his legs against the seat as the horse shifted restlessly, but as it settled, he continued to watch the scene unfolding around and beneath him. The man who had previously called out had disappeared, and the initial disturbance he had caused seemed to have gone with the movement of the crowd. More and more people spilled onto the cobbled sidewalk leading to the edge of the dock where the ships were anchored. As the minutes turned into half an hour, Edward watched closely as each person executed their personal activities, while somehow the composite scene seemed to be a naturally orchestrated symphony of movement.

There was a constant clamor of noise and yelling as seamen on the boats contended with or cajoled the men working on the dockside. Large boxes and weirdly shaped cargo were hauled off and put onto waiting carts or into wheelbarrows. Meanwhile the huge ships seemed to wait patiently as their insides were emptied and spilled onto the dock.

Edward felt a surge of admiration as he watched one young sailor on the nearest boat suddenly haul himself up onto some narrow rungs at the side of the mast. Without hesitation, the sailor then began to ascend the wooden spire, nimbly picking his way up the rungs then climbing over cross masts and rope riggings until he'd reached the final crossbar near the top of the mast. He then wrapped both legs around the mast and sat on the bar as he fiddled with a length of rope. It didn't seem to concern him that he was many feet above the boat and the water, and when he finished his task he climbed down as quickly as he'd gone up.

Most of the boats close by seemed to be emptying of cargo, but there was also a steady stream of people walking unsteadily down the wide wooden planks that ran from the ships' decks onto the dock. Some clutched bags or dragged possessions with them, and they all seemed to be watching for other baggage as the sailors unloaded the cargo beneath them. The majority seemed to draw a deep breath as they set foot on solid land and stood still for several minutes, looking around as if unsure what to do next. A few were more decisive in their movements, men in suits stepping off briskly and heading toward the many shipping offices and freight agents' rooms stationed around the perimeter of the dock.

In contrast, Edward watched an ever-increasing mass of people gathering to the dock, waiting to board the ships. In this group he noticed more children and women along with the men, and their movements were more stilted, as if they were unsure what to do or where they were going. Occasionally, men in businesslike dress would usher them forward, shouting directions and pointing imperiously toward the waiting boats. Then the groups would shuffle themselves and their possessions along the pier, trying to keep family members together and placate young children whose patience was already wearing thin and who seemed completely unimpressed by the adventure they were about to embark on.

"At least they're going somewhere," Edward said to himself as he watched a young girl shaking her head vigorously and refusing to move toward the ship her mother was pointing at. "I'd swap places in a second."

He shook his head slowly as he realized that this was the main reason he still looked forward to accompanying his father on these trips to pick up the raw cotton from the shipping agent. The sights, sounds, and smells of the docks were fuel for many a dream as he lay in his small loft bed at nights.

"Hey, lad!" Edward felt a sudden impact behind his left knee. His leg gave way slightly, and he sat down abruptly, toppling as he nearly missed the edge of his seat. He swung around to his left to see who had spoken, but there didn't appear to be anybody close by except a woman chastising two young children as they tried to keep up with the crowd. Edward started again as he felt another tap on his right shoulder.

He turned quickly the other way and frowned at the man standing behind him who was openly laughing at him.

"Well, lad, you obviously don' have your sea legs yet. I thought you were goin' to take a tumble right then."

The man was quite short, his chest so barrel-shaped that his head appeared to rest directly on his shoulders. The short, dark jacket he wore emphasized the broadness of his chest and shoulders, and his legs seemed skinny in comparison with the rest of his body.

"D'you mind if I come on board, lad?"

"On board?" Edward's scowl deepened, his heavy eyebrows almost forming one brow. "Up here?"

"Well, that figures if it's you I'm askin', don' it?" The man began to move around to the other side of the cart, leaning heavily on a carved wooden walking stick. It was obviously the weapon that he'd hit Edward with, and Edward shook his head in disbelief as the man began to lever himself up into the wagon.

"Hey, I didn't say you could come up. Get off!" Edward made to stand up again. "Get off this cart, right now." He dropped his voice to add emphasis to his words, but the man simply waved his stick dismissively as he sat down heavily.

"Sit down. You'll be making a scene for nothin'." He tapped the front of the cart with the stick then glowered as Edward kept standing. "I said . . . sit down." The words seemed to rumble from deep within his throat like a cartwheel rolling over loose gravel, and Edward felt the command rather than heard the words. He lowered himself back down onto the seat, still staring at the man beside him.

"My da will be back soon." He nodded back toward the public house, and the man merely gave a short laugh.

"I saw your da, and I don't think he'll be back for a long while."

There was a brief silence as his words indicated that he'd been watching the cart for some time. Edward squared his shoulders.

"So what do you want?"

"A wee talk is all." The man coughed and spat onto the cobbles. "And you can call me Doyle."

"I will not," Edward answered flatly, but his curiosity increased with every movement the man made. It was as if the man didn't care at all that he wasn't welcome. Even the way he lifted his hand and tipped back the black wool felt cap on his head seemed nonchalant.

"Well, you can call me cap'n, but then you'd be lyin'." He chuckled at his own joke and spat again, this time a slight dribble wetting the gray-tinged beard that framed his face.

"Then what are you?" Edward leaned forward and rested his elbows on his knees, staring straight ahead but watching the man out of the corner of his eye. A sudden breeze carried a whiff of body odor and sea smells, and Edward turned his head to the side. "What do you want?"

"I'll be lookin' for a young'un to take on board our ship as a cabin boy." Doyle lifted his walking stick and poked at Edward's arm. "You look like you'd be a good one."

"A cabin boy?" Edward scowled. "I don't want to be a cabin boy." He shook his head, offended at being called a boy but also trying not to reveal that he had no idea what a cabin boy was.

"Ah, lad." Doyle closed one eye as he looked straight at him. "I saw the way you were smellin' the air and watchin' all the goings-on around you as you drove in and while you've been waitin'. You have a hankerin' for the sea, I can tell it . . . plain as day. You were born to be a sailor, and bein' a cabin boy is the place to begin."

"Well, then, you'd be wrong, wouldn't you," Edward retaliated. "I'm a farmer." He held up both hands, which, although young, were already heavily calloused. "I work the land."

"Ah . . . that's what you do." Doyle chuckled again, and it was the sort of sound that made you want to laugh with him, a deep rumble with a slight, high-pitched wheeze to it. "I'll be talking about what you want to do . . . what you *really* want to do."

Edward shifted slightly in his seat so that he was facing the sailor, suddenly wondering how he had gotten into this conversation. It had only been a matter of minutes, and the man was telling him what he wanted to do with his life. He glanced back at the tavern and in an instant could visualize his father leaning against a table swilling his ale in a large pewter mug, trying to drink away the thought that he was imbibing his employer's money. The image seemed to grow huge in Edward's mind, and then it wasn't his father sitting at the table—it was his own face and body, only years older. He swallowed hard and ran his hand over his eyes as if to obliterate the clarity of the scene in his thoughts.

"Of course I know what I want to do," he responded irritably, shaken by the image. "I just don't need to tell you or anybody else."

"Aye . . . you have no need to tell me." Doyle leaned forward, matching Edward's stance. "You have no need to tell me at all." He shook his head slowly and looked away toward the ships, seemingly ignoring Edward but making no other attempt to move.

For what seemed an age, Edward stared at him, but neither of them spoke, and gradually the sounds of the dock and all its activity began to grow loud again, intruding on their silence.

"What I really want . . . is to own my own land," Edward finally said quietly. "And plenty of it." He studied his hands again with the palms outspread, then he clenched them into fists. "I want to own my own land and not work for other men for a pittance."

"Aah . . . fightin' words." Doyle shook his head without looking at him. "But it'll not happen here. Not in this land."

"What do you mean?" Edward replied defensively, lifting his head slightly.

"You'll never be a landowner in this land." Doyle lifted one hand dismissively as if to embrace the whole of England. "There's no way you can take land away from the lords and all their inheritances in this country, but," he paused and rubbed his beard thoughtfully, "I've been to places where men like you own more land than the eye can see in one look . . . where you can't even walk a half of it in one day." He finally turned to Edward. "Men just like you," he repeated quietly.

"Like me?" Edward frowned as he visualized the estate on which he lived. It was a large one by county standards, but it was still not even half an hour's walk to the farthest field, and his family was among the poorest of the farm families. He shook his head. "How could that be?"

"Easy, lad. They claimed it. Put their name to it and work it now for their own." Doyle smiled. "I've been there, and I've seen them." He looked away as he pulled his cap down farther over his eyes. "And you could go there too."

"Go where?" Edward didn't wait for long before asking the question.

Doyle took his time answering, then he rested one hand atop his walking stick and used the other to point toward the ocean.

"Anywhere out there." His forefinger was bent and weathered like his face as he indicated far to the left and then swept his hand to the right. "You can go to the northern colonies or to the south . . . to the isles of the sea. There's plenty o' land there for the taking . . . if a man has the guts for it."

"For the taking?" Edward was doubtful. "You mean you can just go and take the land and it belongs to you?"

"Aye, lad." Doyle nodded. "You stake your claim, and it's yours . . . forever, if you want it. They be wanting people to take the land."

"Who's 'they'?" Edward was finding the concept hard to comprehend. "Why don't 'they' take the land themselves?"

"'They' be the government." Doyle gave a brief laugh. "And they don't want little bits o' land. They want our people to take them over so then they can say they own the whole place—all of the colonies."

Edward nodded slowly. He had heard some mention of the colonies when he was in the town of Preston some months ago, but he'd had no idea what the men were talking about at the time. "So . . . you've been to all these places?"

"Aye." Doyle tapped his walking stick on the cart floor. "I've been many times . . . north and south, east and west."

"But where was the best?" Edward asked impatiently.

"Best?" Doyle tipped his cap again. "It depends what you're looking for."

"Land, of course." Edward leaned forward impatiently. "Where is the best land?"

"Well, lad, I'd have to say I've found myself with a hankerin' for the southern seas. The lands down there can be hard on a man, but there's beauty there that . . ." Doyle hesitated and stared out toward the ocean with a clenched fist over his heart. "It holds onto your heart, that it does."

Edward was finding it hard to tell whether Doyle was serious, so even though he was fascinated by the man's words, he was unsure whether to believe him.

"So if it's so beautiful and so good, why don't you go back there?" He folded his arms and leaned back, his head to one side as he studied Doyle's face. "Why are you sitting on a dock in Liverpool if there are such great places to go to?"

Doyle took his time answering, and he finally lifted his stick and pointed toward the other end of the wharf. He jiggled the stick a few times for emphasis.

"I came in on that ship, and we'll be departin' next day to the isles . . . to Australia and to New Zealand. That's why the cap'n sent me to find a new cabin boy. The last one bailed on us in New York." He turned and looked Edward up and down, then he shook his head. "Pity . . . pity . . ."

The very sound of the place names seemed to strike a chord in Edward's chest, and he swallowed hard as he thought about what Doyle was implying. The opportunity was there for him—right now, if he wanted.

"How far is it to Aus . . . Aus . . ." He struggled with the word.

"Australia, lad." Doyle held up his hand with three crooked fingers extended. "And you'll be looking at three to four months at sea . . . on a good trip."

"Three months?" Edward frowned as he thought about three months on the farm. "That's a whole season."

Doyle chuckled as he shook his head again. "Ha . . . you definitely be a farmer. Maybe you should just stay here." He began to move himself to the edge of the wooden seat then turned back. "As for me . . . I be going back to the isles." He tapped his stick against his leg. "This'll be the last voyage for this leg, and then I'll get myself a bit of that land . . . live out my days beholden to no man."

There was something about his words that made Edward hold out his hand as if to stop him from leaving. "Doyle!"

The man hesitated as he prepared to lever himself off the cart, but he didn't turn around. "Aye, lad?"

Edward tried to speak, but the words seemed to stick in his throat, and he slowly lowered his hand. "Nothing."

Doyle took his time getting off the cart and then limped around to the other side as Edward hesitated then jumped nimbly to the ground. They stood facing each other, and although the boy was several inches taller, Doyle closed one eye and looked him up and down again.

"Come to think of it, lad," he shook his head, "I think you'd make a lousy cabin boy."

Edward did nothing to suppress the sudden laugh that rose in his chest, his whole face changing as he grinned broadly. He folded his arms and leaned against the cart. "That may be, but I'll be a great farmer," he stated boldly, and Doyle chuckled.

"Aye, I think you will." He pulled his cap more firmly onto his head and nodded toward the sea. "And maybe I'll even see you in the isles."

Edward stared after Doyle, and it was several moments before he finally spoke to the old man's back as he walked away into the crowd. "Not just maybe."

* * *

IT WAS WELL PAST THE time they were scheduled to pick up their cotton cargo when Edward finally made his way into the tavern to find his father. Immediately on opening the door, his stomach heaved at the smell and suffocating atmosphere. It was so dark that he found it hard to distinguish his father's figure, finally realizing it was the still form slumped in a chair to the side of the room. Edward tried to walk confidently as he crossed the room and shook his father's shoulder.

"Da . . . Da, we need to get the cart loaded." He shook him harder, and Jacob started, his hand going immediately to his shirt pocket. Edward could see that his father had been sleeping rather than just being drunk, but he still felt the anger rise in his chest.

"We've got to go now!" He hissed the words in his father's ear and leaned forward to pull his arm up. The sudden movement seemed to jolt Jacob, and he belched then pulled his arm away.

"I've no need of your help." His speech was slightly slurred, but Edward watched his shoulders relax, so he shook him again, this time gripping his father's thin shoulder extra hard.

"Now, Da!"

Edward's tone finally seemed to get through to Jacob, and he stood up, yawning, then ignored his son as he made his way toward the door. The bright light outside the tavern and the waft of salt air acted like a splash of cold water, and Jacob shook his head and growled in his throat as he pulled himself up onto the cart and slid over into the passenger's place. "The agent . . ."

"I know, Da," Edward muttered grimly as he strode around to the other side of the cart. "And I'll get us there again without your help."

Gathering the reins in his hand, Edward paused to take one final look at the pier. Most of the crowds he'd been watching gather at the boats were now on board, the passengers leaning against the railing or milling in uncertain groups ready for departure. The cargo had been dispatched, although more carts were lining up for new boats to arrive, and the steady stream of people who had been alighting from the boats was dwindling.

He drew a deep breath as several men approached the cart and was surprised when one of them smiled and briefly acknowledged him by tipping his hat as he passed by. Edward turned briefly as the sound of their voices drifted back, a curious inflection on the English he was used to hearing.

"American," he murmured to himself as he swung up onto the cart, remembering his father's observation of the accent on their last trip. He settled onto the seat and clucked his tongue to get the horse moving. As they moved out into the crowd, he looked briefly back at the closest ship. "I wonder what they speak like in the isles of the sea." He liked the sound of the words as they rolled off his tongue, and he repeated them quietly as the cart rumbled over the cobbles toward the agent's office. "The isles of the sea . . ."

Chapter Two

County Cork, Ireland, 1837
A Potato Poem

THERE WAS LITTLE ROOM TO spare in the modest chambers as Father Quinn, the Catholic priest, eased himself through the crowd of people.

He smiled at familiar faces, but as he made his way to a seat behind a long table, the smile disappeared. He hated these meetings, which had become more frequent since the government had tried to nationalize everything in Ireland. They said it was to help unify the country, but Father Quinn couldn't see that ever happening while an English government kept Protestant rule over everything . . . including the Catholic Church.

"Thank you for coming, Father." A small, wiry man leaned close so that Father Quinn could smell the stale odor of whisky on his breath. "Have you prepared thoughts that might be helpful to our cause?"

The elderly priest took a deep breath then nodded. "I have given the idea of a national school a great deal of thought, Mr. Thomas."

"Ah . . . but you won't embarrass us, will you, Father?" Mr. Thomas forced a smile until his cheeks made his eyes appear only slits. "You know what is needed."

"Indeed, I do." Father Quinn turned away, leaving Mr. Thomas nothing more to do than go to the head of the table and call the meeting to order. He had a small gavel that he banged smartly on the table several times but was met with little response. It took a loud bellow from one of the men at the side to get the attention of everybody in the room.

"Ah, thank you, Mr. Kelly." Thomas acknowledged the tall man in a gray, worsted jacket as he lowered the gavel and put his hands behind his back, under the tails of his jacket. "Now, we all know why we're here—"

"Because you think you can force us to do things against our will." A booming voice came from the back of the room, and Thomas's face ran white then began to flush red.

"And we won't." Another voice sounded. A woman's this time.

Thomas held up his hand as the noise level began to rise, but again, it took Mr. Kelly's voice to quell the commotion.

"This meeting is about our national school—"

"That would be your national school. We're happy enough with the hedge school. Our children learn well enough the things that count." A thin woman stood briefly as she spoke.

"Especially their Catholic creed." Another spoke.

"And the hedge school has served well . . . until now!" Thomas spoke far more firmly, his eyes flashing with determination. "But your children need more than to be gathered around and taught folk stories. They need Latin and mathematics and English—"

"The English need English," someone in the back said in Gaelic. "Let us keep our own language. We understand each other!"

The noise continued for a moment, and Thomas's expression gradually hardened. This meeting was merely confounded protocol—and the villagers were annoying him.

He raised the gavel again, but the priest beside him stood up before he could strike it, the crowd hushing as he spoke quietly.

"May I remind you all that this meeting is about education for our little ones." He smiled as he briefly considered his vow of celibacy. "Your children."

"But you teach them, Father." Another voice. "They're as much your children as ours. You taught us."

"Indeed." The priest ran his hand over a strip of silver-gray hair. "But you must remember that the government is giving money to school these children . . ."

"But only if they share with Protestants. We want our children to have a Catholic education!"

Father Quinn paused a moment, then he turned slightly to face Mr. Kelly, who was leaning against the wall watching the proceedings without commenting.

"Mr. Kelly . . ." Father Quinn inclined his head. "You have three daughters at school. Would it not help you financially to have more assistance, more books, more slates?"

Mr. Kelly took his time answering, then he spoke in a full voice that seemed to rumble through the room.

"Aye, Father. My girls are the most important thing to me, and educatin' them is what I desire most. If they need to sit beside a Protestant, then so be it. They should be concentratin' on their work anyway, not socializin'."

There was a low murmur from the crowd, then the priest nodded. "Thank you, Mr. Kelly." He hesitated before turning to Thomas. "I shall teach the curriculum you suggest, but I will make one thing clear. When it comes to scripture, I will not use the King James Version of the Bible. Holy Writ from Rome is all I will need."

* * *

"Lauryn! Lauryn, come quickly," Moira Kelly called to her second daughter, although she was only calling to the open air, as she had no idea where the child was. "Lauryn . . . I need you!"

"She went out to the field, Ma." Megan Kelly looked up from where she sat at a small dining table whose thick wood had been smoothed by countless scrubbings with harsh salty soap and a coarse brush. With a knife that seemed dangerously big in her tiny hand, Megan kept working at peeling a large pile of potatoes from the basket beside her. "She wanted to find Papa. She said she badly needed to tell him something." She looked thoughtful. "Or did she say that she badly wanted to see to something out in the field?"

"Lauryn always needs to do things 'badly.'" Her mother smiled briefly. "Especially if it gets her out of peeling potatoes."

"Oh, she did hers." Megan pointed at the pile of tubers her younger sister had finished before she raced outside. "She's just much faster than me."

Moira looked at her oldest daughter and felt a rush of sympathy. She walked over and touched her on the shoulder. "But you do things so neatly, Megan. You get every eye out of the potato." She picked up one potato from the pile that her younger daughter had peeled. It was much smaller because of the way the skin had been sliced off in chunks. "It's a good thing we know how to use all the potato scraps."

"Potato soup . . . potato bread . . . potato mashed," Megan sang then smiled shyly, her long blond hair falling forward over her face. "Lauryn is writing a potato song. That's probably what she's doing now."

"Ah . . . out with that tin whistle your grandfather gave her." Moira nodded. "I haven't gotten a bit o' sense out of her since he taught her how to play that thing."

"But it sounds wonderful, Ma." Megan rested her hands in her lap, her crippled left hand immediately curling into its customary fist. "I wish I could play it like Lauryn. She seems to have the tunes just waiting inside of her ready to be played."

"But you have your voice, daughter . . . as sweet as a spring stream rippling." Moira bent down to pick up the basket of potatoes. "God gave you the instrument you could use the best, and it brings us all a wealth of pleasure."

She turned away as her eldest daughter's cheeks warmed with the praise and she settled back to her task. It seemed unfair to Moira that her oldest daughter should have been born with such a twisted, frail little body while her younger daughter was well and strong and seemed to have the ability to do anything she set her fiery will to do.

"Lauryn!" Moira walked to the doorway and shielded her eyes against the afternoon sun as she called out to the expanse of green fields and bright blue sky. She took a few steps out along a rough pathway made of stones and stood by the low rock wall that marked the boundary of their house and of the few acres that was their family allotment. Most of the acres were green with the foliage of potato plants—the only crop that the small parcel of land could produce sufficient to feed their family of six—but one small field, lying fallow, was rich with long summer grass waving its yellowing tips in a slight breeze.

Moira smiled as from amongst the long grass she caught the sound of lilting strains of music, sweetly high and tremulous that, suddenly, made all the old stories of wee elfin people seem very possible. The notes were clear but hesitant, though as she walked closer, they seemed to gain momentum as the tune suddenly became louder and stronger and the notes more boisterous.

"Oh, Lauryn . . ." Moira murmured to herself as she watched her daughter rise from the grass and begin to dance with the tin whistle resting against her lips, her slim figure dipping and swaying to the sound of her own music. A thin cotton dress that had once been a shade of pale blue swirled against her body while the grass, catching at its hem, was unable to hold her. Her long brown hair that earlier in the day had been tied into a neat plait was now loose and tumbling around her shoulders.

Suddenly, two more heads popped out above the long grass, and Moira watched her two youngest daughters follow along behind their big sister while they held hands and laughed out loud. For a moment Moira kept still, then she lifted both hands and clapped them in the air. At the sharp sound, all three girls stopped in their dancing and turned to the cottage. The youngest ones began to run toward her straightaway, but Lauryn bent her head as she carefully put the whistle away into a pocket in the side of her dress. Then she ran with long strides through the grass, easily catching up to her sisters and running past them to their mother.

"We have a new song, Ma." Lauryn lurched slightly as her little sisters ran up behind her and grabbed her around the legs.

"Myra, Alice. Inside, now! I need to talk to Lauryn." Moira spoke sharply, but there was no anger in her voice, and her daughters knew it. They both giggled as they ran inside.

"What do you need, Ma?" Lauryn suddenly remembered her braid and attempted to reweave it behind her head. Without a word, Moira turned her daughter by the shoulders and began to braid her hair as she talked.

"'Tis a big thing I'm asking, Lauryn. I need you to take some food to your aunt. I've just gotten word that they haven't been eating much. Apparently, David hasn't been working after hurting hisself, and she has a new baby coming soon." Moira shook her head and the tears glistened in her eyes. "I should have kept touch when that David moved my sister away from here. This was her home . . ." Her voice trailed off.

"But, Ma . . ." Lauryn scrunched up her nose as a hair caught in the braiding. "It's miles over to their house. I wouldn't get back till well after dark is down."

"That's why you must go right away," Moira responded quietly. "You're the only one that can right now, and I hear they really need the food, Lauryn. We don't have much, but I need to help my sister." She spoke more firmly and Lauryn dipped one eyebrow in a frown but didn't protest further.

As Moira finished braiding, Lauryn turned quickly, her face suddenly lighting up. "Does father need anything at the smithy's? I could call in on the way. I was going to go down anyway."

Moira stared at her daughter. For some reason Lauryn delighted in going to the smithy's, and since her father often worked there when not attending the dairy herd, she used any excuse to go and watch him and Mr. Halloran, the smithy, working.

"I believe he could do with some fresh milk." She smiled as Lauryn began to walk inside. "But you must not stay long if you're to get to Jean's place in time."

* * *

THE BASKET LAURYN CARRIED WASN'T large, but it was well packed with bread and potatoes and some eggs carefully wrapped in sacking. In the other hand she carried milk in a lidded tin bucket. The narrow wire handle made grooves in her fingers as she carried it, and she made a game of carefully switching the containers over every hundred steps so her hands wouldn't hurt.

On the final strait of road down to the blacksmith's workshop, Lauryn caught up with the round figure of Father Quinn, walking slowly with his hands clasped behind his back, the hem of his long brown robe fluttering slightly in the breeze.

"Good morning, Father Quinn." Lauryn slowed beside him and took a quick step to get herself in stride with him, then she looked up at the sky. "Or possibly, good afternoon."

"I think my stomach is telling me that its afternoon, Lauryn." Father Quinn smiled as he patted his middle. Lauryn was one of his favorite pupils at school with her ready smile and inquisitive nature. "And where are you off to with all your goods?"

"I'm taking milk to Father, and then I have to go the longest way to take the rest of the food to my aunt." Lauryn rolled her eyes. "But it's very important because they hardly have any food, and I can get there fastest."

"Well, that is a big task, but I think you will manage it well." Father Quinn nodded. "Maybe you can recite your numbers or some poetry as you go along."

"I've already counted one hundred steps eleven times, Father." Lauryn rolled her eyes again. "Do you know how many hundreds I would have to count to my aunt's?"

"No, Lauryn." Father Quinn chuckled at her expression, which he had often seen in class. It was the face she made when she knew the answer but didn't want to be boastful in front of the other children, especially her older sister. "So how about a poem?"

"Oh, I've already written one this morning, Father." Lauryn nodded emphatically so that her braid bounced between her shoulders.

"Written one?" Father Quinn looked mildly surprised. "And what was it about?"

"Potatoes," Lauryn answered promptly. "Would you like me to recite it?" She hesitated then added gravely, "It is meant to be a song, but I haven't quite got the tune on my whistle yet, so it has to stay as a poem for a wee while."

"That will be fine, Lauryn. Tell me the potato poem."

She took a few more steps, her expression fixed in concentration, then she nodded her head and began to recite. Although she was speaking, her voice had a sweet lilt to it.

O little potato, so dirty and brown,
So dirty and brown and asleep in the ground.
Wake up and become some lovely dinner.
Some soup or some bread or some egg-milk dipper.
Wake up and become my fine Irish dinner.

She nodded as she finished, pleased with her performance, then she turned to Father Quinn.

"Do you like it, Father? I am going to write some other verses."

The priest took a moment as he swallowed hard, then he stared straight ahead toward the cluster of houses that was the village. After a moment he nodded.

"It is a fine poem, Lauryn, and it will make a fine song, too." He hesitated then rested his hand on her shoulder. "I should like you to finish the song for me, Lauryn, so I can learn it . . . before I leave."

She responded with concern, as he knew she would.

"Leave, Father? Whatever do you mean?"

"I mean . . . I'm going away, Lauryn." He shrugged his shoulders. "Far, far away."

"But why . . . and when?" Lauryn frowned hard and put her hands on her hips. "You cannot go. You belong to Knockacroghy, Father."

"Oh, a Catholic priest doesn't really belong anywhere, Lauryn, and he never quite knows where the Lord will need him. In fact, I think He may well have forgotten me here because I have been here for such a long time." He took a deep breath. "In any case, Rome has spoken, and I will be leaving Ireland by the end of the month."

"You are leaving Ireland?" Lauryn almost squeaked. "But where else could you live, Father? You're Irish."

"Oh, the Irish can live anywhere, my child, and I'm about to prove it.' He lifted his hand and pointed in a vague, southerly direction. "I am going to the colonies . . . to Australia or Canada or even India."

Lauryn stared as she silently tried to repeat the strange names. She knew of England and that it was over the sea—as was Rome, where the pope lived—but beyond that, she knew only of ships that sailed away and occasionally came back.

"Are there a lot of Catholics there, Father?"

Father Quinn smiled. "Not as many as there should be. The pope has need of priests and nuns to help teach the heathens there."

"What are heathens?"

"Well, how can I describe . . ." Father Quinn tapped his cheek. "They are people who have never known about the goodness of God and who have been sent away by the English government to pay for their crimes."

"Crimes . . . what did they do?" Lauryn's eyes widened. "Did they murder?"

"Ah, not half so grave as that, usually." Father Quinn shook his head. "I believe many have been sent away for very minor infractions, but they have been made to pay a heavy price."

"So will they like you to teach them, Father?" Lauryn looked grave. "They should, for you are a very good teacher."

Father Quinn laughed then, and Lauryn was a bit startled by the loudness of it. It wasn't the priest's usual happy laugh, which seemed to rumble in his chest and made you want to laugh as well. It was hollower, sadder somehow.

His laughter died away as they approached the solid frame of a workshop from which they could hear the rhythmical clanging of metal against metal. There was a shimmer to the air directly outside the building that showed intense heat even in the warmth of the summer's day.

"Does my father know you're going away?" Lauryn turned and frowned again. "He'll not be happy to hear it at all."

"No, you're the first I have told, Lauryn." Father Quinn put his hands into the folds of his gown. "But the others will know soon enough."

Chapter Three

Glasgow, Scotland, 1837
Sgian Dubh

"Skeee . . . skeee . . . yan . . . dooo." Ewen McAlister pronounced the syllables slowly and carefully as he lay on his stomach on the floor in front of his young son. "Skeee . . . yan . . . dooo." He held the long, slim knife just out of the boy's reach. "Let's hear ye say it, laddie. *Sgian dubh.*" He gave the dagger its proper name as the small boy leaned forward to try and grasp it. "The English would have you call it the 'black knife,' but you must remember you're Scottish and that it's *sgian dubh,* and one day it'll be yours."

"If he hasn't cut himself to pieces with it beforehand because his father is careless with it." Ewen's wife, Bess, stirred a pot of oatmeal and water more briskly than usual. It always made her nervous when Ewen brought out the dagger. The title of "black" seemed to fit the mood that usually prevailed when he held it.

"I'm not careless, Bess." Ewen eased himself up to a sitting position and studied the slim steel blade carefully before slipping it into its wood and leather sheath. "The boy needs to learn early of what is rightfully his."

"The boy is not even eleven months old, Ewen. He cannot understand what ye say yet."

Ewen stared at the child, who had lost interest in sitting and was crawling toward one of the two chairs in the room. With a delighted chuckle, he pulled himself up to a standing position and then rocked excitedly as he discovered the power in his short, skinny legs. At nearly a year old, he had finally grown hair that was a fierce coppery red and sat in tight curls over his head in an almost exact replication of his father's dark, auburn hair.

"Good boy, Jimmy." Ewen clapped his hands, and the little boy let go of the chair to clap as well but only succeeded in tipping himself off balance

and landing squarely on his rear. His face immediately crumpled, but his
father held out the knife and the boy's face brightened immediately.

"See that." Ewen glanced up at his wife with a triumphant look. "Even
the sight of *sgian dubh* makes him cheer up. Imagine how happy he'll be
when I teach him how to use it."

Bess said nothing as she lifted the pot off the cast-iron oven plate and
poured the mixture, still steaming, into two small bowls and one large one.
She then laid them out on the table and picked the baby up off the floor.

"I'm not saying it doesn't make him happy, Ewen, but growing up in the
city of Glasgow is a little different than growing up in the Highlands. You
needed to know how to use a knife, but it could get our boy into trouble
if he used one here." She settled the child on her lap and blew on a small
spoonful of oatmeal to cool it. Jimmy puffed his cheeks and tried to blow as
well but only succeeded in spitting so that the spit dribbled down his chin.
"You can see he copies everything we do; we need to teach him what will
help him in this life." She frowned. "After all, we chose it for him."

Ewen sat silently on the floor despite the rumbling in his stomach.
His wife was right. He knew it well enough, but the sight of his young
son growing up so fast and without knowledge of his Highland homeland
seemed lately to gnaw at his heart.

He turned the *sgian dubh* slowly then laid it in the palm of his right
hand and closed his fingers around it. With his eyes shut he could visualize,
exactly, the carved chevron detailing in the black ebony handle and the thin
bands of inlaid silver that matched the slim, thirteen-inch blade. Even after
three generations of use by the McAlister men, it was still as finely honed as
the day it was made.

"Do you ever regret leaving Crianlarich?" Ewen asked quietly, making
Bess pause as she spooned the oatmeal for Jimmy. Her hesitation brought a
quick wail from the child, and she continued feeding him.

"There was nothing for us there," she answered matter-of-factly, as
she was wont to do. Then she gave a slight smile. "Crianlarich served its
purpose."

Ewen raised one eyebrow. "To make us go hungry?"

"No." Bess sighed as she shook her head. "It served to bring us together,
husband. Or have you forgotten?"

Ewen laughed out loud as he pushed himself up off the ground and
walked to the table, pausing to kiss his young wife briefly on the top of her
head before he sat down.

"How could I ever forget the way you cast yourself at me?" He bent to
spoon the oatmeal into his mouth, suddenly realizing how hungry he was

as the thick mixture warmed his throat. "The way you were kicking up your heels in that reel so that I'd notice you above all the other dancers."

Bess blushed unexpectedly as she recalled the evening dance when she had done exactly as he'd said. The sight of the young red-haired Highlander had stirred her heart the moment she'd set eyes on him. "I never did." She concentrated on Jimmy. "You flatter yourself, Ewen McAlister."

"No, you flattered me, my Bess." Ewen reached out to touch her hand then shook his head. "I promised you so much then, but look where we are . . . it's a sad thing, and I don't know how to make it better."

Bess watched her husband's shoulders hunch and felt a surge of hatred for the men who had thrust them into this situation—who had made her husband feel like less than the great man she knew him to be.

"We may miss the Highlands, but they can live in our hearts, Ewen. And meanwhile, Glasgow has more to offer than Crianlarich, and who knows that there isn't something better coming along soon. We just have to be patient."

* * *

The wisps of young Ewen's breath hovered around him as the icy coldness froze them midair. He had long since lost the feeling in his nose, and his eyes were red rimmed, but he pulled the woolen wrap more tightly around his face. He and his father, James, the laird, Dougal McAlister, and three of the other clansmen had been out hunting for nearly four hours. The laird wanted the ultimate trophy, and they had not stopped until they found him.

The stag was amazing to behold.

Even in the mist, its dark coat seemed to shimmer, stained only by the blood from an arrow quivering from its heart and another close below it. As its sides heaved, the men moved in rapidly.

Ewen stared as the men gathered around the still body. Another swift plunge of the sgian dubh *into the heart, and the stag never rose again.*

As he stood back he looked straight into the stag's eye as it stared in a fixed gaze that would never move again. For a moment Ewen imagined the many sights those same eyes would have seen during the stag's life: the towering Highland crags and the lower hills, snow covered in winter and brightened with fields of blue and purple heather in the spring. He saw the stag running freely through the forests, running to protect its own life and that of the does and fawns it had sired, and he suddenly felt sorry.

He raised his hand and gently touched the fine hair on its neck.

"We're always sorry in a way, lad." Dougal McAlister spoke quietly behind him. "But we need him to provide for us."

"But he still looks so strong." Ewen's voice shook slightly. He felt the brief pressure of the laird's hand on his shoulder, then he stood still as his father moved to the animal and laid the blade of the sgian dubh *against its belly. The blade sunk into the hide, and he could see it move the length of the beast up to the ribs where it stopped. As the incision opened he turned and ran.*

It was some minutes before his father came to his side.

"It takes some people like that the first time." James folded his arms. "But we have to do it, lad. It means the difference between life and death for our families."

Ewen nodded as he wiped his lips, then he took a deep breath and straightened his shoulders.

"I'll be fine." He swallowed hard then stared as his father handed him the sgian dubh *in its sheath.*

"One day this will be yours, laddie. You must learn to use it well for it'll bring you honor when you can feed your family . . ." He hesitated and stared toward the south. "Or defend them."

"Aye, Father." Ewen took the knife from its sheath and gripped the handle firmly.

"I'll use it well."

* * *

"Aye, father," Ewen murmured in his sleep as his hand slid beneath the folded cloth that was a pillow and his fingers closed around the knife. "I'll use it well."

He woke with a start and half rose up as Bess moved beside him and Jimmy made a sleepy noise in the small wooden crib at the foot of their bed.

"I'll use it well." Ewen repeated the words as the images in his mind hovered then vanished slowly into the mists he had dreamed. He sat still for a moment watching his wife and son sleeping, then he shook his head. "If only it were that easy."

Chapter Four

Herefordshire, England, 1837
Hedgerows and Handlooms

Dusk was gathering as Edward and his father tied the last bale of cotton onto the cart. As usual, the bales seemed to dwarf the wagon and bulge over the sides until it looked as if the wagon and horse would simply topple over, but Jacob surveyed the load with a practiced eye and nodded curtly.

"She'll do." He had sobered up considerably while they drove to the freight office, and Edward quietly marveled at how directly his father spoke to the red-faced agent. Although his breath was still stale, Jacob somehow managed to give every appearance of being completely in command of the situation. Even when it came to haggling over the price the agent was asking, he managed to convince him on grounds of something about weight, and Edward realized he had negotiated at least the amount he had just drunk at the tavern—and probably a little more besides.

But the assertive manner disappeared as soon as they left the agents, and within a short distance, Jacob murmured something about keeping on the old Scotland Road then settled himself back against the backrest of the cotton bale. He was soon asleep, snoring deeply with his chin wedged against his neck and his hat pulled down over his eyes

Edward breathed a sigh of relief as his father's breathing became deep and regular. It meant that he didn't have to make conversation—or worse, listen to his father's ongoing criticism of the cotton import agent, the cotton industry in general, the state of the farm, or the silly young woman who was about to be crowned Queen of England.

"Oh, Queen Victoria . . . if only you knew how much you need my father's help to run the country." Edward smiled to himself, and the feelings of frustration he'd been experiencing all day slowly ebbed away. The sudden image of his father dressed in the regalia of the royal court and offering advice to the eighteen-year-old queen appealed to him, and he gave a wry chuckle as he addressed the space between the horse's ears in front of him. "But, on a more serious note, Your Highness, contrary to my father's thoughts, I would be interested in having the opportunity to represent yourself and the other lords in the isles of the sea. I think a medium-sized farm would do . . . perhaps, oh, a thousand acres."

He chuckled again as the horse's ears twitched backward, listening to him.

"Well, maybe two thousand, then. I would want to represent Your Majesty well." He paused and inclined his head slightly as if listening to the unseen partner in his conversation. "Well, certainly . . . I could leave tomorrow if Your Majesty desired it. I am sure the Lord Clitheroe could find somebody to replace me in the fields."

The smile suddenly died on Edward's face as he pondered what he had just said. Yes, there was no doubt in his mind that Lord Clitheroe would indeed be able to find somebody to replace him quickly and his father as well for that matter. The upsurge in the growth of huge cotton mills in the Lancashire area had seen to it that many of the people working handlooms in their homes were being done out of work. Much as Lord Clitheroe desired adequate employment for his farm workers, it was becoming increasingly difficult for him to pay the higher price for raw cotton and justify the much smaller output from his estate workers. The industrial revolution had brought progress to the English counties, but it was also bringing increased poverty for many of the cottage workers.

A sudden snort from Jacob made Edward glance sideways, but his father remained asleep as he settled himself more comfortably. Even if he had woken, Edward doubted that he would have let on that he had. Over the last two years, Jacob Morgan seemed to have drifted into a state where sleep was the preferred option to talking or discussing anything with his family. It was only the effect of cheap ale that loosened his tongue these days, and it was often to a point that his family wished he had gone to sleep.

The cart continued to roll along the narrow streets leading out of Liverpool, and as the dusk gathered, so did the amount of smoke, especially along the roadsides. Soon, the only lights were the smoldering embers of small fires lit in drums by people gathering around them.

From the darkened alleys that ran perpendicular to the main road, Edward watched as silent shapes, darkened in the gathering mist, drew closer to the fires. They were all shapes and sizes, some hobbling, some leaning on sticks. All looked hunched as they bent into the breeze that blew from the sea and formed a thickening mist along the street. There was little noise, so the clattering of the wagon wheels on the cobbles seemed almost deafening, but the wagon's presence seemed to draw little attention from the gathering groups.

Edward shifted on his seat and clucked at the horse to move it more quickly along the road. The sight of these figures huddling together for warmth sent an uneasy shiver down his spine. His family was going through difficult times, but he knew that right now his mother would be putting his youngest brother and sister to bed in their tiny loft beds. They would have had a small bowl of soup and a new loaf for dinner. There wouldn't have been much, but it would be enough to fill their stomachs, and there would be more for him and his father when they finally arrived home.

Edward shivered again and glanced back at the group he had just passed. The sight of the children bothered him the most.

Close to every lighted drum and holding tiny hands out to the glowing embers, clusters of young children huddled together. It was difficult to tell their age, as their thin frames, clad in scarcely more than rags, had lost the ability to grow older. Their dirty, pinched faces had also lost a fight with time.

Edward swallowed hard. At least his two sisters had died quickly when the illness had struck them down. These children looked as if they were dying as they stood there, wasting away in the evening gloom.

"Why do the little ones have to suffer?" Edward whispered and gripped the reins more tightly, slapping them down on the horse's back. The horse jerked its head in surprise then moved forward more quickly. "If I were king, there would be none of this," he muttered grimly as he deliberately turned his head away from the roadside gatherings. Then he shook his head and stared up into the dark sky that held very few stars. "And that's got to be one of the daftest things you've ever uttered, Edward Morgan."

* * *

Jacob hadn't mentioned stopping before they left Liverpool, so Edward kept driving the wagon without thinking to find lodging for the night.

"You should be making better time than this," Jacob said suddenly beside him, and Edward frowned as he started slightly. A second ago his father had been breathing deeply.

"It's dark, Da." He raised one hand briefly toward the lane they were moving along. "I can hardly see the hedgerow let alone the road. I don't want the horse to stumble."

Jacob straightened and stretched both arms out to his sides, then he rolled his shoulders and adjusted his hat again. Edward gave a wry smile. His father always adjusted his well-worn felt hat before he tried to assert his authority, so he wondered what he might be about to say.

"You're probably right," Jacob mumbled, and Edward resisted the urge to stare at his father. Instead, he raised one eyebrow and focused on the sound of the wheels. If they ran silently, they were too close to the grassy edge of the road and possible ditches. His father was silent for a long time, but Edward was aware of him staring up at the night sky. Now that they were out in the open countryside, the sky was clearer and more stars glittered over their heads.

"Are you all right to keep driving?" Jacob asked quietly, and Edward frowned again at his father's mellow tone.

"I'm fine." Edward nodded but felt no need to say anything else.

The wheels rolled on, accompanied by the muffled, rhythmic thud of the horse's hooves on the dirt road.

"The horse'll be weary. We should probably give her a spell." Jacob nodded toward the horse's rump. "She'll be working the fields tomorrow."

Edward didn't look at his father but kept listening to the clumping of the horse's hooves as he stared up at the sky.

"Do you think the stars look the same in other places?" He might well have been addressing the question to the stillness of the night rather than to his father, but Jacob looked at his son briefly.

"What other places?"

"Places . . . across the sea." Edward made a sideways movement with the reins. "North, south . . . east, west."

"You've been watching those ships again." Jacob grunted, but his tone wasn't hard.

"I had plenty of time," Edward answered briefly then held his breath as he waited for his father's reaction. When none came, he breathed out quietly.

"I was talking to an old sailor off one of the boats. He's been to all those places." He waited again for a reaction then abruptly decided to tell his father about Doyle's suggestion. "He asked me if I wanted to be a cabin boy on his boat."

"So that's what's been putting ideas in your head?" Edward heard the clipped tone working its way back into his father's voice.

"No . . . I told him I was a farmer." He glanced at his father but couldn't see the expression on his face. "He did tell me that there was land aplenty in those places . . . for the taking."

"He's a sailor. He'll be telling you all sorts for the sake of it." Jacob dismissed the statement with a snort. "You can't trust a sailor."

His abrupt response seemed to add fuel to Edward's desire to get a reaction from his father, and he pointed south. "He said that to the south there are the isles of the sea, Da. He said there's more land than there are people to look after it and that a man like me can get as much as he wants."

"And I said that a seafarer like that is only having you on, son." Jacob thrust out his chin stubbornly. "Land for the taking!" He spat out into the darkness of the lane. "We should all be so lucky."

Edward sat silently. Somehow the act of telling his father seemed to fix the idea more firmly in his mind, and the more contemptuous Jacob sounded, the more Edward felt the idea impress itself into his mind.

"Pull in over there by that gate." Jacob pointed a short way down the lane. "You and the horse can both take a rest. We'll wait till there's a bit more light to go on."

Edward made no comment as he followed his father's directions, pulling the horse to a halt where a driveway widened the road. There was plenty of grass beneath the hedgerow, and the horse began to graze immediately after Edward loosed it from its harness, and he marveled that it would rather graze than go to sleep. As he had jumped down from the wagon, he'd felt his own muscles protest from sitting so long, and so he took his time stretching as he lay out on top of the cotton bales. The desire to sleep soon filtered into his brain and through his body.

Jacob had pulled out the small wooden pipe he had carved himself, and Edward watched a pale light glow in the darkness as his father lit the pungent tobacco. Often Jacob would simply hold the pipe between his teeth, unlit, but tonight it held a red ember that ebbed and glowed with his breath. It was an oddly comforting smell that reminded Edward of the fireplace at home and happier times with his parents and siblings.

He settled back on the rough Hessian bales and lay with both arms raised behind him and his head resting in his hands. Again the sights of the stars above his head seemed to loose the thoughts in his mind. "What if the sailor wasn't lying?" Edward addressed the silence that had come to rest between him and his father. "What if there is plenty of land across the sea?"

It seemed an age before Jacob answered. "Then I wonder why God put it there and not here where we could use it better," he finally responded. "I wonder why He put an ocean between us and that land aplenty."

Edward nodded thoughtfully. He'd never considered God as part of the equation.

"What makes you think God has anything to do with it?" he dared ask the darkness and was surprised to hear his father give a quiet snort almost like a chuckle.

"Your mother does," he answered briefly, and Edward heard his teeth clamp back onto his pipe.

Somehow it was much easier to think of questions in the deep darkness and even more so while his father seemed in such an affable mood.

"Do you think God put us here . . . in our country?" Edward finally ventured. He had never talked to his parents about God before. Religion to him was based on sitting and listening while his mother read to them from a worn copy of the Bible that Lord Clitheroe had given her when she married Jacob. It was the only book in their house, and she diligently read it every day. At times over the last few years when she thought her family was asleep, Edward's mother read the Bible in the dim light of a candle lamp. He had watched her sit in her chair, her lips moving soundlessly as she rocked her body gently back and forth. Sometimes her cheeks would be wet with tears while she read, but he never heard her cry. It was as though she was in a silent world that no one else was allowed to enter.

"I only think what I know," Jacob responded briefly. "My parents put me here and their parents before them and theirs before them."

"So . . ." Edward hesitated, his fingers clenched behind his head. "Does that mean I'm meant to stay here too?" He turned his head to watch the pipe ember flare red in the darkness as his father breathed heavily.

"That decision may be taken out of our hands." Jacob's voice was barely audible. "For us right now . . . Lord Clitheroe is God."

* * *

THE EARLY MORNING MIST WRAPPED itself around the wagon, and Edward's clothes were wet with dew droplets when he woke suddenly a few hours later, disturbed by the motion of the cart as it lurched along the lane. Jacob sat stolidly in the driver's seat, his shoulders hunched against the coolness of the new day.

Edward raised himself up on one elbow and rubbed the sleep from his eyes then shook his hair vigorously before smoothing it back against his head. He was tempted to lie back down for a few minutes, but he slowly sat up and looked around for a landmark to determine how far they were from home.

"I didn't know I'd slept that long," he said out loud to his father, who offered a barely perceptible nod in reply. "I thought you wanted to stop in Preston."

"Another day." Jacob straightened, and Edward noticed that he kept his hand pressed against his lower back. "Too much to do."

There was something in the tone of his voice and the brief responses that made Edward sit quietly. The silver morning light seemed to make everything more transparent, including feelings and expressions, and he realized that the open conversation he'd had with his father the night before was past. The only sounds for the next few miles were birds chirping and calling to each other and the occasional lowing of cows and bleating of sheep echoing across the fields. Still, they were the music of the countryside that he loved, and Edward let the gentle lurching of the cart and the noises soothe his mind as they traveled the road home to Downham.

Now in familiar territory, Edward could name the farms and the lords of the estates as far as he could see across the gently rolling fields and toward the hills in the distance. He could also pick out many of the small farmlets and give names to the families that lived in them. Some families like his had lived in the same place for generations while they worked the land for the estate owner, one of the landed gentry. Most were happy to stay where they were, grateful for a home and place to work with a regular wage and food on the table. Often it was meager food, but at least most could rely on the lord of the estate to care for their well-being. After all, as Jacob often commented in one of his more eloquent drunken states, the lords needed them, the workers. They were nothing without them.

Edward frowned as he glanced down at his father's hunched shoulders. It was strange how alcohol gave a man temporary stature and bravado. When his father had drunk a reasonable amount, he had an opinion on many things and was not afraid to state them, but as the effects of the ale wore off, he seemed to diminish in size and courage and looked like he did now, small and stooped.

"You can take over." Jacob spoke suddenly without turning around, but the tone of his voice made Edward sit up immediately. He took a second to test the stability of the bales before he slithered down the front of them and eased himself onto the wagon seat beside his father. Jacob handed him the reins then pushed himself back against the wall of bales behind him. His hat was drawn down low over his face, but Edward was startled to see the ashen gray color of his father's cheeks before he turned his head away.

"Da . . . are you all right?" Edward kept one eye on the horse as it negotiated a large dip in the road. The wagon lurched slightly, and he saw his father bend forward and hold his stomach before sitting up again. "Da?"

"I'm all right." Jacob made a gesture with his hand and turned his head away so that Edward knew he wasn't going to say any more. He stayed that way until a narrow wooden sign directed the way to Downham, and Edward directed the horse to turn off the main road and begin the slight descent into their village.

Normally Edward enjoyed the feeling of coming home as the number of dark, steely gray brick houses increased in number along the sides of the narrow lane. He liked to close his eyes and hear the change in the sound of the wagon wheels as they first clattered then rumbled as they crossed the wooden bridge across the stream running through the village. Then there was another change in the sound as the horse would strain slightly up the sloping hill toward their home.

But today Edward didn't hear any of these sounds. He glanced often at his father, but Jacob was silent and still until they reached the middle of the village.

"Stop here, lad." He made a slight movement with his head toward the ale house. "Tell your mother I'll be home soon." He took a deep breath and slid down off the wagon seat without looking at Edward. "Business," he muttered briefly as he walked toward the tavern, and Edward watched him pause before the door and draw his shoulders back before stepping inside.

* * *

"WHERE'S YOUR FATHER?" NORAH MORGAN glanced up briefly from the cotton loom she was operating as Edward let himself in through the front door, but though her eyes were on her son, her hands never ceased in their endless movement, sending the shuttle back and forth between the rows of fine threads.

"He stopped off in the village for a spell." Edward glanced over his shoulder. "He'll be back soon."

"After he's spent the lord's money," Norah murmured quietly.

"He said it was his wage." Edward felt compelled to speak for his father, but his sympathy lay with the frail woman working in front of him. She was usually working by the time he rose in the morning and often when he went to bed. Most of the meals were made by his sister.

"Where's Emma?" He walked toward the other room in the house, which was used to prepare the food and was also where he slept.

"She went with Lizzy to fetch some milk. The cow is still dry, so Lizzy's mother said she could spare some." Norah shook her head. "I hate being beholden to people."

"Ma, you're not beholden. You gave plenty when Lizzy's family was sick." Edward walked back and rested a hand on his mother's shoulder. He could feel the tightness in her muscles through the thin cloth of her dress, but he also felt her relax as he kept his hand there. Finally she stopped working and laid her hand on his. Then he could feel the calluses on her fingers and noticed that her fingers were more misshapen than ever, the knuckles swollen and red.

"I wish I could make things better for you." Edward felt his chest tighten, and he clenched his teeth. The thought of taking on the strongest man in the village inspired in him no fear, but the sight of his mother's helplessness made him fight back tears.

"You make things better by just being here, Edward." His mother's chin quivered, then she smiled. "You and Emma and William . . . and your father."

As if on cue, the door suddenly burst open, and a young woman came through dragging a younger boy behind her. In the other hand she held a tin pitcher in which the contents could be heard sloshing gently from side to side.

"I have the milk and William." Emma Morgan smiled broadly as she placed the pitcher on the table then turned to Edward. "And what took you so long? Did the horse go lame? Surely you could have carried him?"

"And surely your mouth will get you in trouble." Edward grinned as his twin sister gave him a hug, then he sat down on a short stool beside the table. "But before it does, I'd love a drink of milk."

"And surely you're capable of getting it yourself." Emma placed her hands on her hips before she turned and fetched a pewter mug and poured a small amount of milk into it. She then turned and curtsied in front of Edward before presenting him with the mug.

Edward grinned and took a drink. He saw that his mother had paused in her weaving and sat, uncharacteristically still, watching her twins with a slight smile playing on her lips. With a shake of her head, she turned bright, tired eyes back to the loom.

Chapter Five

THE BLACKSMITH'S WORKSHOP WAS A deep room with thick walls and an open front to the roadway. A heavy rock fireplace sat to one side, and there Lauryn's father, Kevin Kelly, braced his arm against the wall as he held a thin piece of iron in the grip of long, pincerlike tongs. Both the metal and the end of the tongs glowed in tones from fiery red to yellow-white as the flames licked around them. Sweat was running from Kevin's brow and shoulders as he glanced up at the visitors and acknowledged them with a brief nod.

Lauryn waited to approach her father, knowing better than to interrupt while he was working at the fire or the anvil. She let her attention wander to the horse that was standing patiently with its back leg raised while Mr. Halloran nailed a heavy rounded shoe onto its hoof. It was a tall, dark-brown beast with a long Roman nose that it peered down the length of at Lauryn as she edged closer.

Occasionally, Lauryn would watch the family from the lord's estate riding down the lanes or across the fields, the young girls mounted carefully sidesaddle, their gowns tucked around them while their felt hats sat perkily on their long ringlets of hair, and Lauryn would try to imagine the freedom of riding such noble animals, so different from the pigs and cows she was used to seeing daily.

"Ye'll be standing back now, girlie." The smithy didn't even look up from his hammering, and Lauryn took a quick step backward as she glanced at her father. He was now busy at the massive iron anvil, beating the iron strip with a heavy mallet that rang as it connected with the iron. A few more strokes and he held up the glowing shoe to check its shape then plunged it into a wooden barrel full of water. The hiss of steam and the cloud of vapor that rose from the barrel made Lauryn's eyes water, and she took a step outside.

"So, Father . . . what's my daughter been doing that you have to bring her to me?" Kevin Kelly left the cooling horseshoe on the anvil and walked out to stand beside Father Quinn. Lauryn immediately lifted the tin pail for him to have a drink of milk, but her father gave her a quick frown as he shook his head and offered it to the priest first.

Father Quinn hesitated only briefly as he took the pail and lifted it to his lips for a quick drink. Then he lowered the pail and handed it back to Kevin.

"She'll not be doing anything wrong, Mr. Kelly." Father Quinn smiled. "No, not at all, but she has come to help me while I bring not-so-good news."

Lauryn nodded as her father glanced at her. "Father Quinn is going away . . . far across the sea to teach heatin' people." She paused. "The pope himself is sending him away with some nuns to O . . ." She frowned. "O . . . stray . . ."

"Australia," Father Quinn filled in for her quietly. "Or Canada."

Kevin Kelly stared at the man he had known since he was a lad. "How can it be, Father?" He shook his head slowly, then suddenly shook it more firmly. "You cannot go. Who will teach the children?"

"Another priest will be sent to take my place." Father Quinn tilted his head to the side and shrugged. "Someone younger and perhaps . . . more ready to work alongside the Protestants."

"But you've done that, Father, and with far more patience than they deserve, more often than not." Kevin folded his arms across his chest. "We'll complain—if this is about the schools, then we'll . . ."

"And it will do you no good at all, Mr. Kelly." Father Quinn shook his head resignedly. "I have already pleaded, but minds have been made up, and I will leave in a few weeks."

There seemed to be nothing more to say, but Lauryn held her breath. If anyone could help her beloved Father Quinn stay, it would be her father. She trusted him completely.

* * *

THE SUN WAS HIGH OVERHEAD as Lauryn walked quickly along the stony lanes toward her aunt's home. She frowned in concentration as she walked, her thoughts taken up with the problem of Father Quinn.

It had never occurred to her that Father Quinn might not always be her teacher. She had been so excited to start school two years ago, and she took pleasure in each new school day. She never could understand why some of the children fretted about going. Lauryn never tired of the thrill of learning something new—knowing it would stay in her mind forever and no one could take it away from her.

She unconsciously began to walk more slowly, the basket absently bumping against the side of her leg as she thought about her mother's determination to have her daughters educated. Some children, she often told them, didn't have the privilege of an education.

Some children, she said, were put down mines under the ground and hardly ever saw the light of day. Lauryn stared up at the bright blue sky and then across the fields that glowed bright green in the afternoon sun. Oh, how sad it would be to never see the sun and the sky and the fields that she loved.

Lauryn began to notice, however, that the closer she got to her aunt's, the less beautiful the fields seemed. She also observed that the houses, instead of being squat rock or plastered cottages like her family lived in, were now merely rough, dirty-looking dwellings, built haphazardly against a bank of rock, with a thin layer of thatched grass for the roof. Lauryn had heard her mother and father speak of the landlord her aunt and uncle worked for—a man who was infamous for his poor treatment of his workers—but it was the first time Lauryn had really noticed the difference. She shivered as she turned into the path that led to Jean's house and felt a cold knot prickle in the base of her stomach.

"Is it Lauryn?"

Lauryn looked up as she heard her name called and saw two children standing at the door of the nearest house. Another smaller child hung on a long piece of rag that served as a door. Both of the older children had lank hair falling across their eyes and were dressed in shapeless, sacklike covers that hung from their shoulders. Their faces were dirty and pinched, and their eyes seemed huge.

"Tommy?" Lauryn stared at the taller child, who responded with a grin that showed all of his front teeth missing. He was only three years younger than she was, but suddenly she felt very big. It had been a while since she'd seen her cousins, and the sight of them left her feeling oddly sick. Theirs had always been a sad-looking dwelling, but the children had at least appeared to be clean. She swallowed hard and walked toward the door, holding out the basket. "Tommy, Sarah . . . I have some food for you. Where is your *máthair*?"

The girl, Sarah, pointed inside with her fingers while her thumb stayed firmly in her mouth.

"She's not well." Tommy spoke with a bad lisp. "She thinks the baby's a comin'."

"The baby?" Lauryn stared at him then felt a surge of relief as her aunt appeared in the doorway. Once again, Lauryn almost didn't recognize the woman who had always looked so much like her own mother but was now so thin that it was difficult to see any resemblance. Her dress hung off her frame except for the bulge that protruded where a waistline should have been.

"Oh, Lauryn." Her aunt's voice was barely a whisper as she leaned against the doorway and stared down at the basket Tommy was now holding. "Your *máthair* is a very good woman."

"Are you all right, Aunt?" Lauryn asked the question but felt silly saying the words. Of course nothing was right, but she didn't know how to fix it and her father and mother were too far away right now.

"We're fine, dear." Jean nodded and laid her hand over her stomach. "You'd think it would be easier after seven babies, but they all have their own ways, and this one is training for a circus, I do believe."

Lauryn stared. Seven babies? She had only ever known four cousins, and one of them had died last year. She suddenly remembered that this was the last time her mother had seen her sister, such was her dislike for her brother-in-law.

"Ma sent some bread, potatoes, and eggs." Lauryn suddenly felt desperate to leave. "But I . . . I'd better be getting home now." She pointed to the sky. "For it'll be dark before long, and I'm by myself." She swallowed again and put her hands behind her back. "I'll tell Ma the baby is nearly coming."

"Thank you, child." Jean nodded and made no attempt to stop her. "And tell your *máthair* thank you again."

"For sure." Lauryn began to walk backward down the rough stones that made a short path to the door. As she reached the lane she hesitated and looked back at the forlorn group that was her family. She bit her lip, then fumbled in her pocket and held up the tin whistle.

"I . . . I've learned how to play the whistle. Grandfather Kelly taught me. Would you like me to play you a little tune?"

Chapter Six

Glasgow, Scotland, 1837
Moving On

THE SUN WASN'T EVEN BEGINNING to try to show through the gloominess when Ewen walked the road to the face of the coal mine as he did every day except Sunday. He always started work in the darkness, before five in the morning, and the sun was long gone again when he made his way home at night, no earlier than seven o'clock. Although the mine owners had made some changes in conditions in the last year or so, the hours the men worked had only been lessened by one hour. If they complained, there were a hundred other men moving into Glasgow every day from the Highlands or from Ireland, waiting to take their place. The mine owners knew they had the upper hand, and their show of benevolence pleased the English government but did nothing to ease the burden of the working-class Scots. Long hours and low pay for the privilege of working.

As he walked, Ewen became part of a gathering group of men, women, and children filing out of the endless rows of single-story houses owned by the mining company and rented to the workers. Nobody spoke much, although there were nods of greeting. The workers knew one another well, but there wasn't anything to talk about.

Ewen shook his head as a woman walked past him, hurrying as she dragged a small boy with her closely followed by another boy who was slightly older. Her heavy Irish brogue indicated that she was one of the thousands of Irish migrants who had fled their country in an attempt to find a better life in Scotland or England. Now, as she ushered her sons to the mine face, Ewen frowned as he thought about the day ahead of the children. Fourteen hours underground, drawing carts along narrow passages hundreds of feet below the surface. Even though there were some schools available, none of the workers could afford to send their children, so these boys, like hundreds of others, were destined to spend their lives working in the mines.

"I shall not send Jimmy down there," he muttered with a clenched jaw.

"Ye say something?" A man spoke close behind him, and Ewen started. The man was a stranger, but he had a familiar accent.

"No . . . just talking to myself," Ewen responded and immediately saw the man's face light up. "From Kintyre?"

"Aye . . . a while ago now, though." Ewen smiled, and the man touched his cap brim and fell into step beside him.

"Ian MacDonald." He pointed to his chest. "Moved down from Kintyre about two weeks ago. We've been in Crianlarich for the last two years and on the south coast before that."

"Och . . . you must have arrived as we left." Ewen nodded knowingly. The man's story was the same as many walking alongside them. So many people from the Highlands had been dispossessed of their land and forced to move to the lowland cities. "How did you come to be here?"

"Just lucky." Ian pointed in the direction of Glasgow, which lay to the south. "My brother has still not found work, even in the new foundries. At least we have a house here."

"How many of you?"

"My wife and four bairns." Ian held up four fingers then put two down. "Two of my sons will be starting work as drawers next week." He stated it matter-of-factly and Ewen stared ahead, suddenly sickened by the power of the mine owners who could force a man to sign his children up as workers and deed them over to the mining company for the rest of their lives. It meant that the mine owners were literally that—they owned the workers and their families, body and soul.

"How about you?" Ian asked.

Ewen held up one finger. "One wee boy of nearly a year, and my wife. She used to work down the mine but stopped to have the bairn."

"So you'll have a worker soon then?" Ian nodded. "My daughters are fine lassies, but they're not so useful until they're grown."

Again, Ewen stared ahead. Ian's words brought a lump to his throat as he thought about the two tiny baby girls that he and Bess had buried already. Tiny babes who barely drew a breath before they passed on. Even though most families expected to lose one or two children from their family, it had made it no easier to watch the little girls buried in cold, unforgiving winter ground.

Ewen frowned as he thought about the fight they'd had to bury their babies with a proper service. Miners and their families were not considered fit to worship in most of the local churches, let alone have a decent burial for their dead.

"So which seam are you working on?" Ian asked but didn't wait for an answer. "I'm going down the second."

"I'll be in the second also." Ewen pointed ahead. "Stay with me and I'll show you what to watch for." He almost grinned. "And get ready to spend the rest of your life bent over double. You won't find any straight Highland backs in these mines."

* * *

BESS PRODDED AT THE FIRE to make sure the ashes had some hot embers lying amongst them. Then, while they still glowed orange, she quickly finished kneading some bread dough into a flat, rounded shape. Within seconds, she had dropped the dough into a broad frying pan set atop the ashes.

"We'll make some bannock for your father," she said to Jimmy where he sat on the floor playing with a piece of wood that Ewen had fashioned into a horse. It was serving more to soothe than entertain him as he chewed on it, easing the pain of new teeth coming through. Bess quickly bent to wipe the dampness on his chin with the end of her apron before standing up to flip the bannock in the pan. The familiar smell of the fresh bread wafted through the room as she settled it down flat and Jimmy laughed.

"You know you'd like some too, don't you?" She smiled at her son, and he immediately crawled toward her and grasped the hem of her dress. The dress swung wide and took Jimmy with it. Surprised, he let go and stood on his own, taking a tentative step to steady himself. Then his arms lifted for balance, and he took two quick steps on his own.

"Jimmy!" Bess knelt down on the floor in front of him and held out her hands. Still balancing, the child took another step then fell into her arms. "Oh, my Jimmy!" Bess stood up and swung him round. "You're such a clever wee thing, and your father is going to be so proud of you." She kissed his cheek. "He'll have that knife out soon enough and be wanting to take you hunting now that you can walk!"

She set him down and let him try his steps again, but after several attempts he sat down and began to whimper. Bess gathered him into her arms and sat on the chair, softly crooning a familiar lullaby as she soothed him to sleep. Within minutes, his body relaxed against her, but she held him close rather than put him in his crib.

Still humming the tune of the lullaby, she stared at the wall opposite. It seemed that when she held him lately, thoughts of her two daughters who had passed on filled her mind. They would have been three and two years old now. It had been a short time between the pregnancies, but she had handled it well. What she hadn't handled well was the death of her children.

"Will I ever get to see them again?" She looked up at the ceiling, speaking to be heard but unsure by whom. "Where are my sweet babies?"

She and Ewen had decided to name their tiny girls, even though many said that it was the wrong thing to do.

"Claire and Jean." Bess nodded. It had helped to give the babies names, for it made them more real to her. She even knew what they would have looked like, for in dreams her girls were alive and well . . . one with deep auburn hair and the other with light brown like her own.

She smiled then and bent to kiss her son's forehead. "Maybe you will yet have a sister to play with, young Jimmy."

* * *

EWEN ACHED TO STAND UP straight, but the narrow passage he was working in was only high enough at the sides for him to bend double. With a resigned sigh, he slumped into a crouch and stretched his back as much as he could. He glanced along the tunnel and saw a number of men crouching in the same position. It somehow looked more natural than he felt. He stretched again then leaned forward to resume the constant driving at the wall with the mallet.

The mine's second coal seam already ran deep underground, but the owners had made the decision to drive the tunnel even farther as the demand for coal had escalated in recent months. A large iron foundry had been built in Glasgow that required massive amounts of coal to function.

"And more coal for the works means more coal to make things run at the works." Ewen mimicked the words of the mine's deputy as he'd greeted them that morning. "And that means more money for you, if you're prepared to work for it—and if you're not, then there are plenty of people ready to take your place."

"Are you given to talking to yourself again, or am I meant to be listening harder?" Ian spoke at his elbow. "And aren't we meant to be having something to eat? I need a break before I bust in two."

Even in the dull glow of his tally lamp, Ewen could see that Ian seemed to be in pain, so he put down his tools and nodded toward the part of the tunnel that was wide enough to sit down and eat. Most of the men on their shift joined them as they sat in a long row and opened up the same meal they had every day.

"Bread, water, and cheese." Ian bit into the bannock and chewed slowly with his head resting against the wall. His cap tipped backward, creating a sharp contrast between his white forehead and his coal-darkened face.

"For the rest of your life." Ewen nodded. "There'll be no more haggis for a long while."

"Oh, haggis." Ian smiled and closed his eyes. "All that offal cooked up so fine and spicy and sliced off with my knife."

"Sgian dubh?" Ewen glanced sideways.

"Aye." Ian nodded. "My grandfather's."

Both men sat in silence for a moment, occupied with their own thoughts. Around them the other miners spoke in low tones; a tunnel didn't lend itself to loud talk.

"How old were you when the clearances came?" Ian broke off some cheese. "You must have been only a lad."

Ewen nodded, knowing immediately what Ian was referring to. The "clearances" were indelibly etched in the memory of every Highlander: ten years of brutal eviction of Highland families from their crofts and sometimes eradication of whole families for no reason but to clear the barren land for larger sheep holdings and deer-hunting areas for wealthy English landlords.

"I was fourteen."

"Then you'd remember it well." It was a statement rather than a question.

"Aye." Ewen barely nodded. "Too well at times."

Another long silence fell between them. The bread had suddenly become dry in Ewen's mouth, but he knew he needed to eat it. He swallowed with difficulty before he spoke.

"How about you?"

"I left with a musket pointing at my shoulder blades, carrying my son and my wife heavy with child while my house was burned down," Ian responded in a monotone. "But at least we kept our lives."

They sat in somber silence until Ewen smiled. "My mind can go back to the glen and the forest in a flash, and it is as clear to me as yesterday—yet I canna hardly remember the difference in yesterday and today at the mines." He paused and shook his head. "Probably because there is no difference. Each day is the same—staring at a rock wall for fourteen hours and too tired to think of anything else when you leave it."

"Aye." Ian nodded as he glanced up over his head, the dim light from his lamp etching an arc across the damp rock roof. "I can see that it might be so."

"Oh, it's so." Ewen nodded. "I thought I would go crazy for the first few months, but then it just became . . . normal." He grimaced. "Unless, of course, I am crazy now and just don't know the difference."

They both grunted, and Ian slowly folded up the cloth that had held his food. "What do you remember best of the Highlands?"

Ewen stared at the wall then closed his eyes and took a deep breath. "The mist and the sun breaking through it and lighting up the highest crags and making the heather gleam with the dew . . . hunting the biggest stag I ever laid eyes on and feeling sorry it had to die but proud that I was helping provide food for my family."

Ian nodded. "Oh, I remember . . ."

"The snow lying like the softest white blanket as far as the eye could see, and the fire roaring so we wouldn't freeze and because I'd gathered enough wood." Ewen rubbed his hand across the back of his neck. "I worked hard for a young fellow, but it felt good."

"Because you were free." Ian spoke quietly, and Ewen stared at him. In the light of the lamp the man's face was drawn, and his cheeks seemed sunken.

"Aye . . . I was free."

Again they were silent, then Ian rested both arms on his bent knees and said, "They said we had to leave because there was nothing to make a living from on the Highland soil . . . that it was only fit for sheep." He shook his head. "And we went like lambs to the slaughter, filing off to the coast."

"At least you got to the coast." Ewen swallowed hard. "My brother was killed in front of me and then my father because he tried to help him. I was fourteen and had to look after my mother and sister."

Ian glanced up. "Are they with you?"

"No . . . the cholera took them both a few years back." He breathed deeply. "Sometimes I wish it had gotten me as well." He took a long drink of water. "But at least I have my Bess and Jimmy now, and they make my life worth something even if I'm not."

"Aye." Ian nodded slowly. "Aye, ye're right."

* * *

THE WALK BACK TO EWEN'S house seemed even longer and more dreary than usual, despite Ian keeping up a steady narrative about his first day in the shaft. It was as though he didn't realize that Ewen had been in the same place as he recounted the details from descending in the cage down the shaft, to extracting the first coal and having the drawer boy take away his first cart full of coal, to the deputy making sure the air was fit for them to breathe.

The only thing he didn't mention was the brief time spent with Ewen as they discussed their homeland. It seemed he had sealed that memory and filed it away.

Leaving Ewen with a promise that their wives and children would meet the next morning, Ian entered one of the middle houses on the row while

Ewen kept walking almost to the end of the hundred small dwellings sitting back-to-back with another row of identical houses. Along a narrow space between every second house ran an open drain, and Ewen noted that the smell outside some of the houses was especially bad. Still, the tiny rooms provided a roof over their heads, and for that he had to be thankful.

As he entered the room that was his home, he saw Bess smiling broadly as she looked first at his face and then down to the floor by the bed. He glanced down to where Jimmy was standing, holding on to the bed cover.

"Wait there!" Bess held up her hand as Ewen went to pick up his son. "Just bend down." He smiled at the excitement in her voice as he bent his knees and lowered to the ground in the crouch that had held him captive all day.

"Now call him to you."

Ewen glanced up at his wife, but she only nodded, so he turned to his son.

"Jimmy, my boy. Come and see your daddy." Ewen watched as Jimmy studied his father's face and began to rock on his feet.

"Go to your daddy, Jimmy." Bess moved forward then stood still. "Call him again."

"Jimmy!" Ewen moved a little closer to his son, but in the same instant Jimmy let go of the cover and swung one leg away from the bed, quickly followed by the other and three more steps to follow before he reached his father and was lifted in a tight hug. "Jimmy, my boy!"

But along with pride over his son's accomplishment, Ewen felt as if those five steps had made five tiny incisions into his heart as the tears built in his throat and then coursed down his cheeks. All of the pain and humiliation of the past years suddenly combined in one outburst to mingle with his son's auburn curls.

Bess watched silently as her husband kept a tight grip of their child but would not raise his head. Jimmy stared at her for a moment, then he raised a small hand and rested it against his father's shoulder before giving it tiny pats.

"I canna do it, Bess." Ewen finally raised his head. "I canna see our son learn to walk only to have to crawl the rest of his days." He raised an arm to wipe his face. "We have to get away from the mine."

Bess had never seen such anguish on Ewen's face, even when their babies had passed on, and now it struck at her heart how desperate her husband felt. She was aware that their situation could be better, but long years of fighting for survival had deadened her feelings to any other possibilities.

"But there isn't anywhere else, and it took us so long to get a place here." She shook her head. "We canna leave here, Ewen. Not if there is nothing else to go to."

Ewen heard his wife speaking, but the weight of his son lying quietly in his arms spoke louder.

"We had nothing but hope when we left Crianlarich, Bess." He shook his head. "I canna think but that we might be able to feel the same again if we only try."

Bess walked toward him and stood with her arm around his waist and her other hand stroking her son's head.

"But what if there isn't anything and Jimmy . . ." She hesitated, and her voice caught. "I canna lose another child, Ewen."

Ewen put one arm around her shaking shoulders. "We must do it, Bess." He straightened his shoulders. "In two weeks is Binding Day, and then I'll have just twenty-four hours to tell the mine owners whether I'm staying for another year or not. If I don't do it then, we'll be here forever, Bess . . . and Jimmy'll be due to be baptized, and we'll be expected to sign him over to the company, and that I simply will not do." He rested his chin against Jimmy's curls. "We're going to give our son a better life, Bess. He may not have the Highlands, but he's not going to spend his life underground, either."

"So what shall we do?" Bess moved away from Ewen as Jimmy became restless and wriggled to get out of his father's arms. Ewen gave him a tight squeeze and lowered him to the ground, where the little boy immediately tried to take another step.

"The deputy told us today that the new steel foundry in town is doing more work than anyone thought possible, and a new yard has opened up on the Clyde for building ships the like of which we've never seen before." He nodded as if the idea were making more sense all the time. "We're all having to work harder at the mine, so why wouldn't there be work for me in the town? I heard some say that they're building even more houses and some schools." He looked at his son. "The workers there are able to have their bairns get an education, Bess. Jimmy could go to school when he's old enough."

* * *

"WHAT DO YOU MEAN YOU DON'T want to work here anymore?" Mr. Ross, the mine manager, raised one heavy black eyebrow and peered over his glasses at Ewen. "Are you stupid?"

Ewen felt his neck prickle at the man's tone even more than at his words, but he only worked his cap around in his hands and shook his head. "Just moving." He decided to be noncommittal.

"Moving to what?" The manager almost spat the words out. "You're a miner." His pen hovered over the paper that had Ewen's name at the top alongside a long list of figures in a column marked "wages" and a list that was headed "rent." Even though he was reading the paper upside down, Ewen could see that there was little difference in the amounts.

"We're moving on." Ewen's jaw tightened as he repeated himself slowly.

The manager stared at him for a moment then scored a thick line of ink across the page and scrawled a signature at the bottom. "You're done then."

He didn't even lift his head as Ewen nodded and took a step backward then turned more decisively and walked out, slamming the door just a bit as he walked through it.

"So you're done, then?" Ian shook his head as they walked away from the office that stood in the shadow of the huge chimney stack at the colliery. "I canna believe you did it."

"Neither." Ewen stared straight ahead. "But it's done now. We're moving." He clenched one fist by his side. "I'm going to make a better life for Jimmy."

"And I thought I had made one here." Ian shook his head. "Ye're making me doubt myself now."

Ewen shook his head. "I canna make another man's decisions, Ian. I only know what I need to do. You have four bairns after all."

Ian nodded as he walked with his hands in the pockets of his trousers. They were nearly at his door before he spoke again. "Ewen . . . do you believe in God?"

It was such an unexpected question that Ewen actually stopped walking. Then he shrugged and shook his head. "I haven't thought about it for a long time. My ma'am used to."

"Same." Ian nodded then stopped as well and frowned as he indicated toward the west. "A while ago I listened to a fellow preaching, and it was very different from what my ma'am used to talk about." He scratched his head. "He reckoned that God cared about each one of us and that there shouldn't be any difference in the way we worship . . . like the rich people doing things one way and the poor people doing things another."

He paused as Ewen snorted.

"Well, that's what I thought too." Ian nodded. "But then this fellow said that Jesus Christ was going to come back to the earth and He'd want us all to be treated the same . . . and I got to thinking that that's really the way it ought to be."

Ewen shrugged. "It might be the way things ought to be, but can you see any of us changing the Kirk of Scotland? God Himself, if He exists, would have to do that." He nearly smiled. "It takes money to go to church, and if God wanted us to go then He'd give us some, wouldn't He?"

This seemed to mark the end of the conversation, but as Ian turned to his doorway Ewen hesitated. "Who was this fellow, anyway? The preacher?"

"Oh . . . Irving. Edward Irving," Ian answered. "He was a Presbyterian minister, but he reckoned the Kirk should be thinking more about Jesus Christ and the New Testament rather than living in the past with the Old Testament." He nodded, a slight smile on his lips. "I didn't even really know there was a difference. It was all just the Bible to me." He shrugged. "Anyway, I heard that the Kirk finally threw him out for preaching that Jesus Christ was a man and such."

"A man?" Ewen chuckled. "No wonder he was thrown out."

"Mmm . . . still, he made me think—even hope—for a while." Ian raised his hand in farewell. "Don't really know why I asked you about all that, anyway."

Chapter Seven

Preston, England, 1837
Preachers in Preston

"I THINK I WOULD LIKE to live in the town." Emma Morgan glanced over her shoulder and touched Edward on the arm as he drove the cart toward the middle of Preston. "There are so many fine houses and parks, and look at the shops." She turned on the seat and pointed to a row of slender shop fronts, each with a distinctive painted board mounted at the front door advertising a particular trade. Outside, men in finely tailored coats and fitted trousers walked alongside women in full gowns and matching bonnets.

"They look so pretty," Lizzy Smale said beside Emma, and Edward glanced over at the girl who had been his and Emma's closest friend since they had been little children. There was no doubt in Edward's mind that he would marry the slim, blond girl before long, and the fact that Emma adored Lizzy made it complete.

"You are just as pretty," he stated quickly, rattling the reins on the back of the horse. "In fact, more so." He gestured with his head toward a particularly thin woman walking beside them, her long nose lifted into the air as she negotiated the cobblestone footpath. Edward lifted his chin and nose in imitation, and Emma and Lizzy began to giggle.

"Besides, you have to have money to live in the town." He grinned. "Should we try and find some, or how about we sell the eggs and bacon for one hundred shillings per pound instead of a mere sixpence? I'm sure many will be happy to pay for quality goods."

They were still laughing as they approached the marketplace in the center of town, and as Edward unloaded the produce, the girls took in the sights around them.

"It's always so busy and interesting." Lizzy clasped both hands over her chest.

Emma nodded as she scanned the crowded street. "Look at those preachers over there." She pointed toward the large obelisk that rose some thirty feet above the marketplace. At the base of it, a man was talking to the crowd as he held up a book in his hand. "I heard some of the women saying that there have been some excellent preachers lately. In fact, some of them came to the village of Chatburn the other day."

"I heard that too." Lizzy nodded. "Mother said that her sister said—"

"That her cousin said . . ." Edward interrupted, and Emma nudged him immediately while Lizzy kept talking as though he hadn't spoken.

"That there was such a clamor in the village. She said someone had heard them teaching in Preston and had gone and told the people in the village that they would visit and that people ran from house to house to spread the word of their coming, and everyone in the village—"

"Everyone?" Edward looked skeptical.

". . . came to their doors, and the children all ran to greet them." Lizzy didn't pause. "And the parents were all singing and praising God that they had been sent to them." She finally stopped and took a breath. "I do wish I had seen it."

"But what made them any more special than all the others that come and preach these days?" Emma shrugged. "I know not everyone wants to go to the Church of England or the Methodist Church, but what makes them so different?"

"I believe my aunt said they're from America," Lizzy answered importantly as though her aunt was the source of all knowledge.

"But so have many been who have visited with news of a God who will change our lives." Edward spoke so quickly that his sister glanced at him. "And I don't see many changes happening for us. We still struggle to have enough to eat, and we're still beholden to Lord Clitheroe for the rest of our lives."

His statement seemed to mark the end of the conversation, and the two girls busied themselves with arranging the produce as he unloaded it. As they completed the task, Emma leaned over to Lizzy while staring at Edward.

"Can you look after things here for a moment? I want to go and listen to the preacher."

Lizzy looked aghast as she automatically glanced over her shoulder toward Edward, who was handing produce to a woman a few feet away. " I . . . I don't think Edward . . ."

"I should think Edward would be happy to have some time with you . . . alone." Emma nodded as if that ended the conversation and was already untying the long cotton apron she habitually wore. Her dress underneath was originally brown, but its gathered folds had been sun-washed into shades of beige and tan. Still, she ran her hands over the faded folds and lifted her head a bit higher before she made her way quickly through the gathering crowd. Lizzy held her breath as she watched her become part of the crowd, then she turned quickly as she heard Edward behind her.

"So she did go?" He noticed that Lizzy's cheeks were a shade pinker than usual and realized that he liked it.

"Um, yes." Lizzy frowned slightly as she bent to straighten some produce. "I think she went to look at the shops."

"You mean she'll go to the shops after she's listened to the preacher." Edward smiled as Lizzy's cheeks went a shade pinker. All through their childhood Lizzy had been the one to cover for Emma when Edward wasn't doing so himself. His twin sister seemed to have a compulsion to try things before she really thought about the consequences. He shook his head. "It's no wonder that girl can't find a man who will take her hand. No one is brave enough."

"Oh, that's not true." Lizzy leaped to her friend's defense. "Any number of boys from the villages would court her." She hesitated then took a deep breath. "It is you that they're scared of . . . not Emma."

"Me?" Edward frowned. "What a foolish thought."

"Are you saying I'm foolish?" Lizzy glanced at him.

"Well, no, but . . ." Edward folded his arms as he looked over the crowd. Sure enough, he could see Emma's figure hovering at the back of a large group of people who were gathered around the preacher, and even as he watched, he saw her beginning to wriggle her way through to the front. It was so typical of Emma to be in the thick of things. "Why would they be scared of me?"

"Oh, Edward . . . you are Emma's guardian. You have been since you were babies, and I think . . ." Lizzy paused. "I think it's almost the reason she is so impulsive. She knows you will always be there to fix things up if she gets in trouble."

"But I thought that was your job." Edward frowned. "You always cover for her."

"Then perhaps we are both to blame." Lizzy nodded, then she shrugged. "Maybe we should let her figure things out for herself."

"And concentrate on other things?" Edward's voice dropped slightly, and Lizzy didn't dare to look up. Although she had loved Edward Morgan since she was a young girl, it had always been an unspoken devotion that he seemed to take for granted. For Edward, he had simply always known Lizzy was meant to be with him, and it was only a question of when their marriage would happen. Both of their families expected their union, but he hesitated to take Lizzy's hand, knowing he had little to offer to a new wife and afterward a family.

"I do like to be with you, Lizzy." The words almost caught in his throat as he suddenly realized how much he meant them.

"And I with you, Edward." Lizzy finally looked up and felt a thrill at the way he was looking at her. "I . . ." She began then had no idea what else to say.

Edward smiled and nodded as he reached for her hand and squeezed it briefly before releasing it.

"I'll have four rashers of the bacon . . . and make them good thick pieces too!" A loud voice was strident behind them, and Edward turned quickly as a large woman beneath a billowing white bonnet poked a finger at the piece of salted pork. "And I'll have twelve of the eggs, and they'd better have decent yolks."

"I can certainly check them all for you." Edward spoke calmly as he produced a large knife and whetstone and began to sharpen it directly in front of the woman. "But they'll be harder to carry once they're open."

"Humph." The woman clasped both hands over her stomach and stood back as he sliced off the four pieces of bacon. He took his time and smiled graciously as he handed them over wrapped in a damp cloth while Lizzy placed the eggs carefully in the woman's basket. As the woman dropped coins into Lizzy's hand, she made another gruff sound and walked quickly off to the next cart.

"Oh, Edward, you scared her." Lizzy spoke quietly. "She may not come back again."

"And do I mind?" Edward slid the knife into a leather sleeve. The woman's attitude had stung his pride, and he hated the feeling it roused in him. "She has no right to feel better than us—and where would she get her food if we didn't supply it? She should behave better than that."

"Perhaps." Lizzy nodded, used to both Edward and Emma expressing their feelings about the injustices between the social classes that were so much part of all of their lives. It was a scene she often witnessed in the Morgan home, where Jacob Morgan would expound the problems he saw and propose how they should be righted. No wonder his lively children followed his lead . . . although never when he was speaking.

The rest of the people waiting to be served were pleasant, and the time passed quickly as Lizzy and Edward cleared much of the produce in record time. With only a few items left, Edward began to look over the dwindling crowd to catch sight of Emma.

"Have you seen her at all, Lizzy?" He began to stack baskets against the side of the cart. "She knows not to run off like this."

"Maybe he was a very good preacher." Lizzy worked quietly beside him, her small hands swiftly removing the pieces of straw stuck on the front of her dress.

"And that means we'll have to listen to her all the way home." Edward frowned. "I'm none too fond of this religious nonsense."

"Religion is not nonsense, Edward." Lizzy looked taken aback. "God is not nonsense."

Edward lodged a piece of wood across the back of the cart and then put his hands on his hips as he looked around Preston Square. "Well, then, why can't everybody agree about where they stand with Him?"

As he spoke, the crowd gave way to their right, and Emma pushed her way through, almost stumbling as she walked quickly to the cart. She stopped in front of Lizzy, hands clasped together in excitement.

"Oh, Lizzy," she said, her eyes sparkling, "I do wish you could have listened!" She took a quick breath. "It was an American, and he spoke so wonderfully about the gospel of Jesus Christ being restored on the earth." She pointed to the ground. "Right here . . . in England . . . for the first time since Jesus Christ Himself was on the earth—and exactly as He would have it!"

She turned as Edward made a noise in his throat and gave him the look she always used when she wanted to assert the slight difference in their ages, but he held up his hand.

"Don't give me your older-sister wisdom." He almost laughed but for her serious expression. "And save the telling for on our way home. If we leave now, I can get out to the fields for a time."

Emma barely waited until the cart was beyond the square before she began to recite the sermon that she'd heard, hesitating only occasionally as she tried to remember the words exactly.

"He said that much of the truth and order of the church Jesus Christ established was lost, but that now the Lord has sent forth His servants to preach repentance and baptism for the remission of sins to prepare them . . ." She paused so long that Lizzy glanced at her.

"Prepare them for what?"

"For the Second Coming of Jesus Christ," Emma said breathlessly. She clasped her hands in her lap. "I had such a wonderful feeling when he said it. Like nothing I've felt in church before."

"That's because the only thing you can feel in church is the hardness of those narrow pews." Edward shook his head. "And to think that we pay for the privilege of sitting on them."

"We don't pay pew money." Emma frowned. "Only the rich can afford that; that's why we get the narrow seats, because we don't pay anything."

Edward shrugged and flipped the reins over the horse's rump. "As if only the wealthy can expect to be saved," he muttered.

They traveled without speaking for some time, the only sound the cart's iron wheels rattling on the cobbled street. As they continued through town, they observed a stark difference in the quality of housing as the more elegant two- or three-story buildings with wrought-iron palings suddenly gave way to tightly clustered blocks of brick buildings. The road ran above the enclosed yards of most of these houses, proffering a clear view of squalid spaces with up to eight or ten people simply standing or sitting amongst piles of waste and dirt. Most yards seemed to have a pig rummaging through the litter.

"Oh, it's awful, isn't it?" Lizzy shivered as she wrapped her shawl more tightly around her shoulders.

"All those people living in one house." Emma frowned.

"And there's probably more." Edward's jaw tightened. "Most of these people are workers from the big cotton mills. The mill owners often put three or four families into one house."

Emma put her fingers to her lips then shook her head. "Thank goodness we have our cottage. I shall never complain about sharing the loft with William again."

"I only hope that we keep our cottage." Edward kept his eyes on the road ahead as he suddenly had an image of his father pocketing the handful of coins before entering the inn. "Lord Clitheroe has the power to put us out anytime he wants."

"But he never would!" Emma sat up straighter. "Mother is one of his best weavers, and father . . . works hard."

"Exactly." Edward gave her a knowing look. "But the reason these people are here is because the machinery in the big mills has done them out of their work—and out of their homes. Who knows how long mother will be needed before the mills take over her work. And as for father . . . I'm working as hard as I can, but Lord Clitheroe has already noticed he's not been out in the fields much of late."

"Oh, Edward." Emma barely breathed his name. "It would never happen. Mother and Da were born on the estate, and they married there. They would never be cast off."

Edward took his time answering. Finally he shrugged and said, "Who knows, Emma . . . but do you think God will step in if it does happen?"

Chapter Eight

County Cork, Ireland, 1837
Finnbheara

LAURYN HAD DECIDED THAT SHE wasn't going to say good-bye to Father Quinn, as if in not saying it some miracle might prevent him leaving, but in the end it didn't matter, for when she went to the schoolhouse the following week, he was gone. The small table where he'd once sat was empty of any books, and the three-legged stool was set neatly underneath. In less than a day it was as if Father Quinn had never been, for there was no evidence of him left. Even the room at the side of the small stone church had been emptied of his few possessions.

"Do you think Father Quinn will ever come and see us again?" Megan asked quietly as her family ate dinner that evening. The others were silent as they continued dipping their raw potatoes into egg milk, a favorite dish that Moira prepared only once a week. They were fortunate that their father's main work was as a dairyman, for in looking after the estate herd of cows he was able to glean a full pail of milk every few days.

"I doubt it." Kevin shook his head. "He'll be going a long way away. We shall not see Father Quinn again, I'm afraid."

"But who can take his place?" Lauryn pouted. "I shall not like him at all. I know I won't."

"Now then, daughter. You don't know that a very good priest won't come to us who will teach you even more than Father Quinn. I imagine you will like him just as well," her mother reprimanded her quietly. "After all, even Father Quinn was new here once."

Lauryn shook her head stubbornly. She had already made up her mind. No one could replace her Father Quinn.

* * *

AS THE DAYS TURNED INTO weeks and the summer sun began to drop from
the sky a little earlier each day and still no new priest arrived at the village,
Lauryn began to weaken in her resolve. There were no school classes to
attend, and so the children busied themselves around the village and in their
cottages. Moira made sure that her daughters read from the Bible every day
and were well versed in their catechism, but mostly they played.

For Lauryn, the one good thing about not having school was having
more opportunities to visit her father at the smithy's. Often, she would walk
with him to work in the mornings.

"May I hold the horses while you shoe them?" Lauryn swung on her
father's hand as they walked the distance to the workshop. "Even just the
small ones." She held up two fingers a few inches apart to indicate just how
small she meant, and her father grinned.

"A pony that size is only fit for the little people." He nodded toward the
emerald green fields. "Have you seen any of them riding ponies lately?"

"No." Lauryn chuckled and skipped to keep up with her father's long
strides. "But . . . maybe they sneak into the workshop at night and make
their own tiny horseshoes."

"Ah . . . that would explain the fire still being hot early in the morning
and the tiny pieces of iron that seem to go missing." Kevin pretended to
frown. "I'd been wondering."

"Really?" Lauryn glanced at him quickly then saw his smile and shook her
head, laughing. "Father, do you ever shoe the horses for the daughters at the
estate?" She pointed northward, where the large manor house was located.

"Indeed." Kevin nodded and shook his head. "We have just begun to do
so, and it seems that some of the daughters have very grand ideas of themselves." He looked thoughtful as he briefly squeezed his daughter's hand.
"Promise me that you'll always be true to yourself and what you believe in,
Lauryn. Do not be tempted by the ways of the world or by its wealth, for it
brings its burdens, to be sure."

Lauryn sensed the change in her father's mood, and although she didn't
completely understand what he had just said, she nodded importantly. "Be
true to myself and what I believe in," she repeated and nodded her head.
Then, after a moment, she shyly glanced up at her father. "What do I believe
in, Father?"

Kevin stared ahead for a time, gazing across his beloved country, which
now seemed to hold so many contradictions. Finally, he straightened his
shoulders and said quietly, "You believe in God, Lauryn. First and foremost,

you are a Catholic girl who knows of the everlasting power of God." Kevin stopped suddenly, then he bent down as a sudden wave of emotion coursed through his chest. He held Lauryn gently by the shoulders as he looked her directly in the eye. "And second, you believe in your family and that we are for each other . . . forever."

Lauryn's breath caught in her throat as she felt the seriousness of her father's words. She didn't often see him like this, and as she studied the familiar crinkled lines of his face and the green eyes that were so similar to her own, she sensed a love that was so strong it seemed to fill her whole body. With a tiny cry, she threw herself toward him and immediately felt his strong arms wrap around her slender body and lift her to him.

"Forever, Da," she murmured as tears welled in her eyes and wet his neck.

* * *

HE WAS A GRAND-LOOKING ANIMAL, deep chestnut in color with a broad chest and strong, well-muscled legs. Standing a full eighteen hands high at the shoulder, his massive frame seemed to dwarf the shop and the smithy. Lauryn thought he was magnificent. The horse's owner, one of the new estate managers, obviously had other thoughts as he cursed the animal while having difficulty holding the bridle. The horse incessantly flung its head up, its long golden mane and forelock whipping around its face.

"He's a brute, to be sure." Halloran put his hands on his hips. "Have ye ridden 'im, yet?"

"Not . . . yet." The manager grunted as the horse moved against him, swinging its back legs around. "I won him in a game of cards." He gritted his teeth as he held the reins. "Along with a house, I might add. I've just had him shipped over from England, but he's a thoroughbred, so I need him reshod for these rough Irish roads."

Lauryn watched her father shake his head at the gloating tone of the man's voice, but it was Halloran who voiced his thoughts. "A house won't be much good to ye if the horse kills ye first."

The manager scowled as he handed the reins to Halloran before stepping back quickly. "Just get it done as quickly as possible. I'll be back in an hour."

"Surely." Halloran didn't even glance at the man as he turned his attention to the horse, making quiet clicking sounds with his tongue as he tied the reins to a stout wooden railing then moved to the horse's head.

Perched on top of a large sealed barrel, Lauryn watched the whole proceedings from her seat outside the workshop. She was amazed at how the horse calmed as soon as the manager left, letting Halloran scratch its nose and behind its ears—ears that, a few seconds earlier, had been laid back flat against its head while its mouth frothed flecks of white foam.

"There now, my beauty," Halloran murmured to the horse while he ran his hand gently over its flank. "You can't help who you belong to, can you?" He chuckled quietly. "But I guarantee you'll let 'im know how you feel about 'im before too long."

"He's a grand horse." Kevin had been heating the iron in the fire, and he nodded toward Lauryn as he pulled the smoldering iron out and began to shape it. "What do you think, daughter?"

"I think he's beautiful." Lauryn clasped her hands in her lap and leaned forward. "But why is that man so cruel to him?" She gazed at the horse now standing quietly while Halloran removed its old shoes. "Can't he see that because he's mean he's making the horse be mean back?"

Kevin gave his daughter a thoughtful look, then he nodded and resumed his work.

When the job of shoeing the horse was completed, the animal whiffled slightly and bowed its head against Halloran's chest as he straightened up after fixing the last shoe. "I do believe that was a 'thank ye.'" The rugged man chuckled and ran his hand down the horse's nose, then he turned to Lauryn. "How would you like to sit abroad this fine beast, Lauryn?"

Lauryn looked at her father quickly, and Kevin smiled and nodded. "Just for a second or two." He moved to help her down from the barrel, but she was quicker, leaping to the ground then making herself walk quietly toward Halloran. Her heart was beating so fast that she wondered if the horse could hear it, but it stood quietly.

"Talk to him a little, Lauryn."

Halloran stood carefully near the horse's head as she raised her hand up high to touch its nose. The warmth of its breath on her arm gave her a thrill, and she swallowed quickly. "You are a beauty." She barely whispered as the words stuck in her throat. "And I'm so sorry that you have to live with that man." She looked up into the animal's huge dark eyes. "If I had enough money, I would buy you and keep you forever and ever."

"And I'm sure he'd be happier for it." Halloran nodded at Kevin, and her father came to lift Lauryn up onto the horse's back. She took a second to gauge the distance that was now between her and the ground, and then she smiled. "He must surely be like the horse of Finnbheara, the king of the fairies." She nodded happily as she gently stroked the golden strands of mane. "I shall call him Finnbheara."

The horse pricked up his ears as the name rolled softly off Lauryn's tongue, and she looked at her father. "See, he likes that name. Finn-var-a." She sounded the syllables quietly, and the horse nodded its head.

"Well, Finnbheara looks as if he approves, but I don't know that the manager will if he sees you up there." Kevin held up his hands for her to get back down. "He'll be back soon."

Lauryn took a deep breath then quickly leaned forward and wrapped her arms around the horse's neck. "Thank you, Finnbheara. I shall remember you forever."

She allowed herself to be lifted down and obediently walked out of the shop, pausing at the doorway to look back once more as Halloran loosened the reins from the railing and began to lead the horse outside.

"So, have you finished?" The imperious voice of the manager startled her as he brushed past from behind, completely ignoring her while he walked up to Finnbheara and slapped his rump. The abrupt gesture sparked an instant explosion as the horse, which had been standing so docile a second before, suddenly reared high then landed and swung its back legs as if trying to get as far away from the man as possible. Halloran planted his feet and kept a hold on the reins while Kevin tried to catch Finnbheara from the other side, but the horse lifted his head and swung his hindquarters again. This time he backed against the manager and knocked him to the ground.

Lauryn could see that the manager wasn't hurt, but his scream of anger incensed the horse even more, and he began to lunge again, pivoting on the tight rein Halloran held. In one movement, Finnbheara's back leg caught against the heavy cast-iron anvil, knocking it sideways against the stone fireplace and dislodging some of the stone so that hot coals spilled onto the ground.

With a wide gash on his leg where the anvil slid against it, the horse lunged again, kicking and catching at the coals and splaying them across the workshop.

Lauryn watched, horrified, as the bleeding horse reeled in terror. She distantly heard her father cry out her name, but in the split second that the hem of her long cotton dress alit from a flying ember, the manager raised a whip and began beating the horse against its open wound.

"Finnbheara!" The name was a scream as she felt her body suddenly floating and a pain that didn't feel like pain start from her leg and lift, with the scream, through the top of her head and out into the silent hillside.

* * *

Finnbheara . . . Finnbheara. It seemed she had only to think his name and he would respond, carrying her effortlessly over the tops of rolling green hills and billowing white clouds that curled around her feet and felt cold against her skin before they burst into the brilliant blue sky. The light of the sun warmed her entire body, its brilliance seeming to penetrate right through her skin and bones as if they weren't there.

Ma. She had only to imagine her mother's face and she was there, but yet apart. Finnbheara would not stop. He kept carrying her toward the sun, his powerful legs carrying her forward without wavering. "Ma!"

* * *

"HUSH, DEAR." MOIRA PUT HER hand to her daughter's brow, where tiny beads of perspiration clung no matter how she wiped them away. "Hush, now."

"Well, it's obvious that fairy tales have outweighed the catechism in importance in your household, Mrs. Kelly."

Moira raised her head at the words spoken in a not-so-quiet tone behind her, but she didn't turn around.

"Lauryn loves the folk tales of Ireland," she murmured without changing expression. "But she loves the catechism as well."

"Very good, as that may be all that can save her." A loud cough and the voice whined on. "From all accounts the child is deserving of some form of punishment."

Moira finally turned and stared at the thin, slightly twisted figure of the new priest, Father O'Doherty. Tiny glasses were perched at the end of a long, bony nose, half obscuring his narrowly set pale gray eyes, which now stared back at her without a hint of compassion in them.

Moira opened her mouth to speak then clamped her lips shut and turned back to the still form of her daughter.

Father O'Doherty had arrived in the village the day after Lauryn had been injured in the accident at the workshop. Her dress had caught on fire, and her left leg had been crushed in an instant as the horse had panicked and landed on the small girl. Now Lauryn had lain in bed for more than a week, her body wracked with fever as the infection from the burns and the deep gash in her leg raged inside her.

"I really don't think she's going to make it, Mrs. Kelly." The voice droned on. "You may as well prepare yourselves for the inevitable."

"I will not do that, Father." Moira clenched her jaw. "While she speaks, there is life in her."

"But she is talking to the fairy people." Father O'Doherty clasped his thin, pale hands restlessly in front of his gown. "She should be talking to the saints, whom she has need of, if she be talking to anyone."

"Lauryn is ten years old, Father, and she is very ill." Moira turned her head over her shoulder but did not look up at him. "She does not know that she has need of the saints."

"Well, then perhaps we should prepare her for . . ." The priest frowned at the expression on Moira's face. "Mrs. Kelly, the last rites are what this child needs right now if she is to make peace with God before—"

"Before what, Father?" Moira's voice carried a harsh edge, reflecting her weariness and fear of the unknown. She knew her daughter was seriously ill, but something in her refused to accept that the child was dying. Countless prayers had left her lips over the last week, and she had felt only a comforting peace as she pleaded for Lauryn's life.

"I will let you anoint her, Father—but only if you bless her to live . . . not to die." The words were spoken quietly but emphatically, and Kevin felt the force of them as he entered the room.

"Is she doing any better?" He glanced from his wife to the priest, but when neither responded, he took his cue from the expression on his wife's face and turned to the priest. "I believe we will call for you should we have need of your help, Father."

"Then I sincerely hope that you don't wait until it is too late, Mr. Kelly." Father O'Doherty bent to pick up a small leather bag off the chair beside him then backed out of the room with a brief nod. "And it would probably be of benefit if your wife taught your children more about God than fairies. Then perhaps you wouldn't find yourselves in this situation."

Kevin didn't bother to walk the man to the door but knelt straightaway by his wife's side.

"I certainly hope not many of us fall sick under his watch," Moira murmured as she shook her head. "I do not think God intended blessings to be conditional or reserved only for the dying."

"He does what he thinks best," Kevin replied evenly as he rested a hand against Lauryn's forehead.

"Thinks!" Moira snorted. "He wanted to give Lauryn the last rites." The tears began to slide slowly down her cheeks. "I will not have her die."

"And she won't, Moira." Kevin smiled weakly as he stroked Lauryn's hair back from her face. She moved her head slightly and moaned, but there was no other response. "You know that she'll just be saving her energy for a grand return."

* * *

IT WAS THE CROWN SHE kept seeing . . . moving to and from her. One second so close she could touch it and then drifting away beyond . . . the crown . . . the heart. Backward and forward . . . near yet far. The crown . . . the heart . . . the hands . . . holding on . . . holding the heart.

Whose crown?

Whose heart?

Whose hands?

* * *

"MA?"

Kevin started from his vigil by Lauryn's bed as the name drifted to him. "Ma."

Tears sprang to his eyes as he watched his daughter's eyes flutter open, then the long black lashes settled back against white cheeks.

"She's here, Lauryn. Ma's here." Kevin moved quickly to the other side of the room and laid his hand on his wife's shoulder. She was awake in an instant.

"Lauryn?"

"She's waking," Kevin whispered as Moira threw the thin quilt aside and moved to her daughter's side just as Lauryn's eyes opened again.

Moira raised her hand and began to smooth her daughter's hair away from her forehead, then, as Lauryn mumbled, she leaned closer to hear.

"Your crown."

* * *

"I CAN'T BELIEVE YOU SLEPT for so long." Alice frowned as she tried to weave several long strands of grass together. "And I had to stay quiet all the time, even though you couldn't even hear me." She breathed a long sigh. "I am so glad you're awake now."

Lauryn smiled as she looked at her sisters sitting with her beneath the oak tree. Her mother made sure that one of them was with her all of the time in case she needed help, but the three girls were always close by.

"Why do you think you couldn't wake up?" Myra made tiny pleats of the hem of her dress and then let them fall out again. "Do you think God wanted you to sleep?"

Lauryn glanced at her sister. "Maybe," she answered quietly, then she gazed up at the leaves swaying silently above them. Through the gaps between the leaves she could see tiny glimpses of the blue sky that was threatening to turn gray. Did she remember heaven?

"Did you see God?" Megan finally spoke, and Lauryn looked at her older sister carefully.

"Why do you ask that?"

Megan shrugged as she swallowed. "Oh, I just wondered . . . seeing you weren't quite alive and weren't quite dead . . ." She shrugged again. "I just would so love to see Him."

The sisters sat in silence for a long time, until light splotches of rain began to fall beyond the perimeter of the tree branches.

"Oh, quickly . . ." Myra jumped up and held her hand out to Lauryn. "Ma will be fearfully upset if you catch cold."

With Myra's help and with Alice pushing slightly, Lauryn got to her feet, hopping on her right leg until Megan handed her the wooden crutches that their father had made. With a deft movement she swung them under her arms and began to swing herself toward the cottage. Although she had been able to get out of bed only the week before, Lauryn had mastered the use of the crutches quickly and was almost having fun with the new way of walking.

It had taken five weeks for the infection to run its course and for the swelling in her leg to subside. What was left was an unsightly mess of burnt skin that was rapidly peeling off around the growing tightness of a long scar that extended from below her knee nearly to her ankle. It caused more pain than she ever admitted to have her left foot even touch the ground, but Lauryn listened to her mother's frequent prayers of thanks that she still had her leg and her life, and she knew that she was glad too.

* * *

MOIRA WASN'T SURE WHAT HAD awoken her in the early hours of the morning, but she lay still in her bed, listening to her husband's deep, even breathing, trying to hear beyond the sound to whatever had disturbed her. She finally swung her feet out of the low bed and sat on the edge, listening carefully while she looked over at her daughters all asleep together again in the one large bed. While Lauryn had been ill Megan and Myra had slept on a small bed of straw by the fireplace while the two little girls had shared a bed with their parents.

Suddenly Moira frowned as she noted the forms in the bed under the light cloth cover.

"One, two, three . . ." Moira stood up quickly and walked over to the bed, leaning down to check. "Lauryn?" she whispered as she looked around then walked to the doorway. Carefully moving the heavy wooden bar lodging the door, she slipped outside, shivering slightly as the cool autumn air closed around her. As her eyes adjusted to the darkness, a sense of apprehension began working its hold on her stomach.

"Lauryn?" She kept her voice low but loud enough to be heard out to the oak tree. "Lauryn . . . where are you?" As she walked toward the tree, her breath caught as she recognized the crutches leaning against the trunk. "Lauryn . . . are you all right?"

"I'm fine, Ma." A quiet voice sounded above Moira's head.

"Goodness, child! How did you get up there?" She put her hand to her mouth as Lauryn smiled down from a heavy branch that extended at right angles from the trunk. The children loved playing here, often riding the branch like a horse or imagining it to be a ship sailing away across the ocean.

"I climbed up." Lauryn moved slightly along the branch as if to get down. "I couldn't sleep."

"So you decided to climb a tree in the middle of the night?" Moira shook her head as she moved to the trunk and raised both hands to the worn knots that served as footholds. In a moment she was up the tree and moving sideways along the branch to sit beside Lauryn.

"Ma!" Lauryn smiled through her shock. "You shouldn't . . ."

"And why not?" Moira made herself comfortable. "Do you think I've never climbed a tree before?" She smiled. "Why do you think you like it so much?"

Lauryn grinned as she shrugged then moved closer to her mother on the branch, snuggling against her warmth.

"I kept having the dream." She shook her head. "And then I thought it would feel better out here where I could actually see heaven."

Moira nodded. Ever since her illness, Lauryn had had a recurring dream that she found difficult to explain, though it obviously meant a lot to her.

"Do you think I saw heaven, Ma?" Lauryn stared upward.

"I think so," Moira replied softly. "At least from what you say, I think I would like it to be the place."

"I didn't want to leave there," Lauryn stated simply, and her mother looked at her quickly. "But I think you prayed me back."

Moira sat very still, trying to comprehend her daughter's words as she recalled the countless prayers she had said to keep her daughter safe.

"I think I probably did." She slowly nodded. "Are you sad that I did?"

"Not now." Lauryn shook her head, then she reached over to take hold of her mother's left hand. She gently touched the ring on Moira's finger.

"I remember seeing your ring coming and going, but I thought it was part of heaven."

Moira straightened her hand so the light of the moon shone through the branches to illuminate the ring slightly, although she knew its pattern by heart.

"Tell me about it," Lauren said as she continued staring at the ring, at the crown atop a heart that was held in the clasp of two hands.

"Well," Moira smiled, "your father gave me the *claddagh* ring when he first told Meme that he was interested in me." She nodded, remembering. "At first I wore it on my right hand, but when we were betrothed I wore it on my left hand with the heart facing outward so that everybody knew that I was taken."

Lauryn glanced up. "Taken?"

"By your father. I was promised to him." Moira moved her left hand. "Then when I married your father, I turned the heart inward so that the world would know I was his wife forever." She touched the ring. "The crown means that I will be loyal to him forever, the heart means that I will love him forever, and the hands mean that we will be friends forever. Loyalty, love, and friendship, Lauryn. That is what marriage is about and what you must always strive for when you meet your man someday."

Lauryn wrinkled up her nose as she touched the ring again. "I don't think I will have a ring . . . or a man." She shook her head. "I would rather have a horse like Finnbheara."

Moira laughed quietly then gave her daughter a quick squeeze around the shoulders. "We'll see . . . and in the meantime, I think we had better get out of this tree before we catch our death from the cold." She began to move back along the branch. "I haven't prayed you back from heaven just to lose you again, Miss Lauryn Kelly."

Chapter Nine

Glasgow, Scotland, 1837
Ships and Simple Things

EWEN HELD THE *sgian dubh* for a long time in his hands before he bent down and slid it into the top of his long sock. Only then did he feel complete, and as he stood up straight, he braced his shoulders and lifted his chin.

"Clan McAlister." He spoke more loudly than he had intended, and Jimmy shifted in his crib, his eyes opening and quickly looking around the room. When he saw his father, he rolled to sit up then stared.

"What? Have you not seen your father look quite like this before?" Ewen smiled and put his hands on his hips and stood with his feet apart. "How can you be a Highlander and not have seen a kilt?"

As he said the words he shook his head, realizing that the only reason his son hadn't seen him in full Highland dress was because he'd never worn it.

There was no mirror to see what he looked like, but as Ewen closed his eyes he could visualize his father and the laird, resplendent in their full attire, and his chest swelled.

It had taken him a good while to pleat the full five yards of tightly woven tartan fabric. And then he'd struggled to make it fit across the width of the heavy leather belt he'd lain across the floor. Fitting it around his body to buckle the belt had proved yet another task. Even then it felt heavy and awkward, and he wondered how his father had done it so easily the times he remembered watching him. The ermine sporran came next, then the dark blue hat and socks, and finally *sgian dubh* . . .

"Oh, Ewen!" He turned as Bess gasped from the doorway. "I never . . ."

Her eyes shone with admiration as he stood tall, looking such a different man from the one who had walked into the house earlier, his face bleak and his shoulders hunched. He'd even washed his hair so the auburn curls clung to his head in damp, gleaming spirals. Now he looked like the man who had swept her off her feet when they first met, dressed in this very kilt. "Ewen." She could barely whisper as she repeated herself. "It's been so long . . ."

"Aye. It's given Jimmy a right start." Ewen felt the color mount in his cheeks, and he looked away for a moment. The Highland dress should be worn with pride, and yet he'd waited until Bess went to visit Ian's wife before he'd dressed in his regalia. And now he was feeling conspicuous.

"You do make a fine figure of a man, Ewen McAlister." Bess breathed the words as she stepped into the room. "A true Highlander."

Somehow her words touched him, and he took a deep breath. "Oh, if only, Bess." He shook his head and pointed to the floor where a tin trunk lay open. "I was going to pack, and I opened the chest, and it was there." He began to rub the red woolen plaid, with its stripes of white and green and blue, with his hand. "I canna resist it."

"And you shouldn't." Bess stood in front of him and laid her hand against the heavy cloaklike wrap of plaid that rested over his left shoulder. "The Highlanders wore their kilts going into battle, and I feel that's exactly what we're doing."

Ewen studied his wife's face—the gray-blue eyes and softly arched eyebrows, the slightly turned-up nose, and wide mouth that didn't laugh often enough. He covered her hand with his and drew her close to him.

"Aye, battle it is, Bess. Battle for our son's future . . . for our future." He hesitated. "For our daughter's future."

Bess looked up at him quickly, frowning as she drew back slightly. "How . . . ?"

"I've seen the signs, wife." Ewen drew her back against him, then he whispered in her ear. "And I think I've seen her, Bess. I think I've dreamed her."

Bess breathed deeply as the smell of the tartan mingled with that of the man she adored more than life itself. "I think I have, too, Ewen . . . more than once."

* * *

THEY WALKED TO GLASGOW, TAKING their time, for they didn't exactly know their destination. Ewen carried Jimmy on one arm and in the other hand carried the tin trunk that held nearly everything they owned. Bess carried some blankets and a small wooden box with a hinged lid.

Every now and then Bess glanced down at the box as she walked, admiring the delicately detailed thistle carved into the lid. She knew Ewen's father had done the carving, and her heart suddenly ached. The thistle, with its dark green prickly foliage adorned with a magnificent deep purple flower, was the emblem of the free spirit of the Highlands and yet was not to be seen in the city—where it was considered a weed.

"Do you think there'll be a bad feeling about us in Glasgow?" She raised her head to her husband. "We are still Highlanders even though we've been in the mines for three years."

"Probably." Ewen watched the road ahead. "The Lowlanders canna get it out of their heads that we're a dirty, good-for-nothing lot." He shook his head. "Ian reckoned we were crazy to be leaving the mine and that I'd never get a job in the yards."

"You will." Bess was quietly emphatic. She raised her chin. "I've been praying lately, Ewen."

There was a moment's silence between them; then he simply nodded. "Do you think that will help?"

Bess nodded. "Aye, I do." Her cheeks colored slightly. "I think I've always prayed a little, in my thoughts, but one night . . . after I woke up with the dream of our girl in my head . . . I began to actually say things, Ewen. Very quietly, mind, but it was like I was talking to Him."

Again she waited for some sort of reaction from her husband, but he merely nodded, so she went on.

"So then I started telling Him absolutely everything." A faraway look filled her expression as she recalled her pleas in the darkness of night. "I told him all about leaving the Highlands and losing the babies and trying to have a better life for Jim . . . for our children." She smiled as she laid her hand across her stomach. "I told Him that you needed to find a job in the city, and then I told Him that I'd be more diligent about talking with Him if I could go to the kirk."

"So you made a deal?" Ewen smiled at his wife's forthright manner. "With God?"

"Oh my . . ." Bess put her hand to her cheek. "It doesn't exactly sound like praying when you put it like that." She swallowed. "But I believe I did."

Ewen stopped to shift the sleeping Jimmy from one arm to the other. As he bent to pick up the trunk again, he glanced at Bess. "So do you think He'll answer your prayers?"

"Mmm." She nodded. "I get a feeling He will." She suddenly smiled so that the dimples that lay waiting suddenly appeared in her cheeks. "Maybe it wouldn't hurt if you tried as well."

"What? Praying?" Ewen raised one eyebrow then shook his head. "Maybe He doesn't talk to strangers."

Bess laughed then, a delightful sound that seemed to make the road less stony and their problems less dreary. Soon her husband was laughing as well.

They made a fine sight on the Glasgow road, the tall red-haired Highlander with his tiny wife holding onto his arm and their child asleep on his shoulder.

Dusk was gathering as they reached the outskirts of the city, where long rows of two- and three-story buildings stood so tall that they blocked out the moonlight. Familiar, household sounds echoed in the cooling night air, and occasionally the McAlisters passed people on the cobbled road; however, the passersby usually kept their heads down and didn't acknowledge them.

"So where are we staying?" Bess finally asked the question she had tried not to worry about until now.

Ewen reached into his pocket and took out a grubby piece of paper with a single row of writing on it. "Ian said his family stayed at this place for a spell when they moved here. The woman takes in boarders." He looked up at a street sign. "We just have to find it now."

They asked one man who shrugged his shoulders and moved on without speaking, then a woman who gave vague directions while waving her hand, but it wasn't until they asked a young boy that they got firm directions. Then he walked with them, chattering as he led the way along some narrower alleyways and up to a block that was three stories high.

"Up in top." He pointed to the top level. "Everybody knows Mrs. Wynyard."

And then he was gone.

"Mrs. Wynyard . . . please let us in," Bess murmured as they climbed the stairs, avoiding piles of rubbish and excrement. She put her hand over her mouth as a wave of nausea swept through her body.

"Are you all right?" Ewen stopped, but she only nodded and waved him on.

At the top level Ewen surveyed the doors and finally knocked on one that had dull yellow paint peeling off the wood. They could hear sounds from inside, but it took a while for the door to open a crack. A woman peered out at them.

Before Ewen could speak, she glanced at Bess and Jimmy and nodded. "Ye'll have to have the babe in with ye, and ye share wi' two others." She pointed down the hall. "Privy down there and water fountain that way beside it . . . when it works." She opened the door to reveal her full figure in a stained cotton dress that was mostly obscured by a very large shawl wrapped around her and draped almost to the floor on one side. "Ye pay me by the day and I don't ask any questions." She turned and padded away on feet covered with woolen cloths wrapped around them and tied with string of some sort.

Ewen glanced at Bess, who shrugged and began to walk inside. She was barely through the door when a man sneezed violently beside her and she gasped out loud. He was one of five men sitting, or lying, on narrow mattresses on the floor, each man appearing to be a replica of the other with their disheveled gray clothes and thin, unshaven faces. Two of them looked up and nodded, but the others seemed to be unaware of anyone's arrival. The stale smell of whisky seemed to hang around them.

"No drink allowed here." Mrs. Wynyard stood at the doorway of another room as she gestured toward the men. "But they make up for it in the town. As long as they keep enough for their board, I don't care what they do with the rest of their money."

The room Mrs. Wynard gestured to was slightly smaller, and there was one empty mattress in the corner. Two women occupied the other two cots.

"Och, look at the bairn." One of the women spoke loudly, and Jimmy raised his head, startled by the noise. He looked around and began to whimper at the sight of all the strangers until Ewen put the trunk down and patted his back until he settled. Then he led Bess to the mattress. She stood silently looking at the soiled cotton covering, then quietly put down the blankets she was carrying and used one to cover the bed.

"That won't stop the lice, love." The older woman spoke with an Irish accent. "Where ye from?"

"Lanarkshire."

"Kintyre."

Ewen and Bess spoke at once, and the woman grinned. "Yer Highlanders can never figure out where ye're from." She pointed to her chest and then toward the younger girl. "I'm Molly from Galway, and young Meg here is from Donegal, but she don' talk much. I've bin here two years, and I can tell yer most things yer need to know." She looked at Ewen. "Ye have a job, sonny?"

"Not yet." Ewen shook his head as he sat down on the mattress and nestled Jimmy beside him. "I'm planning to try at the steel works . . ." He stopped as Molly shook her head firmly.

"Not the works, lad." She pointed outside. "The new boatyard is the place. They're askin' for men today, but this lot out here aren't good for a day's work." She sized up Ewen's appearance as he removed his jacket, and she nodded. "Yer'll be fine, sonny. I'll show yer where to go tomorrow."

A while later, as Ewen and Bess lay in the darkness listening to the two women snoring soundly only a few feet away, Bess snuggled in closer to her husband and immediately felt the comfort of his arm around her.

"I do believe my prayers were answered, Ewen." She didn't wait for him to respond. "I asked that someone might help us, and here's Molly saying she knows where you need to go."

"You think an old Irish woman is the answer to your prayers?" Ewen smiled in the darkness. "The Lord surely does work in mysterious ways."

"Well, I think she could be." Bess pouted slightly. "We'll just have to trust that she knows."

Ewen pondered for a moment then squeezed her gently. "Aye, I'll trust her because at the moment I don't have anyone else to trust."

Bess lay quietly so long, Ewen thought she was asleep. Then, just as he began to feel sleep work its way through his tired body, she murmured quietly, "Do you think that's how faith works, Ewen?"

* * *

THEY WALKED THROUGH NARROW STREETS for a good half an hour before the roughly cobbled roads led to the more finely paved streets of Glasgow. Bess walked with her mouth slightly open, in awe, as they passed large, opulent buildings whose ornate frontages towered above them, several stories high and often two to three times as wide.

The roads were constantly busy with carriages wheeling by, drawn by fine horses stepping out briskly, their necks arched and their hooves clattering on the cobbles. Women with parasols and men with walking canes seemed to have no purpose but to wander the streets and parks of smooth green lawn that were laid out neatly alongside the roadways.

Many people stared at the peculiar little group before pretending they simply weren't there. Molly chuckled. "I thought I'd bring yer this way to see how the other half live." She nodded at a couple waiting to cross the road as yet another carriage rumbled by. "Like as not ye won't come this way ever again."

As they continued on, the cream sandstone exterior and high wooden double doors of a large church made Ewen and Bess stop, and Molly watched as they stared upward at the towering steeple. Neither spoke, but Molly caught the look of expectation on Bess's face.

"The likes of us don't go in that church." She nodded in the direction of the crowded housing they'd left that morning. "There's some other churches closer to us that some folk go to. Not as fancy, mind." She shook her head at the ornate wrought-iron fencing. "But God shouldn't mind that, should He?"

She turned down another long street, and they walked in silence until she pointed ahead toward a bridge over a wide river where the dark, murky brown water was barely moving. "There's the River Clyde, and the yard is down a ways."

Ewen felt a prickle of anticipation as Molly led the way along the riverside toward an area where the finely designed buildings of the city were replaced by large, squat industrial buildings with brick walls and rows of long, narrow glass windows.

Beyond these, at the river's edge, boats of all shapes and sizes rocked gently at their moorings while men loaded and unloaded goods. In the middle of the river, a large ship eased its way past the other boats, the water rolling and surging past its sides as the huge hull sliced through the water.

"Ewen, there aren't any sails up on that boat." Bess stared at the ship then along the quay. "But it's moving so fast . . ."

"That's a steam ship, lass." Molly nodded wisely. "They run on coal." She shook her head as Bess frowned. "Don't ask me how it works, but a friend of mine stokes the boiler on one of those boats, and he says it gobbles up coal like a starving man eating pudding."

"And the more ships they make, the more coal they need to make them and to run them." Ewen quietly quoted the mine deputy as he stared at the ship. There was something about the size and strength of it that stirred the blood in his veins, and he gave Jimmy a slight squeeze. "Shall your father make one of those boats, Jimmy?" He pointed to the ship, and Jimmy raised his hand to point as well. "Aye . . . a big one like that. Shall I build one?"

"Aye . . . all on your own." Bess nudged him, but she sensed his excitement. "And you haven't even got a job yet."

"Ah, but you have faith that I will." Ewen began walking again while lifting Jimmy up onto his shoulders, but he continued watching the steam ship as it disappeared around a curve in the river. In that instant, he made a commitment. "I am going to build a ship." He wasn't sure who he was talking to or even why he felt the need to say the words out loud, but his jaw clenched and he nodded his head with resolve. He glanced along the quay at the other ships. "I'm going to build lots of ships that will sail across the sea to places we've not even thought about."

They were nearing a large yard with the sign NAPIER SHIP YARD out front, and Molly stopped and pointed. "Well, that'll be the best place to start if you're going to build all those ships." She shook her head. "I'm not saying you'll get a job, but this is the newest yard, and the boys say that they need men the most." She shrugged. "They say the pay isn't the best but—"

"But I'd be learning how to do something . . . with my hands and my mind." Ewen swallowed hard. "And then I can teach Jimmy."

Bess heard the catch in his voice, and she slipped her hand into the crook of his arm and gave it a squeeze. "Then you'd better go and ask them, hadn't you."

"Aye." Ewen didn't move, and she applied the pressure on his arm a little more firmly.

"You have to do it, Ewen . . . and if they don't have any jobs, then there are plenty of other places here that will. We'll just keep on trying till you find one."

There was something about the quiet confidence in her voice that lifted him, and he straightened up as he lifted Jimmy off his shoulders and handed him to his mother. "Aye." He smiled as he nodded. "Aye . . . the sooner I go, the sooner I start work."

He walked toward the yard entrance with a purposeful stride and didn't turn even when Bess called out with a lilt in her voice, "And who ever heard of a Highlander building ships, Ewen McAlister?"

He had a smile on his face as he entered the yard.

* * *

DAVID ELDER STOOD WITH HIS hands in his pockets as he contemplated the ship's huge iron hull mounted on the slip in front of him. After a moment, he drew a small pulley mechanism from his pocket and considered it carefully. He studied the shape of it and turned it from side to side then looked back at the hull. It seemed incongruous that such a tiny mechanism was so vital to the construction of such a large ship, but he needed it to be more functional still. He gripped the device and put it back into his pocket, nodding as an idea began to solidify, then he turned to walk back to his office.

There was a good feeling about this yard, and the workers were making good progress on the boat, even with some of the innovations that he had insisted on.

"Mr. Elder, sir . . ."

David turned as the yard manager spoke behind him. Donaldson was an excellent manager, and he smiled as he acknowledged him along with the young, taller man standing beside him.

"Looking for work, sir." Donaldson tilted his head toward the man. "By the name of Ewen McAlister. No experience but says he's a hard worker."

The expression on Donaldson's face seemed to say the same as Elder was thinking. *A hard worker—like everybody else who comes here asking for a job.* He kept his hands in his pockets as he studied Ewen's face and then his hands, which immediately stopped playing with the cap he held.

"What work have you done, lad?"

Ewen hesitated. "The mines . . . sir." He swallowed. "I've left there."

Elder frowned. "How did you leave?" He knew the stringent rules the mine owners enforced, often locking the workers and their families into life-long contracts. It was something he detested but recognized would continue as long as there were desperate workers who were prepared to live under such terms just to have work.

"I told them I had to." Ewen nodded. "That I had to move on."

"Move on?" Elder looked puzzled. "Most miners don't simply move on."

Ewen squared his shoulders. "Aye . . . but my son is nearly a year old, and I did not want to have him live his life underground. He's worth more than that." He spoke quickly then frowned at himself as he finished. "And I want to build ships, sir."

It was a simple statement, but Elder sensed the genuine feeling behind it, and it stirred him. There was something about the young man standing in front of him that touched him. He turned to Donaldson. "Weren't we needing extra workers on the plating?"

Donaldson glanced quickly at Ewen then back to his employer. "Aye . . . I think we are a man short." He nodded. "But he would need to start today."

Elder nodded and looked at Ewen. "Do you know anything about plating?"

"No, sir." Ewen felt his stomach knot. "Nothing at all." In that moment, he all but gave up the idea of working in the yard as he realized how much he didn't know. These men must think him a fool. "Nothing at all," he repeated quietly.

"Could you start work immediately?"

Ewen stared, then he stammered, "Aye, sir. Right away . . . if you'll have me."

"We'll have you." Elder nodded. "You'll have to prove yourself, of course . . . a week's trial before you get any pay." He raised one eyebrow as Ewen nodded. "Good . . . Donaldson will show you what to do." Elder waved as if to dismiss him, then he frowned as Ewen took a quick look behind him. "Something wrong?"

"Emm . . ." Ewen coughed and nodded back toward the yard entrance. "I'll just need to tell my family. They're waiting . . . outside."

Elder nodded then pulled out his watch and glanced at it. "Soon as you can, then."

* * *

Bess had been watching the yard entrance the whole time while Molly kept Jimmy entertained. He had accepted the older woman, and she seemed to enjoy making him laugh as much as much as she could. He was gurgling as Bess suddenly pointed. "Here he comes!" She put her hands to her lips. "Oh, Molly . . ."

Ewen swung across the road with long strides, and Bess could see the smile on his face. "Oh, Molly . . ."

"I got it, Bess!" He kept his voice low, but she could sense his excitement. "I start now . . . right now."

He gathered her close to him and gave her a fierce hug, lifting Jimmy up as well. He kissed the boy's forehead then held him slightly away. "Your father's going to build ships, Jimmy." His voice caught. "You'll be proud of me, Jimmy. I'll make sure of that."

* * *

DAVID ELDER WATCHED THE FAMILY from his second-floor office, and a slight smile played on his lips as he turned to Donaldson.

"Work with him, John." He nodded. "I think he'll be good."

* * *

"I PROMISE THAT IT'S ALL there."

Ewen looked up quickly as John Donaldson stood in front of him. A few minutes earlier John had handed Ewen the handful of coins and now, as he sat on a small, upturned barrel counting the change, John watched him.

"Oh, aye . . . I'm sure it is." Ewen ducked his head as he pushed the coins into his pocket. "I'm just doing some figures . . . Bess and I want to move into our own place as soon as we can."

Donaldson nodded. He'd already asked earlier in the week where Ewen was staying, and he'd described one of the worst areas in the city.

"You should be able to get a better place with that." He folded his arms. "Mr. Elder is a very fair man. He makes sure his workers are looked after . . . if they work hard."

"Oh, aye, I'll work hard." Ewen stood up. "I love to work . . . here." He pointed at the ground. "I feel like I've learnt more this week than in my entire life, and when I look out at those big ships and think I'm helping to make one . . . it makes me want to work even harder."

"Good." Donaldson nodded as he recognized the genuineness in Ewen's comment, then he gestured with his thumb toward the office. "Let me tell you a bit about Mr. Elder. He's one of the finest marine engineers in Glasgow." He paused. "No, make that the whole of England."

"But I thought he ran the yard." Ewen frowned as Donaldson shook his head.

"He does this because he wants to make the finest ships." He smiled. "Mr. Elder is a university man, but he's also fascinated by how the simplest tool works and how to improve it. He's in the office, but his mind is every-where."

Ewen nodded. "He seems a very kind man as well."

"Aye." Donaldson nodded again. "There's many that call themselves Christians in these isles but very few that other men can call by the same name." He smiled. "And David Elder is one of those men."

"Aye," Ewen responded quietly. He had already told Bess how different Mr. Elder was compared with the harsh and unpredictable mine owners.

"So, lad, work hard and watch Mr. Elder. See how he treats you and watch how he handles matters." He began to walk away then paused. "Mr. Elder likes you, McAlister. You can learn much from him."

PART TWO

Chapter Ten

Downham, England, 1845
To Zion

"JACOB MORGAN . . . 1800 TO 1840." Edward slowly read the inscription on the narrow gray tombstone then bent to pull away some weeds that had grown up the sides. After five years, the grave was completely grassed over as if it were part of an ordinary field, but as always, he was careful to stand to the side of the grave. It never failed to bother him that his father's remains lay directly beneath him. "Will you always haunt me, Da?"

He stared up at the huge oak tree that, for as long as he could remember, had spread protective arms over the graves in the village cemetery. The last few years had brought many new graves as disease and death had overshadowed the village, with most of the victims being small children. It was now commonplace to walk the main path through the village without hearing a child's voice.

"Edward!"

He turned at the sound of his name, frowning slightly as he recognized his sister, Emma, walking toward him. She was careful to lift the hem of her dress with both hands as she picked her way through the longer grass, but she dropped it to give him a quick hug. "I thought I might find you here." She squinted in the sunlight as she looked down at her father's grave. "Five years is a long time, and yet sometimes it doesn't seem any time at all."

"Mmm," Edward responded quietly. He loved his twin, but she had a gift for turning up at the wrong time. "How is Mother?"

Emma shook her head. "Not well. That is why I've made the trip to tell you. She has been low for the last week."

"Is William with her?" Edward began to walk away from the grave, and she followed behind him, still talking.

"No, William is working, but Patrick is at home. He is helping the new missionary from America set up a meeting at one of the farms." She smiled. "There is so much happening, Edward—so many people who are embracing the gospel. They say that the congregations in Preston are growing so fast we are easily the biggest group in the whole of England and Scotland."

"How nice for you," Edward responded quietly. He found it a bit irritating to listen to Emma when she talked about the church that she and her husband, Patrick, had affiliated themselves with, but he had to admit that her enthusiasm had stood the test of time. She had been a devout follower of the Latter-day Saint religion since the day she had first listened to a missionary preaching in the Preston town square some eight years before.

"I think the missionaries' visits are the one thing Mama looks forward to." Emma smiled. "She likes to ask them a lot of questions about the Bible, but she is also reading the Book of Mormon."

"I thought she was having difficulty seeing anything," Edward interrupted.

"Oh, as long as it's during the daytime and there's plenty of light, she is able to." Emma shook her head. "She reads by day and questions us by night." Emma stole a quick glance at her brother. "Even William is enjoying talking with the missionaries. He says that what they have to say makes a lot of sense."

"William is eighteen." Edward almost snorted. "He doesn't know anything."

"Oh, so does that mean you didn't know anything at eighteen, either?" Emma retorted. "Or is it only William who has the problem?"

"No, William is not alone. Neither you nor I knew much of the world at eighteen." Edward shook his head. It seemed that whenever he spent time with Emma lately there was an underlying friction that he couldn't define. He had felt it come between them when their mother and William had gone to live in Preston with Emma and Patrick.

The sun passed behind a large gray cloud as they reached Emma's horse and cart, and Edward glanced up at the sky. "You might get wet before you get home."

Emma shrugged. "It's only water, and it will be cleaner than the water that we have to wash in." She shuddered. "That is one thing I miss so much about living in Downham. It is so much cleaner here."

"Not clean enough. The cholera still festered."

There was a long silence between them, then Emma took a deep breath. "Anyway, would you be able to come and see Mama soon? She sometimes says your name in her sleep."

"What . . . is she telling me off?" Edward actually smiled, and Emma responded immediately.

"No, she used up all that fire when she lived with you—now she just wants to see you." She touched him gently on the arm. "Please, Edward. I really don't know that she has too much longer."

Edward nodded slowly as he stared up toward the church steeple.

"I'll try and make it next week. I should be finished with the lambing by then."

Emma nodded as she held out her hand to be helped into the cart. Although she was still the exuberant Emma he had grown up with, she had changed since Patrick had been promoted to a manager at the cotton mill. Edward bowed slightly over her hand as he helped her up. "Thank you for taking the time to visit a poor peasant, my lady."

Emma grinned as she swatted the top of his head with her hand before she settled onto the seat. "I am not a lady," she pouted.

"Well, I always knew that," Edward responded quickly, then they both laughed.

"I miss you very much, Edward." Emma was suddenly serious. "You are my other half, after all. I feel for you wherever you are. Remember that."

He knew immediately that she was referring to the special bond they had shared since birth—the ability to sense one another's moods or emotions, whether near or far away. It wasn't a constant connection, but it seemed to manifest itself whenever either of them was troubled in any way.

"I do remember." Edward took his time undoing the rope tethering the horse to a railing. "I remember too well," he finished softly.

"Oh, Edward." Emma shook her head, and the tears formed in her eyes but never spilled. "You must move on. She's gone now." Her voice broke. "Lizzy's dead."

There was a long silence, then Edward slowly shook his head. "Not for me, Emma . . . never for me."

He stood where he was as she moved the buggy on and until he could no longer hear the sound of the wheels on the cobbles, then he turned and contemplated the graveyard entrance. For a moment he lingered, then he wandered back to the graves, passing by his father's to where Lizzy lay.

He knelt where he always did, close to the stone. "Elizabeth Morgan." He ran his fingers over the inscription. "1821 to 1844."

He always hoped that saying the last date would somehow make it more final, but it only made him wonder why she had to go. They had been married three years when the cholera raged through the village. The weaker ones—the old and the young had succumbed early—but Lizzy . . . Lizzy was strong. She and her mother had worked so hard to help where they could, attending to the elderly and placing tiny babies into small coffins when their little bodies couldn't cope with the sickness anymore.

Lizzy would lie in his arms at night crying softly because she hadn't been able to help enough . . . because she couldn't keep them from dying.

"And then it took you, Lizzy . . . and our little one." The words caught in his throat, and he shook his head. They hadn't known for certain whether Lizzy was with child. She had been so busy with helping in the village that it seemed the nausea might simply be from tiredness. And then it was impossible to know as the fever struck and Lizzy never left her bed again.

"Oh, Lizzy." Edward's shoulders shook.

He had stayed in the cottage they had shared since they were married—the cottage he had been born in. He and Lizzy had married the year after his father died, and so Edward had taken over the running of the household, caring for his mother, brother, and wife. Thankfully, his work as a shepherd and laborer on the estate was appreciated by Lord Clitheroe, so they fared well enough.

It had been Emma's suggestion that their mother and William move to Preston to live with her and her husband, Patrick. The handloom weaving his mother had done at the cottage had been done away with as large new factories opened in Preston, and there was no more work for her in the village. The same thing had happened to young William. Struggling to make ends meet on the estate, Lord Clitheroe had no work for William either. It seemed an obvious solution that would provide work and a living for them all and, although Edward had resisted at first, the thought of his own cottage with his wife had made the decision easier.

Three years together . . .

Edward closed his eyes a moment, then glanced at the grave once more before slowly walking away.

* * *

EMMA HELD BACK UNTIL THE cart crossed the bridge over the stream. Then she cried quietly, letting the summer breeze dry the tears as they ran down her cheeks.

"Oh, Edward, if only you knew." She shook her head and swallowed hard. The tune of a favorite hymn worked its way into her mind, and she began to hum, letting the tune pass through her heart rather than just her mind.

By the time she reached the outskirts of Preston, it was getting dark, but she could still see clearly as she guided the horse to the new house, a single-story cottage with three rooms.

She could still clearly hear the astonishment in her mother's voice as Patrick had announced not only his new job, but the news that they were moving away from the crowded tenements into a house with three glorious rooms.

The house was nearer to the factory, and Patrick had reasoned that he would be able to get to work faster—and for longer, if needed. He had definitely been needed longer, and Emma had gotten used to the idea of him going to work at four in the morning and returning after seven at night.

"Emma!" Norah Morgan's voice strained in the darkness even before Emma had closed the door of their house. "Emma, I need you."

Emma quickly crossed the room. "Are you faring better?' She watched as her mother slowly rose off the pillow that was creased under her head.

"A little." Norah's voice shook with the effort of trying to sit up, so she lay back down, easing herself at first then dropping with a quick sigh as she fell back against the bed. "Where have you been?" She put a finely wrinkled hand on Emma's arm. "Patrick said you went up to Downham."

"I did." Emma smiled. "I went to visit Edward, as I hadn't seen him for a long while."

Norah managed a smile as she nodded. "How is he doing?"

"Oh, he's busy with the lambing, and Lord Clitheroe keeps him occupied with other work." Emma slipped the sheet farther up over her mother's thin chest.

"Was he at the farm?"

"No . . ." Emma hesitated then shrugged. "He was at the graveyard."

"Oh." Norah closed her eyes and nodded. "Of course he would be . . . it's lambing time. It's a year ago that Lizzy died."

"Yes . . . and five years since Da passed on." Emma sat down on the edge of the bed. "Do you ever wonder if you will see Da again, Mama?" She listened to her mother's shallow breathing for some time before Norah nodded.

"I've wondered . . . I've hoped." She smiled weakly. "And I know you've always said we'll be together after this life, Emma, and now even William says I will. He says that we'll all be resurrected and then I'll see Jacob again." Her lips quivered. "William has been reading such a lot lately, and he tells me about what he's read. He seems to understand it more than I do, though." She looked up at her daughter. "You've always believed it, haven't you, Emma? About Joseph Smith and the gospel being restored by an angel."

Emma nodded. "I do, Mama. From the very instant I heard Elder Kimball teach it at the marketplace, it's stayed firm in my heart."

"But many say that it's evil." Norah frowned. "I tell them it can't be because you're not . . . and Patrick's not . . . and William definitely isn't."

"Thank you, Mama." Emma smiled. "There are indeed a great many people who misunderstand the missionaries' message, but many others recognize that it is the word of God." She stared across the room, but her mind was much further away. "And God is sending His blessings upon us all the time. Patrick has been given this job above many others, and we can save some money now."

"And maybe the Lord will bless you with a child." Norah spoke very quietly, and Emma simply patted her hand where it lay on the bed cover.

"William is our child right now." She stood up. "And now it's time for you to get some sleep. Then you'll be ready to listen to William tell you more about the things he's discovering. I think you listen to him more than me."

Norah's eyes were closing even as she spoke, but as Emma reached the door her mother said, "Emma . . . I do believe you. I do believe I will see Jacob again—and that can't be evil or dreadful, can it?"

Emma smiled. "Not unless your wife is the Widow Heaphy, who disliked her husband from the very beginning. I should think seeing her again would be dreadful indeed for that poor man."

She heard her mother's quiet chuckle as she closed the door.

"You made good time." Patrick Miller stood in the doorway to the other room. "Did you not spend long with Edward?

"No, he was at the graveyard and not in a talkative mood." Emma shook her head. "In fact, he's never in a talkative mood anymore. It's so unlike my Edward to grieve so, as though Lizzy died only yesterday."

"Maybe that is because it's Lizzy's Edward who is grieving . . . not yours." Patrick held out a plate with a slice of bread and a small piece of cheese on it. "Are you hungry?"

"Not really." Emma shook her head. "I went to tell Edward about Mama but also to tell him about our plans. But . . . I just couldn't."

"Maybe it's too soon." Patrick broke off a small piece of bread and chewed it thoughtfully. "We have this new work, and it will make things happen sooner, but maybe we need to keep our plans to ourselves for now."

Emma stared at her husband and thought once again how fortunate she'd been to meet this gentle man who had embraced the gospel with the same enthusiasm that she had. In fact, they had met the day they were both baptized by the missionaries in the River Ribble. Still soaking wet from his own immersion, Patrick had handed her a wrap as she came out of the water after her baptism. It had taken only a few weeks for the pair to decide they wanted to be married, but there had been months of resistance from both of their families—and especially from Edward.

Thinking of her brother again and especially of his antagonism toward the Latter-day Saint religion, Emma nodded. "You are right, Patrick. I just cannot help longing to share something I feel so strongly about with Edward just like we always have . . ." She hesitated. "Always did."

Patrick put the plate down on the table and held out his arms to her. As she went to him and rested her head against his shoulder, he pressed his lips to the top of her head.

"I can't imagine what it must be like, after all these years, to have the person you were closest to since birth persist in rejecting you." He kissed her again. "You are an amazing woman, Emma Miller."

Emma didn't answer, but she held him closer, the events of the day melting away in his embrace.

"We will tell him . . . soon." Patrick gave her a quick squeeze.

"Tell who what soon?" William Morgan walked into the room and pretended to shield his eyes as he saw his sister embracing her husband. "Me?"

Emma shook her head. As William sat down at the table, she walked over and touched his hair, identical to her own in color, then glanced up at Patrick.

Patrick hesitated a moment before nodding. Emma nodded in return and sat down on the chair in front of him. He was quiet for a moment, then he laid his hands on her shoulders and looked at his young brother-in-law. "William . . . we have something we need to talk to you about." He held up his hand as William immediately jumped halfway out of his chair.

"Mama?"

"No . . . Mama's fine," Emma reassured him. "It's about . . . us."

"You're having a baby?" William stayed standing, looking hopeful.

"No . . . no baby." Patrick shook his head. "This is about . . . Zion."

William put down the bread he had picked up and studied Emma's and Patrick's faces closely. "Zion? In America?"

"We hope that's where it is." Emma smiled as she held Patrick's hand.

"We've been thinking about it for a long time, William." Patrick hesitated. "Ever since Emma and I became Latter-day Saints we have listened to talk of Zion, but now that talk has become so much more . . . it is more like a call."

William nodded, still watching his sister closely. "So . . . what does this mean?" He swallowed the bread with difficulty. "For you . . . for us?"

Patrick shook his head. "Nothing at the moment, but soon . . ." He left the end open.

"Soon?" William stared then glanced toward his mother's room and nodded. "I understand."

"The only thing we need to worry about for now is saving enough money for our fare." Patrick shrugged. "The Lord will decide the rest."

William looked up quickly. "When you say 'our' . . . do you mean *our*?" He pointed toward them then to himself.

Emma watched the look on his face, and then she nodded slowly. "If that's what you want, we will find a way."

She was unprepared for the look of determination that settled over her brother's face as he clenched a fist and pressed it against the table.

"I shall find a way." He looked straight at Emma. "You will not be going to Zion without me."

Chapter Eleven

Downham, England, 1845
Leaving the Valley

THE LAMBS WERE GOOD TO WATCH.

Edward nodded to himself as he watched a group of sheep quickly move into a bunch on the far side of the field as something disturbed them then just as quickly move apart and resume their incessant nibbling at the grass. Each new lamb would follow its mother in a dazed way as she ran then butt up against her stomach as soon as she stopped and begin a frantic feeding, its long tail and rear end wiggling uncontrollably.

Edward walked slowly across the field, keeping an eye out for any lambs that didn't jump and run. The lambing season had been a good one, and Lord Clitheroe was pleased with the growing flock, but Edward was aware that there wasn't much money to be had in a flock of sheep. He cared for this flock, but he was mainly concerned with producing the cash crops that could be sent to market. Oats and barley were being asked for more and more, and Lord Clitheroe was making more use of his fields to harvest those crops. Finance was a real issue on the estates as the booming cotton industry moved into the towns, leaving the cottage craftsmen and women on the estate without work and the estate without income, either from their rent or from their productivity.

Edward whistled, calling the small brown terrier that he used around the farm to his side. Jack was just as happy to chase rabbits instead of sheep, and he had already provided his master with one for the day.

"Come, Jack." Edward clicked his fingers, and the dog wheeled around his heels and followed beside him. "Let's go cook up that rabbit—I'll even share some with you."

They walked back to the cottage, and after setting the meat cooking with some vegetables in a large cast-iron pot, Edward wandered outside, preferring the sounds of the farm to the silence of an empty cottage.

He lit a pipe and leaned up against the low, broad stone wall that ran a few feet away from the cottage. Jack circled a few times then settled at his feet.

"Evening, Edward." A man in his early thirties stopped on the lane running along the stone wall. Like Edward, Matthew Smith had been born and raised in Downham. "Done for the day?"

"All done, Matthew." Edward nodded as Matthew leaned against the other side of the wall. "Last lamb born this morning."

"Ah, we have a few to go." Matthew nodded. "I'll be glad when it's all finished, for then we'll be off."

"Going to take them to the market, then?" Edward frowned. He hadn't heard talk of plans for getting rid of any stock early, but things had certainly been changing in the valley lately.

Matthew shook his head. "Nay . . . we're leaving. Leaving Downham for good." He tilted his head to one side. "Did you not know?"

Edward shook his head. "What's wrong for you to be leaving? You have no need of city work."

"I'm not talking about the city, Edward." Matthew frowned as if he couldn't believe Edward didn't know what he was talking about. "Julie and I are going to join her parents . . . in America." He stared out over the fields. "We've been wanting to go for so long, but we couldn't save the money . . . until now. Now it is possible. The missionaries have arranged an emigration fund. The money is there for us to pay our fares, and then we repay it when we get to Zion."

"But how do they know you will repay it?" Edward was skeptical. "It will take you years."

He stopped as Matthew shook his head. "We are trusted to repay it, Edward, and we surely will." He folded his arms. "And we will be able to repay it because we are going to the city of Nauvoo. Joseph Smith established a new city in Illinois, and it is growing beyond comprehension. It started as a swamp, but it is already the largest city in Illinois with trade and businesses . . . where we can find work readily." He hesitated. "Surely Emma has told you these things?"

Edward drew gently on his pipe. In the years since Emma had affiliated herself with the Latter-day Saints, she had tried to tell him many things, but he had turned a deaf ear. Even when most of the people in the village of Downham had enthusiastically embraced the message of the restored gospel and were baptized by the missionaries, he had stood firm and apart.

"She may have, but . . . I have had other things on my mind, Matthew."

"Yes . . ." Matthew looked at his friend with understanding. "Have you never thought to leave here, Edward? So many people are going overseas— thousands upon thousands leaving to find more opportunities in the colonies." He shook his head. "Even if we were not going to Zion, I feel we would leave . . . somehow. Julie's parents have written of the vast country where there is land for the taking—"

"For a man such as I?" Edward put in quickly, then he looked up at the darkening sky. "I've thought about it. I even looked at the shipping offices in Birmingham once when I was sent up there, but when I talked to Lizzy about it later, she said that she would never leave the valley . . ." He stopped and clenched his teeth on the stem of the pipe.

"And she never will," Matthew finished for him, his voice surprisingly gentle. "But that doesn't mean you can't, Edward."

Matthew walked away then, leaving Edward still standing by the wall, and it wasn't until he became aware of the nearly burning smell from inside the cottage that he moved. He managed to salvage most of the rabbit stew, and Jack happily gulped down most of it anyway as Edward moved restlessly around the room, oblivious to the plate of food he had dished up for himself. It was dark when he finally stopped pacing and picked up a small box that sat in the corner.

He sat down on the edge of the bed as he lifted the lid, then he simply stared at the contents for some time. The box had been Lizzy's sewing box since she was young, handcrafted for her by her father. In it she had stored special things as well as her sewing materials and, after they were married, the small note of their marriage date. Edward held the marriage note for a moment, then he pushed some of the other articles aside. He knew that in the bottom of the box was another piece of paper he had left untouched for the last three years.

As he drew it out, he carefully closed the lid. Then he slowly undid the folds of the paper, staring at a space on the wall above the fireplace and murmuring the words that he knew were on the page.

"The directors of the New Zealand Company do hereby give notice that they are ready to receive applications for a free passage to the town of Wellington . . ." He stopped, surprised that he still remembered that much, then he opened up the paper and kept reading to the end. "Being married and not exceeding forty years of age," he stated as he shook his head. "Single men accompanied by one or more adult sisters . . ." He sighed and lay back on the bed. "So I wouldn't qualify on any count anymore, Matthew," he said to the absent Matthew as he stared up at the ceiling. "I am married but I don't have a wife anymore, and I certainly don't have any available sisters. I also don't have any money to pay my own way . . ."

But that doesn't mean you can't, Edward. The words played in his mind until he folded the paper again and laid it back in the box. As he leaned forward to place the box on the floor again, he noticed a piece of beige linen that had fallen to the floor beside him. He picked it up and studied the rows of fine stitching Lizzy had sewn onto the sampler. A row of capital letters followed by several lines of an intricate leaf design, two rows of lowercase alphabet, and her name.

"Elizabeth Morgan." Edward read the name stitched into the cloth. "Downham, eighteen forty . . ." He stopped, staring at the space where the last number should have been, the needle poked into the fabric with pale blue cotton still threaded, waiting for her to finish the date.

"Eighteen forty-four," Edward finished and closed his eyes as a clear image of Lizzy, sitting in the chair by the fire doing the cross-stitch, came to mind. She was looking up at him, laughing at something he had said then, shaking her head.

I could never leave the valley. Though she had laughed while she said the words, he had known that she meant them.

"And she never will." He shook his head as he slowly replaced the needlework in its box. "Lizzy will stay here forever."

* * *

Within two weeks, most of the difficulties that came with lambing season had been dealt with, and Edward made a trip down to Preston, fitting it, as usual, around a trip to sell produce for the estate.

As his body gently moved with the motion of the cart, he thought back on the first time he had made the journey all the way to Liverpool with his father at the age of nine. The wonder he'd felt upon seeing the ships in their moorings came back to him in a rush, and he recalled with a sad smile the question he'd posed to his father.

"Da . . . can I go on a ship?"

Jacob's response had been immediate. "Nay, lad. *You're a farm boy, and farm boys don't go to sea.*"

"Nay . . . farm boys don't go to sea," Edward spoke out loud, mimicking his father's voice, and shook his head. "Farm boys don't do anything except stay where they are . . . working for others till it's time to hand things over to their sons when they go." He ran a hand over his face. "Except if you don't have any sons—then it's just till you die."

Jack whimpered on the seat beside him as if he was expected to answer, stood up, and rotated once then lay down with a loud sigh. Edward gave a quiet chuckle and rested his hand on the dog's neck. "That goes for you, too, Jack. Just you and me . . ."

The words seemed to drop like pebbles in a pond, and Edward shook his head and rattled the reins. "So let's get nowhere quicker."

* * *

IT WAS LATE IN THE afternoon by the time Edward finished at the market and drove to Emma and Patrick's house. As he looked around at the unfamiliar houses, he wished he'd listened more carefully to the directions she'd given when they'd first moved in.

"You lost, mister?" a voice called out behind him, but Edward chose to ignore it. There were always people begging or looking for ways to earn a few coins these days. Life at the mills did not produce the income that was needed to support the increasingly large families in the tenements, and begging had become a standard practice. "You looking for the Millers, mister?" the voice persisted.

Edward frowned as he looked around, then the frown changed to a grin as the wagon lurched slightly and William climbed up on the seat beside him.

"Afternoon, big brother." William adjusted his cap and pointed ahead and to the left. "You're nearly there."

"I knew that." Edward clicked his tongue at the horse, and it moved more quickly. "I was just waiting for you."

"Oh, and I believe that." William nodded, looking askance at his brother. "Would you even have asked for directions?"

"Probably not." Edward stared straight ahead. He hadn't seen William for some time, and he could already tell that the boy seemed to have grown up. He was more confident than before—more knowing, perhaps. He glanced at William. "How is Mama?"

"Not well." William's smile faded. "She's been coughing bad the last few nights and having real trouble breathing." He rested his arms on his knees and stared at the horse's rump. "She doesn't seem to know us at all. I . . . I don't think she'll be with us much longer."

Edward heard the quiver in his brother's voice, and he rested a hand on his shoulder. Words seemed inadequate somehow. They continued in silence until William pointed to the small dwelling sitting alongside a row of others exactly like it.

"That'll be it." William swung down even before Edward halted the horse. It seemed Emma had been waiting for them, for she was at the doorway before Edward climbed down from the wagon.

"Edward! You did come." She wiped her hands on a cloth as she walked toward him.

"I did come?" Edward frowned. "You sound like you were expecting me. I didn't even know I was coming until yesterday evening."

"I prayed that you would come." Emma shrugged as if that explained everything. "I couldn't leave Mama, and . . ." She glanced at William as she spoke. "You're home early?"

"I'm working the evening shift tomorrow, so I came home earlier." He hesitated. "In case . . ."

"Is Mama that bad?" Edward looked straight at Emma, and she nodded then turned back to the house while talking over her shoulder.

"She's been bad the last three days. She doesn't know us, but she keeps calling out to Da as if he was in the room."

"And you think he is?" Edward asked quietly and wasn't surprised when she nodded but didn't comment. He followed her quietly into the first room and then stood still, staring at the bed. "Mama," he barely whispered.

Norah Morgan was so slight that her body almost didn't make a bump in the spread of the cover over the bed. Her head was back and her mouth slightly open as her breath came in labored, irregular gasps. Her gray hair, lying lankly on the pillow, was only a few shades darker than her face.

"Oh, Mama." Edward finally moved and sank down on his knees beside the bed, covering his mother's hand with his own. He tried to clasp it, but it seemed too small and fragile so he ran his hand gently over it instead.

"She's finding it more difficult to breathe . . . even in the last little while." Emma folded her arms. "It seems as if she's afraid to let go."

"Wouldn't you be?" Edward didn't look at his sister, but he sensed her shake her head.

"I know where we'll go after this life, and there's nothing to be afraid of. Heavenly Father has promised us that." Emma spoke quietly but emphatically then touched Edward on the shoulder. "Why don't you come out here for a moment and let William have some time with Mama?"

Edward glanced toward the doorway, where William stood watching his mother closely, then he nodded and rose slowly to his feet. William moved immediately to take his place by his mother's side.

"How much longer?' Edward asked once they were out of the room, but Emma only shrugged.

"Sister Jones came to visit and she thought tomorrow . . . maybe the next day."

"Shall I stay?" Edward took hold of the back of one of the chairs and leaned against it.

"You're welcome to." Emma took a deep breath and tentatively put her hand on his arm. "I'd really like you to stay, Edward. I need you here."

"You have Patrick."

"I need you." She spoke slowly and precisely, then she rested her head against his shoulder. "She's our mother . . . and William will need us." Edward hesitated for a moment before wrapping his arms around his sister. He felt her relax against his chest.

"I'll stay, Emma. Thank you."

* * *

"EDWARD! EDWARD . . . WAKE UP."

"What?" Edward was awake in an instant, throwing aside the blanket that had covered him as he lay on the floor beside his mother's bed. "Mama?"

"Mama's all right," William whispered close to him. "You were dreaming . . . and calling out." He looked concerned. "I thought it best to wake you."

Edward shook his head to clear it then rested his head in his hand. "Was I calling for Lizzy?"

"Umm . . . no." William hesitated. "No, it was Da you were calling out to."

"Da?"

William nodded. "Several times . . . that I heard. You were asking him to wait."

"Wait?" Edward frowned. "Why would I ask Da to wait?"

His brother shrugged and grinned. "I thought I'd better wake you before you caught up to him. You might have had words."

Edward almost grinned as well as he gently pushed William's shoulder. "Do you remember my arguments with Da?"

"Which ones?" William looked at the ceiling. "The ones about Lizzy or the sheep or your life . . . or the ones about Queen Victoria?"

Edward was silent as he remembered. As he had grown older and his father had grown more unstable, the arguments had increased, neither man content to let the other have the last say. They had usually been pointless quarrels, and it still bothered Edward that the last thing he had said to Jacob before his death was a derogatory comment about not knowing how Queen Victoria ran the country without Jacob Morgan's invaluable advice.

"Have you ever wished you hadn't said or done something . . . after you'd done it?" He stopped speaking as Norah moved slightly. They both waited, but when their mother didn't stir further, William shook his head.

"Probably not as much as you." He grinned slightly. "I got a lot of experience watching you while I was growing up."

"Is that a good thing or a bad thing?" Edward shook his head. "You probably shouldn't answer that."

"It was usually interesting rather than good or bad." William shrugged. "There was a lot I admired and some things I wished I could have unsaid for you . . . or undone."

Edward nodded slowly. "Well put, little brother. And what things would you have undone?"

He thought he knew what William was going to say, but his brother's next words surprised him.

"There were times when you told father off for drinking and then walked away . . . so you didn't see him cry with the pain and Mama crying with him." William swallowed hard. "I think they thought I was asleep or too young to be able to listen, but I did . . . and then I wanted you to come back and see what they were really like." He paused. "How sick Da really was."

"I didn't know he was sick." Edward's voice was barely a whisper. "I thought he was just a weak drunk."

"He didn't want you to know." Emma suddenly spoke from the doorway, and the brothers looked up quickly. "He wanted to be strong . . . like you. Like he once was."

She sat down beside them on the floor.

"Was I the only one who didn't know how sick he was?" Edward frowned. "Was I blind?"

"Blind and proud," Emma said quietly. "You were so like each other."

"But then there's all the good things." William rested both arms on his knees. "That's what I will prefer to remember when we go . . ." He stopped and stared at the ground as Emma put her hand to her mouth.

"Go?" Edward frowned. "Where are you going?"

"Umm . . ." William lowered one eyebrow then glanced up at his sister.

"We'll talk about it all later." She spoke pleasantly and quickly as she stood up, then gasped as her mother's eyes opened.

"Mama," she whispered as Edward and William stood up behind her. "Mama?"

They watched as their mother's lips moved a fraction, and then she struggled to breathe.

"Shh . . . don't worry, Mama," Emma said soothingly as Norah's eyes grew wide.

"Emma." The name was hardly discernible.

"Emma." Her voice was stronger this time, and she lifted her hand off the cover.

"I'm here, Mama." Emma took the hand gently between her own as she looked at her brothers. Their mother hadn't been able to speak for more than four days.

"Emma . . ." Norah Morgan focused her eyes on her daughter then smiled sweetly. "Emma . . . you know . . . the whole truth."

"The whole truth?" Emma stared at her mother as her shoulders began to shake and tears wet her cheeks. She lifted Norah's hand to her lips and kissed it gently. "Thank you, Mama . . . oh, thank you, so much."

There was silence as Norah looked at them all. Then her eyes became fixed on the corner of the room, and they heard one last word.

"Jacob."

* * *

"I'M GLAD WE WERE ABLE to bury them together here." Emma stood beside the newly turned grave that bore her mother's headstone. She glanced around. "Although it is not likely we will be buried here."

"So you are going." Edward responded with a statement rather than a question, and Emma looked at him and slowly nodded.

"You know?"

"I guessed."

"From what William said?"

"From what everyone has said who has an association with a Mormon or is one." Edward toed the ground with his boot. "That you will all leave, sooner or later, to go and find Zion."

Emma nodded in response to the cynical tone in his voice. "Not to find Zion but to be a part of it," she corrected quietly. "We know where it is."

"And you will leave England forever to go and worship this place?" Edward shook his head.

"We are not worshipping the place—"

"Well, Joseph Smith, then," Edward conceded, earning a frustrated look from his sister.

"Joseph Smith is dead, Edward—murdered, along with his brother Hyrum, by a mob. Shot while they were wrongly held in prison." Emma stopped and took a deep breath then lowered her voice. "A year ago."

Edward only shook his head, and Emma pulled her wrap more tightly around her shoulders as a breeze blew through the graveyard.

"No, we are not going to worship Joseph Smith . . . or a place. We're going so we can have the freedom to worship God, Edward . . . to worship in the way He would have us worship, not hindered by other people's disbeliefs or frowned at and—and spat upon—for daring to believe that Jesus Christ lives and loves us." She drew a quick breath, as if it were impossible to stop now. "For seven years I have endured many things because I chose to believe what the missionaries had to say, all because I had a feeling that it was right. Just a feeling, Edward, but . . . such a feeling that I cannot describe it to you. It has carried Patrick and me through so many trials." She paused and looked down at her mother's grave. "Mama knew, Edward . . . before she died, she knew, and she told me." She looked up at him. "She told us."

"She told you," Edward corrected as he shook his head. "I would like to believe as you do, Emma, but it simply isn't in me."

"That's not true, Edward." Emma reached up and hooked her hand at her brother's elbow. "It's just that you don't know how to believe."

Edward raised one eyebrow. "I don't know how . . . ?"

Emma smiled as she nodded. "Faith will not fight against pride."

He didn't respond but stared into the distance for a long time. Finally, he patted her hand where it still rested against his arm. "What if I told you that I was leaving as well?"

"I . . ." She looked puzzled. "I don't know . . ."

"Well, think about it." Edward began to walk toward the road. "I am going to Birmingham to look at the possibility of migrating to the Pacific colonies . . . to New Zealand or Australia."

"But you could come to America." Emma stopped. "It would be perfect. You could come with us." She hesitated as he frowned. "Well, nearby perhaps . . ."

"Or not at all." Edward smiled. "No, if I go, it will be to the South Seas."

"And when would you go?" Emma looked concerned. "Would it be soon?"

"That is most unlikely." He shook his head. "I don't think that I meet any of the requirements to qualify for free passage, so I will have to work for a considerable time to pay my fare, but . . . I will go to Birmingham to find out for sure." He looked straight at his sister. "But, Emma, like you, I have decided . . . somehow I will go."

* * *

THE SCENE WAS SO FAMILIAR that he could almost close his eyes and tell what was going to happen next. The boats rocking at their moorings, the wagons full of goods being loaded onto the ships, the crowds of people milling, uncertain what to do but anxious to board the ships and sail away to their new life. This time, however, it was his own family who was part of that crowd.

Edward watched as a man in a dark, well-worn jacket, trousers, and hat busily organized Emma's group into lines and checked off names on a list. Edward recognized a number of people from Preston and Downham, but there were still a hundred or so that he'd never seen before, among which was a healthy mix of English, Irish, and Scottish accents.

"Do you know where that man is from?" William tapped Edward on the elbow. "He doesn't sound like anyone else here."

Edward listened carefully to the man's accent, then he shrugged. "I think he's from Europe . . . from the north." He looked at Emma. "Are these all Mormons?"

She nodded as she pointed at the man with the list. "The boat is chartered entirely for Church members; they have come from many places to be a part of this gathering."

"The gathering." Edward raised one eyebrow. "That sounds very . . . organized."

"It is." Patrick spoke behind him and moved to stand beside Emma. "And it's time for us to go."

Emma glanced at her twin, and her eyes filled with tears. Gone was the lighthearted conversation that she had tried to maintain on the journey down as she reached out and clung to him. She sobbed as his arms held her tight.

"Oh, Edward, do you think we will ever see each other again?" She rested her hand against his chest and forced a smile. "Do you think you will be able to cope without me?"

"No." Edward swallowed hard. "But my pride will help me to pretend otherwise."

They embraced again, then Emma stood back and held Patrick's hand tightly. "I will write . . . as soon as we reach America and ever after." She nodded. "Until we see each other again."

"And what about when I leave?" Edward teased. "You won't know where to find me with your letters."

"Oh yes . . . I will always find you, brother." She smiled while the tears flowed down her cheeks. "Even on the other side of the world . . . I will find you."

She turned away then, and Patrick placed his arm around her shoulders, leading her away.

"She'll be fine, Edward. Patrick and I will look after her . . . I promise." William spoke quietly beside him, and Edward turned slowly. His younger brother looked far older than he'd ever seen him, and he fought back the tears.

"I should never have given you my jacket, William. You look far better in it than I ever did."

William grinned as he straightened the rough wool overcoat. His lip trembled, and he quickly embraced his older brother, clinging to him as his shoulders shook. For a long time the brothers held the embrace, then William took a step back and wiped his eyes with the jacket sleeve before raising one hand to his forehead in a brief salute.

"I will see you again, Edward. I'll come to . . ." He hesitated and smiled. "I'll come wherever you are. Emma will know where."

"She will." Edward returned the smile and held out his hand. "Farewell, William . . . for now."

"For now." And then William was gone, wending his way through the gathering crowd.

"For now, Will . . . Emma . . . Patrick . . . Mama . . . Da." Edward turned and took a deep breath. "Lizzy . . . till we all meet again."

Chapter Twelve

County Cork, Ireland, 1845
A Plague and a Blessing

"OH, PRAISE BE . . ." LAURYN KELLY muttered to herself as she gathered the edge of her shawl and placed it over her nose and mouth. The coarse woolen fibers tickled her face, but they did seem to filter the stench plucking at the back of her throat. She felt her stomach and chest lurch as a wave of nausea hit. "Ye rotten little beggars." She shook her head and took a deep gulp of the air in the shawl.

It seemed that as soon as she'd walked over the knoll from her own house and down into the valley, the smell had settled around her as thick as if it had substance.

"Mornin', young Lauryn." An elderly man, bent low over a roughly hewn walking stick, raised an arm in greeting as she turned into a narrow lane.

"Mornin' to you too, Mr. Flynn." Lauryn lowered the shawl briefly to show that she was smiling, but the smell immediately filled her nostrils, and she convulsed slightly. "Does the smell not bother you, Mr. Flynn?" She spoke loudly as she put the shawl back over her face

"Aye, it bothers me, lass, but there's nothin' I can do about it." Mr. Flynn shook his head slowly. "Only the good Lord Himself can stop that."

"Then maybe we'd better stop calling him the 'good' Lord," Lauryn responded quickly as she frowned. "For it seems the problem is getting worse the more we pray."

"Now lass, you'd best be stoppin' such words." Mr. Flynn looked genuinely taken aback at her words. "Maybe it's the like of such talk that has got us into this situation already."

"I don't think so, Mr. Flynn." Lauryn shook her head emphatically, and her long brown hair waved across her shoulders. She drew the shawl more tightly around herself and lifted her head high. "Maybe if there was more of such talk, we'd not be lying around waiting to rot in the ground like those stinking potatoes."

"Oh, missy, you be careful now." Mr. Flynn coughed suddenly, and his body was wracked with the effort.

Lauryn shook her head sympathetically and raised her hand briefly in farewell. A few steps on and she stopped and turned in her tracks. "Good-bye, Mr. Flynn." She spoke the words softly, knowing that it was likely the last time she would see Mr. Tom Flynn, a neighbor she'd known her entire life.

Lauryn fought the tears that threatened, swallowing hard as she had learned to do over the last year. It seemed that each day brought more pain and frustration and often tragedy.

She allowed herself the briefest glance over the fields lying dormant along the lane, their rough furrows draped with the wilted leaves of potato plants that would never produce a crop worth eating. What they had produced had succumbed to what the locals called "the blight"—a deadly fungus that ate at the potato, blackening its insides and rotting it while still in the ground. And so each day, the stench of the rotting vegetables rose from the ground and hung like a cloud of death over the Irish countryside— and each day the people suffered from the loss of their only source of food . . . and means of survival.

In contrast to the rotting potatoes were the fields of oats and barley that glowed pale golden-yellow even in the overcast weather. Lauryn could see the bent figures of men and women moving slowly across the fields, their arms swinging large scythes that cut the stalks in wide swaths as the falling crops formed a wave across the land.

She hurried on, and the frown on her face deepened. It was so unjust that the peasants were starving; their only food crop rotted in the ground while they had to work to harvest good food that was sold overseas to line the landlords' pockets. Even now she was hurrying because she was meant to be in the fields herself with her father and sister Alice.

"So we'll work till our backs break to earn a pittance so the landlord can have his feast at his big house." She gritted her teeth and marched on, her head bent to the wind that was building steadily. When she heard the sound of hooves clattering on the road behind her she didn't turn but moved to the side of the lane as far as she could. Anyone who could afford to be riding a horse was someone she wouldn't wish to have contact with.

She felt the horses swing by, the heat of their bodies and their sheer size making the lane seem to shrink around her as she pressed against the wall. Only after they had passed did Lauryn spare a glance and a grudging admiration for the powerful horses. She had always felt a love for horses that had never been quenched, even after being badly hurt by one.

"Finnbheara," she whispered as she watched the horses and their riders disappear around a bend in the lane. The horse had never meant to hurt her; it had only reacted in terror to bad treatment from its owner, an English farm manager. However, as a consequence, Lauryn's leg still bore a deep scar, and she walked with a slight limp, but it was never the horse she blamed. "You could not help being owned by an English Protestant fool." She straightened her shoulders and tried to shake the image from her mind as she rushed through the last glade of trees to the field where her family was working.

"Whoa, there!"

The horse appeared around the corner right in front of her, traveling at such speed that Lauryn fell to the side of the road. She screamed as it bore directly down on her, and she rolled to the side, trying desperately to avoid the enormous hooves flailing over her head.

* * *

" No . . . no!"

The fog in Lauryn's mind cleared for a moment as she tried to focus on the face in front of her; then it closed in again.

She felt herself being moved but wasn't sure how. Then all of her senses seemed to catch fire and she screamed again, her body reacting violently against the force that held it down.

"Wench!" She heard the curse even before her eyes opened properly, and she kicked as hard as she could, scrambling away but stumbling against the folds of her dress.

She felt someone catch and hold her leg as she clawed at the grass, and then her vision cleared. "Let go!" She struggled to pull herself away, but it only seemed to make the strain on her leg greater. She screamed again, but this time because of the pain in her leg as the old scar seemed to rip apart beneath the fingers that held her like a vice.

"Aah!" The grip released instantly and she fell away, struggling to push the folds of her dress down. A sob broke from her throat as she pressed herself against the rough trunk of a tree and searched frantically for a way to escape.

"What a disgusting beast!" She heard the words spat out as the man who had been holding her to the ground reeled back and held up his hands as if they'd been soiled.

"One of the crippled women. Look at that scar!" The other man laughed out loud as his friend stood up, brushing the leaves off his clothes and fixing his trousers. "You chose a cripple for sport!"

"Ah." The younger man screwed up his face in disgust, then he began to walk away, wiping his hands. "Trouble is, that's about all the sport you can get in this godforsaken country . . . either mangy or crippled."

"'Tis hardly sport when you go after the lame ones." His friend laughed out loud again as he hesitated then drew a coin out of his pocket. "I say we leave a donation for . . . services rendered." He stared at Lauryn for a brief moment then flicked the coin so that it landed in her lap.

"Don't leave her anything, man . . ." The other man's voice was scathing. "There weren't any services rendered."

Lauryn stared at the coin that shone insultingly against the rough fabric of her skirt, then she clenched her fingers around it and stood up slowly. As the men mounted their horses and rode away, she sobbed as the full import of the last few minutes wrenched through her body.

There weren't any services rendered. The words pounded in her head.

"Dear God, be thanked . . ." she began. Then, unable to stop the tears, she slumped against the tree, crying softly as she pulled the full hem of her skirt more tightly around her legs.

She knew now who the man was—a friend of the English landlord's son. She'd heard stories about their behavior in the district.

Another loud sob tore through her as she slowly stood up and tried to walk, but her legs gave way and she sank to the ground once more.

* * *

MOIRA SENSED SOMETHING WAS WRONG with her daughter, but she waited until Lauryn had gone outside in the early evening before she wandered out to find her by the oak tree.

"I thought you would be here." Moira sat down beside Lauryn in one of the cradles formed by the tree roots. "Are you going to tell me what's wrong?"

Lauryn stared ahead, but no words would come. Finally, she bowed her head and let the tears fall quietly, leaning against her mother's arm for comfort.

"Someone . . ." She stopped, taking a deep breath. "Someone tried to have their way with me today." She put both hands over her face then let them drop to her lap. "I got knocked over by his horse . . . in the lane, and when I came to, he . . . he . . ." She shuddered, and her mother's grip tightened on her shoulder.

"Oh, my girl . . ." Moira felt her throat tighten as Lauryn lifted her head.

"I didn't know what had happened only . . . only that he was trying . . ." She stopped again and bit her lip. "He stopped . . . because my leg was disgusting."

"Thanks be to God." Moira barely breathed the words as her daughter shook her head.

"He called me a disgusting beast and a cripple." Lauryn's lip quivered as she looked at her mother. "I'm glad that's what he thought because it stopped him, but . . . am I, Ma? Am I disgusting?"

Moira shook her head as she took hold of Lauryn's hand. "He is an ignorant man, Lauryn. Make no mistake about that. We must be thankful that he was so proud that such a thing stopped him. I consider it a blessing what he considers a plague." She stopped and rested her hand on Lauryn's leg. "Show me your leg, daughter."

Lauryn glanced at her mother, then as Moira nodded kindly, she slowly lifted the hem of her dress and put her left leg out to the side. The wound ran from the top of her worn brown boot to just below her knee. The scar itself was a pale brown line, but the skin around it was purple and slightly puckered, fading to white where it had been burnt.

Moira gently touched the scar and let her hand rest over it. "Oh my . . . what a blessing it has been for you, child." She spoke softly. "'Tis not very unsightly at all, and yet it frightened that poor excuse for a man."

Lauryn mustered a smile at her mother's words and laid her head against Moira's shoulder. "'Tis so like you to be positive about the worst things, Ma." She leaned back against the tree. "I look around and see that the potatoes are rotting and we can hardly get enough to eat, and you still thank the Lord for finding one that we can share a piece of."

"Because I truly am thankful." Moira sighed. "And at least we still have a place to live. I just heard that Jean's landlord has evicted them." Tears formed in her eyes. "They must leave their home by week's end."

"But they have nowhere to go." Lauryn frowned. "Should they come here?" She almost dreaded what her mother might say, because there was already so little food left in the house. She glanced down at her own hands, which had become so thin that the veins on top stood out against the bones.

Moira shook her head. "Jean got word to me that they are going to the coast . . . to David's kin." She took a deep breath. "I only hope they get there."

"Is there anything we can do?" Lauryn asked quietly. "Can we help them?"

"We'll go tomorrow or the day after." Moira nodded. "I'll make some bread, and we can still take some milk before the cow dries up." She stopped and stared at the house. "Your father is such a blessing to us, Lauryn. He works so hard and has made himself an asset to the estate." She shook her head. "Otherwise we'd be lost like all the others."

"I heard that there were five more gone in the village this week." Lauryn drew her thin wrap more tightly around her body. "It's such a slow death . . .

just eating less and less and waiting to be gone." She glanced at her mother. "Why does God allow it? Why does He let people suffer if He loves them?"

Moira took her time answering, then she tilted her head to one side and looked up at the sky. "I remember asking that question when I was younger—and a few times since—but I always seem to get the thought that Jesus Christ suffered more than anyone, and He did it for all of us." She smiled. "I only suffer for me and my family, so I figure I can go on."

Lauryn nodded, although the answer didn't quite satisfy her. "Do you sometimes think God has forgotten you, Ma?"

Moira hesitated but shook her head. "No, child. I think I forget Him at times, but He has His ways of reminding me that He's there."

She stood up and dusted off the back of her dress, then she held her hand out to help her daughter, but Lauryn shook her head.

"I'll stay a while longer." She screwed up her nose. "I don't think I'm quite thanking God for what happened yet."

Moira nodded and turned to walk toward the cottage, but after a couple of steps she looked back. "Lauryn?"

"Yes, Ma."

"Whatever happens to you . . . don't be bitter or hard—be strong."

Lauryn stared at her mother as she silently repeated the phrase, then she nodded slowly. "I'll try."

Moira smiled and went into the cottage.

Be strong . . .

* * *

Lauryn watched her mother wrap two small loaves of bread fresh from the oven, and her stomach spoke for her. They had not had bread themselves for over a week, and the sight of it made her mouth water. She ran her tongue over her dry lips and pressed a hand to her stomach to stop the incessant rumbling.

"Did you fetch the milk?" Moira glanced up, and Lauryn held up the small pail.

"Will you be back before supper?" Megan asked quietly from where she lay on her bed against the wall. She had been in the same position for several weeks now, her body seeming to reject the food the rest of her family craved.

"Shall we have supper today?" Moira looked at Lauryn, then she smiled and walked over to Megan's bed, soothing her hair back off her face as she bent and kissed her forehead. "Perhaps a fine lamb roast with all the trimmings." She held up one finger. "Oh, we'd better make twice that, as we'll likely be having guests over."

"And can we have . . . a whisky cake for dessert? Only take it easy on the whisky, because it's heady stuff and . . ." Lauryn tapped her chin. "How about a potato pudding while the oven's hot? Being as how I'm so very, very fond of potatoes."

Megan laughed as her mother and sister prattled on while they wrapped their shawls around their shoulders. She giggled and made to get up. "Off with you both and I'll be getting busy." She leaned on one elbow. "I should have it all done in half an hour, so you'd better hurry."

She sunk back onto the pillow as they waved and walked out the door. "Please hurry," she whispered as the door closed.

Lauryn and her mother walked with their shawls held across their faces, leaning into the wind that cut into their bodies, but the fierce wind was a blessing in that it blew away much of the stench.

It was the same road that Lauryn had taken to the fields and near the glade where she had fallen. As Lauryn's steps faltered, Moira glanced at her daughter's face and then looked around.

"Here?" She pointed to the ground, and Lauryn nodded. She stood still until her mother took her gently by the hand and led her on down the road. Just a few steps on, Lauryn stopped and stared at the ground where a coin lay half hidden in the grass.

"What is it?" Moira bent down and cleared the grass to pick up the coin, then she held it up as Lauryn swallowed hard.

"One of them threw me the coin . . . for services rendered." She faltered. "But the other one said he shouldn't have—for services not rendered."

"Then you knew what you needed to know, and that's what counts." Moira spoke briskly as she dropped the coin into the basket she was carrying.

"What are you doing?" Lauryn frowned. "I don't want their money."

"No, but your aunt will, and it'll be the most money she's ever had from a landlord. It'll bring me much delight to give it where he wouldn't want it to go."

Lauryn smiled as she began to walk again, keeping her eyes averted from the side of the road. Once again she felt her mother's arm across her back, firmly guiding her past.

As they approached the mud hut that had housed Jean and her family for the last few years, Lauryn wondered how it had ever stayed up. The walls were crumbling at the corners, and the stick roof had sunken in such that in places there was no covering. The cloth that had served as a door was now hanging limply to the side, and there were no children watching for them.

"It's very quiet." Lauryn touched her mother's arm. "Are you sure they haven't left already?"

"I'm sure." Moira tightened her jaw, preparing herself for the scene inside, but then she hesitated and turned to Lauryn. "They'll not be good, daughter. Prepare yourself."

Lauryn nodded and stepped in close behind her mother. Then she ducked her head to enter the hut.

"Oh my . . ." Her stomach turned as her eyes adjusted to the darkness inside and she took in the whole room in one glance.

Jean sat, or rather lay, across a small table, her head rolling on her arm as she tried to lift her head. Moira went to her immediately, giving no heed to the excrement on the floor, and within seconds she was holding the pail of milk to Jean's lips and forcing her to drink.

Only then did Lauryn hear the faint murmur in the corner and look over to where two children lay, their eyes enormous in their skulls, their skin stretched over their bones. They were practically naked, but despite the cold they didn't seem to be shivering. It was as though they were past feeling anything.

"Ma . . . the children . . ." She pointed toward the corner as her mother looked up and moaned, shaking her head as she eased Jean back onto the table.

"Oh, the dear ones." As she walked slowly to the corner, the children's eyes followed her, but the children themselves made no attempt to move.

"They're starving right there in their beds," Moira whispered as she looked around. "There should be four of them."

"Yesterday." Jean's voice was the barest noise. "David . . . bury them."

"Oh my." Moira put her hand to her forehead for a second, then she clasped both hands in front of her. Lauryn saw her lips move and knew she was saying a silent prayer. That was her mother's way, and in that instant, she felt the full strength of her faith.

No more words passed between them as they each took a child on their lap and patiently tried to press some milk-soaked bread between their lips. The children's eyes continued to stare, but as the milk trickled into their throats, they slowly responded, whimpering and huddling against Moira and Lauryn.

"Ma . . . we cannot leave them here to die," Lauryn whispered as she rocked the little girl, her youngest cousin, on her lap.

Moira could hardly speak as she rocked her nephew, and when she spoke it was in a whisper. "I cannot believe I have allowed myself to believe they were better off. Jean's messages never . . ." She stopped, swallowing with difficulty then took a deep breath. "We'll be taking them home now . . . where they belong."

Chapter Thirteen

Glasgow, Scotland, 1845
A Wee Talk

"FIONA! JIMMY! WHERE ARE YOU?" Bess McAlister pulled off her gloves as she let herself in the front door of the High Street house. "Children . . . ?" She stopped to put her gloves on a side table by the door and then removed the brown felt hat that she always wore outdoors.

"Fiona? Jimmy?" She called again then frowned. "Molly!"

"Here I am, Bess, but I don't know where those children are." Molly entered the room and held up floured hands. "I was just tossing some bread."

"That's fine, Molly. I'll find them." Bess smiled and began to walk up the narrow staircase to the two bedrooms that sat on either side of the landing. She and Ewen had one room while Jimmy and Fiona shared the other. Molly slept in a small alcove off the kitchen, which she considered a tiny part of heaven.

A glance into the children's bedroom showed they weren't hiding from her, and another quick search of the downstairs failed to reveal them either. Bess frowned as she opened the front door and looked up and down the street. When there was still no sign of them, she walked through the kitchen to where Molly was sliding two loaves into the oven.

"Where on earth could they be?" Bess folded her arms and stared out the small paned window. "They know better than to be out on the streets alone, especially at the moment, with all this fuss from the workers."

"Aye, terrible that is. All of those men threatening everyone about gettin' more money. They should try workin' a bit harder and earnin' it." Molly frowned as she turned from the oven and wiped her hands on her apron. "Maybe we should be goin' out to find the bairns . . . just to be safe, like."

"Exactly what I was thinking, Molly." Bess hurried to put on her hat, but she'd just put the large pearl-tipped pin in place to secure it when the front door squeaked open a fraction and a shock of deep red hair appeared.

"Jimmy McAlister . . . where on earth have you been? And where's your sister?" Bess put her hands on her hips as her son moved slowly inside followed by a smaller version of himself with long hair and wearing a long dress and pinafore.

"Sorry, Mam." Jimmy glanced at his sister, and she looked back at him. "We got held up . . . down at Mr. McGibbon's shop."

"And what were you doing down at the Saltmarket?" Bess frowned. Her children were normally very well behaved. For them to go somewhere they were not typically allowed was unusual. "I hope you have a very good reason."

"Oh yes, Mam." Fiona nodded solemnly and looked at her brother again.

"I was talking to Andrew . . . that goes to the school. He's a bit older than me, but he talks to me . . . sometimes . . . But he said that he was leaving, leaving the city . . . and that Mr. McGibbon would need somebody to take his place working in the shop." Jimmy drew a breath.

"So Jimmy went to ask . . ." Fiona began, but Jimmy nudged her and she stopped immediately.

"I went to see if I could get the job." He stood up and squared his shoulders. "Then I could help with the rent."

Bess stared at her children. Only twenty months apart in age, the McAlister children were inseparable—nine-year-old Jimmy acting as the fearless protector of seven-year-old Fiona, who could not bear to have her brother out of her sight. The mornings that he attended classes, she would sit waiting for him to arrive home.

"Jimmy, that was very thoughtful of you, but . . ." Bess saw his face drop into a frown and quickly turned her next words into a question. "So did Mr. McGibbon need your help?"

"He said that I was a bit young but that by the time Andrew actually left I might be able to do a few things like sweeping." He shook his head. "I didn't know that Andrew was going away on a ship, but that's what Mr. McGibbon said . . . that Andrew and his family are moving to Canada." He frowned again. "Where's Canada?"

"Oh, Canada is away across the ocean, near America," Bess answered simply. "Many people are moving there from Scotland."

"Why?" Fiona folded her arms. "Why do people want to go to Can . . . away?"

"They go because they feel they will have a better life there." Bess moved to give her children a hug, then she guided them into the kitchen.

"There are not quite so many people there, but there is a lot of land and new cities so people think they will have a better chance of making a living."

"Then why don't we go?" Jimmy sat down at the table and breathed in deeply the smell of the baking loaves. "We could go with Andrew's family . . . to Canada."

"Oh, it's not as simple as that." Bess poured the children a small glass of water each from a tin pitcher. "There are many things people have to do before they can even get on a ship. They have to save money to pay their fare, then they have to pack all their belongings, and they canna take much so they have to leave a lot of precious things behind. Then they have to leave their family and friends—"

"But we *are* our family," Jimmy interrupted. "And Molly."

"Well, thank ye, Jimmy." Molly turned from the table where she was cutting potatoes. Ever since Ewen and Bess had arrived in Glasgow with baby Jimmy eight years before, Molly had been their helper and guardian. She had looked after them in the slums, and once Ewen's job had begun paying well and the family had been able to move, they had been adamant that she stay with them. Molly truly had become like family and was totally devoted to the McAlisters.

Bess waited until Molly had given the children a slice of bread each and they were happily eating before she went into the small sitting room next to the front door. She smiled as she surveyed the room with satisfaction. For the first time in her life, she had two comfortable chairs and a small, padded sofa. She sat down on one of the chairs and picked up some fine crocheting she'd been working on for some time. It was a skill she had only recently acquired, so the work was slow but satisfying. She worked a few threads then laid the piece in her lap and looked, instead, out the front window.

From where she sat she could see the fronts of two houses opposite. The houses were a mirror image of her own, and they too were neatly kept and clean as befitting this area of lower middle-class housing. The people here were not wealthy, but they had worked hard and done well enough to buy or rent their homes—located near enough to town but not quite in the established, market areas.

Bess smiled. Her husband had worked hard, and they had saved well. This house was their reward for eight years of diligence. Ewen was now a manager at the Napier shipbuilding yard and, under the watchful eye of Mr. David Elder, had acquired a reputation as a quality shipbuilder. He had recently been given a promotion when his immediate manager had left to begin his own shipbuilding business in Clydeside.

Ewen had steadily overcome the stigma of being a Highlander and had proven himself a man of integrity and industry, and Bess was tremendously proud of him.

She glanced around the room with the furnishings they had slowly acquired over the years and shook her head.

"We don't need to go anywhere." She smiled again as she resumed her crocheting.

"Will Father be home soon, Mam?" Jimmy appeared in the doorway with Fiona close behind.

"We want to tell him about the fair," Fiona announced importantly and received a nudge from her brother.

"What fair?" Bess looked up from her work.

"The big fair . . . at Glasgow Green." Jimmy pointed down the road, his eyes wide with excitement. "We saw the posters down at the store, Mam. There's going to be all sorts of strange things there."

"Strange things that cost money, only to find out they're a trick." Bess pursed her lips. "We'll not be a part of such nonsense, Jimmy."

"But, Mam, the poster said that there'll be a woman who looks like a pig . . ."

"And a worsar—there's going to be a worsar there!" Fiona added.

"And what would a 'worsar' be?" Bess almost laughed at the expression on her daughter's face but managed to look suitably fascinated.

"That's why we have to go, Mam . . . to find out." Jimmy clenched both fists. "Please, Mam."

"Please . . ." Fiona clenched her fists as well.

"Please, what?" A deep voice spoke behind them, and both children jumped then turned and threw themselves at their father. Ewen McAlister bent down as two pairs of arms wrapped tightly around his neck, then he stood back up with both children swinging. He crossed his eyes and held onto Jimmy as the boy's weight almost made him stumble.

"Jimmy, boy . . . what have you been eating? I shan't be able to do that much longer. You'll be lifting me soon." He lowered both children to the ground, and Jimmy flexed his arm.

"I'll be able to go to work soon, Father. I'll be old enough and strong enough to be a shipbuilder."

Ewen tousled his hair affectionately. "And as I've told you before, you'll be an engineer like Mr. Elder. That where your future lies, Jimmy. You can design the ships, not just build them." Ewen looked his boy in the eyes. "That's why you must do well at the school."

"I am, Father. I did all my sums and got them right."

"That's my boy, Jimmy. I'm proud of you." Ewen smiled then turned as he felt a tug on his hand.

"I'll be an engineer too." Fiona looked up at him with a wide smile. He picked her up and swung her around then slid her onto his back.

"And I believe you will if you want to, young lady." He chuckled and winked at Jimmy. "Two engineers will do the McAlister Clan proud."

* * *

"So how was your women's meeting at the church today?" Ewen sat down in the chair opposite his wife after they had put the children to bed. "Are you liking it there?"

"I'm liking it fine." Bess nodded slowly as she picked up the crochet. "They are a devout group of women, but . . . sometimes I feel like I don't quite measure up."

"In what way?" Ewen studied his wife's face, which he could usually read like an open book. Tonight he wasn't quite sure what the small frown indicated.

Bess hesitated before she shrugged. "The Free Kirk is very different from the old Church of Scotland. I thought it might be more . . . progressive . . . but there are so many rules and . . ." She pressed her lips together then shook her head. "Sometimes the reverend says things in those long sermons that make me feel . . . uncomfortable . . . almost as if I'm disagreeing inside, but then I nod my head because I don't want to look like I'm a dissenter."

"And that makes you feel even worse?" Ewen asked quietly, and Bess smiled as she nodded.

"Exactly." She put her head to one side. "Would you not come with me and see what you think?"

"You know what I think," Ewen answered carefully, knowing that the one thing they disagreed on was his reluctance to attend the church meetings with Bess and the children. The last time he had attended was seven years before, when Fiona had been born. Having recently arrived in Glasgow, they had approached the local church to make arrangements to have her baptized but had been refused because they didn't have enough money.

"Yes, I do," Bess responded quietly.

They sat in silence for a few minutes, then Bess chuckled. "Your son forgot to tell you that he applied for a job today . . . at Mr. McGibbon's store."

"At the Saltmarket?" Ewen stared. "Did you know about this?"

Bess shook her head. "Only afterward. They went on their own, he and Fiona. He said he wanted to help pay the rent."

Ewen frowned, then he too chuckled. "How can you be angry when he's so well intended?"

"That's what I thought." Bess smiled. "Apparently the errand boy is migrating with his family to Canada, so the job will be vacant in a few months' time."

Ewen stared then nodded slowly. "There are many people migrating. I swear there are so many shiploads of people ready and waiting that we canna build the ships fast enough. The ship we're working on now is already booked fully for its maiden voyage to New York. Cabin class and steerage—all booked." He sighed. "It means more work for us, which is good, but I canna believe how many are leaving. Thousands every week."

Bess nodded. "I know . . . I read a poster at the church today about it. They're holding a meeting on Saturday about a new colony in New Zealand . . . set up by the Free Kirk and run by those standards. The women are saying that it's going to be like a little Scotland in a new land but without all the poverty and misery we have here."

Ewen raised one eyebrow. "That would indeed be appealing. As I was walking home tonight I ran across a group of union people protesting, making a racket about more wages." He breathed deeply. "I fear that something bad will happen before long . . . especially since so often they get all riled up with the liquor as well."

Bess nodded. "We'll need to keep the children close by . . . especially after today. I think they had a little taste of feeling grown up."

* * *

"REMEMBER, FIONA . . . KEEP A TIGHT grip of my hand so you don't get pulled away from me, and you'll be fine." Jimmy wrapped his fingers firmly around Fiona's. "And don't talk to anyone, understand? Not anyone."

Fiona nodded silently, using a slight skipping walk to keep up with Jimmy. She trusted him completely, and when he had announced the plan to go and watch the fair being set up at Glasgow Green, she had been happy to be included.

Still, as they wended their way through the crowds on Saltmarket Street, she began to feel her breath coming in gasps—and it wasn't because she was walking quickly. The people seemed so dirty, and they stared at her and Jimmy. When Jimmy dodged a man, she ran straight into him, and the man snarled at her, revealing a mouth full of decaying teeth.

Fiona's breaths became sobs, and Jimmy slowed as he felt the strain in his hand.

"Jimmy, I don't like it here." Fiona's lip trembled, but she bravely continued walking. "I want to go home."

Jimmy tried to ignore the looks from the people around them as he pulled on her hand and whispered, "We're nearly there, Fiona . . . and the Green is a good place. Just stay with me . . . okay?"

Fiona gulped and nodded, then she pressed closer to Jimmy's side.

* * *

JIMMY TRIED TO APPEAR CONFIDENT, but he felt his own heart beating harder and almost wished he hadn't decided to bring Fiona with him . . . or come at all.

There were many shops along the street, but nearly all of them were selling alcohol or tobacco. And standing outside or lying on the ground were many people looking and sounding drunk. His own father didn't drink, not even a small dram of whisky like Mr. McInnes next door, so the sight of these people laughing loudly and vomiting in the gutter sent a chill down Jimmy's spine.

He gripped Fiona's hand more tightly.

"We must be nearly there, Fiona," he repeated, keeping his eyes fixed on the end of the street. It seemed a very long way, but from what he'd been able to gather, this was the way they should go.

"Jimmy, I'm scared." He heard the tremble in her voice but refused to look at her face. It had seemed such a grand idea to go with Fiona to see the fair. They wouldn't go inside of course, because their parents had forbidden it, but Jimmy had thought about it long and hard, and "worsars" and pig-women surely needed to go for a walk or eat, so if he and Fiona waited long enough near the fair, they'd be bound to see them.

"I see it, Jimmy. There's the Green!" Fiona jiggled his hand and pointed. "I see it!" She began to run faster then, pulling him with her.

They were puffing as they reached the edge of a large grassy area that stretched as far as they could see. There were many people walking along pathways or standing and talking. Jimmy tugged on Fiona's hand. "It'll be over there, I'm sure of it."

Out of the squalor of Saltmarket Street, Fiona began to relax, but Jimmy still had to pull her along as she became distracted looking at all the sights. It was a good thing she was preoccupied, however, because after walking for a while, Jimmy began to see the same benches and statues for the second time . . . and then the third.

"Where's the fair, Jimmy?" Fiona stopped. "I'm so tired."

"I know you are, Fiona, but maybe the fair people haven't arrived yet." He pointed to a large oak tree with spreading branches that offered shade. He led Fiona there and sat her down.

"I have some bannock for you." He pulled a lump of bread from his pocket and broke it apart, carefully giving her the larger piece. "Eat it slowly, mind."

Fiona obediently nibbled on the bread while Jimmy stood above her. He didn't want her to see his face, for he was beginning to have doubts. Surely the fair would be clearly visible. He strained his eyes to look over the Green, but there was no sign of any cages or tents or sideshows like the older boys at school had described.

He looked down at Fiona chewing happily on her bread and touched her on the shoulder. "I'm just going to ask someone where the fair is." He pointed to a small group of nicely dressed people. One man was speaking while the others listened attentively, so Jimmy waited until he had finished, then he approached a young man at the back of the group.

"Excuse me . . . can you tell me where the fair is?" He tried to stand as tall as he could while he asked the question, but the young man took his time answering. He looked him up and down then finally pointed back in the direction Jimmy and Fiona had first come.

"It'll be over there by the Saltmarket, but . . ." The man hesitated as he glanced at Jimmy then over at Fiona sitting on the grass. "The fair won't be here for another two weeks."

"Two weeks . . . oh no." Jimmy could hardly whisper the words as he stared at the ground. "I thought . . ." He couldn't finish as the foolishness of what he'd done hit home.

"Did you think the fair was on now?" the young man asked quietly, and Jimmy nodded silently. Then he squared his shoulders and looked directly at the man. "Thank you, sir. That was good information."

Jimmy walked slowly back to Fiona, not quite sure how to tell her that she wasn't going to be seeing the fair now . . . or probably ever. He looked up at the sky and the rapidly disappearing sun, and he shivered—not from the cold, but in anticipation of his parents' reaction.

"Jimmy, where's the fair? Is it coming soon?" Fiona was standing beside him now, pulling on his arm.

"Aye . . . soon, Fiona . . . but not right now." Jimmy swallowed. "We'll need to go home now and come again another time."

"Another time?" Fiona's lip quivered again, and he found himself wishing she didn't cry so easily.

"Don't cry, Fiona . . . we just have to go back home." Jimmy tried to take her hand, but she pulled it away and sat back down on the ground, the tears flowing easily down her cheeks now.

"I don't want to go back there, Jimmy. It's scary, and the people will hurt us."

"It'll be all right, Fiona. I promise."

She looked up then and sniffed as she shook her head. "You promised we'd see the worsar."

Jimmy gulped, and he felt his own tears threatening. How could such a grand idea have gone so dreadfully wrong? He'd so wanted to see the fair with Fiona, but now they were lost and she didn't trust him anymore. His shoulders slumped.

"Excuse me, young man . . . are you having some trouble?"

Jimmy looked up into the eyes of the man who had been speaking to the group a few minutes ago under the tree. He was quite stocky, with thick sideburns showing under his tall hat, but he had a kindly face, which was now showing real concern.

"No, sir—" Jimmy shook his head, but Fiona spoke up.

"We came to see the fair, but it's not here . . ." She stopped talking as Jimmy nudged her.

"But the fair's not on for two weeks," said a woman who was standing at the man's side. She knelt down in front of Fiona. "Are you lost?"

"No," Jimmy answered quickly. "We know how to get home."

"But we have to go past the horrible men, and I . . . don't . . . want to . . ." Fiona's voice broke, and she covered her face with her hand.

The man and woman glanced at each other, then the woman looked at Jimmy. "Would you mind if we walked with you to your home . . . just past the bad men?" She smiled, and Jimmy liked the way her eyes smiled, too, but he still hesitated.

"I know where to go," he repeated, and the man nodded.

"We'll only go with you if you want." He nodded toward Fiona. "Just to get your sister past the bad men."

Even Jimmy could see the logic of that, so he nodded and held his hand out to Fiona.

* * *

"Oh, Jimmy . . . Fiona . . . where have you been?" Bess began to sob as soon as her children walked through the door. Moments before, her fear and anger had known no bounds, but with their arrival, the tears broke and she cried as she gathered them close. "I was so very fearful for you." She touched Fiona's hair then hugged her again. "What were you thinking?"

Fiona was happy to submit to her mother's embrace but also impatient to introduce her new friends. "Mam . . . Mam . . ." She tapped her mother's shoulder and pointed behind her.

It was only then that Bess saw that the front door was still open and that a couple about her own age were standing there quietly.

"Oh, I'm so sorry." She quickly wiped at her eyes then stood up. "I was just so pleased to see them . . ."

"We thought you might be." The man spoke first then held out a hand to the woman. "I'm John Fraser, and this is my wife, Ann."

"We saw the children at Glasgow Green, and Fiona was a little upset—" Ann began, but Bess interrupted her as she realized what her children had done.

"Glasgow Green . . . oh, Jimmy, no!" Bess exclaimed as she looked at her son, but he was already blushing fiercely red to the roots of his hair and refusing to look up.

"Jimmy was doing a fine job looking after Fiona, Mrs. McAlister." John Fraser smiled. "And he was very polite asking for help."

Jimmy almost looked up, but his mother spoke again, so he continued staring at the ground.

"He wouldn't have had to ask directions if he hadn't gone in the first place." Bess frowned. "And taken his wee sister with him. He knew he wasn't allowed to go to the fair."

"But we weren't going *into* the fair, Mam." Fiona shook her head vigorously. "Only to watch outside because the worsar would have to eat and then we would see it."

Ann Fraser put a hand to her mouth to disguise the smile, but not before she caught Bess's eye and saw the same expression in her eyes.

"Worsars do have to eat," John said.

Jimmy finally looked up, relieved to hear an adult who understood, then he glanced at his mother, his expression begging understanding.

Finally Bess nodded, but her face was stern as she put a hand on her children's shoulders. "I want you to thank Mr. and Mrs. Fraser for bringing you home, and then off to bed with you . . . and no supper at all."

The children turned, and Jimmy solemnly bobbed his head and thanked the Frasers, but Fiona was not so easily put off. She ran to Ann and threw her arms around the woman's legs then looked up at her.

"Will you come and visit us again? Please . . ." She looked at her mother. "Please . . . so Father can meet them too."

"We'll see." Bess nodded then indicated the stairs. "Now off with you."

She waited until the children had waved once more, then she gestured toward the sitting room.

"Please, come in. My husband will be here soon, and I should think he would like to thank you personally for looking after the children."

The Frasers glanced at each other then nodded as they followed Bess.

"Jimmy really was doing a fine job looking after Fiona." John smiled as he sat down. "I had seen them walking for some time before we actually talked to them, and he never let go of her hand. He had even given her something to eat."

"Well, that is gratifying to know." Bess shook her head. "I've been a bit fearful of him being this age lately. It's not like he has the run of the Highlands like his father used to . . . The city is so much more dangerous, especially down by the Saltmarket."

"Children only think about what they want to do—not the consequences." Ann put her head to one side. "We have three bairns about the same age, and they're the same way . . . though our oldest is a girl and not quite so adventurous as Jimmy."

Bess nodded, then she frowned slightly. "So where are your children now?"

Ann smiled. "They're with my mother while John and I have been teaching at the Green."

"Teaching?" Bess looked puzzled.

"About the restored gospel of Jesus Christ." John smiled. "Which you may find unsettling if you've heard all the rumors."

Bess frowned again. "I haven't heard any rumors . . ."

Ann shook her head. "They're not really rumors. It's just that we teach about the Restoration of the gospel of Jesus Christ that was established on the earth when He was here. We believe that He will come again . . . to reestablish it . . . in order that we might gain salvation." She hesitated then looked straight at Bess. "In order that we might be united with our families . . . forever."

"Because much of the truthfulness of His gospel has been altered," John added. "We teach what we believe to be true, but many disagree with it." He nodded toward the Bible sitting on a side table. "Do you attend the Free Church?"

"I do . . . of late." Bess nodded as she laid her hand on the top of the Bible. "Before that I was with the Kirk of Scotland but never quite allowed to worship." Her cheeks flushed as she remembered the times she had been turned away when the few free pews were full and she had no money to pay for entry. It seemed that her desire to worship God was always restricted—either by society or by the church itself.

"Mr. and Mrs. Fraser, I don't know what is keeping my husband, and I don't want to keep you from your children." She clasped her hands in her lap. "But I do have a question . . ." She hesitated. "You said just now that you teach that families can be united together forever." She licked at dry lips. "We, Ewen and I . . . had two little girls . . . they died soon after they were born. Is it your understanding . . . I mean, do you think that I will ever see them again? Be reunited with them?"

* * *

JIMMY WAS DREADING HIS FATHER'S return, and as he lay awake in his cot, he strained his ears to hear the click of the front door latch. He heard nothing for a long time after he went to bed, and then he heard the sounds of the Frasers leaving and his mother's invitation to them to come again.

Why would she want them to come again? He lay on his back with his hands under his head. Did his mother want them to speak against him in front of his father? Jimmy moaned slightly and closed his eyes. He opened them again quickly as he heard the front door once more then the sound of his mother greeting his father. How long would it take her to tell him what a fool his son had been?

"Jimmy?" His father's voice was very low in the darkness some time later, but Jimmy nodded his head, still wide awake.

"Yes."

"So you're awake." He felt the weight of his father on the side of the cot. "I thought you might be."

"Aye." Jimmy nodded but still couldn't look at his father, even in the darkness.

"I want you to come into my room for a while, Jimmy." Ewen stood up. "I think we need a wee talk."

Jimmy slid out of bed and padded after his father, blinking in the light from a glass lamp beside his father's bed. His mother wasn't in the room, so Jimmy took a deep breath. His father had never beaten him, but he'd never done anything like this before either.

"I'm so sorry . . ." He hadn't even finished his sentence before his father held his finger to his lips.

"I know you are, Jimmy. Your mam's told me." Ewen walked to a trunk that sat at the end of the bed then lifted the lid and rummaged around for a moment, finally lifting out a wooden box. He motioned with his head to the bed, and Jimmy climbed up beside him. Ewen opened the box and lifted out a knife in a wooden sheath covered in leather. Putting the box aside, he slowly drew the knife from its sheath, and Jimmy gasped as the light from the lamp reflected off the slim, steel blade.

"Oh, Dad." Jimmy looked at his father with wide eyes, but his father smiled.

"I'll not be doing anything to you, Jimmy . . . but I think it's time you learned about *sgian dubh* . . . and about responsibility." Ewen returned the dagger to its sheath, then he carefully handed it to Jimmy. "I want you to hold this while I tell you something."

Jimmy swallowed as he felt the weight of the knife in his hand and his fingers closed around it.

"I was your age when my father first let me use *sgian dubh*." Ewen nodded as Jimmy looked at him again. "Just nine, and my father and the laird took me on a hunt for a red deer . . . a stag . . . the biggest I've ever seen, with antlers as wide as I am tall."

Jimmy stared. "What does a stag look like?"

Ewen stopped, then he shook his head. Truly, his son had lived in the city his whole life, first at the coal mines then in the city center. He knew little of the things that were precious to Ewen. He took a deep breath and held his hands out wide.

"Imagine an animal, four . . . five times bigger than a dog, with horns, huge horns growing out of its head like small trees." Ewen watched Jimmy frown at the concept, and he nodded. "That's the sort of animal you find in the Highlands, laddie, and when I was nine, we went to hunt one and we found him."

"What did you do?" Jimmy frowned. "Did you kill him?"

"Aye, we did . . . we had to provide food for our family." Ewen held up one hand. "But that wasn't the main thing about the hunt, Jimmy, even though I'll remember it to my dying day. The main thing was that it was my father who decided that I was old enough to go on the hunt. Remember, it was a very dangerous thing to be doing—but important." Ewen laid his hand across *sgian dubh*. "He not only taught me how to hunt, but how to use *sgian dubh* so that I could provide for my family. But, Jimmy, don't you see?" Ewen looked directly at his son. "It was my *father* who decided I was big enough to go on the hunt, and he decided that only after I'd shown that I could be trusted, and then . . . he came with me so that he could look after me while I learned."

Ewen watched his son's eyes begin to glisten, and he felt his throat constrict.

"If I or your mother ask you not to do something, Jimmy, it's because we care about you and want to protect you until you're ready." He tapped the knife. "One day I'll teach you how to use *sgian dubh,* Jimmy, but now I think I'll have to wait a while. What do you think?"

Jimmy sat very still, feeling the weight of the knife in his hands, then he slowly nodded and set his jaw firmly.

"You'll not have to wait long, Dad." He solemnly handed the dagger back to his father. "I promise you that."

Chapter Fourteen

County Cork, Ireland, 1845
A Wild Will and a Fast Tongue

"THE SOLUTION IS SIMPLE, FATHER." Lauryn stood to the side of the black-smith's shop while her father beat the red-hot iron on the anvil. The sparks flew yellow with each blow, and she could see that he had already beaten it as much as he needed to. Still the hammer flew up and down.

"I'll not have you going over the sea alone." Kevin swung the hammer harder. "It's not right for a lass."

"But it's only to England." Lauryn folded her arms and took a deep breath. "I've thought about it a lot, Father, and this is what makes the most sense. You have three extra mouths to feed now, with Jean moving in, and I'd be one less. I could also send money home to help out."

Kevin picked up the iron and turned to plunge it into the water barrel. The hiss of steam seemed to deflate his resolve, and his shoulders slumped. "I don't want you to do it, Lauryn." He shook his head. "You shouldn't have to do it."

"People shouldn't have to die, Father. People shouldn't have to be leaving Ireland in the thousands because they'll starve if they stay." Lauryn shrugged her shoulders. "I'd rather go with your blessing, Father."

Kevin slowly lifted his head as she spoke, and she could see that he was relenting. "Have you spoken to your *máthair*?"

Lauryn shook her head. "Not yet. I wanted to speak to you first." She slowly walked toward him and stood still until he put the hammer and tongs down. With a sigh he took her in his arms and hugged her tightly.

"My Lauryn . . . my strong girl." He stared over her head at the cluster of village houses that she'd been part of her entire life and shook his head. "I have no idea what you're going to, girl. No idea at all. What would I be doing sending you away to something we don't know?"

"You won't be sending me away, Father." Lauryn squeezed him around the waist. "This is my decision."

He nodded as she moved away. "You know your *máthair* won't let you go."

"I know." Lauryn smiled, but her lips trembled. "But I could not leave without the image of Ma frowning at me. That will be what keeps me on the strait and narrow when I'm gone."

Kevin studied his daughter silently. Then, as if trying to seal her image in his mind, he gently touched her cheek. "Just remember, daughter—wherever you are, whatever happens to you . . . Remember that we're one heart. One Irish heart that beats as strongly together as it does when we're apart . . . as long as we don't forget each other."

"Yes, Father." Lauryn put her hand over his. "We're one heart . . . always."

* * *

SURPRISINGLY, MOIRA SAID LITTLE WHEN Lauryn told her of her decision. As Moira sat in a chair with a child on her lap and her eye on Megan lying in the bed with the other little one curled up beside her, she only nodded as if such a thing were inevitable.

"I'll send money back as soon as I begin earning." Lauryn pulled up the other chair. "Father O'Doherty said that there are jobs aplenty in Birmingham and that I can find lodgings—"

"And since when have you ever listened to anything Father O'Doherty had to say?" Moira's lips twitched. Since Lauryn's beloved Father Quinn had left, Lauryn had steadfastly refused to allow that his replacement might speak the same word of God.

"Since I needed him to be useful." Lauryn was blunt as she shrugged. "I think he cooperated because he'll be glad to see the last of me."

"There could be something in that." Moira nodded. "What else did he say?"

Lauryn stared at an empty plate on the table as she silently recalled the many things Father O'Doherty had had to say—much of it having to do with repenting of her wild will and fast tongue.

"Not much . . . just that I could get some work in Cork to begin with to pay for my fare and lodging."

"I see . . ." Moira shifted her position on the chair so that she could rock the little boy, then she pointed toward a small jar above the fireplace. "Bring it to me."

Lauryn walked over and picked up the jar. Hearing it rattle, she frowned as she handed it to her mother. A long time ago it had held coins from when they had sold extra eggs and milk, but it had been empty for many months.

She watched as her mother tipped it up and a single coin rolled out then spun and dropped on the table.

Lauryn stared at it then looked at her mother.

Moira rocked, but she didn't look at her daughter as she indicated the coin. "You can use it or you can keep it as a reminder that you don't need the English money—you're simply choosing to use it for the time being."

"For the time being." Lauryn stared at the coin. "And then I can help you and Da and the others."

"You help yourself first, daughter." Moira rested her head against the child's. "Just be sure you make the right choices."

* * *

FATHER O'DOHERTY PROVED TO BE surprisingly helpful as Lauryn made her preparations to leave. He somehow arranged for her to travel to Cork and then on to London and Birmingham, with one of the woman parishioners of the local Protestant church. She was to travel as a temporary waiting maid and would be leaving in just a few days. The news of her departure had come unexpectedly, and Lauryn had not even time to wonder how he might have arranged such a thing as she had been immediately caught up with preparing to leave. Although she did not have much in the way of possessions, her mother wanted her to leave looking respectable.

The night before she was to leave, Father O'Doherty arrived at the cottage late in the evening with a parcel wrapped in a piece of cloth and fixed with twine.

"Father . . . please, come in." Kevin opened the door and stood back in surprise as the thin figure of the priest seemed to slide in through the doorway.

"I won't be long." Father O'Doherty placed the parcel on the table and stood back quickly, not looking at Lauryn or Moira. "This was given to me with some other clothes . . . a dead woman . . . so the clothes were given to me . . . to give to the poor. Miss Lauryn could probably use them . . ." He hesitated then turned toward the door.

"Thank you, Father . . . for everything you've done for me." Lauryn spoke quietly behind her mother.

"You're welcome, Miss Lauryn." He took one step forward then turned back slightly, still not looking directly at her. "I . . . ah . . . I have also included a letter . . . to the effect that you have been my best student at the school and that I would highly recommend your employment." He rushed the final statement then finally raised his eyes to look straight at her. "I don't

know that the recommendation of an old Catholic priest will hold any sway
in England, so I had the landlord sign it as well. You may find it helpful."

There was total silence in the room, then Lauryn moved forward. "Oh,
Father . . ."

Her lip trembled at the unexpected kindness, and she held out both
hands in a gesture of gratitude. Father O'Doherty bobbed his head in a
quick nod, seeming to recognize what she was trying to say, then he walked
to the door.

"Our prayers are with you, Miss Lauryn. *Rath de ort* . . . the grace of
God be with you."

Nobody moved for some time after the door closed behind him, then
Lauryn slowly pulled the twine on the parcel and undid the cloth. Inside
was a pale yellow, cotton dress, its high-necked, pin-tucked bodice and long
puffed sleeves trimmed with fine white lace. She could hardly breathe as she
pulled it up and held it against her body, the long skirt falling to the floor.
As it came off the table, a plain white envelope fell to the floor. It wasn't
sealed, and as Moira picked it up, she glanced at her daughter. Lauryn
nodded as she kept the dress pressed against her, swaying gently so that the
fabric moved beneath her hands.

Moira read the letter first. She put her hand to her heart as she read
it again. "Oh, Lauryn." She lowered the letter and shook her head. "Such
kindly things he's said about you."

Lauryn finally put the dress down and went to look over her mother's
shoulder. "Oh . . ." Lauryn gasped as she read the first few lines. "This could
never be me he's talking about." She frowned and put her head to the side.
"A quick mind and a cheerful spirit? Industrious and worthy of high levels
of trust . . ." She lowered the letter, but her father, who had not had the
chance to learn to read like his wife and daughter, tapped it impatiently.

"Never mind the tiny bits . . . read me the whole letter."

Lauryn did read the whole letter—many times that evening and
through the next day until finally her mother took it from her and placed it
back in the envelope.

"You'll be wearing it out, and then it'll be no use to you at all," she reprimanded Lauryn softly as she laid it in the small bag that held all of her daughter's possessions. "Now I think that'll be all you'll be needing." Her voice
trembled, then she took a quick breath. "There's one last thing though . . ."

Lauryn looked at the bag. "There isn't any room, Ma, and I have all I need."

Moira smiled, then she began to twist the ring on her finger. "This won't
take any room." She held out the ring. "Your father and I want you to take
this with you."

Lauryn stared then began to shake her head. "No . . . I cannot take your wedding ring. The *claddagh,* Ma, is yours, and after that it will be Megan's . . ." Lauryn felt the tears thick in her eyes, and her throat swelled as she felt her mother's hand under hers then the ring placed in it.

"It is yours now, Lauryn. Wear it well."

"Ma . . ." Through a blur of tears, Lauryn slid the ring onto her right hand then closed her other hand around it as her mother's arms came around her.

"May God hold you in the hollow of His hand, my daughter."

* * *

Lauryn's whole family managed to make it to the village to say farewell. Megan and Myra took turns riding on their father's back, and the two babies were able to walk with occasional help from Alice and Moira. Even Jean was walking well now. Lauryn felt a rush of love for all of them as they grouped together outside of the Catholic church, each one in turn looking anxiously along the road that led up to the grand building.

Finally, the rattle of carriage wheels sounded, and Lauryn felt her heart skip a beat.

"It's here," Alice squealed and pointed needlessly as the dark blue carriage rolled into sight. "Oh, Lauryn . . . to think you will travel in such a fine buggy."

Lauryn had seen the closed-in carriage rolling along the lanes before and had always wondered who might be riding inside. Now she stared as it pulled up alongside the church, the horse panting as it jerked its head and lifted its feet. When it settled, the driver fastened the reins and swung down off the carriage seat to open the door.

It took a moment before one beige leather shoe emerged, followed by a hat of black velvet topped with a short feather. The rest of the passenger followed in a tumble of green velvet.

"Oh my, I do hate getting in and out of these carriages, but it would be most rude to stay in there, wouldn't it?" The rotund woman fanned herself with a finely carved ivory fan then smiled at the group as she quickly summed them all up. She fixed her gaze on Lauryn. "And you must be Lauryn, the girl who is brave enough to help an old woman like me to get back to England."

Lauryn glanced at her mother, then she nodded and dropped in a quick curtsy, though the gesture felt unnatural. "I . . . yes, I'm Lauryn . . . Mistress . . . Lady Farnsworth," she stammered, hoping that she'd said the name correctly. "I'm pleased to meet you."

"Pretty and good manners . . . we should get along very well." Lady Farnsworth nodded then looked around. "And is Father O'Doherty anywhere to be seen?"

As if on cue, the priest stepped out from the church doorway, and, with his hands clasped in front, he walked the few steps to the carriage and bowed slightly to Lady Farnsworth.

"As promised, my lady, your companion for the voyage, Miss Lauryn Kelly." He nodded toward Lauryn but did not look at either her or her family. "She will serve you well."

"I am sure of that, Father." Lady Farnsworth chuckled. "How I love the thought of being a Presbyterian old maid, turning up in England with a pretty young Irish Catholic companion." She turned to Kevin and Moira. "It is good your daughter is able to come with me. My own maid is ill and unable to travel, and I have to get back to Birmingham urgently, so this girl is a godsend. I will make sure she settles well."

With that, she held out her hand to the driver and waited to be helped back into the carriage. Once inside she leaned out and beckoned to Lauryn. "Come quickly, young lady . . . farewells are never nice."

"Ah . . . coming, your . . . Lady . . . ma'am . . ." Lauryn looked at her mother with wide eyes then gave her a tight hug. She continued along the line, embracing everyone in the family until she came to Father O'Doherty.

"Thank you, Father . . . for everything. I will do you proud." She smiled then very quickly leaned forward and gave him a hug before turning and stepping up into the carriage. She was already halfway inside before she realized that the driver had held out his hand.

"Oh, dear . . ." She hesitated then hurriedly sat down inside, admiring the dark brown leather seats that smelled of polish and sank beneath her as she sat down.

"Oh . . ." She couldn't help running her hand gently over the leather. She looked up at Lady Farnsworth with wide eyes as the old lady smiled.

"I forget how much I take for granted." Lady Farnsworth nodded and folded her hands across her ample stomach. "I think you and I are going to have fun on this trip, young lady."

Lauryn nodded absently, looking out the carriage to catch a last glimpse of her family. Her father was standing with his arm around his wife's shoulder. Megan, Myra, and Alice were crying together while Jean and the children and Father O'Doherty stood slightly apart.

"*Rath de ort,*" she whispered as she drew back against the soft leather seat and stared at the mirrored pane opposite, frowning slightly as she saw a clear reflection of herself for the first time. Her newly washed long brown hair was pulled tightly back off her face and fell softly over the shoulders of her new yellow dress. She raised a hand to her face, and the sun glittered off the silver ring on her finger.

"Love, loyalty, and friendship," Lady Farnsworth said quietly beside her. "I like the concept of the Irish ring." She nodded as her whole body moved with the motion of the carriage. "Stay true to those things, my dear, and life will treat you well."

"'Tis my *máthair*'s ring," Lauryn said quietly. Then the tears began to slide down her cheeks. She kept her face turned away to the window, but she managed a smile as her companion finally responded.

"I don't you suppose you own a handkerchief, do you child?" She rummaged in a large, beaded black bag and then triumphantly waved a white hanky toward Lauryn. "I see we have many things to teach one another."

* * *

ALTHOUGH THE VILLAGE WAS ONLY fifteen miles from the city of Cork, Lauryn had never been there, and the promise of an excellent view from the carriage as they traveled the streets through the town kept her close to the windowed door as she tried to take everything in.

The wide streets were full of people, but the carriage moved without slowing its pace. The crowds of people seemed to simply move and swell in a tide around it, parting as it approached and falling in behind as it passed. Other carriages were part of the mass, but much of the crowd consisted of wretched-looking children and adults, raggedly clothed and barefoot, many holding out their hands and begging from more finely dressed people who passed them by as if they didn't exist.

"It's a sad state of affairs, isn't it?" Lady Farnsworth tut-tutted beside her. "These poor people get forced off their land and come to the town thinking there'll be more for them—but there's even less here and more to share it between."

"There's people starving on the land," Lauryn said quietly. "My cousins were starving. Some of them died."

"That's the pity of it." Lady Farnsworth nodded. "So many dying. I find the whole situation here in Ireland deplorable, but I'm not sure what I can do about it because it's so . . . huge." She frowned and fanned herself. "At least I can help one . . . I think you should come to Birmingham, Lauryn."

"But . . . I am, ma'am . . . aren't I?" Bewildered, Lauryn looked at her companion, who tapped her fan against her chin. "I was to stay with you until you got to Birmingham."

"Yes, yes . . . but that was only until we got there, and then you were to find your own work." She nodded happily. "The more I think about it, the more I think you should stay with me once we get to Birmingham."

There didn't seem to be much else to say on the subject, and so Lauryn sat quietly as the carriage plied its way through the city and down to the harborside. As the carriage drew to a stop, Lauryn tried frantically to think what she should be doing to assist her employer. What did a lady's maid do? She glanced around as the door was flung open and the driver held out his hand. Lauryn took it this time and felt her cheeks flush. She pulled her features into what she hoped was a refined expression then stepped out of the carriage. The cobbles were uneven beneath her feet, and she stumbled slightly and again felt the driver's hand beneath her elbow.

"Careful, miss," he said with an English accent, and Lauryn stared then nodded. "And I suggest you help me with the smaller bags that the lady will need immediately . . . and stay right beside her. She sometimes forgets where she's going."

"Oh . . . right." Lauryn smiled her thanks and took a step back as Lady Farnsworth began to step out of the carriage.

Lady Farnsworth looked around her. "Let's get on board quickly and out of this rabble." She fanned herself again. "Lauryn . . . stay with me and we'll find our cabin while Potter gets the bags."

Potter smiled and bowed slightly as he handed Lauryn her own bag plus two others then turned back to the carriage to unload several large trunks.

"It's absolutely ridiculous how much I carry with me." Lady Farnsworth chuckled. "I never use it all, but my brother and sister-in-law will think less of me if I don't look like I'm ready for high society."

The corner of Lauryn's mouth twitched as she began to glean an idea of what actually took place in the strands of English society she had only ever seen at a great distance. It seemed certain that Lady Farnsworth would provide some interesting insights, and Lauryn felt her spirits lift for the first time that day.

"Actually, what I'm most ready for is a good lunch." Lady Farnsworth looked toward the large boat that swayed gently at anchor to their left. She pointed and beckoned Lauryn. "Come on, child. Let's see that you get some decent food into you. You probably haven't had any for a while."

They made their way through the crowd, and once again Lauryn found herself wondering at the vastness of the throng. To one side, people were stepping out of carriages and filing up a long wooden gangplank onto the ship. Servants or crewmen followed, carrying luggage. There were even several dogs in the mix—elegant, long-haired hounds with slim, pointed snouts. Most of the passengers wore fine gowns, and the women carried parasols, which they held at an angle against the few rays of sun struggling to shine through the gray skies overhead. Children scampered about, waiting to get on board, and each seemed to have a nanny nearby while parents walked ahead with hardly a glance at their children.

Lauryn swallowed hard as she looked toward the rear of the ship, where a growing mass of people was crushing together near another gangplank. Their clothes were a uniform drab gray or brown, and many of the men were unshaven and obviously unwashed. The women didn't fare much better, and their clothes had no shape or semblance of fashion. Most people were barefoot, and many carried no luggage with them at all. Children were scattered in amongst the adults, but most clung to a parent, not daring to move from their sides.

Lauryn felt a lump in her throat as she realized that without Father O'Doherty's intervention, she would be walking that gangplank, surrounded by the penniless, rather than where she stood now, surrounded by gentry. She frowned as she wondered at the workings of fate that had changed her path, and then she remembered the earnest prayers of her family, and suddenly she felt their spirit—and their faith.

"Come, Lauryn. We need to go down to our cabin so Potter can get back to the buggy." She glanced back on the dock. "Unless someone's sold it by now." Chuckling at the mere possibility of such a thing happening, Lady Farnsworth moved along the deck and toward the central stairwell, negotiating the narrow, steep stairs with amazing grace in spite of her size. Lauryn followed quickly, trying to focus on what was happening around her. Everything was new, everything was different, and everything seemed to be happening so fast that her head was spinning.

She gulped for a breath as she realized that everything actually *was* spinning and her stomach was churning. She stopped and leaned against the wall, gasping. After a moment, she looked up into the understanding eyes of her employer.

"You're just feeling the movement, dear. That's all it is. Boat rocking and these narrow corridors with no air . . ." She fanned herself. "You'll be fine when you get your sea legs."

"Sea legs," Lauryn repeated as she swallowed hard then kept her lips tightly pressed together. Potter was right behind her, and he leaned closer.

"Deep breaths through your nose, miss, and take long, slow steps . . . get used to the rocking."

Lauryn nodded and tried to smile as she took a deep breath, but her eyes welled up as she looked at Potter's face. Suddenly a sneeze overtook her. The bags she was carrying went flying, and with the intensity of the sneeze and the tears that were already in her eyes, Lauryn felt her nose and eyes running all at once. The woman behind Potter stared in horror, and suddenly it all seemed so ridiculous that Lauryn began to laugh. Oblivious to the line of people now gathering behind Potter in the hallway, she picked the bags back up and quickly retrieved the handkerchief Lady Farnsworth had given her earlier. Potter stood patiently, the smile on his face growing as Lauryn chuckled, blew her nose, and straightened her shoulders.

"There now . . . nothin' like a good sneeze to fix things." She smiled broadly at the woman still staring, nodded, and walked on to catch up with Lady Farnsworth.

"Well done, Miss Lauryn," Potter murmured as he followed behind. "You'll do well."

The cabin was small, especially with Lady Farnsworth standing in the middle of it, and by the time Potter had stashed the luggage to one side beside a hand basin, Lauryn was pressed against the wall. She glanced at the two slim wooden bunks with crisp white linens beside her, and as she looked back, Lady Farnsworth nodded.

"Normally you would have separate quarters, but for a short trip like this I'll keep you close by. You, of course, will take the top bunk, Lauryn, and I will let the right half of me sleep for the first few hours and then the left." She laughed out loud as she shook her head. "They may not let those poor, unfortunate beggars into cabin class, but the ships surely provide beds only big enough to fit them." She removed her gloves and set them on the table. "However, in a storm I never worry, because once I'm wedged into the silly little bed, King Neptune himself couldn't get me out."

Lauryn glanced at Potter and suppressed a grin as she shook her head. She had no idea who King Neptune was, but her preconceived ideas about the English nobility were flying out the window the more time she spent with Lady Farnsworth. Her smile faded as Potter frowned slightly and nodded toward the bags Lauryn had carried then toward some wooden drawers beside the bunk.

"Um . . . should I put anything in the drawers, m'lady?" She raised one eyebrow at Potter, and he inclined his head very slightly.

"Yes." Lady Farnsworth glanced around. "Good thinking, young lady. Let's get organized quickly so we can get down to the dining room." She looked at Potter. "And you had better get back to the buggy, Potter, before someone steals it." She chuckled again as she searched through her purse.

"Now here's a little money to get something to eat on the way back, Potter, and thank you for your help." She glanced at Lauryn then back to Potter. "Such a shame you couldn't come with us."

"It is indeed, m'lady." Potter bowed slightly, giving Lauryn a quick look as he tapped one finger to his forehead in salute and backed out of the cabin. As the door closed behind him, Lady Farnsworth gave Lauryn a broad smile.

"Well, I can see I'll have to stay on my toes to keep my new maid." She swung around and clapped her hands. "But enough of that—let's get on with the unpacking."

Lauryn hurried to the task, her cheeks still pink from the look Potter had flashed her way as he'd departed. She worked as fast as she could, unpacking the bags and trying hard to anticipate what Lady Farnsworth wanted. As she unpacked voluminous silken underwear and petticoats and large-boned corsets, she tried not to marvel at everything she touched; however, she was unconsciously shaking her head by the third bag.

"It's a bit much, isn't it, Lauryn?" Lady Farnsworth stood in front of the wall mirror. She was pinning her hair but also watching Lauryn behind her.

"M'lady?" Lauryn stood up holding a black silk stole in one hand while the heavily embroidered end with long silken tassels draped over her other hand.

"So many things." She turned from the mirror and walked over to run her hand over the stole. "I think this is my favorite, though . . . given to me many years ago by an admirer . . . when I had admirers." She smiled at Lauryn, but it didn't reach her eyes. "Put it on."

"Ma'am?" Lauryn asked, puzzled.

"Put the stole on." Lady Farnsworth held up one finger and spun it round in a circle. "Let me see it on you."

"Um . . . all right." Lauryn tentatively held out the stole then flicked it over her shoulder as she had done thousands of times before with her own cotton shawl. But as the silk closed around her, she couldn't resist running her fingers over the fabric and the thick embroidered roses and vines. "It's so beautiful," she murmured softly then glanced up and stood straighter, unsure what to do next. Lady Farnsworth merely smiled and pointed to the drawer.

"Put it in the middle drawer. I'll wear it to dinner tonight." She gathered up her bag again. "And now lunch awaits us."

* * *

THEY HAD BEEN AT SEA for three days, and during lunch on the third day, Lauryn felt sure she couldn't take another mouthful of the vast amounts of food that seemed to appear like magic on the tables every time they sat down. For the three days she had never left her employer's side—partly because she wanted to make sure she was doing everything right and partly because she was fearful of venturing beyond the security of Lady Farnsworth.

Everything around her was so foreign as to render her completely silent, except when they were alone. At the dining table, which they shared with an elderly couple and two middle-aged businessmen, she was never included in the conversation, and it suited her perfectly. She quickly learned to eat with her eyes slightly downcast so that she was there but not there, yet always attentive to her mistress's needs.

On this third day, however, the table conversation lasted a lot longer than usual while Lady Farnsworth engaged in a lively discussion on the virtues of the cotton trade with the two gentlemen. Lauryn was impressed with Lady Farnsworth's knowledge and confidence in the subject, but after an hour and a half she struggled to suppress a yawn.

"We are boring aren't we, young lady? Why don't you go for a little walk while I put these gentlemen to rights about international trade," Lady Farnsworth said as she waved her hand toward the deck. "I'll be at least another hour."

Lauryn stood up slowly to make sure Lady Farnsworth meant what she said, but when she waved her away again, Lauryn slid quickly out of her seat. "I'll come back in one hour, ma'am."

As she walked away she thought she heard the words "An Irish gem."

Out on deck she was surprised to find a large crowd of people, all of them from the steerage class, pressed into the area, many of them leaning over the rails. The breeze carried the smell of the group toward her in a wave, and Lauryn put her hand to her face. It was the same smell she remembered from her cousin's house and from the crowded part of the dock and from certain city streets they had passed through—the stale stench of unwashed bodies and clothes.

She turned toward the other end of the boat, but she was inexplicably drawn back, and she walked slowly toward the thick rope that divided the deck area. Several people watched her approach with sour expressions and dark, hooded eyes.

"Miss!" She turned as a voice called out close by and a tall man in a ship's officer's uniform walked toward her. "Best you stay below during this time, miss." He clasped his hands behind his back and nodded. "Not a good time to be on deck."

"I . . . I see." Lauryn glanced back at the mass of people, then she nodded and lifted her hem before turning back to the doorway.

"Any money, miss?"

She heard the voice through the rabble, and she turned back. A young woman leaned against the rope, one hand held out while the other hand rested on a protruding stomach. She might have been about the same age as Lauryn, but it was difficult to tell, as starvation had etched years onto her face and body.

"I wouldn't, miss," the officer warned at Lauryn's elbow, and she looked up quickly. "She probably stole the four pence for the fare." He nodded toward the woman then extended a hand back toward the stairwell. "This way, miss."

Lauryn nodded slowly and began to walk back with the officer close behind her. At the door she hesitated again, tempted to look back, but then she stepped over the doorjamb and let the door close firmly behind her.

* * *

"It's such a relief we won't have to go by carriage to Birmingham." Lady Farnsworth fanned herself as fine beads of perspiration trembled perpetually on her brow. "The train is so much faster and smoother."

"Train, ma'am?" Lauryn frowned, and her mistress raised a delighted eyebrow.

"Yes, the train, Lauryn." She held both hands apart. "It's a very large engine that pulls carriages of people all at once . . . all the way from London to Birmingham." She shook her head at Lauryn's blank expression. "You'll see."

And Lauryn did see. She took in the sights of the London docks, which were so much bigger than those at Cork and where there were five times as many ships and people and buildings. She saw the rows of fine houses, three stories high, that graced the city streets along the route to the train station. She saw markets where people cried out to advertise their goods. She saw row upon row of shops with their front glass windows full of goods of every description, each one selling something different.

"London is a wonderful place to visit about once a year, in my opinion." Lady Farnsworth glanced out of the carriage window. "I'm a country person at heart—I prefer the quiet, and animals often make far better conversationalists." She smiled at Lauryn's startled look. "Don't you agree?"

Lauryn nodded as she smiled back, quickly catching on to her employer's sense of humor. "Pigs are very good company, but they tend to have too much to say. Horses are my favorites because they're good listeners."

"Did you have a horse in Ireland?"

"Oh, goodness me, no." Lauryn shook her head. "Horses were for the likes of . . ." She hesitated. "Well, you know."

"For the likes of us English." Lady Farnsworth nodded.

"But my father is a blacksmith, so I used to sit and watch the horses while he did their shoes. They all have different personalities, you know. Just like people."

Lady Farnsworth nodded and smiled, clearly enjoying Lauryn's perspective. As Lauryn became more confident around Lady Farnsworth, she found she had more to say, and the two had many interesting conversations.

"The most beautiful horse in the world was Finnbheara," Lauryn finished.

"Finn . . . var?" She attempted the Irish pronunciation and the rolling "r" sound, and Lauryn smiled as she nodded.

"He was a huge horse . . . all golden with two white socks at the front." Lauryn shook her head. "He hurt me, but it was not his fault. It was the manager who owned him that made him so frightened."

Lady Farnsworth looked concerned and asked, "Is that how your leg got hurt?"

There was a short silence, then Lauryn nodded. She had tried hard to conceal her leg while changing, but her mistress had obviously seen the scar.

"When the manager beat him, he went crazy and sent the fire onto me then landed on my leg with his foot." A pained look crossed Lady Farnsworth's face, and she shook her head. "But it was an accident, mind. He didn't mean to hurt me."

"I'm sure he didn't." The woman frowned. "Did the manager make amends . . . did he help you?"

"I don't know how he could have, ma'am. I could only get better or worse on my own. My ma cared for me, and when I woke up I only had to learn to walk again." She nodded. "At least I only have a tiny limp now while my sister Megan will be a cripple her whole life, and then there are those who have suffered worse things." She hesitated, realizing she was perhaps talking too much. "Not like being hurt by a horse . . . other things." She stopped talking and turned her head to the window, uncertain why she had suddenly shared so much.

"Yes, I understand . . . other things." Lady Farnsworth nodded slowly as she studied Lauryn's profile.

* * *

THE TRAIN STATION MADE THE docks seem like a restful place. Not only were there people milling around everywhere in tight crowds, but the train itself, a huge, black iron engine, sat hissing and billowing puffs of steam from its black chimney. Lauryn stayed close to Lady Farnsworth as she glanced around, not wanting to miss anything but trying to avoid it at the same time.

"You've got the look of a hare being chased by the dogs." Lady Farnsworth tapped her on the arm. "We'll get settled into the carriage as soon as we get our tickets."

They were escorted onto the train by a conductor, and Lauryn sat watching the crowds of unkempt people crushing against each other to fit into some carriages at the end of the train.

"That's the trouble with these trains—they're spreading the riffraff around the countryside." Lauryn turned slightly as a woman spoke clearly behind her, standing in the aisle. A large feather hat almost obscured the woman's face, but Lauryn could see an elegantly gloved hand gesturing toward the crowd. "At least when they all had to walk they stayed mostly where they belonged."

"Ah, that's the price of progress, my dear. The rail has opened up many opportunities, but it has brought its problems as well." The man standing beside her bent his head to the side as he spoke and curled the end of a long blond mustache between his fingertips. "Unfortunately, we need the likes of these to go down the mines to get coal so that we can run the trains."

"We *need* them but we don't *want* them." The woman smiled and nodded, and the feathers on her hat fluttered. "Such an unfortunate quandary."

They passed by, and Lauryn stared after them.

"An unfortunate quandary," she repeated softly with one last glance out the window. Is that what she felt too?

The carriage had been a bumpy ride, and the ship had lulled her with its rolling motion, but the train had Lauryn sitting on the edge of her seat nearly the whole way from London to Birmingham as she took in the speed at which it clattered along the metal tracks and the thick clouds of dark gray smoke that it belched into the air.

"Quite alarming, isn't it?" Lady Farnsworth nodded with the movement of the train. "But one does get used to it, and then it's a nice long ride to fall asleep on." She settled back against the seat and into the corner. "In fact, wake me when we get to the station—although I'll probably hear those terrible screeching brakes. A train tends not to do anything quietly."

She closed her eyes, and Lauryn sat quietly, trying to make her eyes move quickly enough to absorb all the new scenery before it rushed past her window. Traveling at such speeds, she noticed how quickly the landscape changed from dirty brown towns to green fields then back to the towns.

Occasionally, she caught sight of a few small groups of houses nestled in a valley between rolling hills.

"Like home." She breathed in deeply. Had it only been four days since she'd left her home, her village? Left Ireland . . . possibly for good? She closed her eyes and thought of all that had happened in the last four days. The number of different people she'd seen and met . . . the different transport . . . the food—so much food it could have fed her family for months!

Had it only been four days? It already felt like a lifetime . . .

* * *

THEY GOT OFF THE TRAIN at the Curzon Street Station, in the heart of Birmingham, and once again Lady Farnsworth stepped off the train and called immediately for a porter to bring their luggage, then led the way through the station. Like a ship under full sail, Lady Farnsworth led the way, and Lauryn followed in her wake.

"I wrote that we were arriving today, so there should be a carriage waiting." She pulled on her gloves as she walked. "I'll be most upset if it isn't there." She turned to Lauryn and chuckled. "Actually, I wouldn't really, as then we could stay the evening and do some shopping on Union Street, but it never pays to let them know that. They need to be kept on their toes."

"They" were ready and waiting outside the station—a shiny dark blue carriage with a black leather top and silver trim. Two men in dark livery stood waiting to load their luggage. The younger one loaded the luggage in the back while the older, silver-haired man greeted Lady Farnsworth with a wide smile and a chuckle. "So you've bin shoppin' in Ireland, m'lady?"

"Shopping in Ireland?" Lady Farnsworth looked puzzled, then she glanced at Lauryn and flapped her hand. "Jamie . . . you've always been a rascal." She held a hand out toward Lauryn. "Miss Lauryn Kelly, meet Mr. Jamie Field, head of the stable and head of the estate if you listen to him tell the story." She turned as the younger man jumped down from the back of the carriage. "And this is Master James Field, son of Mr. Jamie."

Master James was much taller than his father and had a full head of black hair that seemed to match his dark eyes. Lauryn stared, fascinated; they reminded her of the deep brown eyes of Finnbheara.

"Very pleased to meet you, Miss Kelly." Jamie nodded toward her and she started, realizing that he was speaking to her.

"I'm . . . I—pleased to meet you." She dropped in a slight curtsy, and Jamie chuckled.

"Well, fancy getting a curtsy. She's a good girl." He glanced at Lady Farnsworth and swung into a deep bow as he directed them into the carriage. Lauryn smiled, taking an instant liking to the old man, but it was his son who held out his hand to help her into the carriage, and she couldn't suppress a slight intake of breath as she laid her hand in his.

"Miss." He bowed very slightly, and she bobbed her head in response as she climbed into the carriage.

"Jamie, I'd like to stop on Union Street and pick up some books and maybe spend a half hour or so to have a little look around," Lady Farnsworth called from inside the carriage, and Jamie nodded.

"Half an hour, m'lady."

Lady Farnsworth turned to Lauryn. "I'll go to the bookstore, and I'd like to order a new hat, so you can have a little look around the shops on your own if you like." She patted Lauryn on the arm. "On your own in the big city."

"Thank you, ma'am." Lauryn nodded, but she gripped her bag tightly.

They reached Union Street in a matter of minutes, and after she had followed her mistress past a few stores, they stopped outside a shop that had an impressive array of hats sitting on wooden stands in the window.

"Just stay within a few shops so I can find you easily." Lady Farnsworth pointed up and down the street. "Half an hour."

Lauryn glanced up at the sky to get an idea of where the sun sat, as was her usual way of guessing time, but there was no sky, the air being filled with a fine layer of dark smoke that seemed to hover above the buildings. She glanced around then decided that she would stay within three shops so she couldn't be late.

There was plenty to see in just six shops, and Lauryn gazed long and hard at the variety of goods—tobacco products, knives, men's outfits, ladies' hats, a lawyer's office and . . . She glanced up at the sign, for there was no window display like the others.

"New Zealand Company," she read then glanced back at the window. The sole decor was a yellowing poster. She took her time, reading it quietly out loud, grateful for the chance to practice her English. "Free passage to the town of Wellington . . . New Zealand . . ."

She became aware of someone standing behind her, and she moved to the side without turning then kept reading the poster silently.

"So nothing's changed."

She turned, startled, as the man behind her spoke sharply.

"I'm sorry?" She frowned, annoyed by his tone and the fact that he had startled her.

"Nothing has changed—a man still needs to be married or have sisters to get free passage." He was obviously talking to himself more than to her as he took off his cap and ran his hand through his hair. "So I either have to find a wife or some sisters or another option."

He was quite a bit taller than Lauryn with light brown hair and pale blue eyes that only now seemed to take notice of her.

"I should think you'd better rely on the last option," she muttered as she moved out of his way, but he was standing on the hem of her dress, so as she turned smartly she was pulled back just as quickly. She stumbled back, only to have a strong hand grip her arm and steady her.

"Thank you . . ." She steadied herself and plucked the offending hem from under the foot he lifted. "For nothing," she muttered as she pulled away.

"Ah, Lauryn. There you are, right on time." Lady Farnsworth swept out of the hat shop with a large round box clasped firmly in her hand. She promptly handed it to Lauryn. "That didn't take long at all. I knew it was right for me as soon as I walked in, but I had to try a few on just in case . . ." She stopped and glanced at the poster Lauryn had been reading, catching the gist of it quickly. "Now don't tell me you're thinking of migrating already . . . I'm not going to let you get away that easily." She turned and waved as their carriage pulled in beside them. "Mind you, it's something I've often thought about—going somewhere exotic. I was born in India, you know, so it's in my blood."

James helped Lady Farnsworth into the carriage, then Lauryn extended her own hand for assistance. She looked straight ahead as she entered the buggy but couldn't resist a glimpse back at the man outside the shipping office as she sat down. He was staring at the carriage, but then he turned slightly, looked straight at her, and with a slight smile he tipped the edge of his cap.

With a tilt of her chin, she inclined her head in what she hoped was a gracious nod. "May you be blessed with the other option . . . before you find some poor woman to be your wife," she murmured under her breath as the carriage rolled away.

Chapter Fifteen

Glasgow, Scotland, 1845
"Never But One Gospel"

"So, TELL ME MORE ABOUT this couple . . . the Frasers." Ewen settled himself onto the sofa beside Bess after he had seen Jimmy back to bed.

"I will . . . after you tell me what you said to Jimmy." Bess smiled. "Was he terribly upset?"

Ewen shook his head. "I decided not to talk about what he'd done." He leaned his head against the back of the sofa. "I showed him *sgian dubh* and explained that my father had made the decision about when I was old enough to do something difficult . . . that I didn't make the decision on my own."

Bess nodded. "So when did you tell him you were going to show him how to use *sgian dubh*?" She glanced at her husband and watched the smile on his face grow.

"You know me too well, wife." He stared at her for a moment then frowned. "Bess, I went to tell Jimmy about hunting the stag, and when I said the word *stag* he just looked at me. He had no idea what I was talking about."

"Well, he wouldn't, would he . . . living in the city his whole life?"

"Aye, but don't you see, Bess? All the things that were a part of me when I was a bairn . . . he'll never know." He shook his head. "He'll never know the freedom of the Highlands . . ."

"Or the hardship." Bess picked up her crochet. "Would you prefer the crofter's hut to this, Ewen?"

Ewen took his time looking around the room, then he slowly shook his head. "I suppose not, but it pains me to know that Jimmy and Fiona won't know of the Highlands."

"They will if you tell them," Bess answered simply. "They're old enough to listen now—and maybe if Jimmy had known about the stag and *sgian dubh,* he might not have gone to Glasgow Green."

Ewen nodded, and Bess could see the faraway look in his eye. In a moment his mind would be back in the Highlands of his youth, so she cleared her throat and set the needlework down again.

"Anyway, you asked me to tell you more about the Frasers . . . Ann and John," she said. "They appear to be a very fine couple, and they have three children near the same age as Jimmy and Fiona."

"But you said they were preaching at the park." Ewen frowned. "Were their children with them?"

"No, the children were with their grandmother," Bess replied. "But what I found interesting was that Ann was teaching as well as John. She said she doesn't speak in public like he does, but she had so much knowledge and could answer my questions as well as John could." She stopped as she realized what she'd said.

"So you were asking them questions?" Ewen asked.

"Well, yes." Bess nodded and pretended to study her crochet. "I was interested to hear what they had to say, especially about babies dying."

"Oh, Bess." Ewen sighed and shook his head. "What did they say?"

"Well . . ." Bess bit at her bottom lip, then she looked at the ceiling. "They quoted a scripture that said that little children were alive in Christ and that He loved them, and . . . and that it was wickedness to think that God would save one child because of baptism and that another should perish because he or she hadn't been baptized." She clasped her hands. "Do you not see what that means, Ewen? Our children have not gone to hell. They are alive in Christ."

Ewen watched the expression on his wife's face and the peace that seemed to have rested on her, and he nodded. "'Tis what I have always felt should be the way." He leaned one arm against the sofa. "So what other questions did you ask? Jimmy mentioned they were here for a while."

Bess nodded. "I'm afraid they might have been a little bit late returning to their children, but it seemed that every question I asked they had an answer that made sense to me." She studied her hands. "I cannot explain it, Ewen, but I didn't feel the concern that I mentioned to you the other day."

Ewen nodded, then he raised one eyebrow. "So what do they preach . . . what is different?"

"They preach that the gospel of Jesus Christ has been restored to the earth in exactly the way that Jesus Christ Himself established it when He was on the earth . . . and that He will come again." She took a deep breath.

"And that the gospel needs to be preached to all men, Ewen—not just to the rich but to *everybody*."

"There's many that say that's the way, Bess. There's always mention of the Kirk missionaries going overseas to teach the heathen nations."

"Aye, they do—and yet they turn away their own at their own doorstep." Bess shook her head. "I'm not saying who is right or wrong, Ewen, but I am saying that I felt very good listening to what they had to say."

Her husband studied her face for a moment then said, "It seems to me that I've heard this sort of thing before." He frowned, then his expression cleared. "Do you remember Ian . . . at the mine? He came just before we left."

"Aye, he was a Highlander as well."

Ewen nodded. "One night we were walking home and, all of a sudden, he told me about a man who had been preaching that Jesus wants His gospel to come back to the world and that He will come back as well." He frowned and tapped his head. "Irving . . . that was the man. Ian said that he was a Presbyterian minister, but he got struck off from the Kirk because of teaching such things."

"I imagine he would." Bess nodded, then she shook her head. "But that is not who the Frasers profess to follow. They say that they have been taught by missionaries from America."

"Not English or Scot?" Ewen grinned. "How could that possibly be true then?"

Bess recognized the teasing tone in her husband's voice and she smiled, relieved that he had reacted so well to her news. Then the butterflies returned as she took a deep breath. "Would you be happy with me going to their meeting, Ewen? I should dearly like to."

Ewen sat quietly for a moment, then he nodded. "I think that would be fine, Bess. And maybe . . ." He hesitated then nodded again. "Maybe the children and I should come with you."

* * *

EWEN FOUND HIS MIND PREOCCUPIED while he worked at the shipyard the next week. Though he was grateful his children had not come to any harm on their outing, he could not help but remember time and again that it had been a close call. Then there was the matter of the preachers. He was intrigued by his wife's fascination with this new religion but was beginning to wonder if it had been wise to consent to go with her.

"Where would your mind be, I wonder?" Ewen started as Benjamin Staples spoke beside him. "You've screwed that bolt on and off at least three times."

Ewen glanced down at the bolt in his hand and shook his head. "Sorry, I am thinking of other things."

Benjamin chuckled. "It's all right with me, but I'd hate to think the ship might sink because you had something on your mind, lad." He pointed at the bolt. "I'll have to admit though—you may have done it three times, but you've done it very thoroughly each time. 'Tis not likely to come loose in a hurry."

Ewen smiled as he reset the bolt, carefully counting how many he had already tightened.

"So, what's on your mind, lad?" Benjamin kept working alongside him, and Ewen knew he was also keeping an eye on him.

"Ah, my bairns had a wee adventure on their own the other day." Ewen shook his head. "They're fine, but I keep thinking I don't know what I would have done if they'd been hurt."

Benjamin nodded. "Aye, that's tough when a bairn is hurt—or worse, dies, especially if you could have done something about it."

"Aye, it's not like if they're ill with the cholera or such and it's out of your control." Ewen frowned. "We've already lost two wee girls. I don't think I could handle losing another."

Benjamin studied the bolts in his hand. "We lost three before we moved. I thank God for this job that let us move somewhere decent."

Ewen nodded in agreement then leaned against the vast iron hull of the ship they were working on and looked at Benjamin. "Speaking of God . . . have you ever heard of some preachers that come from America?"

"The Mormons?" Benjamin responded immediately. "They're an odd bunch, but they're great for the shipping trade."

Ewen frowned. "What do you mean by that?"

"Well, I'm surprised you haven't heard mention of it," Benjamin said. "Those Mormon missionaries came to England about five or six years ago teaching about Jesus coming again and telling everyone that they should get together to prepare and that they could do it best back in America." He indicated the ship they were building. "For the last few years they've been chartering boats as big as this, filling them with people that've joined up with them, and taking them to America." He put his hands on his hips and stood back to look at the size of the ship. "That's a lot of people, Ewen . . . and there's more going all the time by the sounds of it."

Ewen rolled the bolts in his hand and shrugged. "I don't know if this is the same group. It might be."

"Well, if they talk about 'gathering' you'll know it's them." Benjamin grinned. "And if I hear that you've decided to head off to America, I'll know they've got you."

Ewen smiled and went back to securing the bolts, but he glanced at Benjamin. "Have you ever thought about migrating, Benjamin . . . to Canada or the like?"

"Not me." Benjamin shook his head. "But I have a brother who went to Canada about seven years ago, and my sister lives in Australia now with her husband. There's talk of finding gold down there, and he wants to strike it rich." He shook his head. "I tell him just work harder, the lazy beggar. He'll have my sister doing the panning while he tells everyone how he's going to be rich."

Ewen smiled. "So do you ever hear from them?"

Benjamin nodded. "My brother writes pretty regularly—twice a year— and I've heard from my sister once since she reached . . . Sydney, I think it was." He glanced at Ewen. "Are you thinking of it yourself, lad?"

"Oh no . . ." Ewen shook his head. "But I was talking to my lad, Jimmy, the other night and realized that he doesn't really know anything about the Highlands, where we come from. It's not that far away and not long since we left there." He shrugged. "It made me wonder if people forget where they come from when they migrate."

Benjamin stared up at the steel hull then slapped the side of it with the flat of his hand. "I don't know what happens when they get there, lad, but the more of these beasties we build, the more people are going to find out how Scottish they really are when they leave Caledonia."

* * *

SUNDAY DAWNED AND THE CHILDREN woke early, eager to go to the new church. Ewen lay in bed listening to their excited chatter, then he closed his eyes and pretended to be asleep as he heard them at the door.

"Dad . . . are you ready?" Fiona climbed up on the bed.

"Do I look ready?" Ewen didn't open his eyes, so she tried to lift one of the lids.

"You have to be ready." She patted his shoulder. "We're going to meet Mrs. Fraser's little girl who's my age."

"I thought we were going to church," Ewen mumbled, trying not to smile as Fiona patted him again.

Bess watched, smiling as her husband kept teasing. It was amazing to her that he would be coming with them. And to see the children happily encouraging him was beyond anything she could have dreamed of.

"We are going to church," Jimmy finally spoke, and he smiled as he pronounced the news he'd been saving for two days. "And Molly's going to come as well."

"Molly?" Ewen's eyes opened wide. "Molly's going to come to church?"

"Aye . . . she said she didn't want to be left out if the whole family was planning to go."

Bess felt tears pricking her eyes, and she turned busily to the door and held it open. "Off with you both, now. Breakfast first, then we'll get you into your nice clothes."

"How nice?" Ewen asked when the children had rushed downstairs. "I only have my work clothes."

"You'll scrub up fine in your jacket and brown trousers." Bess smiled as she sat down on the bed beside him. "I'm so happy that we're all going, Ewen."

"I got that impression, Mrs. McAlister. You've been looking like the cat that got the cream all week." Ewen reached out and took hold of her hand. "Bess . . . you have to understand, I'm not promising anything here. I'm interested in what these people have to say, but I'm not committing to anything." He made sure she was looking at him. "You do understand?"

"I understand." She nodded and traced the veins on the top of his hand. "I don't even know that I'll be interested either, but I feel good about it, Ewen, and that's enough for me at the moment." She leaned forward and kissed him gently on the lips. "Thank you."

Ewen held onto her hand and pulled her closer. "Maybe I should come to church more often."

* * *

THE LARGE HALL WAS NEARLY full of people, and Ewen noted that there was a mix of well-dressed people sitting alongside those who obviously did not have much money. Children were part of the congregation, sitting with their parents, and there was a group of men sitting up front, not just one preacher.

Ann and John Fraser greeted them as soon as they walked through the door, and the children of both families became firm friends within minutes. Fiona was soon walking hand in hand with six-year-old Kitty, and though Jimmy took a moment longer he was soon busily talking to ten-year-old Milly and nine-year-old Ethan. Molly stayed close to Bess, but she was obviously taken with the setting.

"Well, it didn't take the children long to get to know each other," Ann commented to Bess as she led them to some seats about halfway to the front. "The problem will be keeping them quiet."

"The problem is usually keeping them awake." Bess smiled. "They're not fond of our reverend's long sermons, I'm afraid."

"Oh, there will be more than one person speaking." Ann pointed up to the front. "Each of the brethren will speak, and sometimes one or two members of the congregation."

"The congregation speak?" Ewen caught up with the conversation as John stood up to let him into a seat.

"That's right." John sat down beside him. "We don't have a paid pastor. The brethren are called to serve as leaders, but they only serve for a period of time, then someone else takes over." He pointed to one of the men up front. "Except the elder up there. He's a Church leader visiting from America for a time and is a full-time missionary. He's in charge of the Church over the whole of the country . . . England, Scotland, Ireland, and Wales. His name is Wilford Woodruff."

Ewen took his time studying the man who sat quietly watching the congregation file into their seats. He had a firm set to his jaw, accentuated by chin whiskers and sideburns and thick hair brushed back from his brow. His bushy eyebrows seemed inclined to furrow into a frown, but occasionally, when he acknowledged somebody or said something, his eyes and smile seemed to light up his whole face.

"He has been personally responsible for bringing hundreds of people into the gospel." John shook his head.

"How?" Ewen frowned, but he couldn't keep his eyes off the man's face.

"You'll see." John smiled. "He'll be speaking soon."

The children joined them in their pew, and the congregation settled quickly as one of the men stood up at the wooden pulpit.

"Good morning, brothers and sisters and visitors." He inclined his head toward Ewen and Bess and another couple behind them. "We hope that you enjoy your worship with us this morning and that you might feel of the Spirit of the Lord."

The meeting progressed with the singing of hymns and the offering of bread and water as a sacrament, then Wilford Woodruff stood to speak. He began slowly, then picked up speed, sweeping the congregation along with his words. He never used any written notes but kept his eyes firmly on the congregation as he spoke of the gospel of Jesus Christ being restored to the earth in the latter days. He said that those opting to accept this message now numbered over one hundred thousand.

"The condition of the Church in America is more encouraging than at any former period in the history of the Church because the Saints are more universally of one heart and one mind." His eyebrows furrowed slightly. "But opposition does arise . . . I exhort you, in all cases, to abide by the laws of the land. No man, by keeping the laws of the kingdom of God, need violate the laws of the realm; no one who infringes those laws will be sustained by the authorities of the Church."

"Sometimes that's hard . . . when there is opposition," John whispered, and Ewen nodded.

"The kingdom of God is a kingdom of order, and a spirit of order should characterize every branch of the Church. I rejoice in assembling with you this day and rejoice also in finding things throughout the land in so good a condition as they are." His eyes twinkled as he glanced at the man who had opened the meeting. "Elder James Houston has informed me that the branches in the Glasgow conference are in a very prosperous condition, full of union and love in their counsels, and that Lanark, where he has been laboring, has seen a further sixty-four souls embrace the gospel in the last six months."

There was a murmur of recognition amongst the congregation, and Elder Woodruff nodded.

"I find the general condition of the Church to be most satisfactory and encouraging, but I feel to exhort you here today . . ." He paused, and Ewen watched him struggle against emotion for composure. "Please . . . do not be discouraged by your trials. Contemplate, rather, the course of the Savior, from the manger to the cross. He sought not for peace or prosperity, but for the salvation of men. It was no sign, because men were poor, that they could not be useful and successful in propagating the principles of truth. Let us but remember from whence our power comes and forget not that union is strength, that the grand secret of our success lies in being of one heart and one mind. On the contrary." He paused and held up one hand. "Division stops all blessings and closes the heavens against us. The heavens are full of blessings for the Saints, and union and peace among us can alone call them down upon us, but . . ." He paused again and nodded slowly. "I call upon you all, in the name of God, to be united in all things pertaining to the rolling onward of the kingdom of our Lord and Savior Jesus Christ."

As he concluded speaking and returned to his seat, Ewen found that he was nodding in agreement with what had been said. Bess was fully on the edge of her seat, and she glanced at him to see if he had been listening and smiled warmly when he nodded.

"Well, now I feel like I'm worth something in the eyes of God!" Molly gave a brief nod of approval as they filed out of their seats at the conclusion of the meeting. "Nobody's told me that I'm a child of God before." She wiped a tear from her eye and sniffed loudly. "I thought that bein' poor stopped me from gettin' anywhere near 'im."

She took hold of Fiona's hand and walked ahead with all of the children.

"That wasn't what I was expecting," Ewen said to John as Ann drew Bess away to talk with some of the other women. He shook his head. "In fact, I didn't know what I was expecting, but . . ."

"You felt different?" John asked quietly, and Ewen nodded.

"It's been a long time since I went into any church, and I always felt that it was wrong that I should be turned away, but when that second man spoke . . ." He hesitated. "He read from that book, and it said that the people were cast out of the synagogues because they were poor—even though they were the ones who had built it with their own hands. They weren't allowed in, so they thought they couldn't worship God . . ."

"But then God told them that because they'd been shut out, they had been humbled and were ready to hear the word of God." John nodded. "Do you think you are ready to hear, Ewen?"

Ewen stood still with his hands in his pockets and watched his wife talking with the group of women. She was smiling, and he couldn't help thinking of the pensive expression she usually wore after attending Sunday sermons. He didn't know what he wanted yet, particularly, but he could see what Bess wanted, and he knew he felt good about what he had heard and seen so far.

"I think I'm ready to hear, John . . . but I don't know that I'm ready to accept anything yet." He didn't smile as he looked over to where Elder Woodruff was talking to some men in a small group. He had a book of scripture open and was pointing to a passage. "But I do have questions." He pointed to a similar book that John held in his hand. "What is this book you keep reading from?"

John held up the book, then he pointed toward the American preacher. "I think I'll let Elder Woodruff explain. I had the same question a long time ago, and he really helped me understand." He smiled and led the way across the room. "Elder Woodruff, my friend Ewen McAlister would like to learn more about the Book of Mormon."

"Well, then." Wilford Woodruff smiled and held out his hand to shake Ewen's. "How much time do you have, Brother McAlister?"

Ewen glanced across to where Bess was still talking, and he nodded. "Plenty of time, I think."

They all laughed, and there was a moment while Ewen felt his gaze held by the American, then Wilford Woodruff nodded. He held up two books, one in each hand, and indicated the one in his left hand.

"Here is the Bible, Brother McAlister . . . the record of the Jews, given by the inspiration of the Lord through Moses and the ancient patriarchs and prophets. Is it an imposture, and as the infidels say, the work of man? No, it is not in the power of any man who ever breathed the breath of life to make such a book without the inspiration of the Almighty." He paused then held up the other book.

"It is just so with the Book of Mormon—does the Book of Mormon contain a different gospel to that contained in the Bible? It does not. It gives a history of the people who dwelt upon the American continent anciently, tells where they came from and how they got there, tells of the dealings of God with them and the establishment of the Church of Christ among them. They were visited by Jesus after His resurrection. Hence He said, 'Other sheep I have, which are not of this fold: them also I must bring and they shall hear my voice; and there shall be one fold, and one shepherd.'" He nodded emphatically. "I testify to you, Brother McAlister, that both books contain the same gospel. There was never but one gospel, and there never will be any other revealed to the human family."

Ewen simply stared for a moment, then he frowned. "So, you're saying that this book is the same as the Bible?"

"It supports what is told in the Bible." John pointed to the two books. "The Book of Mormon tells about Jesus Christ . . . but from a different place and people." He pointed across to where Jimmy was talking to Ethan. "Bess mentioned that you were from the Highlands, but Jimmy and Fiona have never been there. Does that mean that if they find and read a book about that place in a few years that they mustn't believe it . . . just because they've never been there?"

"Well, no . . ." Ewen replied.

"A man named Joseph Smith found some records—gold plates—and he found them with the Lord's help." John touched the cover of the Book of Mormon. "Then he translated them . . . into this."

Doubt clouded over Ewen's face, and he shook his head.

Wilford Woodruff spoke then. "All the ingenuity of all the men under heaven could not compose and present to the world a book like the Book of Mormon. It could never emanate from the mind of an impostor, or from the mind of a person writing a novel. Why? Because the promises and prophecies it contains are being fulfilled in the sight of all the earth." He paused and studied Ewen's face again then held out the Book of Mormon. "Take this, Brother McAlister. Keep it . . . read it . . . and know that its principles are divine—they are from God."

Ewen stared at the book as he slowly raised one hand to accept it. Then he looked to one side and shook his head.

"Do you think you are ready to hear, Ewen?" John asked quietly.

Ewen's expression softened, then he nodded and slowly took hold of the book. "I'm ready to have a look . . . only a look, mind." He held up one finger, and Wilford Woodruff smiled.

"A look is a good place to start, Brother McAlister."

* * *

"I BELIEVE THAT IT IS God's message, Ewen." Bess brushed her hair thought-fully as they prepared for bed that evening. "Ann was telling me about an experience Elder Woodruff had when he first came to England . . . when the Frasers joined the Church."

"When was that?" Ewen unbuttoned his shirt.

"About five years ago." Bess laid the brush in her lap. "She said that he went to preach in the south of England—that the Lord told him to—and that even though he was meant to be somewhere else, he went, and when he got to this place, he met a man named John Benbow, who introduced him to the members of a congregation that he belonged to—"

"The Church of England?" Ewen sat on the bed to remove his boots.

"No . . . that was the thing of it . . ." Bess shook her head. "He was part of a group that felt that the old church was not teaching the way Jesus would have wanted these days. This group wanted apostles and the like, just like Jesus had organized things, and so they formed their own kirk and called themselves the United Brethren or such." Bess took a breath. "Anyway, Ann said that along came Elder Woodruff with the very same message they were waiting for, and they were all baptized . . . their superin-tendent, forty preachers, and some six hundred members."

"Six hundred?" Ewen placed his boot on the ground. "Six hundred . . . at once?"

"Over the space of a few days, apparently." Bess nodded then began brushing her hair again. "It seems that if that many people felt good about it, then we should at least think about it."

"I am thinking about it, Bess." Ewen leaned back on the bed. "I have agreed to read the book, but . . . I have heard a bit about the Mormons lately." He frowned. "Benjamin, at the yard, says they're a strange lot and that they are moving in great numbers to America."

Bess kept brushing. "Ann and John are still here." She pursed her lips. "Not everyone feels the need to move, Ewen."

"Aye, Bess, you're right." Ewen lay back against the pillow and picked up the book, rubbing the tan leather with his thumb before he opened the front cover. "The Book of Mormon: An account written by the hand of Mormon, upon plates taken from the plates of . . . Ne-phi." He stopped and looked at Bess. "I thought it was written by someone called Smith."

Bess shrugged, although there was a sparkle to her eyes. "I don't know . . . read it a bit more and find out."

PART THREE

1849

Chapter Sixteen

MASTS AND ROPE.

For as far as the eye could see from one redbrick wall at the side of the dock to the other, the skyline was a rocking mass of tall, wooden, brass-bound masts set with hundreds of knotted ropes binding hundreds of yards of canvas sails to the rigging. The sails were all tied up while the ships sat in dock so that the rope riggings formed a giant mesh that seemed to lock the sky and sun out and contain the London dock in perpetual gray.

With nearly two hundred ships in port and room for one hundred more coming and going, the dockside seethed with movement. The tide ebbed and flowed along with the surging tide of humanity that swarmed onto the dock daily to fill the bellies of the emptied vessels.

"Oh my . . ." Lady Farnsworth fanned her face rapidly as she peered out of the carriage window. "However are we supposed to know which ship we're meant to get on? We could end up in America . . . heaven forbid." She leaned out to look the other way. "Well, that doesn't help. It looks exactly the same wherever you look."

Lauryn smiled as she drew a small envelope of papers from her bag. She flipped through them until she reached the one she was searching for.

"We're meant to be at Woolwich dock, and I believe that is where we are." She slipped the tickets back into her bag. "Besides, James knew exactly where to come. He told me."

"I'm sure he's told you a good many things in the last few weeks." Lady Farnsworth nodded her head knowingly as she moved forward on the seat. "I wouldn't be surprised if that young man turned up in the luggage once we're out to sea."

Lauryn's cheeks colored, but she simply closed her eyes and took a deep breath. Her employer was right about one thing—her family in Ireland were not the only ones to be sorry that she and Lady Farnsworth were migrating to New Zealand.

She waited as the carriage slowed to a stop, then she moved quickly to precede Lady Farnsworth out the door. However, the driver was quicker and was waiting at the door with his hand extended to assist them in alighting. Lauryn smiled and bobbed her head in acknowledgment as James Field took her hand and gave it a slight squeeze as he helped her out.

"Thank you, James." She barely whispered the words as it occurred that this was the last time she would feel her hand in his. For the last four years he had always been there. She looked at him quickly. How would it feel to not have James Field always there?

"Well, I'm surely going to miss you, young James." Lady Farnsworth breathed heavily as she folded up to get out of the carriage then used his hand as leverage to drag herself through the door. "Lauryn's going to have to build some muscles in the antipodes, or we may have to just walk everywhere."

The thought of Lady Francis Farnsworth walking anywhere suddenly appealed to the lady herself as much to Lauryn and James, and they all laughed together. That was the delightful part of being the lady's waiting maid—her attitude always included a blend of respect and a good dose of humor.

James moved quickly to assist the ladies with the smaller bags, then he went around the back to unpack the larger trunks.

"I know we probably should have ridden by train from Birmingham, but I wanted this last carriage ride before we set out on the ocean." Lady Farnsworth took a moment to study the ships rocking alongside the dock. "I just hope it wasn't my last carriage ride." She shook her head as she shaded her eyes and studied the full length of the tallest mast. "Close up, these ships really don't look as if they would carry a lot of people and things safely, all that way. Still, that's what adventure is all about, isn't it? Doing things we normally wouldn't do."

Lauryn studied the ships as well while her mistress began to rummage in her bag. Then she turned to look at the woman who had become her minder and friend during the last four years. At sixty-three years of age, Francis Farnsworth had remained single after losing her husband after only a year and a half of marriage. Her family regarded her as their slightly obnoxious maiden aunt, and she was happy to live up to their expectations. Then Lauryn had appeared in her life, and Lady Farnsworth had taken it upon herself to see that Lauryn had every opportunity to learn and study while she had worked as her maidservant. And she felt that those opportunities would be doubled in a new land, in a new experience.

Now Lauryn could hardly believe they were embarking on such a grand adventure together. She had been surprised at first that Lady Farnsworth would leave her comfortable home in search of adventure, but the assurance of meeting her nephew in New Zealand, who would hopefully have things ready for them there, and the knowledge that the Birmingham estate would be left in the very capable hands of James Field and his father had Lady Farnsworth feeling confident about the move. Since the day they'd seen the notice at the New Zealand Company shipping office, Lady Farnsworth had spoken of little else. Lauryn supposed it was as the lady herself had averred—it was in her blood to travel.

"Don't we have to do something before we board?" Lady Farnsworth frowned as she struggled to remember—a consequence of aging that Lauryn dealt with on a daily basis.

"We have to have a final medical check with the surgeon superintendent." Lauryn looked around. "I imagine that will happen on board the ship. His name is Dr. Appleby."

"I do like the way you keep track of everything, Lauryn. A most admirable trait." Lady Farnsworth straightened her shoulders, lifted her chin, and began to march toward a large ship. "Let's be on our way, then. No point lingering now."

Lauryn picked up her bag as James loudly cleared his throat and pointed toward another slightly larger vessel moored in the other direction farther along the quay.

"I think you'll find it'll be that one, ma'am." He glanced at Lauryn and raised one eyebrow.

"Oh, good." Lady Farnsworth never skipped a beat as she turned in her tracks and headed the other way. "That one's much bigger, thank goodness."

She hesitated as a sudden commotion broke out further down the dock, by the side of one of the ships. A large crowd of people were being herded onto the boat by a battery of men, including several in police uniform. Using their batons and with arms outspread, they had the group packed so tightly that they were moving at a shuffle. Lauryn saw, even from a distance, that there were men and women bunched together and that nobody was exempt from the occasional hard swipe of the policemen's batons. She started as she saw several women stumble and fall amongst the feet of the group that kept moving. A moment later she heard screams then several splashes.

"Oh dear, someone's gone into the water." Lady Farnsworth fanned herself faster as she peered toward the group.

"They won't care." A man walking beside them with a large crate on his shoulder nodded his head toward the commotion. "They'll all be criminals . . . headed for Australia." He grimaced. "Most of 'em probably stole one loaf of bread too many."

"All criminals?" Lauryn frowned as she stared at the melee of people stumbling over each other as they were forced onto the ship by the constabulary. She saw several policemen bring their batons down hard onto people's heads and shoulders. One woman fell and never rose. "For a loaf of bread?"

"Come, my dear . . . it's too depressing," Lady Farnsworth said as they watched a man briefly check the woman who had fallen then roll her aside with his foot. The color drained from Lauryn's face, and Lady Farnsworth put her hand on Lauryn's arm and drew her gently away toward their vessel.

* * *

THEY FOUND THE SURGEON'S QUARTERS on board, and while Lady Farnsworth was busy talking to the doctor, Lauryn waited outside in the narrow hallway. There were people coming and going past her but, as she stared at the wall opposite, all she could see were the looks of desperation on the faces of the people being herded onto the convict ship. She'd learned that the ships full of "criminals" were being sent to the penal colonies for even the smallest crimes. There weren't enough prisons in England, so they were bundled off to whatever fate awaited them on the other side of the world. Nobody cared if they survived the voyage. Nobody cared about them at all. Lauryn shook her head. Those people had looked just like the people she had once worked and lived beside in Ireland.

Eventually, she became aware of someone watching her, and she turned slowly. "Oh, James . . . you managed to find us." Lauryn smiled as her heart leapt a little at the way he was staring at her. He looked so strong and familiar among the throng of strangers.

"Miss Lauryn . . ." He twisted the brown tweed cap in his hands and frowned as he spoke. "I need to talk to you . . . while m'lady is busy."

Lauryn glanced at the door of the surgeon's room, then she looked at James uncertainly. "I cannot leave here, James. Tell me what it is you want."

She saw the frustration on his face, and his grip tightened on his hat, then he walked to her side and placed a hand on her elbow. There was a small alcove behind them in the hallway, and he drew her there. Another woman and child passed by, but he kept his hand on her arm.

"Miss Lauryn, I need to tell you . . . before you leave . . . that I will miss you." James swallowed and drew himself up a fraction taller. "I think you know that if you had stayed in England . . . I would most certainly have asked you to be my wife."

Lauryn stared at his chin and nodded slowly. She was fully aware of the expectation James had had. They would have been the perfect couple—well matched, both physically and socially, similarly employed in the same household with the prospect of a lifetime of secure engagement. There had been an attraction since their first meeting, but their relationship had always been strictly governed by James's desire to reach the status of head of the estate staff, a position held by his father. The one time he had professed his feelings for Lauryn, he had also expressed that they could only consider marriage once he had attained this position.

She laid her hand on his arm and looked up at his face. It was so familiar and had become so dear to her, but in that instant she realized that part of her was glad for the journey to New Zealand. This realization was something of a shock, and his face was already coming closer. She suddenly knew he was going to break all his rules of personal conduct and kiss her in public.

"Jame—" His lips closed against hers, lingering there, and she tried to feel some emotion, with little success.

When James pulled away, neither Lauryn nor James spoke for a moment, then the door across the hallway opened and Lady Farnsworth erupted through the small opening, catching sight of Lauryn and beckoning her quickly with her fan.

"Lauryn, dear, the good doctor needs to see that you're fit and well. I've already told him that the nasty scar on your leg will not render you any less fit for travel or service in New Zealand . . ." She paused for breath and quickly assessed the situation with James. "So have you two said your farewells, then . . . not really the place in a narrow hallway with the world watching?" She flicked her fan. "But, best to make these things fast." She ushered James back and took hold of Lauryn's hand. "We'll meet you on deck shortly, James, by the gangway. Lauryn, the doctor has some questions for you."

Dr. Appleby was surprisingly young, and Lauryn felt a bit awkward as he listened to her heartbeat and checked her eyes, ears, and throat, but Lady Farnsworth kept up a constant prattle so that the time passed quickly.

Once the doctor had noted down a few words on a page beside her name, he sat down opposite her and looked at her kindly. "There now, that's as much as I shall ask of you. You're obviously very healthy . . . far more so than most of our Irish passengers." He glanced at the page, which had a list of names from top to bottom. "We have a real mix this voyage—Irish, English, Scots, a couple of Germans."

"What about in the forecabin, Doctor?" Lady Farnsworth peered over the list. "Who are our neighbors going to be?"

"Ah, on this trip," Dr. Appleby lowered his glasses on his nose as he glanced over the list, "we have . . . an accountant and his family of four children, a dressmaker . . . a spinster . . . two farmers, and a merchant." He looked up. "And yourselves, of course." He laid his glasses down and looked at Lauryn.

"Miss Kelly, your employer leads me to understand that you are well read and have considerable ability in writing and music."

Lauryn glanced quickly at Lady Farnsworth, who responded with a slight nod.

Lauryn nodded as well and said, "I have had the opportunity to study since I was a child and especially of late . . . thanks to Lady Farnsworth." She smiled her appreciation to her mistress as she thought about the many hours in which Francis Farnsworth had tutored Lauryn in academic subjects and taught her to play the piano, insisting that it was her way of keeping herself amused and useful in her old age.

"Well, perhaps we can put all of that study to good use aboard ship." Dr. Appleby cleared his throat. "As the surgeon superintendent, I employ numerous tactics to facilitate a smooth journey for the passengers." He gave a rueful smile. "The captain tries to keep the boat sailing smoothly, and I try to see that the passengers' lives do the same."

"So you're not just the doctor?" Lady Farnsworth asked, and the doctor shook his head.

"Indeed, no." He pointed to the ship's passenger list. "Daily roll calls, entertainment, health, diet, relationships, schooling . . ." He waved his hand and smiled. "A doctor of all trades."

"So what do you want of me?" Lauryn felt her heart beat faster as he appraised her once more then sat back in his chair.

"We have, as usual, a rather large contingent of young children on board this trip . . . about twenty-two, I believe, if we count the young babies. About fifteen are between the age of five and twelve, and I'd like to provide classes for them each day—twice a day for an hour each time—where they will be taught basic reading and writing and stories and games." Dr. Appleby pressed his fingertips together. "I think you would be an excellent person to fill the role as schoolteacher, Miss Kelly, and your employer thinks so too."

"A schoolteacher?" Lauryn's eyes were wide as she stared at him then glanced at Lady Farnsworth. The woman had a wide grin on her face as she nodded.

"Don't you think that's a wonderful idea, Lauryn?" She folded her arms across her stomach. "You'd be so good with the children, and especially teaching them about music . . . with that wonderful pennywhistle of yours."

Lauryn felt the color rise in her cheeks as the doctor smiled.

"I'm sure that when you play the whistle it's as if the Irish hills are right around you, Miss Kelly."

Lauryn smiled as she unconsciously touched the pocket insert sewn into the seam of her dress that held the thin tin whistle she'd had since she was a child.

"I like to imagine that they are, Doctor." She nodded. "If I can be of assistance with the children, I'd be happy to help."

"Excellent." Dr. Appleby stood immediately as if to hesitate would negate the agreement. "I will introduce you at the first roll call after we set sail, and classes can begin immediately. I will provide you with some slates, but it's likely that most of the children will not know how to write, so it may not be necessary."

Lauryn tried not to feel too overwhelmed at the prospect as she stood up and smiled. "I'll see you at roll call, then."

* * *

Dr. Appleby sat for some time in his chair after he'd seen the two ladies out of the infirmary, then he picked up the passenger list and ran his finger down the lines of names. Just under two hundred passengers. He knew that likely ten, maybe fifteen, would not reach their destination because they would succumb to one of the maladies that often beset passengers on these long ocean voyages. It was what made a job such as his so difficult—not just trying to keep the passengers happy but to keep them alive.

A good journey would mean at least one hundred and ten days at sea, but voyages usually ran longer. Those who had not traveled this route thought it was the storms that took their toll, but it was the disease that invariably got on board through infected food or passengers that exacted the greatest casualties. All those on board were planning to go to a new life in a new land, but some would arrive as widows or widowers, and some might even arrive as orphans.

He put down the list and stared at the wood paneling on the ceiling. This would be his last voyage. He intended to stay in New Zealand once they docked and set up a practice in one of the new settlements—Canterbury probably.

"And spend the rest of my days there," he whispered then tapped his hands on the arms of his chair before picking up the list again.

* * *

LOADING HIS GOODS ONTO THE ship took far longer than expected, and Edward took a quick look at his fob watch before he strode back up the gangplank for the tenth time. It was bad enough getting his personal luggage on board in one piece, but he had felt bound to oversee the safe storage of all his shop goods into the hold. He would not see them for another four months, at least, so he felt compelled to make sure they were as secure as possible. There were numerous large crates and boxes of merchandise, and so he had tried to have it all stashed in one area rather than risk it being lost among the other passengers' goods. And even with everything secure, he had arranged with the captain to inspect it on a regular basis in case anyone felt the need to go "shopping" during the voyage. He'd heard numerous rumors of goods being stolen at sea.

He took long, impatient strides up the plank then was forced to wait for a family just stepping onto the deck. He drummed his fingers on the wooden rail as he waited for an opportunity to pass by them.

He gradually became aware of the boy in the family watching him and found himself the object of an unwavering stare. The child was no more than ten or twelve years of age, and he had a shock of dark red hair and freckles that seemed to make his green eyes even more focused.

Edward folded his arms and looked up toward the mast, then he turned back and stared hard at the boy, willing himself not to blink until the child looked away . . . but there was no change.

"Jimmy, hurry on now." Edward heard a woman's voice, but he kept his gaze focused. The boy, however, responded to the voice, and his eyes flickered. Then he screwed up his nose as if admitting defeat and nodded at Edward. As he adjusted a small knapsack on his shoulder, he tipped a finger to his forehead and saluted Edward then ran after his family.

A smile crept onto Edward's face as he watched the boy merge into the crowd of people descending below the decks. He shook his head. He hadn't had a stare-out since his brother William had been little.

"But you haven't lost your skill, Edward Morgan . . . you can still stare 'em down . . . even if they are a child," he said to himself.

He made his way along the deck, measuring his stride to the increasing movement of the boat. The skies had clouded over in the time he had been loading his boxes, and the sea was becoming increasingly choppy. He watched one woman teeter slightly then fall against the railing. He shook his head. They hadn't even left port yet—what were these people going to be like out on the open sea?

"Mr. Morgan . . . can I see you for a moment, please?"

Edward turned as he heard his name and saw a man walking over to him with papers in one hand and his other hand extended. He responded to the handshake as the man introduced himself.

"Doctor Michael Appleby . . . I'm the ship's surgeon, and I need to do a last-minute medical check, if you don't mind . . . down in the infirmary."

"Not at all," Edward said as the doctor pointed the way. "I was just making sure my cargo was loaded properly." He ducked his head as they entered the stairwell. "It took longer than I expected."

"That is often the way with ocean voyages, unfortunately." Dr. Appleby stopped at the door to his infirmary and unlocked the door. "I see you are a merchant, Mr. Morgan. Any specialty?"

Edward shook his head as he entered the cabin. "No specialty—simply supplying as many goods to as many people as I can." He frowned at the smell of carbolic that permeated the room. "It worked here." He shrugged. "I assume it will work in the colonies."

"And I daresay you will be successful." The doctor pulled a tongue depressor from a jar and held it up. When Edward nodded, he did a quick examination then leaned back against the desk. "So, which port are you destined for, Mr. Morgan?

Edward shrugged. "I plan to go ashore in Sydney, where I have a consignment to deliver as well as plans to sell my own goods. Since being in London I have heard much talk about the potential in Australia—as well as some rumors about a gold strike, so I believe it's a good choice"

"Ah, gold fever." Dr. Appleby nodded. "I intend to be well off the seas before that ensues."

"And yourself? Are you going to settle in New Zealand or Australia?" Edward asked.

"New Zealand . . . Port Chalmers, probably—as is the case with most of the passengers on the ship." Dr. Appleby smiled. "But I'll decide that when I get there." He ran a hand over his chin. "I intend to set up a practice, but I've always had a yearning to establish a small holding . . . some acreage."

Edward nodded, feeling a growing respect for the doctor. "That is my intention as well. I'm a farmer at heart, but the farm will become possible when I have the funds . . . and mercantile will provide that." He stood up. "In the meantime, I am a shopkeeper."

"Well, you have two farmers traveling in the forecabins with you, so I daresay your conversation will get around to the land at some point in the next three or four months."

"Three months . . ." Edward mused. "That will be a whole season." He stepped toward the door. "I think I shall find that conversation more to my liking than prices of goods, but one will serve the other."

As the men parted, Edward shook the doctor's hand firmly. "I don't envy you your job, Doctor, on a voyage such as this."

Dr. Appleby nodded and smiled, but he looked tired. "There is an interesting variety of jobs I oversee—and I try to get the passengers engaged in helping where possible. I have just recruited a schoolteacher, but I will also be needing assistance at roll call, and I'll even appoint constables to keep the peace. I'll also need help making a check for stowaways—standard practice while the passengers are at roll call." He raised one eyebrow. "The crew usually conducts that search, but I try to involve a few helpers so they don't get too carried away."

"Carried away?" Edward frowned as Dr. Appleby nodded.

"There are always people trying to stow away. They either sneak aboard or their families hide them in crates or barrels with the idea of letting them out after a few days. It sometimes works . . ." He sighed. "But the captain and crew tend to favor the use of very sharp poles to poke into the usual hiding places."

"Ouch." Edward caught his meaning and grimaced.

"Yes." Dr. Appleby smiled wanly. "So, if I could engage your help, it would be appreciated. I'm sure you wouldn't be as ruthless."

Edward gave a short laugh. "Well, I know I'd be more useful as a constable than a schoolteacher, but I'd be happy to help, Doctor. I'm used to working long hours, and so the thought of sitting around for these months is not appealing."

Appleby chuckled as well then indicated the deck above their heads. "And from the sight of some of the children coming on board, we may need a constable to keep law and order so the schoolteacher can teach."

Chapter Seventeen

Liverpool, England, 1849
The First Leg of the Journey

THE CAPTAIN CALLED TO DROP anchor three times during the first night, so by six o'clock in the morning, they were still not far beyond Gravesend, and Lauryn felt that her stomach had switched places with her head. Lady Farnsworth was wedged into her narrow bunk and was still snoring loudly when Lauryn tried to stand up from her bunk and only succeeded in stumbling sideways into the wall. As the ship rolled from side to side she put her hand to her head and fought to keep the contents of her stomach in place.

"Oh, please let this not be the state of the whole journey," she whispered as she drew in a deep breath then slowly exhaled. After a few such breaths she felt much better and prepared to get dressed, quickly pulling on the blue dress she had worn on board yesterday and rebraiding her long brown hair. She decided to pin it up into a tight coil, thinking this might make her look more like a schoolteacher. Once that was done she sat back on her bunk and tried to prepare a lesson; however, with the pitching of the ship she only succeeded in rolling into the bunk again, so she lay still, staring up at the ceiling, trying to visualize the children she had seen so far and what sort of students they might be. The thought of teaching was frightening and thrilling all at once, so she lay for a long time.

Against all odds, sleep must have sneaked up on her, for the next thing she knew, there was a loud rapping on their cabin door.

"Mrs. Francis Farnsworth?" The deep voice seemed to reverberate inside the tiny cabin with its thin, plank walls. "Miss Lauryn Kelly?"

Lady Farnsworth gave a deep snort and tried to raise herself up as Lauryn quickly sat up and glanced at the lady's small brass travel clock.

"Oh, my goodness." Lauryn swung her feet over the side. "It's a quarter past nine. We should have been up on deck for roll call."

"Roll call . . . what a disgusting idea." Lady Farnsworth put her hand to her eyes and shuddered. "Tell them I'm ill and dare them to find out."

"But . . ." Lauryn hesitated.

"Mrs. Farnsworth? Miss Kelly? This is roll call." The voice was quieter and held a tone of concern. "Are you all right?"

"M'lady . . . I'm meant to be up there . . . because of teaching school." Lauryn spread both hands in a helpless gesture. "How can I help you if . . . ?"

"You can't help me—you've got a job to do." Lady Farnsworth shooed her toward the door. "I'm Mrs. Farnsworth for the purpose of this trip, and I'll help myself." She chuckled. "But you'd better come back in a while and just see where I am."

"Miss . . ."

"Coming!" Lauryn called out and turned swiftly to the door, pulling it open just as the man raised his hand to knock again. His clenched fist came within an inch or two of her nose, and she gasped as she pulled back.

"Mrs. Farnsworth?" He stepped back and consulted a paper with a list of names.

"Miss Kelly," Lauryn corrected him. "Mrs. Farnsworth is not feeling well and will be up later."

"Lauryn!" She heard a loud gasp behind her. "I'm stuck!"

Lauryn saw the twinkle in the man's light blue eyes as he hid a smile.

"Um . . ." She glanced behind her then backed back into the cabin. "We'll both be up soon." She bit her lip. "Could you please tell the doctor that I will be there to teach the children in time for school?"

"Certainly," the man said as the door closed.

* * *

EDWARD NODDED AS HE TICKED off the two names on the list. "Lauryn Kelly . . . Lauryn . . . Lauryn." He began to walk away then stopped and stared at the door that was only a few feet from his own cabin. "Lauryn . . . I should think you'd better rely on the other option." He repeated the phrase in an Irish accent—the same phrase that he had told himself time and time again over the last four years since the girl had spoken to him so abruptly outside the New Zealand Company office in Birmingham. It was this comment that had prompted him to think of any other option that might help him raise the fare for his passage.

That other option had come to him when he had returned to Preston and met an old merchant who was giving up his trade because of illness. The merchant had been happy to share his knowledge with Edward in return for his strength and agility and gradually allowed him to take over the business and buy him out. The price had been a pittance compared to what the business was worth, but with only a few months left to live, the old man had seen Edward's intervention as a godsend.

"You were a godsend for me, Mr. Jones," Edward murmured as he shook his head. "You were definitely the other option." He began to walk up the passageway. Lauryn Kelly was a beautiful young woman who now seemed to possess a dignity that made her difficult to distinguish from the feisty young Irish girl whose dress he'd stepped on.

"Miss Lauryn Kelly. Fancy that . . ." He shook his head as he walked back up to the deck. "And she's the schoolteacher."

* * *

INSIDE THE CABIN, LAURYN HAD extracted Lady Farnsworth from the bunk and gotten her ready without too much fuss.

"Was that the doctor at the door?" Lady Farnsworth leaned against the bed end and did up a button on her cuff.

"No . . . it was another gentleman." Lauryn shook her head. "The doctor must have sent him down. I told him to let the doctor know I'd be there to teach school later." She frowned. "Are you sure you don't mind my doing that?"

"Mind? I suggested it!" The lady waved her hand. "But I should like to sit in on some of the lessons, if I may." She looked thoughtful as she slid down to sit on the edge of the bunk. "I know I seem to have made some unusual decisions regarding this trip, Lauryn, but I do actually know what I'm doing." She smiled vaguely. "My brother wanted us to travel in the cabin class, but I felt that we would be more comfortable here. I decided that I didn't want to be 'Lady Farnsworth' for this voyage. 'Mrs. Farnsworth' seemed so much more friendly somehow."

"'Mrs. Farnsworth' it shall be then." Lauryn smiled.

"And that leads me to another thing, child." The new Mrs. Farnsworth looked directly at Lauryn. "I heard a delightful Scottish child address her mother as 'Mam' yesterday, and it has been on my mind. I should like you to call me that, Lauryn. I should like you to call me 'Mam.'"

Lauryn frowned slightly as she nodded. "Well, yes ma'am . . . anything you want."

"You do know what I mean, don't you, Lauryn . . . not just ma'am but 'Mam'—as a child would address her mother."

Lauryn stared. She had come to regard this woman as much more than an employer, but it had never crossed her mind that their relationship would ever be regarded in such a light.

"I know that it's an unusual request, Lauryn, but I have my reasons." Mrs. Farnsworth smiled. There was something wistful about it that touched Lauryn, and she felt tears in the back of her eyes. "I never really had a husband, as he was taken so soon after we married, but our joy together was so complete that I could never bear to think of replacing him with somebody else. I remained faithful to his memory, but in so doing, I never had the opportunity to bear children. That has been the other source of grief to me." She stopped, and her lip trembled. "When I picked you up in the carriage that day in Ireland, I got a feeling that you were special . . . and you have been, Lauryn. You have listened and learned and tolerated me, and now . . . I feel that on this trip, I would like you to think of me as . . . if not your mother, then as someone who you would like to be related to." She stopped and nodded in the decisive way so characteristic of her. "That is why I want to be 'Mrs. Farnsworth' . . . . or 'Mam' to you."

A myriad of memories tumbled through Lauryn's mind, of her time spent with this woman—almost twenty-four hours a day for the last four years.

"I should be honored to call you that . . . Mam." She smiled and then did something she had never presumed to do before. She took two steps across the cabin and gave Lady—Mrs.—Farnsworth a warm hug. Then she stepped back quickly with a brief curtsy.

"And that was perfect." Lady Farnsworth smiled then waved toward the door. "Now go and teach those children what I've been trying to teach you all these years."

* * *

WHETHER THE SEA WAS CALMER or she had simply acquired her sea legs, Lauryn didn't notice the rolling motion as much as she made her way up onto the deck. Once there, she looked around, uncertain which way she should go. The doctor had mentioned the forward deck, but it seemed so filled with people that she hesitated to go there on her own.

She took a deep breath and began to make her way forward, excusing herself as she sometimes had to push past small groups of people who seemed reluctant to move. Near the front of the ship, she suddenly heard her name called.

"Miss Kelly . . . over here."

She saw the doctor beckoning, and she flashed a grateful smile as she walked toward him. He already had a group of four children gathered around him, and he spread his hands out above them.

"'Here are some members of your class, Miss Kelly . . . with quite a few more to come, if they can be persuaded."

"They'll not come," a short, thin boy with tousled brown hair said with a broad Irish accent. "They're scared."

"Now why would they be scared?" Lauryn asked the genuine question, and a young girl with long, red braids nodded knowingly.

"They'll be scared that they don't know enough," she said with a Scottish accent.

Right behind her, an older boy who could only be her brother spoke up with a slight scowl on his face.

"Or they might feel too old to be in classes."

Lauryn glanced at the boy. "I do hope some older children come so they can help me teach." She shrugged. "I cannot teach everybody, so I'll need good helpers."

"Jimmy can teach . . . he's been going to education classes for the longest time." The girl moved slightly as her brother nudged her.

"Hush, Fiona, that'll do." But he was smiling slightly.

Lauryn smiled too as she glanced up at the doctor then back at the group. "How about the first job I give my helpers is to find some more children for class? Then we'll start with a music lesson." She slipped her hand into the secret pocket of her dress and drew out the tin whistle. Raising it to her lips, she played a few notes of a familiar tune, then she put down the whistle and waved her hands. "Now go—find yourselves some classmates . . . quickly."

As the children scattered, she put the whistle back into her pocket then looked at the doctor. "Will that be all right . . . to begin with?"

"To begin with, and in the middle, and the end." Dr. Appleby smiled. "Whatever you feel will keep them attentive and possibly learning."

Lauryn laughed then, relieved that her first encounter with the children had gone reasonably well. She put her hand to her throat as she felt a wave of emotion. "Thank you, Doctor . . . for trusting me. I'll do my very best."

"I'm sure you will, Miss Kelly." The doctor nodded then looked behind her and raised his hand in greeting. "Mr. Morgan . . . another job for you." He gestured toward Lauryn. "If you could be on hand for the first few lessons . . . to help Miss Kelly keep an eye on the children."

"My pleasure, Doctor . . . Miss Kelly." Edward nodded to both of them in turn and put his hands behind his back. "And how much discipline am I allowed to enforce?"

Something in the tone made Lauryn look up quickly. When she did, she gasped as his blue eyes seemed to reflect her expression.

"Oh . . ." she stumbled. "Oh . . . you . . ."

"I believe it was Birmingham, Miss Kelly." Edward nodded as she continued to stare. "The New Zealand Company office . . . where you offered the advice for me to try another option rather than finding a wife."

"Or a sister . . ." Lauryn swallowed as she remembered the scene vividly—how he'd startled her with his exclamation about migration rules and then stood on her dress and made her stumble before he caught her again. She'd been on the defensive as a newly arrived young woman in Birmingham, and she'd retaliated with a smart remark. Her cheeks colored as she remembered her muttered comment as they'd parted. *May you be blessed with the better option . . . before you find some poor woman to be your wife.*

"I'm glad to have the opportunity to thank you for your advice, Miss Kelly." Edward kept talking. "I did explore another option and left the wife idea well alone, and it was by far the better choice."

Lauryn stared then clasped her hands in front of her and nodded. "I'm pleased to have been of assistance, Mr. . . . Morgan." She glanced at the doctor, who mouthed the name, and she smiled her thanks. "Irish blessings must work, after all, and I'm sure some woman must be truly grateful."

He looked at her a moment then spoke directly to the doctor above her head.

"I'll be back in half an hour if that's what you need me to do." He tipped his cap again and was gone, wending his way through the crowd.

"A small world, it seems," Dr. Appleby said, watching Lauryn's face closely.

"Very small indeed," Lauryn agreed, then she smiled as if the incident hadn't occurred. "So, do you have a list of the children, Doctor? The sooner I get to know them, the sooner we will no longer have need of additional supervision."

* * *

"So, how did your first lesson go?" Lady Farnsworth asked as soon as Lauryn walked into the cabin. "Have you charmed them already?"

"I don't know if *charmed* is the right word." Lauryn crossed her eyes as she sat down on the bunk and sank into it. "We ended up with eleven children between the ages of six and twelve, and they were all very shy to begin with, but most of them warmed up." She blew a long breath. "I hate to admit it, but Mr. Morgan was extremely useful as a policeman."

"Mr. Morgan?" Lady Farnsworth asked, immediately interested.

"The man whom the good doctor asked to help me with supervising the children." Lauryn frowned. "We had actually met before . . . on my first day in Birmingham. It wasn't a good meeting." She shrugged and waved her hand dismissively. "But that's neither here nor there. He was useful today . . . if a bit overbearing."

Lady Farnsworth studied Lauryn for a moment then picked up two small books off the end of her bunk. "I had a look through my things and thought that these might be useful to you. Some books of verse. Do you remember them?"

Lauryn took the books, one red and one green, and turned them over gently. "I remember these well. You taught me my first verses from them when I arrived in England." She laid down the red one and opened the green. "I remember thinking that I wasn't being a good Irish girl if I was learning English poetry."

"You did start slowly." Lady Farnsworth smiled. "But I loved the way your Irish accent treated the words and gave them a whole different feeling."

They were both silent for a moment, remembering, then Lauryn looked up. "I believe I have the perfect child to share these with." She touched her hair. "A little Scottish girl. Her name is Fiona, and she has an amazing memory for verse. She even speaks in a kind of rhyme, and when I played the whistle it was as if she already knew the Irish tunes. She was humming along with me in seconds."

Lady Farnsworth nodded. "Some children simply have the gift in them. The shame of it is that much of the time they never come to learn that they have it."

"Fiona's a bit like that, but I think her parents are goodly folk." Lauryn smiled. "She has an older brother who was not too happy about being in class with little ones, but I made him a junior teacher, and Mr. Morgan made him a deputy, so now he's proud as can be."

Lady Farnsworth smiled. "And have you decided what you're doing with them this afternoon?" She glanced at the clock. "You only have three hours before you start again."

Lauryn nodded as she held up the green book. "I shall teach them some verse, and then Dr. Appleby is going to give them some instruction on behavior aboard the ship as well as hygiene." She wrinkled her nose. "Some of the folk seem to have little knowledge of washing. I can only be grateful that we're up on deck with a breeze blowing."

"Yes . . ." Lady Farnsworth shook her head. "It really doesn't bear thinking about how bad the smell will get in the steerage compartment with all those bodies in together."

Lauryn rolled her eyes. "Can you imagine what it's going to be like after three months at sea?"

"Well, one pamphlet described it as 'a wonderful summer holiday,' so I'm going to think about that, and then, before we know it, we'll be landing in New Zealand and ready to start our new life on my brother's holdings." Lady Farnsworth hesitated. "You don't have any regrets, do you child . . . about following an old woman to the other side of the world?"

Lauryn thought about her more recent life on the estate and then about her mother and father and sisters still living in Ireland. She had tried to convince them to come and live in England on the estate after she'd been there for two years, but they had refused to leave Ireland, intent on making life better where they lived, as her father had become actively involved in the struggle for equality for the laborers.

She shook her head. "None whatsoever. Maybe I can convince my parents to come to New Zealand one day . . . who knows."

"And James Field?"

"James will do well on the estate, and he'll find a nice woman to help him." Lauryn smiled. "I think I might have married James, but now I don't need to, and I feel fine about that." She smiled. "Maybe I don't need to marry at all. I'm perfectly happy."

* * *

DR. APPLEBY STUDIED THE PASSENGER list as he placed a tick beside the names of all the pregnant women on board. There were six in all, and though only four of them were due to give birth while on board, he fully expected, with the trials of sea voyage, that all six would produce before they reached dry land again. He ran his hand over his face as he studied the names and wondered how many of the babes would survive their introduction to the world. It was not uncommon for either mother or baby or both to pass on during childbirth.

He stood up and studied the contents of the medicine cupboard then wrote down some notes beside each name. The best he could do was to be prepared . . . but for what, he was never quite sure.

* * *

THERE WAS A MASS OF stars the like of which were never seen in a Glasgow sky, and Ewen McAlister stood with his family on deck as long as they could before they had to be downstairs for the ten o'clock curfew. The ship was rolling gently as it cut through the water, its full sails heaving with slow thuds in the breeze.

"Don't you love the sea air?" Bess breathed deeply beside him as she laid her hand across her slightly protruding stomach. "I'm so glad this baby will breathe fresh air when it's born."

"Do you think it will be born while we're on the ocean, Mam?" Fiona pressed her hand against her mother's stomach.

"It shouldn't." Ewen shook his head. "We should only be at sea for three months and 'tis not due until after that. We should be safely settled in Port Chalmers by then, and Jimmy will be helping me set up our engineering business."

"Aye." Jimmy nodded and pointed to his chest. "I was the only one who could do the sums in class today."

"I told Miss Kelly you were going to be an engineer, and she was much impressed." Fiona smiled proudly then looked up at her mother. "Jimmy is a teacher's helper, and Mr. Morgan made him a deputy as well."

"What sort of deputy?" Ewen asked. "And do you have two teachers?"

"No. Miss Kelly is our teacher and Mr. Morgan is there to help keep everybody good. The doctor said that he was one of the ship's constables," Jimmy answered importantly. "Mr. Morgan said that he needed a level-headed youngster to be an example to the others." He shook his head. "There's many there that have a lot to learn about education classes."

Ewen caught his wife's look over their children's heads and suppressed a smile. Jimmy took responsibility very seriously.

"So, do you like your teacher?" Bess kept her hands on her daughter's shoulders as they stood near the side of the boat. "Does she teach you well?"

"Oh, aye." Fiona looked up at her mother with shining eyes as she touched her hair. "She has pretty brown hair and pure white skin and the finest green eyes, and when she laughs she gets the very deepest dimple right here." She pressed her finger to her cheek. "And she loves poetry and reading, and she plays the tin whistle so that we can dance, and she plays the piano, but, of course, there is none, so she sings for us, and her voice is so fine—"

"And she does numbers very quickly." Jimmy held up his hand. "We had a race to add up numbers, and she won every time."

"Well, she sounds just about perfect." Bess smiled at their enthusiasm and felt a sense of relief. Keeping the children happy at sea for three months had seemed a daunting prospect, and it looked like Miss Kelly was an answer to her prayers.

They lingered a while longer on deck until the ship's bell rang, signaling that all should go below, but as the family moved toward the stairwell, Jimmy suddenly called out to a man swinging down from the rigging.

"Mr. Morgan!"

The man looked behind him as he jumped the last few feet onto the deck, having apparently been helping one of the sailors. He had to squint slightly in the darkness to see who had called, then he smiled broadly.

"Jimmy! Fiona!" He made his way toward them and held out his hand to Ewen as he approached. "Mr. McAlister . . . and Mrs. McAlister, I presume." He turned to Bess and bowed slightly. "It's a pleasure to meet the parents of such fine students."

He placed his hand on Jimmy's shoulder. "This young man here is proving especially helpful in setting up school."

"We've been hearing about it, Mr. Morgan." Ewen shook his hand firmly.

"All about it." Bess smiled. "I feel we will come out a poor second to the likes of yourself and Miss Kelly by the end of the trip."

"Well, I would be surprised if Jimmy isn't helping to sail the ship by the end of the trip." Edward grinned, then he saw the expression on Fiona's face. "And Fiona will be helping, of course."

"Of course." Bess nodded, knowing full well her daughter's need to do everything her brother did. "Every good captain needs a good first mate."

The ship's bell sounded again as they reached the top of the stairs.

"Jimmy tells us you are one of the appointed constables on board, Mr. Morgan." Ewen paused. "Dr. Appleby has asked that I too fill that job, so I imagine we may do some shifts together."

"I'd look forward to that," Edward said. "I'm trying to keep busy so that the time passes more quickly; maybe we should offer our help in other ways as well."

"That would suit me fine. I'm a mechanic by trade and build ships." Ewen glanced around the boat deck. "I'm looking forward to actually seeing one in action."

"And if anything breaks on board we can call on you." Edward laughed and indicated the stairs in front of him. His own cabin was on deck, but he felt compelled to see how the McAlisters were housed in the steerage compartment. There was already talk of unsanitary conditions, and the doctor had expressed fears of an outbreak of cholera, which had scourged the last ships he'd traveled on.

The McAlisters stopped in front of two level wooden bunk structures among the many that ran the full length of both sides of the ship. Each bunk measured around six feet deep, two feet wide, and four feet high and was meant to house up to four people, a husband and wife and two children. As they passed by some of the bunks it was obvious that more than five children were being crammed into one sleeping space.

"This is my bed that I share with Mam and the baby." Fiona indicated the bottom bunk then pointed to the top. "Father and Jimmy share the top bunk because they're better at climbing up."

Edward nodded as he thought about the extra seven guineas he had paid to have a forecabin and now considered it money well spent. He glanced around the compartment with the long tables running down the middle where everyone ate together, and then he took in the thin curtains slung across the fronts of the bunks for privacy. He turned to Ewen.

"I only have a small cabin up fore, but it would be good to have company occasionally, if you and your wife would like to join me . . . and the children, of course," he added when he saw Fiona's face.

Ewen nodded and extended his hand once again toward Edward. "I would appreciate that, Mr. Morgan, and please, my name is Ewen and this is Bess."

Edward nodded thoughtfully then grasped Ewen's hand firmly. "Ewen . . . Bess . . . and Fiona and Jimmy. I consider it a privilege to have met the whole McAlister clan, and I look forward to our journey together." He moved forward slightly as the ship suddenly rocked. "And let's hope that it's a good one."

When Edward had gone and the children were fast asleep, Ewen held Bess close as they sat on the edge of her bunk. He felt assured that the decision to come had been a good one. He'd left a good job with David Elder but felt that his chances of establishing a business for himself in a new land were promising. He also looked forward to being able to worship with the Saints in a new place where they could build up the Church.

It wasn't long after his reading of the Book of Mormon that the entire family had joined the Church. He would be eternally grateful to Bess for being open to the Frasers and the message they brought. Bess had been as determined in her decision to become Mormon as she was in her decision to follow Ewen to New Zealand. Still, he worried about her and the baby on such a long journey.

"Are you still glad we've come?" he whispered to Bess as she leaned against him.

"Aye. You know that I am—as long as we're together. It was hard leavin' Molly, but with her new job, she'll fare well. It's unfortunate we couldn't afford to pay her fare."

"She'll be fine. God will look after her, I'm sure."

"Just as He will look after us."

Chapter Eighteen

Atlantic Ocean, 1849
The Pattern of Ship Life

WITHIN FOUR DAYS, THERE HAD been a pattern established to life aboard ship, and Lauryn found that the time was passing more quickly than she had anticipated. She and Lady Farnsworth joined the other passengers in the forecabins for breakfast on deck, which Edward and a Mr. Atkins—the captains of the mess—took turns bringing to them. It was always simple fare of a hefty ship's biscuit with salt butter and a cup of tea or coffee.

Roll call followed soon after, then Lauryn prepared and taught classes until lunchtime. Lunch usually consisted of a serving of meat with some dried potatoes and a small piece of something that was called pudding but in reality defied description.

Lady Farnsworth typically spent the morning in conversation with the ship's other spinster and one of the older gentleman farmers who she seemed to have a fondness for. After lunch, she often retired, so Lauryn spent the time on deck with the children until class began again.

Supper was a repetition of breakfast, but the evening's activities seemed designed to take the mind off the stomach, as the sailors often arranged a boisterous musical get-together, which involved singing and dancing.

"I do believe that I will finish this voyage being half the woman I used to be." Lady Farnsworth used both hands to hold her ship's biscuit as she tried to bite into it. "Or at least my teeth will be half what they used to be." She held the biscuit in front of her and frowned. "How do those poor men in steerage cope?' She looked up at Edward as he placed a pot of hot water on the table between them. "The ones with hardly any teeth."

"I've seen them sucking on the biscuits for many an hour." Edward laughed. "Finishing about in time for lunch, so it passes the day well for them."

Lauryn smiled as she picked up the pot to pour water into cups for her and Lady Farnsworth. She enjoyed being a part of the conversation, but with Edward around she found herself holding back a bit. It was almost as if he was waiting for the chance to say something critical, and she felt compelled to say something first. She far preferred the relaxed discussions she had had with Dr. Appleby several times after class.

"Well, the children have discovered that the biscuits make excellent pieces to play deck games with . . . because they don't break." She held up one piece of biscuit. "Personally I have become a dipper. I'll let the hot tea do its work on them."

She dipped the biscuit then let it sit in her mouth a while before eating it, but Lady Farnsworth scrunched up her nose.

"I can't bear them soggy like that." She shook her head and pushed the biscuit away. "I have some dried dates downstairs. I'll wait for those." She sipped the tea then turned to Edward. "So, do we know what is planned for entertainment tonight? I rather enjoyed those shanties we were singing last evening. I didn't know most of the words, but there's always a good chorus to exercise the lungs."

"I love how a group of complete strangers can get together and form a musical band with so many instruments." Lauryn held up her hand and counted off her fingers. "The boatswain and the man from steerage had their fiddles, the second mate had his mouth organ, and there were two accordions and three whistles." She laughed as she shook her head. "It was a trial at first to even find a common tune, but once everybody was dancing it didn't matter anyway."

"And I have the sore feet to prove it." Edward sat down for the first time and, using brute force, cracked his biscuit into several pieces with his hands and calmly chewed on a small bit. Lady Farnsworth stared then chuckled again.

"I think I may have to sit close by and eat your crumbs, Edward." She had established early on that she was going to call the men in the forecabins by their first names, and they, accordingly, now all called her Francis.

Edward paused then passed her a small piece, which she happily accepted. Then he leaned his elbows on the table so that he was looking straight at Lauryn. "I didn't notice you dancing at all last evening, Miss Kelly. Are you bound to be a full-time musician for the duration of the voyage?"

"It would suit me well, Mr. Morgan." Lauryn didn't look at him as she dunked another piece of biscuit. "I enjoy making the music."

"But you're also a fine dancer, Lauryn," Lady Farnsworth interrupted. "You should be dancing, and there's plenty who would be delighted to partner you . . . wouldn't they, Edward?"

Edward nodded as he stared at the sky.

"I would say that there's at least eight young men from steerage and a couple from cabin class who have an eye out. There aren't so many ladies in that class to keep their eyes occupied . . ." He hesitated. "And there's always the good doctor, who is surely in sore need of some lighthearted entertainment."

"See, Lauryn . . . endless opportunity." Lady Farnsworth nudged her again then turned to Edward. "Why, even Edward might be persuaded to have a reel or two. The children would love that, wouldn't they . . . the teacher and the constable?"

"Oh, I think it would be best to keep any gossip about the teacher at bay." Lauryn began to get up from the table, suddenly uncomfortable with the turn of conversation. She had noted Edward wheeling around the deck last night with a number of young women who were traveling to the colonies as paid servants, and she had seen the delight on their faces. "Best to keep the teacher . . . and the constable . . . quite separate."

Edward almost smiled as he caught her eye, and she blushed slightly then hastily picked up her cup and took it to the bucket to clean it.

"There'll be enough swooning below deck already among those young women who have no more to think about than who they danced with last evening." She pressed the front of her dress with her hands and stood by Lady Farnsworth. "And you would be well advised not to feed their egos, Mr. Morgan."

"And suppose I am not trying to 'feed their egos,' Miss Kelly? What if I am merely endeavoring to ensure that their journey has an element of enjoyment?" Edward's eyes hardened. "And should I not point out that you were the only woman playing a musical instrument among a group of men who were obviously enjoying your presence?"

"I . . ." Lauryn opened her mouth then shut it as she recognized his argument and nodded. "I see your point, Mr. Morgan, and please feel free to dance with whomever you choose."

"Thank you, Miss Kelly. That is very gracious of you." He stood up as well and gathered the biscuit pieces. He put them in his pocket, then he hesitated. "I will be arranging for Mr. McAlister to supervise at class today." He held up one finger and wagged it back and forth. "The teacher and the constable . . . let's keep them quite separate."

* * *

"Well, that was a splendid display," Lady Farnsworth said in a huff as they walked back to the cabin. "One of the finest young men on board ship, and you were quite rude to him." She put her hand on the door handle then turned to look at Lauryn. "I really think you should go and apologize."

"But I told him that I saw his point about playing with the musicians." Lauryn frowned. "And he *was* making those young ladies swoon. I can just imagine the conversation going on right now in their sewing class." She waited for Lady Farnsworth to enter the room in front of her. "In my opinion, Mr. Morgan is undoubtedly looking for a wife to help him set up house in the colonies, and three months on board ship is a perfect opportunity for him to do that." She paused. "I just happen to know that he sees finding a wife as a purely . . . practical exercise, and it offends me to see him pursuing those women in such a blatant fashion."

She stopped and took a breath, realizing she had nothing more to say, having voiced the thoughts that had been bothering her since she realized Edward Morgan's identity.

"Well then . . . perhaps you aren't interested in what Edward's true situation is—seeing you have already summed him up so well." Lady Farnsworth sat down heavily on the edge of the bunk and eased her slippers off. She didn't look at Lauryn.

"I . . . I think it is probably none of my business." Lauryn studied her fingers carefully. "And I'm not saying that Mr. Morgan isn't a fine gentleman, but—"

"But there's something about him that makes you act very differently." Lady Farnsworth nodded. "And I shall tell you anyway . . . not that you deserve it, but I think he does."

In the four years that she'd been with her employer, Lauryn had never heard Lady Farnsworth speak to her in such a tone, and she lowered her head.

"There is an advantage to being an elderly widow . . ." Lady Farnsworth settled herself in the bunk. "Men of any age seem to feel quite comfortable sharing things with me that they wouldn't normally divulge." She pulled a white lawn handkerchief from her sleeve. "The other evening I had occasion to admonish Edward for not joining in the dancing—"

"For not . . . ?" Lauryn frowned as Lady Farnsworth held up a hand to stop her interrupting.

"He was up on the forward deck watching the ocean while everyone was having a lively time, and I happened to find him and ask why he wasn't joining in, to which he responded that he wasn't one for parties." She nodded at Lauryn as if making a point. "I then felt fit to ask him why not, when there was such an abundance of young ladies who would love to make merry with him. He took his time responding but then told me that he was already married."

"Married?" Lauryn felt her mouth drop open as she stared at Lady Farnsworth.

"Indeed." Her mistress nodded. "To which I responded by asking where the dear lady was now and whether she would be joining him in the colonies. He then said that she wouldn't be joining him anywhere as she had died . . . some five years ago." She raised her handkerchief to her eye and wiped a tear. "He told me a little about her and how she had become ill after helping fight a plague in their village, and that . . . she had died with a baby inside." Lady Farnsworth's expression crumpled, and she put her handkerchief fully over her face. "He said that he would always consider himself married to Lizzy, and so he had no need to dance or make merry with others." She cried quietly for a moment then looked at Lauryn. "And I knew exactly how he felt."

Lauryn sat very still for a long time while Lady Farnsworth cried as if releasing years of pain. As the tears subsided, Lauryn quietly walked to the lady's bunk and put her arm around her shoulders.

"Oh, Mam . . . I had no idea." She felt the older woman relax against her, and she squeezed a bit more tightly. "I need to apologize . . . to both of you."

Lady Farnsworth shook her head. "I don't think Edward would appreciate your knowing something he shared in confidence, but I simply had to say something, Lauryn, because you seemed to be judging the poor man so wrongly."

"I was," Lauryn admitted and shook her head as she recalled some of the conversations she'd had with Edward. Then she frowned.

"But what made him come and dance when he said he wasn't going to?"

Lady Farnsworth smiled as she laid her hands in her lap. "I told him my story . . . about Richard dying . . . and then I told him that I'd discovered the one true way to make my life feel not so bad: make someone else's feel better."

Lauryn nodded slowly. "And so he took your advice, and I told him off for it." She covered her face with her hand. "I feel awful." She looked up. "And what can I possibly do to make amends without telling him that I know his story?"

She sat staring at the floor until Lady Farnsworth finally spoke. "Just be yourself, Lauryn . . . be the lovely person everyone enjoys. And let him enjoy it as well."

* * *

It was as if Edward Morgan had vanished off the boat. He had not appeared at the activities in two nights, and Ewen McAlister had supervised in class again. Lauryn found it difficult to concentrate, as every time a man walked along the deck near where the class was held, she would look up, expecting to see him.

"I enjoyed class today, Miss Kelly," Ewen said. He and Bess joined her as she tidied some of her books into a bag. Bess had stayed nearby while her husband was supervising, and Lauryn had been delighted to see her actively listening. She had the same enthusiasm that Fiona showed and the same appreciation for the smallest details. "Particularly the story about your home in Ireland." He pushed a hand through his coarse auburn hair. "Sometimes I get to thinking that the Highlanders were treated the worst, but I realize that there's others who had it just as tough."

Lauryn nodded as she held the bag against her. "It has been good for me to teach about their struggles. It's easy for me to forget when I have been living so well for so long." She smiled wistfully. "My parents are still there fighting for a better land. I can't change anything in my homeland, but I can try to make things better where we're going." She shrugged. "At least try to make sure the same mistakes don't happen."

"Aye . . . there is that hope." Ewen nodded and put his arm around his wife. "'Tis what we are hoping for our children anyway."

Lauryn saw the glance that passed between the two of them, and she felt a pang of envy for this little family—so complete and determined in what they were doing. She smiled and looked around the deck. "I don't suppose you've seen Mr. Morgan recently." She tried to sound casual as she held out the books. "I was thinking he might like a read of some of these. He seems to appreciate good stories."

Ewen shook his head, and his brow furrowed. "I haven't seen him since he asked me to look after things yesterday, and he wasn't on deck last night."

"He wasn't?" Lauryn smiled in an effort to hide her surprise at that information. "I thought I was the only one feeling tired. Maybe the voyage is taking its toll already." She gestured toward the cabin. "I had better be checking on Mam. She didn't want to miss another evening."

"It may be the last evening activity for a while." Bess looked concerned. "I heard the captain say that we'll likely be running into bad weather in the next day or two and that everything will need to be well secured." She put her hand to her chest. "I do get so concerned when I think about a storm . . . especially for the children's sakes."

"Och, you've no need to worry, Bess." Ewen put his arm around her shoulders. "We've weathered a few storms of different kinds. We'll handle a real one . . . you'll see."

Lauryn watched as they gathered the children around them and took a walk around the deck. It was not uncommon for people to walk back and forth on the deck many times a day simply to avoid going downstairs, where the stench and heat made resting unbearable.

She gathered up her things and made her way quickly to her own cabin, which at least had some ventilation since it was located above the deck. As she had done many times, she offered a quick breath of thanks for being able to lodge in a better location than steerage. She was nearly at her cabin door when Edward stepped out of his cabin. She stopped as she felt a sudden desire to flee. Instead she took a deep breath. *Just be yourself, Lauryn . . . be the lovely person everyone enjoys—and let him enjoy it as well.*

She'd never thought of herself as a lovely person, but she tried to smile as she nodded and clasped the bag in front of her. Edward was looking straight at her now, and she felt her resolve fading fast so she took a step forward.

"The children have been missing you, Mr. Morgan." She paused as her voice caught in her throat, then she coughed. "They were wondering if you were ill."

Edward didn't respond, so she determined to try another approach. "Um . . . I would like to say that I feel badly about my behavior the other day, Mr. Morgan. It was not my place to make a judgment on your activities . . . nor on the young women."

"You're right about that, Miss Kelly." His tone was not abrupt . . . just tired. She looked at him squarely and noticed the darkness under his eyes and his disheveled hair.

"Are you all right, Mr. Morgan?" She found herself genuinely concerned as thoughts of fever immediately came to mind. The doctor had her ever vigilant, watching for symptoms among the children, and she instinctively put out a hand then withdrew it as he seemed to recoil from her.

"I don't have a fever, if that's what you mean, Miss Kelly." He rubbed his chin, which was dark with stubble, and shook his head. "I have simply been taking some time to deal with matters . . . which required some peace and quiet." He stared at her for a moment, then he leaned against the wall. "Matters that you have, in complete innocence, caused me to confront— while I have been avoiding them." He managed a wistful smile and put his hand against her cabin door. "Please tell Francis thank you from me. She'll know what I mean."

"I . . . of course," Lauryn stammered slightly then attempted a smile, but her stomach was churning. "Perhaps we will see you on deck tonight."

He took a moment to respond. Then he barely nodded. "Perhaps."

* * *

"DO YOU THINK MR. MORGAN is all right, Father?" Jimmy looked up and down the deck. "I haven't seen him for nearly two days."

"I'm sure he's fine, Jimmy. I asked the doctor, and he said that Mr. Morgan just needs some quiet time. He has a lot on his mind with taking his business to the colony." Ewen leaned against the railing. "Just like us—but he has more stock to think about."

"Do you think we could set up our business near Mr. Morgan?" Jimmy's eyes grew wide with anticipation. "Then I could work for both of you."

"And you'd be the richest man in town in no time at all." Ewen smiled at his son. "You'd be employing us before long."

"Och, no . . . you'll always be my dad, so I cannot employ you." Jimmy shook his head, then he brightened. "But I do think we should stay in touch with Mr. Morgan. I'd like him to be our friend in New Zealand."

"Aye, Jimmy. I would too, though he'll be travelin' on to Australia." Ewen looked out at the ocean and put an arm around his son's shoulders. "Let me tell you, Jimmy . . . Mr. Morgan is a good man, and you should stay acquainted with good men. Don't waste your life spending time with people who don't make you want to be a better person. Do you understand me?" He smiled and gave Jimmy a soft nudge on the shoulder. "Now let's see if your mother and sister would like to dance a bit of a Scottish reel."

They gathered Bess and Fiona and walked along the deck toward the place where the music was usually organized and met Edward just as he came out from the cabin area. Jimmy was beside him in a second.

"We wondered if you were ill, Mr. Morgan." Jimmy spoke first as Edward greeted them. "We missed you."

"Well, thank you for noticing, Jimmy." Edward looked at Ewen and nodded to indicate the whole family. "Thank you, indeed."

"Are you going to dance with me tonight, Mr. Morgan?" Fiona asked, holding out her hand as she spoke. "I didn't have anyone to dance with last night . . . except Father, and he wants to dance with Mam."

"What about Jimmy?" Edward watched her, amused by her confidence as she shook her head.

"Jimmy still has some learning to do. Girls are better dancers than boys."

"Then I hope I dance well enough for you." Edward slipped her hand through the crook of his arm as they continued along the deck, and she skipped between him and her parents.

The music was already starting as the crowd made space for their group against one of the small upturned boats that were on hand in case the ship had to be evacuated. Everybody knew that there were only enough boats to carry one-third of the passengers, but this fact was not spoken of. Everybody also knew that priority would automatically go to the cabin-class passengers—that the rest would fend for themselves.

Edward looked around for Lauryn and Francis as he sat down, but there was no sign of them until after the first two songs—two shanties. Then, as he turned around, he saw Lauryn slip in beside the other two whistle players, sharing a bright smile with them before she began to get the beat of the music with her foot then put the whistle to her lips and joined in the tune. She played two songs before the dancing really began. As the second song ended, he saw her look around, stopping when she saw him. He saw her whisper something to the player beside her, then she pocketed the whistle and made her way toward him and the McAlisters.

"Good evening." She bobbed a slight curtsy in front of them, and Fiona giggled and tried to copy the motion. "I thought I might try dancing tonight instead of playing." She smiled at Jimmy. "Do you think I might have the pleasure, Jimmy?"

Edward watched as Jimmy's ears flushed a bright pink and he looked at his father and mother. When they nodded, he took a deep breath and nodded as well, then he walked out to where the dancers were assembling in a circle, not waiting to see if Lauryn was following. She raised both hands and hurried after him.

* * *

It was only as Lauryn and Jimmy walked back to his parents that Lauryn noticed Edward escorting Fiona back from the crowd of dancers as well. The child was glowing as she took hold of her mother's hand and swung it.

"I danced well, Mam. Edward said I did." She stopped and put her hand to her mouth in horror as she realized, too late, that she had said his first name. "Oh!"

"Out of the mouths of babes." Edward shrugged. "'Edward' it'll have to be, Fiona."

The music started again, and Lauryn felt her heart beating faster than the music as she listened to the bantering tone in Edward's voice. With Lady Farnsworth's voice still sounding in her mind, she turned back to him and again curtsied slightly in front of him.

"May I have the pleasure of this dance, Edward?" she asked quickly and turned toward the dancers before she heard, very slowly and clearly . . .

"No, thank you."

She stopped in her stride as the words seemed to hang in the air between them, then she slowly took one step backward, then a second. She would not turn her head, and her hand instinctively reached for the whistle in her pocket. She should have stayed with the musicians. Her cheeks drained of color as she fought the indignity of being refused, then she felt a shadow cross her face and saw that he was standing in front of her, his hand extended.

"I'll do the asking. May I have the pleasure of this dance . . . Lauryn?"

Her pride instructed her to refuse, but she somehow found the courage to look up and straight into his eyes.

Pale blue and unfathomable . . . but with a hopeful light there that seemed to close around her heart.

She raised one hand and inclined her head as she took a step toward him. "I'd be delighted . . . Edward."

Chapter Nineteen

Atlantic Ocean, Near Portugal, 1849
The Sabbath

LAURYN LAY STILL FOR THE first hour after waking, when she had woken up enough to realize that it was Sunday. Lady Farnsworth was still breathing heavily in the next bunk, so she made no attempt to move, knowing that today she didn't have to teach school. As much as she loved instructing the children, it was, nevertheless, a tiring time—especially when the seas were a little swollen and she had to hold on tight to continue teaching. Added to that was the task of thinking of something new to teach every day, and she had come to the end of the week feeling quite tired.

"But not too tired to dance." She smiled with her eyes closed as she relived the evening before.

Following the near disaster when Edward had refused her offer to dance and then promptly asked her to dance with him, their relationship had risen to a new level. He had proven to be a competent though careful dancer, but his spontaneous laugh when he got the steps wrong more than made up for his mistakes. Lauryn had laughed with him, and they had swiftly danced their way through three reels and a number of shanties before they realized that much of the crowd was watching them rather than dancing.

It was as if the barriers between them had dissolved as they danced. She had only to extend her hand and he was there, taking her fingers in a firm grip before propelling her to the next step. The more confident she had become, the lighter she had felt on her feet, and the dancing had been endless fun.

She wriggled her feet beneath the coverlet and found that they were a bit stiff, but she rubbed them together happily, already planning how they would enjoy the next dance.

"Are you awake, dear?" Lady Farnsworth spoke quietly from the other bunk.

"Yes, Mam." Lauryn sat up quickly only to be waved back down again.

"Let's not rush this morning. I have some figs and apricots, and I can do without a cup of tea for one morning." She hesitated, and Lauryn could hear the smile in her voice. "Unless you want to go up to breakfast for some reason."

Lauryn smiled as well as she remembered how delighted Lady Farnsworth had been when she had come on deck to find her dancing with Edward.

"I could go and get you a cup of tea and bring it back down."

"Now that would be nice, and you could find out what is going to be happening for the church service." She coughed slightly and tried to roll over. "The good doctor did say that church would be at eleven and that he had an offer from one of the gentlemen in cabin class to give the sermon, but I want to be sure before I go up."

"So there really is no preacher?" Lauryn lay with her hands behind her head. "I thought the doctor might give a sermon. He has a nice manner, which is what really counts, I think."

"He told me that he would if he had to but that he would prefer others to do it." Lady Farnsworth sighed. "The problem is that the ones who think they can do it are most often the ones who have the least ability or qualification . . . except for a large dose of self-righteousness."

Lauryn smiled as she thought about the services she had attended since she was a child. Strictly Catholic sermons had been the rule until she left Ireland, but she had sometimes attended the Presbyterian services with Lady Farnsworth over the past four years.

She felt no great compulsion to attend church except for the notion that it was good and appropriate and through a sense of gratitude that Father O'Doherty had helped make her life so successful. He was a priest, and therefore she should express her gratitude by attending church.

However, Lauryn often felt unsettled about the idea of religion. She wrestled with the fact that there was so much pain in the world, and she wondered why God didn't fix things if He was so powerful. And so the conflict lingered on—not raging, but present enough to make her noncommittal.

"I do wish Dr. Appleby would reconsider. He has such a gentle voice and a great knowledge of humanity." Lauryn frowned. "Do you know if he is a religious man?"

"He said that he relies on God but that he doesn't know if God knows him too well." Lady Farnsworth smiled. "I think that would make an interesting sermon in itself."

"Well, why don't I bring you some tea, and then we'll go up for the service at eleven?" Lauryn swung her feet to the floor then grimaced slightly as they tingled.

"Painful feet?" Lady Farnsworth didn't miss the look on Lauryn's face, and she chuckled. "I wonder how Edward's feet are today."

"His should be fine . . . it was mine that got trodden on." Lauryn hobbled a step or two then sat down again as her feet began to really hurt as the blood circulated. "I do hope my shoes fit on my feet." She pulled her slippers to her with her toes and tried to put them on, but her feet were noticeably swollen. She looked up at Lady Farnsworth with wide eyes. "What shall I do?"

"Limp," the lady offered as she chuckled merrily from her bunk.

* * *

PRIDE PREVENTED LAURYN FROM GOING to breakfast, but by eleven o'clock she was able to ease her shoes on and affect a slow, deliberate walk. She took her time walking along the deck and made sure that she kept slightly behind Lady Farnsworth at all times so that her shuffling walk was not readily discernible. She also persuaded Lady Farnsworth to sit near the back, pleading more protection from the wind, and sat down quickly.

Dr. Appleby was at the front listening to a gentleman Lauryn recognized as being one of the cabin-class passengers who had frowned intensely when she had taken the children up for some games on the deck. He was using his hands a lot, and she could see his mouth working fast even from a distance.

"Oh my . . . it looks like he's only just getting warmed up." Lady Farnsworth frowned and settled herself onto the wooden seat. "I do hope he doesn't go too long. I dislike feeling unrighteous because I'm uncomfortable."

Lauryn smiled as she looked around the gathering crowd. The pipe music that signaled the beginning of the service had only just been played, so many people were still wandering to find a space to sit on the deck. By the number of people she had seen appear for roll call every morning, it seemed that most of the passengers had a desire to listen to the preaching.

At precisely eleven o'clock, Dr. Appleby introduced Mr. Pilcher as the presenter of the sermon, and at precisely half past twelve, Lady Farnsworth groaned and fanned herself impatiently.

"I have no idea what that man is saying, and I don't intend to stay a moment longer." She scowled at Mr. Pilcher as he said something in a strident tone and actually shook his fist at the congregation. She held out her hand to Lauryn for assistance to stand up. This required Lauryn to stand first, which she did slowly and carefully, hoping not to attract any undue attention. The two women received some envious glances from a few of the steerage passengers as they walked away, but Lauryn tried to keep her gaze fixed on the door to the cabins.

"I didn't see Edward or the McAlisters at the sermon . . . did you?" Lady Farnsworth asked as she eased herself onto the bed. She seemed to be finding it less difficult as she lost more weight. "I had the impression that the McAlisters were a religious family."

"So did I." Lauryn nodded as she pulled her shoes off slowly and breathed a sigh of relief. "They seem like good, church-going people." She frowned as she tried to recall something Fiona had said at class, then she nodded. "That's right . . . Fiona mentioned that her father gave talks in church, but then Jimmy told her to be quiet."

"But that would make Ewen a preacher, surely?" Lady Farnsworth looked interested. "I would think he'd do a far better job than that obnoxious Mr. Pilcher calling us all to repentance." She paused to consider the possibility and nodded. "Yes, far nicer. I shall talk to Dr. Appleby about it."

"But you don't even know if Ewen is a preacher," Lauryn protested, but Lady Farnsworth waved her hand as if to dismiss the protest.

"Then we'll just have to find out for sure, won't we?" She nodded decisively. "I think you should ask Edward if he knows about Ewen. If he does then it might tell us a little more about Edward as well—whether he's a church-goer."

"I thought Edward had confided everything to you." Lauryn felt slightly put out, but she knew it was impossible to argue. "Somehow I really can't imagine him sitting in a pew."

"Well, you can be sure that if he does attend church, it is because he made a conscious decision to do so—not because it's just something that he's expected to do." Lady Farnsworth smiled knowingly. "I don't think Edward Morgan has ever been forced into doing anything he doesn't want to do. He's such a determined man."

Lauryn nodded gently as she tried to visualize Edward sitting in a church, but the picture just wouldn't form.

* * *

EDWARD HAD COME ON DECK for the sermon just after eleven o'clock, but he'd been forced to stand at the very back, where the sound of the waves washing against the prow of the boat was clearer than the sound of Mr. Pilcher's voice. He only watched for a moment before he found himself frowning at the man's impassioned antics, so he quickly wended his way through the stragglers behind him and began to walk toward the front of the boat. Since most of the passengers were clustered in the middle, the front area was clear except for one or two who were taking advantage of the relative solitude to enjoy the view of the rolling ocean.

Up above the main deck, he could see that the second level was nearly completely deserted, and he made his way to the ladder. Though he had sequestered himself in his cabin all night, his mind was still running with many thoughts, not the least of which included Miss Lauryn Kelly and an evening of dancing the like of which he had never been a part of before. In retrospect, in the quiet of his cabin, he had admonished himself for a complete lack of control, but he knew that the smile on his face at the end of the evening was a better indication of his feelings.

"Edward!" He heard Fiona's voice before he saw her head pop out from behind one of the upturned small boats, then he watched as Jimmy's head also appeared. They looked so comical that he chuckled as he walked toward them. At the same time, he watched Ewen's taller figure roll onto his knees from behind the boat and wave a hand in greeting.

"Good morning, Edward. You're not attending the service below, then?"

"No, not this morning." Edward strolled toward them with his hands in his pockets. "I might ask you the same question, though. I thought you were God-fearing people."

"Oh, we are." Ewen held out a hand to help Bess to her feet. "But we're used to having our own little services, so we thought we'd take the time while it was quiet to have our church meeting."

"If you don't mind my asking, what is the difference if you all use the same Bible?" Edward leaned against the side of the boat and folded his arms. "Although I'm not saying you're missing much from the looks of the gentleman preaching now."

"I'm sure he has a strong conviction." Ewen nodded. "And we do use the same Bible, but we have some . . . other teachings of Jesus Christ that we also like to study."

Fiona patted the book in her father's hand. "We like these stories about Jesus."

Ewen smiled as briefly he held up the book. "The children enjoy studying . . ." He stopped as he saw the look on Edward's face, then he glanced down at the book.

"Do you know this book?" Bess had seen Edward's expression as well, and she took as step forward.

"Yes . . ." Edward answered slowly as he held out his hand and Ewen placed the book in it. He studied the cover for a moment, then he turned it over slowly and opened it.

"The Book of Mormon." He started to shake his head and gave a slow smile.

"You do know it." Ewen's voice was very quiet. "Where from, Edward?"

The boat rose and fell several times before Edward answered, then he shook his head as he handed the book back.

"My twin sister became a Mormon . . . when we were only seventeen years old . . . then she married a fellow who had also joined the faith. My younger brother joined also . . . after they went to Zion." He couldn't help the slightly derogatory tone that crept into his voice as he said the word *Zion,* but the McAlisters didn't seem to notice as their faces lit up.

"Your sister is a Latter-day Saint? Oh, my goodness!" Bess clasped her hands in front of her. "What miracles keep happening!"

"It was hardly a miracle." Edward's tone was dry as he shook his head. "She joined against my and everybody's better judgment and suffered many persecutions because of it."

"But you say she is in Zion now?" Bess remained focused.

"She is . . . with her husband and William." He paused. "And two new daughters, I believe."

"So they have been there a while, if you haven't seen your nieces," Ewen said.

"They're not my nieces." Edward frowned. "My sister couldn't have children . . . these are orphans from some journey that went dreadfully wrong. Their parents died, so Emma and Patrick adopted them."

"Oh, that is so good to hear," Bess murmured as she made no attempt to disguise the tears glistening in her eyes. "I have heard of much suffering on the treks to Utah, but how wonderful it is that your sister gets to have her wish for children and those little girls will fulfill their parents' dream."

Edward stared at Bess, finding her compassion amazingly simplistic. He had read Emma's letter with her news and had felt immediately annoyed that, firstly, this journey to Zion had taken lives instead of fulfilling expectations and also that Emma would accept another person's children as her own.

He finally shrugged and looked down at Fiona and Jimmy, who had been listening carefully to their parents' conversation.

"So, what do you like about this book?" Edward kept his hands in his pockets as he studied their eager faces. "What makes you think it's so special?"

"Umm . . . I like the stories about the people traveling from Jerusalem and . . . the tree of life and . . . when Jesus talks to the children with the angels." Fiona looked up at her mother. "Are those all my favorites?"

Bess nodded as Edward raised an eyebrow at the flow of information, then he looked at Jimmy. "And what about you, Jimmy?"

The boy looked straight back as if he were measuring his response carefully, then he nodded. "I like it because it's the word of God."

Edward watched Ewen put his arm around his son's shoulders, and in that instant he sensed the same conviction that he'd often seen on Emma's face and which he'd witnessed with William just before he left. He couldn't define it, but it seemed to be the same quiet assurance that had frustrated him so much.

He nodded as he glanced from Fiona to Jimmy then back to their parents.

"Well, then . . . do you mind if I join you for a while and see if I think it's the word of God?"

* * *

EDWARD FELT A SENSE OF relief as he made his way to his cabin without meeting anybody. As he passed Lauryn's door, he hesitated for a moment as he heard voices inside, but then he shook his head and quickly opened his own door. Without pausing, he walked straight to the small tin trunk beneath his bunk, pulled it out, and opened it. Inside, a smaller wooden box rested on some clothes, and this one he opened more thoughtfully then stared at the two letters sitting on top.

"Mr. Edward Morgan." He read his sister's firm, precise handwriting on the envelope as he put the box down on the bed and sat down beside it. He held the letter for a moment as he visualized the text that he'd read only once just before he left for London.

"Just read it again, man," he muttered as he slid the folded pages out of the envelope. It was quite a thick bundle, and Edward smiled as he pictured Emma writing it. She wrote the same way she talked, and her personality seemed to bounce off the pages as the ink flowed.

Salt Lake City, Utah

April 1849

My dearest brother,

I hope that this letter reaches you before you set off on your own adventures across the world. At the moment I feel fairly certain that it will, but once you have left English shores, who knows how long it will be before you think to write to your poor sister and let her know your address. I know it will take a long time to get yourself established, but be sure that any mail will reach this address as we are bound to stay here in Salt Lake City for a long time to come.

So much has happened since I last wrote . . . but don't I say that every time? At any rate, it has again, and a single letter will not do it justice, but I will try . . .

We are now in our new home, a two-story weatherboard house with three rooms up top and two down, with a kitchen. Patrick and William have done most of the building themselves, but there are always plenty of helping hands from our neighbors. It is quite humbling to live in a community where everybody is literally of one heart and one mind. I know you were critical of that concept, but here it is a reality. Everyone has come from different places and circumstances, but we are able to live the gospel here as the Lord wants it to be lived.

Do you remember how you said that the Church would fall apart when Joseph and Hyrum Smith were murdered? I confess I did feel some apprehension myself, but quite the opposite has been true. The Saints have rallied, and President Brigham Young is a strong and valiant replacement for Joseph. Certainly I feel a great confidence in the man, especially when he speaks and shows us how Zion will build now that the Saints have settled in the Salt Lake Valley.

I truly believe that you would love it here, Edward, with the snow-capped mountains towering high above us and endless fields and valleys to cultivate. It is hard work, but we are all used to that. At least here we get our own reward and don't see it go to a landlord.

We also have great cause to rejoice, although our rejoicing comes with sadness. A while ago, some families endured many hardships while crossing the plains. A number of people died, including a particular husband and wife; their daughters had to travel the remainder of the journey in the care of others. When they reached Salt Lake, Brother Brigham asked if there was anybody who would take the responsibility of these children and raise them as their own.

Oh, Edward, there was no hesitation as Patrick and I looked at each other and then at those little girls. We are now the parents of two wonderful little children—Kirsty and, would you believe, Emma. They are six and four, respectively, and although they sorely miss their dear parents, they have settled in with us well and now enjoy our company. I am delighting in making them new dresses and bonnets as the dear things had nothing to wear when they arrived and not even shoes on their feet.

But then, dear Edward, the Lord didn't stop sending His blessings upon us. Shortly after we took the girls into our home I found out that I am to have a child! I still cannot quite believe such a miracle could happen, but part of me knows that the Lord was waiting to bless us here in Zion.

So the next time you see us, and I remain fixed in that hope, our family will number five . . . or six, depending on William's position. Currently he is with us, but as a strong, handsome bachelor, he is the target of many a winsome glance from a number of young ladies in the city. He has been taken on as an apprentice to one of the wheelwrights here, but I know that his heart lies with the land. He talks often of learning his trade and earning the money to buy his own land outside the city. He has grown to be a fine young man, Edward, and is strong and valiant in the gospel. You and our parents would be proud of him.

Well, I delight in saying that my daughters are calling for me, and though I fight off feelings of sickness on a regular basis, my cup is full and I thank the Lord for my blessings.

My sincere hope is that you will also find what you desire, Edward. It is difficult to comprehend that we are so far apart, but a part of my heart will always be with you. I continue to feel your pain at times, dear brother, and I grieve for you. Lizzy was such a dear person, and we were privileged to have her in our lives, but Edward . . . I do feel strongly that we were not meant to live our lives alone. You are still allowed to have joy. And enough . . . there I go again. I will stop now. Be assured of my abiding love and affection.

Your sister,

Emma

. . . and don't forget to write as soon as you settle!

Edward smiled as he looked up from the pages. Somehow, in his reading of the letter this time, he sensed more of his sister's joy.

"Joy." He murmured the word as he read the final paragraphs again. Then, keeping the letter in his hand, he lay back on the bunk and closed his eyes.

Lizzy was such a dear person, and we were privileged to have her in our lives. Was that how you dismissed someone after they died? Was that how he was meant to think of Lizzy . . . as simply part of the past?

You are still allowed to have joy.

"Joy." He repeated the word then cast his mind back to that feeling he had known with Lizzy . . . running together down the hill, eating a meal together that she had cooked, being together in their own home. He frowned as he tried to remember other incidents, but they were vague, and he ran a hand over his eyes.

"But I don't want to forget you, Lizzy."

He felt the grief then, as a physical knot somewhere near his heart that rose to his throat and escaped in a muffled sob as he turned his face to the pillow.

"I shouldn't forget you." He clenched his fist over his closed eyes and pressed hard.

You are still allowed to have joy, Edward.

He lay completely still, and his eyes slowly opened as he seemed to hear a woman's voice in his head. He swallowed with difficulty as he shook his head and stared at the ceiling.

"Lizzy?"

* * *

It was far more blustery on deck than she'd seen on the entire journey so far, and Lauryn had to hold onto the railing firmly as she slowly made her way to the dining area. She'd already seen a number of people fall as they'd come up from steerage to get their pots of hot water, and most had lost their precious allowance of fresh water on the deck. She felt for them as they cursed in frustration, knowing that they now had to face those who remained downstairs who wouldn't have any liquid with their dry biscuits that evening.

She bent her head to the wind and limped through the doorway, searching for Lady Farnsworth, who had come along earlier.

"Good evening, Miss . . . Lauryn." She turned quickly as she recognized Edward's voice and felt the warmth rise in her cheeks.

"Well, good evening, Mr. . . . Edward." She gave him a quick nod then grimaced as the ship moved and she stumbled against the table leg. "Ouch!" She bit her lip as the offending toes were stubbed against the wood and the tears sprang to her eyes.

"Are you all right?" Edward put down the plate he was holding and took hold of her arm to steady her.

"I'm fine." She stood very still to allow the pain to subside, then she nodded and pointed to her feet. "Sore toes."

"Sore?" Edward looked confused for a moment then nodded. "Sore toes . . . from last night?"

Lauryn nodded and attempted a smile. "I shouldn't have been so vain as to wear new slippers."

Edward seemed to be suppressing a smile as she reached out a hand to the table and tried to take a dignified step toward the seat on the other side of the table.

"Can I be of any assistance?" He offered his arm, but she shook her head, aware that Lady Farnsworth was now watching her closely. She had been determined to make her next meeting with Edward one in which she talked confidently and amiably with him . . . as friends. She had practiced all day what she might say, and now he was standing offering his arm while she limped away . . .

"No, I'm really quite all right." Lauryn heard her own voice sounding distant and impatient, and she groaned inside as she saw Lady Farnsworth roll her eyes.

"I don't think so." She heard Edward's abrupt tone, then she felt herself lifted and carried swiftly around the table, where the lady slid the chair out and Lauryn was placed firmly in her seat.

"Oh my . . . I do love a gallant gentleman!" Lady Farnsworth clapped her hands in delight as Edward stood back then walked around the table to pour himself a drink as if nothing had happened. "How I wish I had sore feet!" She laughed out loud then and shook her head. "Now, that, my boy, would really test your strength . . . and your chivalrous nature."

Even Lauryn couldn't suppress a slight smile at the image, but she kept her eyes firmly fixed on the small plate of biscuits in front of her. Her heart was still pounding vigorously, and she refused to look in Edward's direction. She could still feel exactly where his arms had tightened around her body, how small she had felt against him, and, incredibly, how his heart had felt beating against her.

"I saw a need," Edward responded quietly as he broke a biscuit. "I have a twin sister who has trained me well over the years."

"Now, why on earth would your sister be teaching you that sort of gallantry?" Lady Farnsworth was still chuckling.

"Not exactly gallantry," Edward corrected as he held up one hand and began to touch each finger in turn. "My sister, Emma, is an intrepid and often thoughtless young woman. By the time we were fifteen, I had rescued her from, let's see . . . a charging bull, a swollen stream, a water wheel, and a swarm of bees—very angry bees." He shook his head. "One learns to respond to needs."

"Whether they are actually needs or not." Lauryn spoke primly at the plate of biscuits.

"Perceived needs," Edward countered immediately. "My experiences with my sister taught me not to wait until the need was past and have to suffer the consequences."

"Well, your sister sounds like a lady I'd like to meet." Lady Farnsworth shook her head slightly as she looked at Lauryn then back to Edward. "It must have been difficult to leave your twin sister behind in England. It sounds like you are very close."

"I didn't leave Emma. She left me . . . at least she left England some time ago. She is married now and has migrated to America with her husband." He hesitated. "And my younger brother . . .William."

"And you didn't go with them?" Lady Farnsworth looked puzzled. "You're going to the other side of the world."

"We had different motivations." Edward shrugged. "They were driven by religious belief while I have always had a desire to go to the South Seas . . . the isles of the sea."

"So, you haven't seen them for a while?" Lauryn finally spoke quietly, and Edward glanced at her.

"Not since just before I met you in Birmingham." He inclined his head. "About the same time you must have left your family."

His response was pleasant enough, but somehow the reference to their first meeting seemed to make their relationship more intimate and caused the color to spread up Lauryn's cheeks. She looked down again. There was a brief silence, which Lady Farnsworth brought to a halt by tapping her fingers on the table.

"So, Edward, you are going to be a merchant in the isles of the seas? Does that mean you have brought a lot of goods with you?"

"I have." Edward took her lead and nodded toward the floor. "I have a large amount in the hold below."

"Well, then, I should like to see it all if I might." Lady Farnsworth looked straight at him. "I'm always keen to see a good business get up and running. Do you have investors?"

Edward smiled at her forthright approach. "No, no investors. I'm a lone trader. I prefer to pay for my own mistakes."

"And reap your own rewards." Lady Farnsworth chuckled as she leaned on the table. "I appreciate independence, but I also like to see resourcefulness rewarded. Don't be afraid to share what you're doing, young man."

Edward laughed then, and Lauryn looked up quickly as he shook his head.

"I'm not afraid, Francis, and I have no reservations about showing you my cargo, although the hold is hardly a delightful place to visit." He raised one eyebrow toward Lauryn. "Anyway, perhaps we should wait until your companion's toes can handle the walk."

"A very good idea." Lady Farnsworth slapped the table gently as if the decision had been made. "Lauryn will be fine by tomorrow, so we can go down after she has taught the morning class."

"That would work." Edward nodded. "I believe I'm helping her with the children tomorrow."

Lauryn kept silent as the conversation about her didn't seem to include her, then she coughed and straightened in her chair. Even that movement made the blood rush to her feet, and she grimaced slightly then affected a smile.

"Well, I believe that's all decided then. My feet will be just fine by morning, and a visit to the dark and smelly belly of the ship sounds delightful." She folded her hands in her lap. "I can't wait."

Her indignant comments were nearly lost on her employer as Lady Farnsworth chuckled again and began to stand up.

"The dark and smelly belly of the ship." She wagged a finger at Lauryn. "You should be writing more poetry, my dear. Dark and smelly belly," she repeated as she moved away form the table. She took a few steps then glanced back at Lauryn, who was still sitting at the table. "Are you coming, Lauryn?"

"I . . . I think I'll just stay here for a while." Lauryn ignored Edward as he stood up. She patted her bag. "I have a book I need to read."

Another brief silence followed as Lady Farnsworth glanced at Edward, then she nodded.

"Of course, dear. But don't be too long." She walked to the doorway and turned. "You don't want Edward to give you a hand, do you?"

Lauryn could hear her chuckling again as she walked down the hallway from the dining area. She also saw Edward hesitate, but as she bent her head to rummage in her bag, looking for a book that wouldn't be found, she heard him quietly leave the room.

As the sound of his steps on the wooden floor died away, Lauryn laid her bag aside, rested her elbows on the table, and covered her face with her hands. The heat of her cheeks warmed the palms of her hands, and she shook her head slightly as she gave a small groan.

It's your Irish pride, Lauryn Kelly. You're too proud to limp in front of the man. She rubbed her forehead. *Too proud to accept his help—even if you enjoyed it . . . like you enjoyed his company so much the other night.*

"It was nothing like James Field," she murmured into her hands as she recalled trying to generate some response when James had kissed her. The time she had spent in Edward's arms had had her pulse leaping far more than James's determined embrace. "Nothing like it at all."

So why, then, did she always become so churlish and indignant toward Edward? Why did she always have such a reaction to him whether it was in pleasure, like the dancing . . . or in pain? Lauryn wiggled her toes and felt the prickling sensation intensify.

"Joy or pain?"

* * *

EDWARD WALKED SLOWLY ALONG THE deck after he left the dining area . . .
and Lauryn. He could easily visualize her still sitting at the table, her lips
slightly pursed, her hands clasped in her lap as she stared at the plate of salt
biscuits, refusing to look at him.

What on earth had possessed him to pick her up and put her on the chair?

"Impulsive." He pushed his hands into the pockets of his trousers.
"Childishly impulsive."

He'd come to pride himself on his quietly resolute demeanor, realizing
that in not revealing too much of himself he gained the upper hand with
most people in his business dealings. It also gave him time to watch people
and analyze their behavior and then to respond to their strengths . . . or
weaknesses. While not ruthless, he didn't hesitate to take advantage of those
who might otherwise take advantage of him. Edward Morgan considered
himself a good judge of people, and of himself, which was why he now felt
tormented about his behavior toward Lauryn.

There was no doubt that he felt attracted to her. She was a bright, beautiful woman, and there was definitely something about her slightly defiant
personality that appealed to him or at least made him react to her. Nobody
else had ever had him dancing all evening and enjoying it. He'd danced with
the other young women after Lizzy, but it had felt obligatory, and his face
had ached from trying to smile at each new one. But dancing with Lauryn
had been pure pleasure.

Edward shook his head as he thought about the pleasure he had come to
find in overseeing the school lessons. He had originally consented to the job
from a sense of obligation to the doctor, but he knew he'd probably learned
more than any of the children as he listened carefully while Lauryn taught,
her bright voice with the gentle Irish lilt seeming to give the information
more meaning somehow.

"More meaning somehow. More enjoyable." Edward nodded slowly.
That was what Lauryn did for him, and even when she was being silent or
defiant, he enjoyed the challenge of getting a reaction from her. Was that
why he'd carried her to the chair? Because he knew he'd get a reaction?

He grimaced slightly. He hadn't meant to hurt her feelings, though.

Edward stopped walking and leaned against the deck railing. Even in
the darkness he could make out the foaming crests of the waves flowing
against the side of the ship as the wooden hull relentlessly sliced its way
through the water. Given good conditions the voyage would continue this
way for another eleven weeks.

"Eleven weeks." Edward pulled his gaze away from the water as he
straightened up and began to walk back toward the dining area.

The two farmers were talking quietly when he reached the doorway, sitting in the chairs Lauryn and Lady Farnsworth had previously sat in. Edward gave the doorjamb a slight thump with his fist then turned back to the cabin area. In a matter of seconds, he reached the hallway to his cabin just as Lauryn reached her own door.

"Lauryn!" Edward called out before she turned the handle. She looked up, gasping slightly with surprise.

"Oh, you startled me." She put her hand to her chest then tightened her hold on the handle.

"I'm sorry . . ." Edward walked slowly down the hallway. "I'm sorry I startled you, and I'm sorry if I embarrassed you . . . before . . . in the dining room." He finished lamely. "I should have asked you first."

Lauryn hesitated, but then her expression softened. "Yes, you should have asked." She nodded as she smiled slightly. "Then at least I would have had the opportunity to say 'No, thank you.'"

He smiled and shook his head as he recognized her reference to her asking him to dance and his refusal.

"But would you have asked me right back?"

Lauryn lifted her chin and looked at the wooden paneling above her head. "No . . . probably not," she answered quietly.

"Then I would have missed an opportunity." Edward leaned against the doorjamb and folded his arms. "To help you."

"Yes." Lauryn nodded and almost smiled. "Yes, you would have," she repeated quietly as she turned back to the door. "I'll work on being more gracious."

"And I'll keep looking for opportunities . . . to help." Edward made to step forward, then he stopped. "Good night, Lauryn."

"Good night, Edward."

* * *

Lady Farnsworth was true to her word about wanting to see the extent of the merchandise Edward had stored in the hold, and next day she was waiting alongside Edward at the back of the group of children as Lauryn dismissed the class.

"Are you ready, Lauryn? Edward, shall we go?" She took his arm then hesitated and looked down at Lauryn, still sitting on her stool. "Oh, how silly of me . . . you should be helping Lauryn."

"Lauryn is just fine." Lauryn stood up from her seat and took a step without limping. "The swelling has gone right down after a good night's sleep." She smiled and nodded toward Edward. "Besides, the gentleman has two arms. We could take one each."

"Why not?" Edward responded easily as he held out both arms, and Lady Farnsworth chuckled as she promptly grasped one arm and waited while Lauryn moved to the other side.

"No carrying anyone today, Edward?"

"Not without asking first." He looked down at Lauryn, but she only smiled and looked straight ahead. She and Edward had parted on good terms the night before, but she had been surprised how earnestly she had wanted to see him again this morning. She hadn't been disappointed when he had arrived shortly after the class had started and had greeted her with a broad smile and a brief salute before sitting down with the older boys at the back of the class.

"Oh, here, I brought you something to eat, Lauryn." Lady Farnsworth delved into her bag and handed her three biscuits. "I know you didn't have breakfast this morning. You must be starving, dear, so chew on those for an hour or so."

Lauryn smiled her thanks as she took the biscuits, but they held no appeal, so she slipped them into her bag.

There was a member of the crew sitting outside the entrance to the hold as they approached, but he didn't even bother to get up as Edward moved toward him.

"Af'ernoon, sir." He tipped his cap. "Ladies. Checking up, sir?"

"Just giving the ladies a quick look, Albie." Edward nodded. "We're short on entertainment this afternoon, so they want to see cargo."

"Aye . . . it'll be a long trip if this be entertainment." Albie rolled his eyes as they walked past him and began to ascend through a large opening in the deck.

As her eyes became accustomed to the darkness, Lauryn could see row upon row of boxes and crates of all shapes and sizes, stacked several high with thick ropes securing them together. Stenciled onto the side or top of many of the wooden crates were names she recognized from either the roll call or her class.

"Adams—Lyttleton. Drake—Port Chalmers, Wilson . . ." She read sideways. "Port Chalmers."

"E. J. Morgan. Here we are." Lady Farnsworth pointed to a large crate and then to another and another with the same name. "My goodness, how long did it take to put your name on everything? I felt quite overwhelmed with only two trunks." She fanned herself as she stood on tiptoe and surveyed more rows. "You really are taking a shop load, aren't you?"

"As much as I can." Edward nodded thoughtfully. "I had to find a balance between necessary goods and goods that people in the colonies might not have been able to obtain for a while—things they would purchase quickly at a higher price. That way I can afford to send back for more."

Lauryn stared at the stack of crates and shook her head. "It's amazing to think how much people need to get by . . . or expect they need." She touched one of the crates. "It makes me realize how little we made do with back in Ireland . . . just the barest essentials."

Lady Farnsworth was surprisingly sober. "It makes me realize how much I've had over the years that I didn't really need."

They stood quietly for a moment, then she pointed at one of the crates. "Edward, I think I'd prefer to see Lyttleton written on your crates instead of Sydney." She shook her head. "I really don't think Australia will need you as much as New Zealand."

Edward gave a brief laugh. "Actually, it's more that I need Australia." He slapped his hand against one of the boxes. "The market is bigger there, and I hear it's more ready for these goods. I need to make a fast turnover, and the news of the gold rush seems to indicate that this is the better place to be at the moment."

Lauryn listened quietly as he continued to respond to Lady Farnsworth's questions about markets and establishment costs and to outline the types of products he was shipping. He sounded confident and informed, and she marveled at the courage it must take to invest in so much then move it to the other side of the world.

Edward and Lady Farnsworth continued to talk while Lauryn began to move along a narrow aisle between the boxes, trying to get an idea of how many belonged to Edward. She had not previously given much thought to whether he was wealthy or not, but then, nobody would know that Lady Farnsworth had money, considering she was traveling in the forward cabins and not in cabin class.

Lauryn smiled as she thought about the two people behind her. An unlikely pair, but they got on so well, and she was fortunate to be friends with both of them. She nodded as she thought about the good fortune that had led her to her situation.

"Oh . . ." She gasped and looked down quickly as something moved against her foot, and for a moment she panicked as she thought it might be a rat. Edward had warned that there were probably vermin amongst the crates, but she saw nothing as she carefully lifted her skirt to check. She turned to look behind her, and her foot touched something again.

"What?" she barely whispered as she bent down to pick up the thin metal tube that had rolled from beneath the hem of her dress. It felt familiar between her fingers, and she recognized a tin whistle almost identical to her own. Instinctively, Lauryn put her hand to the pocket insert at the side of her dress, but the familiar shape of her own whistle lay comfortably along the seam. In the same moment she heard a soft scratching to her left, and she slowly looked up.

It was difficult to tell what age the man was, as a long shadow lay across the narrow space that he was wedged in, but as he leaned forward, Lauryn could see that he had a black beard and long hair that fell across part of his face. His dark eyes glistened as they looked directly into hers, and she could feel the scream mounting in her throat. In the same instant, he raised a finger to his lips. With his other hand, he pointed to the whistle in her hands. In a swift movement he used both hands to mimic playing the whistle then gestured in the space between Lauryn and himself. Surprisingly, a broad smile showed through his beard. He put his hand over his heart and pointed to her then raised one finger.

"Heart . . . one . . ." The tightness in Lauryn's throat seemed to disappear as she slowly crouched down, trying to fathom what the man was miming with his hands. She looked at the whistle in her hands. It was his Irish tin whistle . . . just like hers . . .

"Ireland . . . one heart," she whispered as she looked back to where the man lay and nodded. Yes, she was Irish, too. For some reason, the fear she had felt just a few seconds before seemed to disappear as she watched him rub his stomach then put his hands together in a begging motion. Her mind raced as she realized he was begging for food.

"Lauryn . . . where are you, dear?' Lady Farnsworth's voice echoed in the hold, and Lauryn jumped, falling slightly against the crate behind her.

"Coming . . . I . . . was just counting Edward's crates." Lauryn glanced quickly at the man and raised her shoulders to indicate that she didn't have any food. She felt a keen sense of disappointment as she watched his shoulders slump, and she sensed his complete helplessness.

"Lauryn?" Edward's voice sounded closer, and Lauryn stood up quickly as he walked around the corner of the narrow aisle.

"I . . ." She held up her bag. "I dropped something, and I couldn't find it in the dark."

"Your tin whistle?" Edward smiled as he looked down at her hand. "You can't afford to lose that. The children would be really upset if they had to miss their music and dancing."

"My . . ." Lauryn looked down at her other hand, which still held the other flute. "I . . . yes . . . I'd be lost without it." She opened her bag to put the whistle inside and saw the three biscuits that Lady Farnsworth had brought her for lunch. "Um . . . I think I dropped a pencil as well." She turned back quickly and bent down to the floor.

"Is this an opportunity for me to help?" Edward began to walk down the aisle, but she gave a short laugh.

"No, no . . . I see it." She moved toward the narrow space where the man was hidden and quickly placed the three biscuits on the floor, then stood up and turned toward Edward. "I have it!"

"Good, now we'd better get back up on deck. I don't like to stay down here too long." Edward stood aside as she squeezed past him, and though she felt the gentle pressure of his hand behind her back, she was moving too quickly to appreciate it.

"I agree." Lady Farnsworth moved in front of Lauryn up the narrow set of stairs. "A few minutes is quite long enough, but thank you for showing us your cargo, Edward. It's given us a much better idea of what you do, hasn't it Lauryn?"

"Um, yes . . . much better." Lauryn nodded, but she frowned as she climbed the steps. Had they only been in the hold a few minutes?

"Well, I'm glad." Edward was right behind her, and she jumped slightly as he touched her elbow. "Now would you like to sit down to eat your lunch?"

"Lunch?" Lauryn looked at him blankly, then she shook her head. "Actually, I need to go and prepare some things for the next lesson . . . some verse . . . in my cabin."

She could see the inquiring look on Edward's face as she smiled then quickly gathered her skirts a little higher and turned away. "I'll see you this afternoon . . . Edward . . . Mam."

Moments later, when her cabin door clicked shut behind her, Lauryn finally relaxed and closed her eyes. Everything had happened so quickly . . . What had she just done? Who was that man and why was he in the hold?

She stared at the wall as her mind began to process the facts, then she put her hand to her mouth.

"A stowaway. He must be a stowaway." She leaned her head against the door and groaned. There had been such a fuss made about stowaways when they'd boarded the ship. She had watched the delight on the captain's face when two had been found hiding—a man and a boy. He had held them up to public humiliation then had them dumped off the ship and handed to the police.

"How did he escape?" Lauryn murmured to herself as she walked forward and put her bag on the table. As she set it down, she saw the shape of the whistle still inside. Very slowly, she pulled it out and turned it between her fingers.

"An Irish stowaway who plays the tin whistle." She shook her head as she thought about the lack of fear she'd felt as she'd watched the man miming his plight. Although she couldn't tell his age, he somehow seemed a familiar soul. "He can't be that bad of a man . . . but he must be starving if he's been down in the hold since we sailed." She put the whistle back in the bag. "And how can he possibly stay there for another ten weeks?"

Chapter Twenty

Atlantic Ocean, Near Africa, 1849
Just Connor

LAURYN'S CONCERN FOR THE MAN in the hold was forced aside as the storm rapidly reached its full fury. All passengers were given strict instructions to stay in their berths, and for once the narrow confines of the bunks proved their worth as the ship pitched and rolled. Any possessions that weren't secured were thrown from side to side in the compartments, as was anyone who ventured out. Cutlery and crockery became flying weapons until they were stored under bedding, and even heavy trunks slid across the floor to crash against the side of the berth.

Added to the misery were the violent bouts of seasickness that most of the passengers had avoided on the hitherto calm seas. Now, most of the people on board were subject to surges of vomiting that left the compartment stinking and vile to stumble through.

Lauryn lay in her bunk with hands outstretched to wedge herself against the endless rising and plummeting of the ship's prow into and over the huge waves. Lady Farnsworth had long since decided that the journey was over and simply rolled with the movement, waiting for the worst to happen.

Amidst the screaming wind and the loud groaning of the ship's structure as it struggled against the waves, the smashing of the water on the deck provided a regular pounding noise that oddly enough lulled the senses.

And then, suddenly, it was gone—leaving an eerie silence as the boat itself seemed to hang suspended.

She heard the screams before she felt the impact, and by then it was too late to brace herself as the ship swung fully over on its side, listing at such an angle as to make her feel as if she were upside down.

"There's water coming in!" Lady Farnsworth pointed in horror as water welled through the joints in the wall planks and poured onto the floor. She looked at Lauryn and shook her head violently as she closed her eyes.

Amidst the tumult, Lauryn tried to focus on what might be happening outside in the rest of the ship. Where were all of the children she'd been teaching? Were any of them lost or hurt? Where was Edward, and what about the Irishman?

She fought a surge of nausea as the ship seemed to convulse and began to move back to an upright position. Water raced back across the floor and then pooled where it was, sloshing from side to side as the ship stabilized. There were a few more deep dips as the ship lifted through smaller waves, but the worst was obviously past, and Lauryn began to sense a more regular swelling motion in the movement.

"Do you think it's over?" Lauryn asked very quietly as she stared at the ceiling.

"I hope so," Lady Farnsworth responded in a monotone. "I swear that was as close to death as I have ever been."

Lauryn could only nod in agreement as she tried to sit up but fell back against a sodden pillow. She looked sideways at the contents of the cabin and groaned slightly. "I think every single thing must be wet."

There was silence, then Lady Farnsworth gasped. "Can you imagine what it must be like down in steerage? The poor souls!"

"I was thinking about the children. They must have been thrown around like rag dolls." Lauryn sat up. "Perhaps we should go and see."

"I doubt they'll let you." Lady Farnsworth waved her back down. "I'm sure Edward will let us know soon enough. He's bound to be there with the doctor."

Lauryn nodded. The doctor had come to rely on Edward's assistance in many activities and issues that had developed, above and beyond the proffered assistance from those who assisted him in cabin class. Some had not taken to the situation kindly, but Edward seemed to continue doing as the doctor asked, regardless of any ill will.

"I hope he's all right." She frowned slightly at the thought that he might have been trying to help too much during the storm. "And what about the poor doctor? He's going to have his hands full if people are hurt."

"Oh, I'm sure people will be fine once they dry out. It's being wet and dirty that makes people feel ill. There's always sunshine after there's rain, so I expect we'll be fine in a few days." Lady Farnsworth pulled herself up. "You'll see. We'll be entering the tropics soon, and everything will dry out nicely."

"Ladies . . . are you both all right?" Lauryn heard Edward's voice outside the door, and her heart beat more quickly.

"We're both well." She pulled herself out of the bunk and sloshed through the inch or so of water to the door. As she opened the door, she saw the look of relief on Edward's face a split second before her eyes were drawn to the bleeding gash on the side of his head above his left ear. "But you're hurt!"

He gave her a puzzled look as she stared at his head, then he put his hand up and brought it down covered in blood.

"I must have hit something . . . or it hit me." He gave a short laugh. "It's hard to tell when you're upside down."

Lauryn laughed weakly as she leaned against the doorjamb. Then she remembered her earlier concerns.

"Was anybody else hurt, Edward . . . any of the children?"

He nodded slowly as he pointed up to the deck. "One of the sailors was washed overboard, and a small child is unconscious from falling onto its head."

"Oh, dear." Lauryn closed her eyes briefly then looked at him. "What do we do . . . if someone dies?"

Edward took a moment to respond. "I really don't know yet."

* * *

THE ENORMOUS WAVE THAT HAD washed over Lauryn's cabin had dumped a deluge of water into the steerage compartment, leaving several inches of water swilling around with excrement and vomit. There was no way to empty it, and the only solution was to pour a layer of sand over it and let it gradually dry out. Entering the tropics had produced another problem as the soaked compartment created high humidity and a potential breeding ground for disease.

Dr. Appleby drew Lauryn aside after the first lesson back on deck two days later. He looked tired and was not quite as neatly shaven as usual, but he maintained the pleasant smile that seemed to endear him to most people. As the children began to leave the class, he pointed to two who had been listless since the storm.

"Miss Kelly, I'm concerned that some of the children might be feeling more than just the effects of seasickness." He frowned as he watched the children carefully. "With all this humidity, I want to be made aware of any symptoms at all that you might see . . . or not see . . . Stay aware of any children who aren't coming to class."

Lauryn nodded as she studied his face.

"So what sort of symptoms should I be looking for—other than the usual signs of fever?"

"Obvious things like diarrhea, vomiting, or extreme listlessness." He shook his head. "Our main concern is cholera, and unfortunately, it often strikes so quickly as to render any form of relief useless."

"And do you think it might—"

"I hope it won't," Dr. Appleby interrupted. "But it has been my experience that it intensifies in these conditions, and I have limited resources to deal with it. If we see any indication at all, we will need to isolate the individuals immediately." He stared into the distance. "The children are particularly prone, but the adults also succumb in these conditions. One of the last sailings ended up with fifteen children orphaned."

"Fifteen." Lauryn barely whispered the word as she realized the implications. "But what did they do . . . without parents?"

"They were simply given to people, Miss Kelly . . . people who would hopefully care for them in their new land." He shook his head. "That is why this will be my last voyage. Sickness takes a toll even as death does by rendering one either too careless . . . or too caring." He took a deep breath. "I have alerted the constables to be watchful as well, and now . . . I must tend to the child with the head injury."

"Is he going to be all right?" Lauryn almost didn't dare ask, but the doctor shrugged his shoulders.

"He might make it, but he is the youngest of nine children, three of whom died before they came on board ship, so I don't know that the parents hold out much hope." He turned to face the door down to the infirmary. "But I do care."

As Lauryn watched him walk away, she felt a great sense of compassion for the soft-spoken man who seemed to bear the burdens of life on board the ship far more than the captain himself. She had hardly seen Captain Bayliss since coming on board, and rumor had it that he kept silent watch with a whisky bottle near his side. Certainly, most of the orders seemed to come from the second in command, Mr. Frew.

"So, what was the doctor looking so concerned about?" Lady Farnsworth came to stand beside Lauryn from where she'd been talking to the two gentlemen farmers. "And please don't tell me we're heading for another storm."

"No, he was just telling me about the child who was hurt during the storm." Lauryn didn't look at her employer, deciding not to cause her extra worry by telling her about Dr. Appleby's concerns.

"You're not very good at telling stories, are you dear?" Lady Farnsworth fanned her face without looking at Lauryn. "What was it really?"

Lauryn smiled slightly and shook her head. "He's concerned we might have an outbreak of sickness with all the humidity, and he was asking me to look out for symptoms amongst the children." She stopped, and Lady Farnsworth glanced at her.

"And that was it?"

"Yes."

"Well . . . I don't know why you should feel to keep that from me, dear. I was a nurse . . . of sorts . . . a long time ago." She corrected herself further. "A very long time ago, but I'd rather deal with sickness than that frightful storm any day."

"I think we'd all rather not deal with any of it." Lauryn bent to pick up her bag. "Have you seen Edward today?"

Lady Farnsworth nodded happily as she began to walk ahead of Lauryn. "I was talking to him after lunch. He asked where you were."

"Did he?" Lauryn concentrated on the short flight of stairs. "And is his injury better?"

"Oh, that wee bump . . . it's not even showing, but he did say it would take more than a wooden jib to dent his thick head."

"I'm glad he's well, then." Lauryn nodded thoughtfully. "I think he was helping the crew during the storm. He seems to be in the middle of things a lot."

"He's that kind of person, child . . . just as you are." Lady Farnsworth halted suddenly in her tracks and turned to face Lauryn. "You are fond of him, aren't you, Lauryn?"

"I . . ." Lauryn stuttered, then she smiled shyly. "I believe I think about him more than I ever did about James."

"And you knew James for four years." Lady Farnsworth winked at her. "Thank goodness we left England before you did something silly there."

They walked in silence along the deck, then Lauryn coughed. "Mam . . . do you remember what the captain said at the beginning of the trip?"

"My goodness, he said a lot of things. What was I supposed to remember?" Lady Farnsworth chuckled.

"He said something about stowaways and . . ." Lauryn deliberately left the sentence unfinished, and Lady Farnsworth finished for her.

"Stowaways wouldn't be tolerated, and if discovered out at sea they would be branded and given the foulest of work to do."

"But how would they survive out at sea, anyway . . . if they were hiding?" Lauryn tried to sound casual. "Surely they would starve."

"I imagine they would wait and then turn themselves in." Lady Farnsworth fanned her face. "My understanding is that most would prefer the worst journey than have to stay in England." She glanced at Lauryn. "But whatever brought that subject up?"

"Oh, I was just thinking about the children playing hide-and-seek and wondered how anybody could stay hidden on board ship. There's so little space."

"Well, if they haven't any food, they're not going to take up much space, are they?" The lady laughed and turned away to the cabins, but Lauryn followed more slowly.

The Irishman was clearly hungry, so he must be intending to turn himself in soon.

"He must . . . or he'll die down there." Lauryn frowned as she recalled the man's dark face and his sudden, hopeful smile. She bit at her bottom lip and glanced along the deck. There was still another hour before the afternoon class.

"Mam!" She called to Lady Farnsworth, who was already in conversation with one of the women from steerage as she made her way downstairs. She had no qualms about mixing with the lower-class passengers, although many of the cabin class openly frowned at her.

"Mam!" Lauryn pointed back they way they'd come as Lady Farnsworth turned. "I forgot some things."

* * *

It only took a few minutes to walk to the dining area, and because the set time to eat was tightly adhered to, there was no one at the table. Lauryn quickly grabbed a handful of biscuits and a slice of the fruit pudding, but there was nothing to hold water in except tin cups, which would be too obvious to carry on deck.

She took a moment to mentally review the items in her cabin and nodded as she remembered a pewter flask that Lady Farnsworth kept in the small dresser. When she arrived back at the cabin, she pushed the food and flask tightly into the bag and let herself out again.

"Lauryn . . . I've been wondering where you were." Edward spoke behind her, and Lauryn froze, her hand automatically trying to cover the bulging drawstring bag she held in front of her. "Francis said you had gone to get some things." He stood right behind her so that she had to turn to face him.

"I . . . yes." She closed her eyes briefly, feeling a twinge of guilt for lying, then turned with a bright smile, holding up the bag. "I thought I'd do a memory bag game for the children. I'll show them lots of little things and see who can remember the most."

"Which, of course, Jimmy will win because he remembers everything." Edward smiled and put his hand out to the bag. "Do I get a preview?"

"No!" Lauryn gripped the bag tightly, then realized she had reacted a little too quickly. She smiled again and used her other hand to pretend to push him away. "We'll see how you fare against the children . . . or at least Jimmy." She drew a quick breath. "Now I really must get organized."

"Can I help at all?" Edward seemed reluctant to move, and Lauryn felt a knot forming in her stomach. He obviously wanted to spend time with her, and normally, she would have happily obliged.

"Ah . . . yes, you could help me by putting the children's stools into two teams. Then we can start directly when they come to class." She made to walk by him. "I'll be up there as soon as I can." She held up the bag. "Just a few more items."

She knew he was watching her as she quickly walked away, and it actually made her hold her breath to think that she was trying to deceive him. For a second she wondered why she was even trying to do so. A few seconds' interaction with the Irishman, and she was now acting like she was the fugitive. It didn't make sense, but she somehow felt compelled to confront the man first . . . on her own.

* * *

THE SAME SAILOR WAS SITTING tipped back on his chair at the entrance to the hold. He appeared to be asleep, but he cocked one eye open as she approached.

"Afternoon, missy." He didn't move his head, but Lauryn could tell he was watching her carefully.

"Afternoon, Albie." Lauryn felt a sense of relief as she remembered his name, and he almost smiled in return. "I seem to have dropped a trinket, and I think it was when I visited the hold with Mr. Morgan yesterday. Do you mind if I take a look?" She smiled pleasantly. "I'll be very quick. I don't want to spend more time there than I need to."

Albie nodded as he began to move off his seat.

"Surely, miss. I'll show you down."

"Oh, that won't be necessary." Lauryn tried to sound flippant. "I know exactly where it'll be." She began to walk toward the opening, then she turned and put her head to one side. "I would appreciate it if you could stand at the door though, Albie . . . just in case."

"Of course, missy." Albie grinned and folded his arms. "Just watch for the rats on the second aisle."

She wasted no time going down the steps, and as soon as her eyes adjusted to the darkness, she made her way quickly toward the rows of Edward's stock. Near where she had seen the Irishman behind the crates, she stopped and pulled the tin whistle out of her pocket. She realized she'd been holding her breath, as she had to take another breath just to blow a few soft notes. Then she lowered the whistle and cleared her throat.

"Are you there? It's me . . . the Irish girl." She kept her voice to a very low whisper then strained her ears to hear any response. But there was nothing except the usual sound of the waves on the side of the boat. "I've brought you some food." She hesitated. "I'm alone."

Only then did she hear a faint scratching noise from behind her, then she saw a hand with beckoning fingers emerge from the gap. She felt her heart pounding as she moved closer and knelt down to peer around the corner.

"Oh!" She jumped as she came almost face-to-face with him and fell back against the crate. Close up, his matted hair and filthy skin not only smelled but gave him a sinister look, and she shivered then took a shallow breath. "I brought you food," she repeated, but her hands refused to move as they clutched the bag.

He still didn't speak, but his eyes watched her carefully as he held out his hand.

"Um . . . I wanted to speak to you." She finally got her fingers to move and quickly undid the drawstring and took out the biscuits and cake. His eyes flicked to the food. "I brought you some water as well." This time he shook his head as he took the flask and opened it carefully, as if he were handling something precious.

"Don't drink it too quickly." Lauryn watched him open the flask and sip a few drops. "I don't know if I can come back down again."

He looked up at her then, and she saw the smile cross his face.

"Go raibh maith agat." His voice was coarse and deep, and it made him sound older than he looked. She thought he must be in his mid-twenties.

Lauryn inclined her head to acknowledge his thanks as she felt a surge of emotion at the familiar tones of the Gaelic language. She struggled for a moment then bit at her lip as she fumbled with the bag.

"Oh, I nearly forgot your whistle." She handed it to him and he took it, spinning it between his fingers then clasping it tightly in his hand. At the same time she put her hand into her dress pocket and pulled out her own whistle. "I thought I had dropped my own when yours rolled on the floor."

The man stared at the whistle then back at her, and the smile appeared again.

"Where are you from?" It seemed the water had soothed his throat, and his voice was soft.

"Um, County Cork . . . near Blarney." Lauryn faltered. She hadn't said that for a long time. "And you?"

"Tipperary." He tried to bite on a biscuit, but it was too hard. "I'll just have to lick it." He managed a low chuckle, but his breath seemed to catch with the effort. "My mouth's . . . forgotten how to eat."

"Missy!" They both jumped as Albie's voice echoed through the hold. "Ye all right down there?"

"Um . . . fine, Albie! Coming!" Lauryn pressed fingers to her forehead as she tried to think quickly, then she scrambled to her feet. "I won't be able to come back, but I think you should give yourself up or you'll starve down here. My friends said that you'll be all right—the captain will just give you dirty jobs to do."

"You told them?" He looked at her quickly, but she shook her head.

"I only asked about stowaways." She looked back toward the entrance. "Look, I have to go, but please . . . give yourself up or you might die down here, and no one would know."

"Oh, they'd smell me soon enough." He attempted a grin again, and she wondered what sort of person he was. How had he gotten to this state?

"Why did you stow away?" She frowned.

"Running from the police." He stopped as a shiver seemed to wrack his thin frame and he coughed quietly. "I jumped off the convict ship . . . at the dock . . . this was the closest boat when I surfaced." He drew a breath with difficulty. "I waited 'til a big load came on board . . . they were more concerned about what was on top than underneath."

"But why . . . were you a convict?" She almost didn't want to ask, but she had to know. "What did you do?"

He shook his head, and a slight smile tipped the side of his mouth, though it did not reach his eyes, which looked sunken and listless. "You should be worried . . . it was a terrible crime I committed." He shrugged. "I took an apple . . . to feed my sister and my mum, but I wasn't quick enough . . . got caught and taken away, and now they've probably starved."

His voice became monotone as he talked about his family. Then there didn't seem to be anything else to say. They were of a similar age and from a similar place and yet, by a quirk of fate their circumstances were so very different.

"I'm sorry." Lauryn barely murmured the words then took a deep breath as she began to walk away.

"What's your name?" His voice was a whisper behind her, and her step faltered.

"Lauryn . . . Lauryn Kelly." She turned her head slightly. "And yours?"

"Connor." She waited for more, but he simply looked straight at her.

"Is that all? Just . . . Connor?"

"It's all . . . I need."

Lauryn heard Albie's shuffling steps coming closer, and she turned to leave. However, she had only taken a few steps when she heard a slight moan behind her. When she glanced back she saw that Connor had slumped forward, his head lolling on his chest.

"No!" she gasped, just as Albie's form came into view.

* * *

"Is Lauryn not feeling well?" Edward placed his plate on the table beside Lady Farnsworth's as he stared back toward the doorway to the dining area. "I just passed her leaving, and she said she wasn't hungry then mumbled something about preparing the lesson." He picked up a knife and fork. "She seems to be acting very differently."

He waited as Lady Farnsworth took her time responding. Her forehead creased in a deep frown.

"I'm glad I'm not the only one thinking that way." She slowly pushed a lump of dry meat around her plate with her fork. "Lauryn has been behaving strangely . . . and not just during the day." She looked up at Edward, and he could see the concern in her eyes. "She normally sleeps like a baby, but the last few days she . . ." She hesitated. "It's like she's tormented. She's been talking in her sleep . . . lots of names, and sometimes it sounds as if she's in pain."

"In pain?" Edward frowned.

"Not in pain now, but like she's feeling some pain . . . reliving it." Lady Farnsworth shook her head. "I woke the other night when she called out, but then she went very quiet, so I didn't know whether to go to her or not." She smiled, but her lips trembled. "I wonder if I have done something that might have hurt her in some way. I have been known to offend people."

Edward smiled at her deliberate understatement. "Then I must have offended her as well, because she has barely spoken to me since the other day. In fact, it's almost as if she's avoiding me." He shrugged. "And I have no idea what I might have done.

Lady Farnsworth laid a hand on his arm, and her voice dropped to a whisper. "Edward, I've been thinking a lot about it, and I believe this all began when we went down to look at your merchandise in the hold. I remember she made a comment about not realizing how little she'd had in Ireland, and then she said something later about how much you seemed to have." She nodded thoughtfully. "Maybe she's worried about her family in Ireland. They have so very little, and she may never see them again—now that a silly old English woman has decided to take her to the other side of the world."

Edward watched a film of tears form over her eyes as Lady Farnsworth shook her head.

"I tend to forget that she's not mine—that she has others she still cares about . . . deeply." She gave a brief smile.

They both sat quietly through the rest of their meal. As they finished, Edward glanced at his companion.

"Do you think I should try and talk to her about it?" He tapped one finger on the table. "I wanted to ask her to accompany me to the dancing this evening but . . ."

"But you don't feel like being rejected." Lady Farnsworth smiled. "I'm not sure that I'd mention dancing right now, but perhaps an inquiry after her health might help show that you are concerned about her."

Edward nodded as he rose from the table then offered to take Lady Farnsworth's plate.

"I'll talk to her after class this afternoon." He shrugged. "It's funny . . . she seems to be able to muster a degree of brightness when she's with the children, but it disappears right after class." He took a deep breath and glanced at his watch. "And now I need to go and check on my merchandise again. The guard said he found some dead rats by the crates."

"Well, better dead than alive." Lady Farnsworth raised one eyebrow. "Right?"

Edward took his time walking to the hold and couldn't help glancing around to see if Lauryn was still on deck. It bothered him that the more she ignored him, the more he wanted to gain her attention, but the longer it lasted the more he realized how much he actually appreciated her company.

He stood for a moment with his hands in his pockets, staring at the place set apart as the classroom area on deck. He was beginning to realize how much he enjoyed listening to the lilt of her voice as she shared the poetry and numbers and games with the children.

"The Irish lilt," Edward murmured. He had never stopped to think about what life might have been like for Lauryn before she came to England—before that day they'd met in Birmingham. He tried to imagine a very young Lauryn living in poverty, the likes of which he'd seen in the hand-drawn sketches in the newspapers—scrawny waiflike creatures of skin and bone living in mud huts.

Edward shook his head. He'd had poor beginnings, but perhaps Lauryn's were even worse, and if her family was still suffering . . .

"Then how must she be suffering?" He shook his head as he turned toward the hold, absently making note that there was no sailor tending the opening.

He ducked his head as he began to ease his way down the narrow steps then began looking for signs of the large ship rats that seemed to be able to remain unseen and yet make great holes in the wooden boxes. He heard Albie's voice before he saw anybody, and as he walked around the highest stack of crates he almost bumped into the sailor, who was standing with his arms folded across his chest and a large knife in his hand.

"Albie . . . threatening the rats, are you?" he began to joke, but the sailor shook his head.

"Not the ship's rats, Mr. Morgan. They'll be bigger 'n that." He nodded his head to his right and called out, "Ye have to come out now . . . both of ye . . . for I heard you talking to someone."

There was a long pause, and Edward moved forward to see who the sailor was talking to.

"Lauryn!" He pushed past Albie as Lauryn straightened up in front of them, staring at something beyond the crates, her arms hanging by her sides. "What on earth . . . ?"

She made no move as he reached her.

"I cannot help him anymore." Her voice was barely a whisper as the tears began to slide down her cheeks. "He wouldn't listen to me."

"Who?" Edward frowned as he followed her gaze then knelt down to see into the slim gap between the crates. "Good grief!"

It was difficult for him to tell exactly what the man looked like because his arm lay awkwardly across his face, but at close quarters Edward recoiled from the stench that emanated from the man's body. He covered his face with his hand then leaned closer to him, easing away some of the dark, greasy hair to feel near his throat.

"He'll be a stowaway," Albie offered knowingly as he edged closer. "They often come to a nasty end if they last this long . . ."

He stopped as Lauryn gave a choked gasp and put her hand to her mouth.

"Get a blanket, Albie!" Edward stood up and placed himself in front of Lauryn so she couldn't see. "And get someone to help you take him to the infirmary."

"The infirmary?" Albie frowned. "There's no need for that, Mr. Morgan, sir . . . the captain will have us put 'im straight overboard . . . so as not to disturb the passengers, like."

Edward saw the expression on Lauryn's face, and he shook his head.

"A blanket and to the infirmary," he repeated firmly. "He's still breathing." Edward could hear Albie mumbling as he turned back to the entrance.

"Albie!"

"Yes, sir." The sailor halted in his tracks.

"I'm the only one here . . . understand." Edward paused. "You were helping me with my inspection when we found him."

Albie turned and glanced at Lauryn's back as he nodded slowly. "Aye, sir . . . helping you inspect those crates of . . . tobaccy?"

Edward breathed slowly as he nodded. "I think it's the sort you like, Albie."

"Aye, sir . . . I like it a lot. And I'll be sure to help you when you off-load."

Then he was gone and Edward was left staring at Lauryn. Her face was almost devoid of color, and her arms were now wrapped around her body as she shivered slightly.

"Lauryn, you need to go to your cabin," Edward said quietly, but she shook her head.

"Do you think he'll live?"

"I don't know. His pulse was very weak." Edward looked down at the floor rather than at Lauryn. His impulse was to put his arms around her and comfort her—and then ask the many questions that were racing through his mind. Instead, he clenched his fist by his side and took a deep breath.

"Lauryn, I'm going to have to insist that you leave here before they move him." He cleared his throat. "It won't be pleasant, and it isn't appropriate for you to be here." He hesitated. "It was never appropriate."

Something in the tone of his voice finally connected with Lauryn, and she looked straight at him.

"Appropriate?" She repeated the word as if she didn't understand the meaning.

"If the captain finds out you knew he was here, Lauryn . . . he'll consider you just as guilty for helping him to stow away." Edward spoke quietly and firmly. "You must go . . . now."

He put out his hand to guide her away, but she recoiled slightly and took a step backward. Then she hesitated.

"He didn't do anything wrong. I know he didn't." Her eyes began to fill with tears again, and she shook her head. "He said we were of . . . one heart. One Irish heart."

* * *

Dr. Appleby stood silently with his hand on the man's wrist while Edward waited behind him.

"I think he'll pull through." The doctor nodded. "Plenty of fluid will make a difference. I doubt he's drunk much for a long time." He glanced back at Edward and shook his head. "He's a hardy beggar." He pointed to a deep wound on the man's leg, where the blood had congealed on the trouser fabric around it. "It looks like one of the sailors got him with a prod when they were searching for stowaways, but he must have kept quiet . . . somehow."

"He's kept quiet for a long time." Edward shook his head. "But he can speak . . ." He stopped before he mentioned Lauryn, but the doctor noticed his hesitation.

"So he spoke before he passed out?"

"Ah . . . so Albie said," Edward answered cautiously. Of any of the people on board ship, Dr. Appleby could be trusted with his concerns. "Actually, Doctor . . . Albie wasn't the one who found him. It was Lauryn."

"Lauryn?" Dr. Appleby looked genuinely surprised. "How on earth did Lauryn find him? Didn't you say he was down in the hold?"

"He was." Edward hesitated. "I don't know how she knew he was there, but Albie . . . found them." He swallowed and nodded toward the man on the infirmary table. "Lauryn thought he was dead and . . . well, she was devastated."

"Devastated?" The doctor frowned. "That doesn't make sense. I mean . . . she must have been upset upon finding what she thought was a body, but . . . why was she down there in the first place?"

Edward took a moment to respond, then he pushed his hands into his pockets. "I get the feeling she knows him." He tilted his head to the side and studied the doctor's face. "She said that they were of one heart . . . one Irish heart."

"One heart?" Dr. Appleby stared at the man then back at Edward.

"One Irish heart," Edward repeated slowly as he turned away. "At least we know he's Irish." He began to walk toward the door, then he hesitated. "I'll bring some clothes down and help you clean him up. He'll stand a better chance before the captain if he looks presentable."

"You want him to have a better chance?" Dr. Appleby raised one eyebrow.

"I believe Lauryn wants him to."

Chapter Twenty-One

Atlantic Ocean, Off Africa, 1849
The Trial

"Miss Kelly!" Fiona let go of her mother's hand and ran forward to Lauryn's side as they walked along the deck. "Miss Kelly . . . I missed you. Are you well enough now?"

Lauryn stopped as Fiona took hold of her hand. Under the strict instructions of Lady Farnsworth, she had stayed in her cabin for the last two days, so she hadn't seen the children for nearly three.

"Fiona." She swung the little girl's hand gently. "I missed you too."

"And are you well now, Lauryn?" Bess McAlister arrived by her daughter's side with Jimmy.

"I'm fine, Bess. Thank you." Lauryn smiled. "And thank you for taking over the classes for me. When Mam said you were teaching . . ." She hesitated. "I was very grateful."

"Oh, it was a pleasure." Bess laughed as she glanced at her children. "At least it was for me. I don't know about Jimmy and Fiona."

"Och, you were fine, Mam," Jimmy responded immediately. "Although I did like it when Edward taught us about the stars."

"And the weather," Fiona added. "And his sheep."

"Edward?" Lauryn glanced at Jimmy. "Sheep?"

"Aye, he took over some of the classes as well." Jimmy folded his arms. "Although . . . I had to help him a bit."

"Jimmy had to pretend he was a farmer looking after sheep." Fiona swung Lauryn's hand. "Just like Edward did when he was his age."

"Aye . . . I think I might like to be a farmer." Jimmy nodded. "Edward says he will be again someday, so maybe I could help him."

"I see." Lauryn hesitated, trying to grasp both the idea of Edward teaching and the notion of him being a farmer. For the last two days she had resolutely refused to let herself think about him at all—especially the look on his face when he'd seen her down in the hold.

"Did you know there's going to be a stowaway at roll call this morning, Miss Kelly?" Fiona was a mine of information. "He stayed hidden for days amongst the rats, but then he nearly died."

Lauryn glanced quickly at Bess, who nodded.

"While you've been ill there's been such a commotion about a stowaway they found in the hold. Ewen said he nearly died, but he's all right now—though the captain has called for him to appear for trial at roll call this morning."

"Trial?" Lauryn's voice caught in her throat.

"Aye, Dad said the captain will punish him well enough for sneaking on board." Jimmy looked serious. "Although my dad says he's already nearly paid the price."

Lauryn fumbled for composure as she realized that there were now a good number of people milling around them as they walked quickly to the roll call area on the deck. She heard the word *stowaway* on several people's lips.

She didn't speak again as they walked with the crowd, and even when they stopped she avoided looking at anyone in particular, especially when Lady Farnsworth beckoned to her from a seat near the front of the crowd. The lady persisted, and several people turned to stare as Lauryn tried to blend into the crowd.

"I think Francis has saved a seat for you."

Lauryn started as she heard Edward's quiet voice behind her. She hadn't seen him for several days, and her heart pounded in response. "I think she's saved one for you, as well."

It might have simply been the movement of the crowd, but Lauryn felt as if she were being propelled forward as the crowd seemed to open in front of her.

"I thought it might be a long meeting this morning." Lady Farnsworth patted the seat beside her and smiled happily. "I didn't think you should be on your feet too long."

Lauryn attempted a smile as she sat down and felt a sense of relief as Edward moved to the other side of Lady Farnsworth and took his seat. Though she kept facing forward, Lauryn could see him out of the corner of her eye. He was busy leaning down to listen to something Lady Farnsworth was saying.

"Good morning, everybody!" Dr. Appleby made his way to his usual place at the front of the group. "A slight change in procedure this morning."

He paused and took a deep breath then finished quietly. "As you are all probably aware, Captain Bayliss has . . . some issues he wishes to discuss."

The very fact that Captain Bayliss was actually in attendance was cause for murmuring, but it was the slight flurry of activity to the right that drew most of the crowd's attention away from the captain's portly figure.

"Oh, my word . . ."

"It's the stowaway."

"He don't look like no stowaway . . ."

Lauryn heard the murmuring around her before she finally gathered the courage to look up. When she did, she had to stifle the gasp that rose in her throat.

The thick black beard was gone completely, and the matted hair had been washed and pulled back into a long ponytail, revealing high cheekbones that, though gaunt, emphasized thick, dark eyebrows and brown eyes that stared straight ahead. Even the man's lean frame emphasized the breadth of his shoulders beneath a full white shirt that lay open at the throat.

Lauryn felt her breath catch in her throat.

"Well, 'e can stowaway in my quarters anytime." A woman's voice broke the silence behind Lauryn, and a ripple of laughter ran through the crowd.

Two sailors escorted Connor as he was walked forward to stand beside the captain, just a few feet in front of Lauryn.

Out of the corner of her eye, Lauryn could see that Edward was watching her closely. His gaze flicked to the Irishman for a moment, and then he turned his gaze beyond the ship.

Captain Bayliss took his time looking the man up and down, then he cleared his throat and thrust his thumbs behind his jacket lapels.

"This morning . . ." His voice boomed then cracked, and he cleared his throat. "This morning we stand in judgment of this man, who has violated the standards of this ship, a common thief who has attempted to hide away to avoid paying the fare that many of you have given your life savings for." He hesitated but didn't get any reaction. "Therefore, it is my duty to impose a punishment on this decrepit individual. Death will seem to have been a better option by the time he finishes paying his dues." Captain Bayliss paused again, waiting for his words to have an effect, but most of the crowd were watching the prisoner rather than listening to him. He cleared his throat again.

"As captain, I feel bound to not only punish him but to brand him as befitting his crime." He nodded at one of the sailors to his left, and the man walked forward holding a long iron. This time many in the crowd did gasp as another sailor produced a small brazier filled with hot coals.

"He's really going to brand him!" One of the cabin class woman passengers swooned slightly against her husband's shoulder.

"Quite rightly, too." Mr. Pilcher, the self-professed preacher, rose from his seat. "The punishment befitting the crime."

Lauryn sat rigidly as the crowd began to debate the matter, and the color drained from her cheeks as the iron hissed on contact with the hot coals. It was a familiar sound from her days spent watching her father in the blacksmith's workshop, but she swallowed hard as she suddenly relived the searing heat of the coals on her own leg. Her hand involuntarily slipped to the side of her leg, and she closed her eyes as she felt the scar beneath the folds of her dress.

Lauryn felt the seat move as Lady Farnsworth suddenly rose beside her. "I think this is absolutely ridiculous and barbaric behavior!" Her voice rose well above the crowd's noise, which stopped almost immediately as she moved toward the captain, precisely unbuttoning her glove as she walked. "Captain Bayliss, I am a mere woman, but in this instance I must object to this action." She stopped in front of the Irishman and looked him up and down. Her expression was severe as she then turned and surveyed the crowd. "The shipping company has exacted some form of payment from most of us in exchange for being carried across to the other side of the world. Some have paid more, some less, depending on their circumstance, and we have been assigned appropriate accommodation in accordance with our payment." She looked at the section where most of the passengers from steerage were gathered. "This man may have not paid, but he hasn't had anything in return either. Some of you have not had to pay because you have assisted passage, but you have at least had a compartment. This man has had nothing." She turned to the cabin-class passengers and looked pointedly at Mr. Pilcher.

"Mr. Pilcher, you rehearsed so eloquently, and at great length, in your sermon about the mercy of the Lord and how we have such great need for the righteous to demonstrate that mercy and follow His divine example and yet . . ." She shook her head as if in pity. "Yet you would demand something as barbaric as branding someone who has only the same desires as yourself . . . to forge a new life in a new land."

"But . . ." Mr. Pilcher raised his hand to protest, but his wife pulled it back down.

Lady Farnsworth stared at him for a moment, then she turned to the captain and held out her arm.

"If you feel to brand this man for surviving in subhuman conditions, then you must brand me as well, Captain, for you have literally stowed me away in conditions far below what I am accustomed to."

There was a moment's silence, then someone called out a single word. "Aye!"

In an instant the crowd was shouting, and the tone was not lost on Captain Bayliss. He looked at Lady Farnsworth for a long moment, then he turned and shook his head at the sailors holding the iron and brazier. He glanced at the Irishman, then he held up one hand.

"I'm nothing if not a fair man." He coughed. "I shall forego the branding, but . . ." He looked around the crowd then back at his prisoner. "This man will be assigned to clean the privies and any manner of lowly chore as befitting his status, and he shall sleep on the floor . . . where he belongs. And he may not converse with anyone for . . . seven days. It will be as if he doesn't exist!" He fairly spat the last few words, then he slowly looked Connor up and down. "And when we reach port in New Zealand, he will go before the local judiciary and be tried as the common criminal that he is." Bayliss gave the crowd one last glance before he turned and marched toward his quarters.

The crowd stood silently for a moment, then Dr. Appleby moved quickly forward and undid the rope around Connor's wrists. There was a cheer from many of the passengers, but the Irishman stood still as he rubbed his wrists, his gaze directed straight at Lady Farnsworth. He looked at her for a long moment, then he raised one hand to his forehead in a slow salute and bowed slightly from the waist. Not a word was spoken as she acknowledged him with a slight smile. Then she put her glove back on and turned to Lauryn.

"My dear . . . I think we need a good breakfast, don't you?"

* * *

FOR A FEW DAYS THE silent Irishman was a novelty amongst the passengers, especially in steerage, where he spent most of his time. It appeared that he was complying completely with the captain's instructions and didn't engage in any conversation, although many tried to joke him out of it. At night he made his bed on the floor close to the McAlister family.

"He plays the tin whistle just like you do, Miss Kelly," Fiona said as she rushed to class the first morning after the trial. "He sat on the floor on his blanket and played the softest wee tune." She began to rock slowly from side to side. "My mam said it reminded her of mist falling on the heather in the Highlands."

"The ship seems a lot quieter around him." Jimmy chuckled. "He won't speak, so a lot of the children see how long they can go without speaking either. They want to beat him."

"But they can't because he's so good at it." Fiona nodded her head then frowned. "Do you think he can talk?"

"Oh, I think he can." Lauryn folded her hands in her lap as she sat down. "I think he's trying to show the captain that he's an honest person. He was told not to talk, and so he's not going to." She hesitated then added softly, "Do you think you could trust a person like that?"

"Aye." Jimmy nodded. "My dad says that a man is as good as his word."

Lauryn nodded. "That's right, Jimmy. That he is."

* * *

"THAT WAS QUITE A SPEECH yesterday." Edward fell into step beside Lady Farnsworth as she strolled along the deck. "You would do very well in a court of law."

"Tchh . . . leave that to those pompous lawyers." Lady Farnsworth smiled but nodded her head in acknowledgment. "At least the boy is unscarred and will have a degree of freedom for the rest of the journey." She fanned her face she glanced sideways at Edward. "He certainly scrubbed up well for the trial. It was very good of someone to find clothes for him, for they definitely won him the favor of the crowd, if not Captain Bayliss."

"I think Bayliss was enjoying the whole process until you burst his bubble." Edward nodded. "I hate to think what he would have done if you hadn't spoken up." He looked straight ahead. "It was a lesson to me. I should have spoken up sooner."

Lady Farnsworth nodded.

"Perhaps . . . or perhaps you'd already done enough. I recognized the shirt he was wearing."

"Possibly." Edward hesitated, then he shook his head. "Or perhaps I wasn't sure how much I wanted to intervene."

"Because of Lauryn?" Lady Farnsworth stopped and turned toward the deck railing, and Edward automatically stopped by her side. "You obviously sense some sort of connection between the two of them."

"You obviously do as well." He knew she was baiting him, and he considered for a moment as he leaned his elbows on the railing. "Has Lauryn mentioned anything about him . . . since the trial?"

"Only that she was pleased that the captain had been lenient with Connor." Lady Farnsworth glanced at Edward, and he looked up quickly. "Exactly. I never heard a name mentioned at the trial, did you? And yet she said his name quite naturally . . . without thinking. But it's what she said before the trial that causes me concern." She shook her head. "I mentioned the other day how she was having difficulty sleeping and that she was calling out names and crying." She paused. "Connor was one of the names I heard most frequently."

Edward took a moment to respond. "Meaning?"

"Meaning that I think she knew the man before she saw him at the trial." Lady Farnsworth nodded knowingly. "I think he's part of her past."

Edward frowned, then he leaned back and gripped the rail. "Lauryn was down in the hold with him when I found him."

"With him?" Lady Farnsworth stared at him, then she turned to look out at the ocean. "So she does know him."

"It appears that way, though for how long I really have no idea." Edward shrugged. "She was very upset when she thought he was dead, and then she said that they were 'of one heart.'"

"One heart? But . . ." She frowned.

Edward nodded. "I am completely at a loss as to what it all means. I would love to find out, but I don't feel that I have the right to ask Lauryn, and as for . . . Connor . . ." He looked up at the sky. "I don't know that I want to ask."

"Well, then, it must be up to me." Lady Farnsworth tapped her fan decisively against the palm of her hand. "I may have stood up for the man because I didn't want to see him ill-treated, but that's where my obligation to him ended. My duty is to safeguard Lauryn." She straightened her shoulders. "And that means I need to talk to her immediately."

"And if she chooses not to say anything?"

"Oh, she will." Lady Farnsworth smiled then frowned. "At least, I hope so." She straightened the front of her gown as if preparing for battle. "I will sort this out, Edward, and then we can get back to normal."

She didn't wait for a response as she left, but he watched her determined walk with a slight frown.

"I hope you can, too, Francis. I really hope you can."

* * *

"Miss Kelly!" Fiona tapped Lauryn on the arm, and Lauryn started and looked around quickly. She had retreated to a quiet space on the deck in between classes, and the gentle movement of the ship had momentarily lulled her to sleep. "Miss Kelly . . . look at what Jimmy has!"

Jimmy stood behind his sister, proudly displaying a piece of paper with one word written on it.

"I asked him to write his name, seeing as he wouldn't say it." He held out the piece of paper with the name "Connor" written in bold irregular letters. "'Tis Connor." He tapped the paper. "He would not write anything more, but he wouldn't write it for anyone else either."

Lauryn looked at the handwriting then back at Jimmy and Fiona, smiling at the satisfaction she saw in their eyes over the one-word scrawl.

"I think he could do with help with his letters." She attempted to joke gently, but Fiona shook her head so that her red braids swung.

"Connor may not write well, but he does many other good things."

"Aye." Jimmy folded the piece of paper and put it in his pocket. "He helped us clean all of the bunks on our side of the cabin, and when the others complained—"

"He helped them too," Fiona finished for him.

"And last night some of the babies were crying, and he played his whistle for them and they stopped." Jimmy mimicked the whistle playing.

"And then he kept playing, and the children were all dancing."

"Are you two telling more stowaway stories?" Bess walked up behind her children and put her hands on both their shoulders. "I'm sure Miss Kelly has heard enough of them by now."

Lauryn nodded as she moved over to make room on the seat. "I do get to hear a lot of stowaway stories, and not just from Jimmy and Fiona. It seems the Irishman has won a few friends among the children."

Bess smiled as she sat down, her hands resting on top of her bulging stomach.

"And their parents," Bess noted. "He can keep them entertained for hours just with that whistle. And because he mimes anything he wants to say, the children actually listen more . . . and then they do what he asks!" She shook her head. "It's wonderful to watch, and between having you for their teacher and the Irishman down in the cabin, the journey is actually becoming quite restful."

Lauryn half listened as Fiona recounted another story, but she was concentrating more on Bess and the delighted way she watched her daughter, her eyes wide, as if she were hearing the story for the first time and her mouth half open, ready to smile or laugh in response. It seemed that the Scottish woman was always serene somehow, as if she knew exactly what her purpose was as a mother and as a wife, and she delighted in it.

"Bess." Lauryn leaned forward. "Do you mind if I ask the children to do an errand for me?"

"Of course. They'd love to." Bess motioned to the children, and they both jumped up.

"Could you please find Mr. Morgan and ask if he's going to be at class today?" Lauryn thought quickly. "And then make sure that our class area is tidy . . . and that my books are on my seat." She picked up two volumes from beside her and handed them to Jimmy. "And could you stay and make sure nobody moves these? Thank you, children."

Bess watched with a slight smile on her lips as her children walked off quickly, then she turned to Lauryn.

"And what have my bairns been doing that you need to talk to me privately?" She put her head to one side. "Has Jimmy been acting beyond his years?"

"Oh no." Lauryn shook her head, slightly taken aback by Bess's direct approach. Had it been that obvious that she wanted to remove the children? "I . . . I did want to talk to you, but not about the children."

Bess nodded as she studied Lauryn's face, then she simply waited as Lauryn stared up at a blue sky almost devoid of clouds.

"Bess . . . do you ever have dreams . . . or nightmares?" She looked down at her hands in her lap. "Not just ordinary dreams, but ones where you feel like you're actually in them and that the people . . . It's like they're part of you, and you can feel their joy and their . . . pain?"

"Aye." Bess nodded solemnly without hesitating. "I know what you mean . . . and I have." She glanced at Lauryn. "Are you being troubled?"

It was such a simple question, but Lauryn felt as if a load had been lifted off her shoulders as she nodded then thought carefully before she spoke.

"Bess . . . I knew the Irish stowaway was on board." She heard Bess gasp slightly, but she kept going. "I saw him . . . when Edward took us down to the hold, but he asked me to keep it a secret . . . and I did." She took a deep breath. "It all happened so quickly, and it was the hardest thing not to tell Mam . . . or Edward . . . but somehow, because I knew he was Irish and he was in trouble, it was like he was all of my childhood rolled into one person, and I had to be loyal to him . . . to keep him safe." She put her hand to her face and felt the heat of her cheeks. "Does that make sense?"

"Of course it does," Bess responded quietly and patted Lauryn's arm. "It's loyalty . . . to the past. I still feel it for Scotland. For the Highlands."

Lauryn closed her eyes. "But, Bess . . . the dreams . . . the nightmares . . . they started happening that night, and it was always the same. I would see Connor's face—"

"Connor? The stowaway?" Bess frowned.

"His face would be all dark and dirty, and then it would disappear and I'd see my family . . . my parents and my sisters and sometimes my cousins, and they were in pain or starving and helpless, and sometimes . . ." She hesitated, feeling the pain afresh, then she straightened her shoulders. "Sometimes it was terrible things that had happened to me when I was young, and I was terrified, but . . . but then almost straightaway there were peaceful moments, and the dark face became much lighter and clearer, and instead of confusion there were lots of people. Some people I knew, but others . . . I have no idea except that they felt familiar." She glanced at Bess and shrugged. "And then it would stop, but I would feel like I wanted to stay in the dream. I wanted to stay with all of them and not wake up."

There were tears in Bess's eyes as she put an arm around Lauryn's shoulders and gave her a tight hug. Then the two women sat silently for some time.

"I don't know why I told you all that, Bess." Lauryn gave a short laugh. "But somehow I thought you'd understand . . . or help me understand." She put her face in her hands. "Why did it all start with Connor?"

"He made you remember." Bess didn't hesitate, and Lauryn slowly turned to look at her sideways.

"I didn't think I'd forgotten." She spoke quietly, and Bess nodded.

"I've had dreams sometimes . . . many times . . . of my wee girls." She smiled at Lauryn's puzzled expression. "Ewen and I lost two daughters before Jimmy and Fiona were born, and I would often dream of them reaching out to me. I'd be trying to reach them as well . . ." She paused. "Sometimes I'd get to them, and then I didn't want to come back."

Lauryn nodded as she recognized the longing tone in Bess's voice. "Do you still dream about them?"

"Not as often." Bess smiled. "Not since I found out for certain that I'll be with them again . . . sometime. It was the not knowing that made the dreams painful." She put her hand on her stomach as the baby inside her moved. "Now I know that one day our Father in Heaven will allow us to be together as a family . . . forever."

"You *know* that?" Lauryn stared at Bess, and she could almost feel her contentment as she nodded.

"Aye, Lauryn . . . I know it. I asked the Lord, and His answer came through Jesus Christ and the restored gospel." She rested her hand over Lauryn's. "One day, you'll know it too."

Lauryn sat for a moment, trying to comprehend what Bess was saying.

"It may not make sense now, Lauryn," Bess continued softly. "But your dreams took you from dark to light, and the light was where you felt peace. One day you'll recognize that peace."

"But . . ." Lauryn began to protest, then she shook her head. "I think I see what you're saying, Bess, and I can understand now why the nightmares started with finding Connor, but . . ." She frowned. "I only knew Connor as a dark figure in the shadows. I didn't even really see what he looked like and yet . . ." She hesitated. "In my dream, when the face got lighter and almost seemed to glow . . . it was Connor's face. I didn't know that at first, but I recognized him when he was all cleaned up." She shook her head. "Why was it Connor?"

Bess watched her carefully, then she shook her head slowly. "Why was it Connor . . . and not Edward?" Lauryn's shoulders stiffened, and Bess continued gently. "I can't answer that, Lauryn. All I know is that the Lord talks to us through our dreams, but often He gives us people right beside us to help them come true."

Lauryn sat very still, then she wiped at the tears that began to gather in her eyes. "Edward *is* in my dream, Bess." Her voice was almost a whisper. "The dream stops . . . when he stops me from leaving."

Chapter Twenty-Two

Atlantic Ocean, Off Africa, 1849
The Scourge

WHILE MOST PEOPLE WERE HAVING breakfast, a Mrs. Bridges in steerage class began complaining of severe stomach cramps. Soon after, her body began purging at such a rate that she could not leave her bed.

When one of her young children began showing the same symptoms, the news traveled like the plague itself. Edward was with Dr. Appleby when Mr. Bridges rushed on deck, his face red with panic and screaming that his wife was dying and that his child was nearly there as well.

The doctor looked at Edward then spoke quietly to the man sobbing beside him. "Tell me quickly what has happened . . . so I can bring a treatment."

"She's been purgin' . . . can't stop, and now her face be turnin' blue and the young'un's the same." The man gasped. "I thought she were jus' seasick."

Dr. Appleby's brow furrowed deeply as he stared at the man then at Edward.

"I believe we have a problem." He said the words calmly, but Edward saw the fear in his face.

"Cholera?" He had a sudden vision of Lizzy, and his heart sank as the doctor nodded.

"You're familiar with it?"

"My wife died of it." Edward steeled his jaw. "Just tell me what to do."

They were already moving together as the doctor pointed toward the end of the deck. "We'll need to set up an isolation tent and keep everyone well away . . . keep people confined to cabins where possible." He turned toward the infirmary then hesitated as he banged his fist against the door.

By the end of the day, three more people had the symptoms, and by noon the next day, another four—including two of the first three—had already died. One woman lingered, but their attempts to rid her of the disease only caused her to linger longer than the others. By evening she too had succumbed, and her body was cast overboard like the others.

With the danger of contagion, the captain had insisted that bodies be disposed of immediately and so, in lieu of a funeral, the barest of words were spoken about the person, for the sake of their family. And then, as the family turned away, the sailors quickly disposed of the corpse over the side of the ship. It seemed heartless, but everyone recognized the need to cleanse the ship as quickly as possible, so little was said, and those in mourning lapsed into a grim silence.

Edward took a moment to lean against the deck railing as he watched three crew members slide the latest body off the back of the ship. The speed at which the sickness was spreading was hard to fathom, and he felt the terror of it closing in around everyone on board. At times, when he stopped, thoughts of Lizzy would creep into his mind, and then he would drive himself on, cleaning up and moving people and generally trying to make it easier for the doctor to function. He noticed that most of the time Connor worked silently near him. They would acknowledge one another's efforts as a grim smile passed between them—two strangers united by the scourge of sickness. It seemed to Edward that there was no need for the Irishman to maintain his silence any longer, but he chose to do so anyway, using his silence to observe people, and as a result he was always among the first to see the need for help . . . and to offer it.

"Edward . . . have you eaten?" He heard Lauryn's voice behind him, and he turned slowly to see her tentatively holding out a cup of broth and a biscuit. He had hardly spoken to her since the day of Connor's trial, their only contact an occasional nod at the beginning and end of class before they went their separate ways. Several times he had determined to speak with her, but she had remained elusive, and since the cholera had struck he had confined himself to his room when not helping the doctor.

Now he could see the concern on her face, and he felt a sudden rush of gratitude that she would think of his needs. Somehow the simple act of her bringing him something to eat stood as a peace offering of sorts, and he was anxious to accept it.

"No . . . no, I haven't. Not for a while." He took the cup and tried to bite into the biscuit, making several attempts before he managed to break off a piece.

"'Tis better to dunk," Lauryn murmured, and she smiled as he took her advice. "Um . . . what news do you have?"

"Nothing good . . . another three have the symptoms. All in steerage." He shook his head. "It'll be a miracle if a soul survives from down there . . ."

"Then are the McAlisters all right?" Lauryn put her hand to her mouth. "Should I bring them up here?"

"No . . . we can't." Edward shook his head. "We must concentrate our efforts on containing the outbreak, and I've seen to it that the area around their bunks is clean, which will be the best thing to keep it at bay." He ran a hand through his hair then and looked directly at her.

"Lauryn . . . I want you to promise me that you'll stay in your cabin as much as you can." He swallowed hard, and suddenly it was if the difficult weeks between them had never happened. "I could not bear to lose you, too."

She barely had time to nod before he was gone, striding along the deck toward the stairwell to steerage and out of sight.

"I could not bear to lose you, either, Edward."

* * *

Bess held Fiona close to her and put a hand over the girl's ear as another scream echoed through steerage. It was closely followed by wild sobbing and cursing, and Bess knew without looking past the curtain hanging at the end of their bunk the process that was now taking place.

Dr. Appleby would be there, his face ashen gray, as he helped Edward and whoever would assist them to pull the body from the bunk and carry it upstairs wrapped in the blanket the person had died under.

Bess rocked slowly as Fiona cried, a quiet whimper that had become as much a part of the process as the screams and cursing.

"Are you well, Bess?" Ewen pulled back the curtain a fraction.

"Aye." She smiled at him and lifted her hand to stroke his face, then she grimaced slightly. "I don't think the baby's too happy, though . . . sitting in here all day all cramped up." She looked at him pleadingly. "Do you think we could have just a wee walk up on the deck?"

She watched him look back along the compartment, then he nodded. "We'll go aft . . . it's very dark, and not many people will be about." He helped her out of the narrow opening, and Fiona scrambled out behind them. Ewen tapped on the outside of the top bunk and Jimmy's head appeared straightaway. "We're just going upstairs . . . hurry."

They walked quickly, and soon they were standing on the deck with only the rays from a few lamps shedding light around them. Overhead, the sky seemed thick black, but the stars were like a bright carpet.

"Oh, they're like little jewels." Fiona stared upward then reached for her mother's hand. "Don't you wish you could hold them?" She frowned. "I wonder what they feel like to hold."

"You can't hold stars, Fiona. They're too big," Jimmy responded practically, but he kept looking as well.

"You can wish upon a star." Bess closed her eyes and thought for a moment as Ewen drew her closer.

"Isn't it meant to be a shooting star that you wish on?" He leaned down and kissed her forehead as it rested pale against his shoulder.

"I can wish on any star I want." Bess smiled. "Mothers are allowed to."

They stood for a while before one of the crew called behind them, "Everybody down! 'Tis past ten."

Ewen breathed deeply as he shook his head then ushered them all back to the stairs. However, near the bottom stair, Bess suddenly doubled up with a little cry.

"Ewen . . . the baby!"

It was Jimmy who ran for Dr. Appleby, finding both him and Edward in the infirmary.

"Doctor . . . Edward . . . my mam's having the baby! Father said to come quick!"

Neither man hesitated as the doctor reached for his bag and he and Edward ran along the deck. Down the stairs they could hear deep moans coming from the McAlister bunks, where Fiona stared wide-eyed from the top bunk while Ewen knelt on the floor trying to calm his wife. He looked up as the doctor sank to his knees beside him.

"The pains started a while back. I took her for a walk up top, but now they've gotten worse." He shook his head. "The babe's not due for another three months."

Dr. Appleby reached into the bunk and laid his hand on Bess's stomach. She moaned again, and he felt her body convulse. Then there was an overwhelming stench. He hung his head and tried to control his expression as he turned to Ewen and Edward. "I think you should take the children up to Lauryn's cabin."

Ewen refused to leave, and so it was Edward who took the children to the forecabin, a hand on each child's shoulder until he knocked on Lauryn's cabin door. He simply stood there as she opened the door and looked at them all, the question in her eyes.

"My mam's having the baby." Fiona looked up. "But it's too early."

Lauryn's breath came in a gasp, then she quickly gathered both of the children to her and nodded to Edward as he motioned toward his cabin.

"You're welcome to stay with them there, so you don't disturb Francis."

She nodded again and began to move them into the passageway as Edward turned away.

"I'll be back in the morning."

* * *

EWEN WAS STILL ON HIS knees talking softly to Bess as he smoothed her forehead. He stayed that way for the next two hours while Dr. Appleby tried to help her in some way. He gave her opium for the pain, but the purging only intensified. After five hours the baby delivered, but Bess was beyond knowing as she writhed and fought to breathe.

Edward watched the doctor's hands shaking as he cut the cord and the tears ran unchecked down his face as he placed the tiny infant in the crook of her father's arm.

"She's breathing, Ewen . . . I don't know how, but she is." His voice shook. "Will you name her?"

Ewen stared at the wee girl then at his wife, and Edward could hardly hear the words as he laid his cheek against his child's.

"She'll be Bessie McAlister. . . the same as her mam."

Edward watched as he gently laid the child beside her mother, who suddenly became calm. The writhing stopped and her breathing eased almost as the baby's chest stopped rising and falling. Bess's eyelids quivered, then she looked directly at her husband.

"I'll be seeing my girls then, Ewen."

"Aye, Bess . . . they'll be waitin' for ye in heaven."

He didn't cry when her eyes closed, but he calmly folded her arms around the baby and straightened her hair. He tucked the blanket around the two of them then looked up at Edward. "I'd like the bairns to say good-bye to their mam."

"But . . ." Dr. Appleby hesitated, but Edward laid his hand on his friend's shoulder.

"I'll get them now."

Lauryn opened the door when he knocked and had only to look into his eyes to know what had happened. She bit on her lip as the tears began to fall, and he wrapped his arms tightly around her.

"Ewen wants the children to say good-bye to Bess," he whispered over her head.

"I'll take them now."

They woke the children, and neither one asked any questions as they walked with Edward down to their bunks. Ewen stood up slowly as they reached him, and only then did Fiona start sobbing, wrapping her arms around her father and refusing to look at the bed where her mother lay.

Edward kept his hands on Jimmy's shoulders, but the boy pulled away and knelt down by his mother. He simply stared for a moment, then he gently kissed her forehead. Only then did he notice the tiny baby, and he turned to his father.

"A wee girl, Jimmy. We'll call her Bessie." Ewen's voice caught, and he stared up at the ceiling.

"Bessie," Jimmy whispered as he reached out and touched the tiny cheek. Then he turned and gave Fiona's dress a gentle tug. "Fiona, you need to say good-bye to Mam and wee Bessie."

Her sobbing seemed to stop instantly, and Jimmy moved to the side as Fiona knelt beside him. She stared at her mother for a moment, then she too bent and kissed her head.

"Oh, Mam . . . I'll miss you." She began to cry again, then she took a deep breath and looked up at her father. "We need to say a prayer so Mam and Bessie can go straight to Heavenly Father and the girls."

"Aye, Fiona." There was no hesitation as Ewen sank to his knees beside his children and wife and took hold of Fiona's hand. Then the only sound was the deep Scottish voice asking for a safe journey for all of them until they would be together again.

* * *

"Are you all right, Lauryn Kelly?"

She knew, without looking up, that it was Connor speaking, and she felt no surprise as she shook her head without answering. She'd somehow known he would come.

"It's a bitter thing to lose a friend." His voice was gentle with a soft, familiar lilt, and for a moment it was as if she were sitting close beside her father with the peat fire burning in the small cottage while her mother made fresh bread.

"She was a wonderful woman," Lauryn managed to speak into her handkerchief. "She should not have been allowed to die when others deserve to."

"But we're not the ones who decide that." His tone was even but firm. "She said that the other night."

"Bess did?" Lauryn looked up for the first time and stared at his dark silhouette as the setting sun shone directly behind him.

"I made my bed close to their bunk of late, and they've included me in their time together . . . and their prayers. She was telling the children that no one knew when their time would be up, but that they had to be grateful because they knew where they were going and that they'd be together." He stopped as Lauryn closed her eyes.

"As a family . . . forever." Her voice was a whisper as she remembered Bess's words. "Did she say that?"

"Yes, she did." Connor moved so that she could see his face, and for the second time Lauryn found herself looking straight at him, feeling as if their conversation flowed on from a myriad of yesterdays.

"Do you think she knew she was going to die?" Lauryn asked quietly.

"I think she was prepared to die . . . under the circumstances." His tone was even. "I don't think she was scared."

"She said that she knew where she was going . . . that she'd asked the Lord." Lauryn bit at her bottom lip to keep control.

"She told me that I had to ask the Lord." She could hear the smile in his voice. "She said that I needed to."

"She told me that I would know one day . . . just like her." Lauryn smiled as well, imagining Bess's firm but kindly tone.

"Since when did the Irish ever listen to a Scot?" Connor knelt down in front of her, his elbow resting on his leg.

"Since when did the Irish listen to anyone?" Lauryn countered, and he grinned the wide smile that felt so familiar.

"Maybe the Irish should listen to each other." He paused as he looked at her. "I've never thanked you for helping me, Lauryn Kelly."

"You didn't have to." A slight frown creased her forehead. "I nearly let you down."

"You could never have done that." Connor shook his head. "Between you and your friends, you literally saved my skin."

"My friends?" Lauryn looked puzzled. "Oh . . . Lady Farnsworth!"

"Lady Farnsworth . . . and Edward Morgan." Connor made to walk away but stopped as he saw the confused expression on her face.

"Edward?"

"Yes . . . Dr. Appleby told me that Edward had looked after me and given me new clothes."

"Edward?" Lauryn repeated as she stared toward the forecabins. "He did that?"

"Yes, he did," Connor said quietly. "He's a good man . . . even though he's not Irish."

They were quiet for a moment, then he reached back into his trouser pocket. "I've been waiting to give this back to you. I've not known the right time to do so . . . or whether I should." He held out the small pewter flask that Lauryn had taken him water in. "It's been easier to stay below deck."

She slowly reached out her hand, and he placed the flask in it, their fingers touching briefly, then he closed his other hand over hers. It felt warm against the cold of the pewter, and she looked up, a question in her eyes as she studied his face.

"I don't know, either, Lauryn Kelly." He smiled then, and she felt a load lift from her heart. "I only knew I could trust you as soon as I heard your voice down in the hold."

She nodded. "And I knew I had to help you. As soon as you said . . . 'one heart' . . ." She faltered. "What made you say that?" She pulled her hand from his and placed it against her heart, then held up one finger, imitating his action.

"It's what I felt," Connor answered quietly. "Somehow, I knew you'd know . . . the whistle . . . the heart."

Lauryn nodded again, then she smiled as tears brimmed in her eyes. "'Tis what my father said to me when I left Ireland. He told me that we would always be . . . of one heart." Her voice broke, and she felt his arm tight around her shoulders as more tears came. "Wherever I was . . . to remember we were of one heart."

"Then your father is a wise man, Lauryn Kelly," Connor spoke gently as she cried quietly against his chest. Then she felt his hand against her cheek, and the lightest kiss brushed her brow.

* * *

LAURYN TOOK HER TIME WALKING back to the cabin, and as she let herself in, Lady Farnsworth looked up immediately, concern evident on her face as she rose from sitting on her bunk. Neither woman spoke as Lauryn turned but kept her back to the door, her gaze directed at the small bedside table. She lifted her hand and held out the pewter flask. "I took this from you." She walked slowly across the cabin toward Lady Farnsworth. "I haven't been honest with you, and . . . I'm so very sorry." Her voice trembled, and she bit at her lip.

For a long moment Lady Farnsworth simply looked at the flask, then she held out her hand and closed Lauryn's fingers around it.

"You borrowed it . . . and you've had other things on your mind." She smiled. "There's no need to apologize, my dear."

Lauryn shook her head. "No, I must apologize, for I've treated you badly by not being honest with you, and you did nothing to deserve it." She looked up. "Thank you . . . for everything you have done for me . . . ever."

Lady Farnsworth did not hesitate as she held out her arms and drew Lauryn close to her. "Oh, my dear girl . . . what torment have you been going through?"

Lauryn only shook her head as she held the older woman tightly. Then Lady Farnsworth eased her away.

"Do you feel you can talk to me now?" She studied Lauryn's face. "Though I don't wish to pry." She gave a short laugh. "Actually, I'd love to pry more than anything—you know me. I even told Edward that I would to find out what was going on with you."

Lauryn pulled back slightly. "Why did you tell Edward that?"

"Because he was as concerned about you as I was." Lady Farnsworth didn't hesitate. "Very concerned."

Lauryn felt the color rising in her cheeks as she took a step back and put her hand to her forehead. "I . . ." She stopped and frowned. "I feel so confused."

"I get that impression." Lady Farnsworth sat down on the edge of her bunk and patted the space beside her. "Sit down, Lauryn, and let's try and sort things out."

Lauryn slowly sat down. There was something in the tone of her employer's voice that made her take a quick breath.

"Edward told me that you knew the stowaway was there." Lady Farnsworth wasted no time in getting to the point, and this time Lauryn didn't even feel surprised as she nodded. "And he also said that you said you were 'of one heart' with the man." She hesitated. "I'm presuming that meant that you are both Irish."

Lauryn glanced at her then nodded. "He said the very same words that my father said when I left Ireland."

"And that struck a chord." Lady Farnsworth waited as Lauryn nodded again, then she patted her on the knee. "So, it wasn't that you felt any other . . . connection with the man." She paused. "What is his name again?"

Lauryn smiled as she listened to Lady Farnsworth's businesslike tone. It was as if everything that had troubled her was now being neatly placed in order.

"His name is Connor."

"Is that his first name or his last?"

"His only one . . . he said he doesn't have need for any other." Lauryn shrugged while Lady Farnsworth gave a brief snort.

"Connor, then. Is there any other connection?" She repeated the question then waited while Lauryn stared at the ground.

Just a short while ago she had stood in the safety of Connor's arms, his hand on her cheek while she felt his gentle kiss on her forehead. She closed her eyes as the memory brought a warm feeling to her heart.

"Is there, Lauryn?" Lady Farnsworth's voice had lost its businesslike tone, and she spoke very gently then waited until Lauryn slowly shook her head.

"I really don't know, Mam."

Lady Farnsworth sat without speaking for a time then folded her hands in her lap. "Well then, I don't want to be an interfering old woman, but . . . is there any connection . . . with Edward Morgan?"

She waited as Lauryn continued to stare at the floor. When the silence went too long to be comfortable, she sighed. "So, there isn't." She did little to disguise the disappointment in her voice, but then Lauryn shook her head. "So, there is?"

Lauryn nodded very slightly, then she shook her head and buried her face in her hands.

"I don't know," she repeated quietly. "I really don't know."

After a long pause, Lady Farnsworth gave a low chuckle. "I hadn't realized what I missed out on by falling in love with Charles." She smiled as Lauryn looked up. "He was the first man I ever noticed, and I never ever wanted to look at anyone else. It was so simple."

Lauryn studied her for a moment, suddenly wishing with all her heart that her 'mam' could have held onto the love of her life. She sat back and only hesitated slightly before she rested her head against Lady Farnsworth's shoulder. Immediately she felt the lady's head rest against her own, and she felt the comfort of her own mother.

"Do you think it's possible to love two people?" Lauryn stared across the room without seeing.

"Yes, I do." Lady Farnsworth nodded. "But in different ways . . . or at different times."

"Not at the same time?" Lauryn held her breath and was surprised to feel Lady Farnsworth laugh beside her.

"Now that would be greedy, my dear."

"But easier to understand." Lauryn folded her arms across her body and lowered her head. "Right now, I don't understand myself. I loved Bess . . . as a friend, and I miss her dreadfully. I love the children, and I even love Ewen for who he is, and my heart just aches for him . . ." She frowned. "And I . . . love being with Edward. I do know that, but now I also feel . . . something . . . when I'm with Connor." She stopped and looked at her companion. Then she could only shake her head helplessly.

Lady Farnsworth smiled. "And I never even got a mention."

Lauryn looked up quickly, then she put her arms around her. "Oh, Mam . . . you know how I love you."

"Well, good. I'd hate to be forgotten." Lady Farnsworth gave her a tight hug, then she stood up, picked up her fan, and pointed it at Lauryn. "As for your . . . problems, my dear, we have many, many more weeks on board and nowhere to go, so I suggest you treat everybody as a friend. And, as I've said before . . . just be yourself." She was suddenly serious. "I think the children, especially, are going to need you to be that . . . more than anyone else."

Chapter Twenty-Three

Atlantic Ocean, Off Africa, 1849
The Message

EVERY PASSENGER ON BOARD SHIP had known that once they were at sea, there would be no landing and no turning back, and so the endless miles of ocean stretched in front of them with no hope of reprieve from the constant horror of the scourge of cholera. For twelve days it raged amongst crew and passengers with no deference to status or wealth. Eleven souls succumbed and were hastily buried at sea. Seven children were left without a single parent, and four were left with just one.

As one whole day passed without any symptom rearing its head, Dr. Appleby dared to sit in his infirmary and simply wait.

On the second day he ventured back down into steerage, but apart from those in mourning there were no signs of sickness. Still, he went back to the infirmary and waited.

At the end of the third day, he ran a pencil down the passenger list and placed a careful line under the name of each person who had died. He merely noted the cause of death as "disease." When the task was completed, he wandered up on deck and went to the very front, where the wind was strongest against his face and body. There he stood for a full hour, letting the wind do as much as it could to blow away the horrors of the journey.

"Are you seriously thinking of going over?" A voice spoke quietly behind him, and he half turned and smiled as Edward came to stand beside him.

The doctor sighed. "This is my third time on as many ships." He looked back out to the ocean. "This has been the worst."

"And the last," Edward reminded him quietly.

"And the last." Appleby nodded, then he raised his chin to the wind. "The problem is, Edward, I worry too much . . . I care too much. I should be like some of the other physicians who simply take their twenty-five pounds for safely delivering the majority of the passengers, minus a pound or two for those who die, and get off at the other end ready for the next trip. As long as they have a full load of whisky and rum in the infirmary, they can cope with anything." He shook his head. "But I actually care whether they all get there, and it tears me apart when I cannot save a family."

They stood in silence for a long time, then Edward rested his hand on the doctor's shoulder. "If it's any help, I'd like you to know that I've never worked with a man who I've admired more. You did far more than a man should be asked to do, yet I never heard you complain . . . even when they abused you because you couldn't stop it happening."

Dr. Appleby smiled grimly. "It is ironic, isn't it . . . they verbally abuse the only person that might be able to help, then promptly ask for more help." He turned back to the ocean. "Thank you for everything you did, Edward. Your assistance was priceless. And I should say also that I've never had such a supportive person to work beside."

They shook hands firmly then began the walk back to the cabins. As they reached the forecabin, Dr. Appleby hesitated, then he smiled.

"It would please me if you were to call me Michael from now on, Edward. I think we've been through too much to remain on formal terms, and it would be nice to think that I had a friend rather than an acquaintance."

Edward smiled then and nodded as he reached out to shake hands once more.

"I'd be honored, Michael."

* * *

ALL OF THE PASSENGERS ASSEMBLED for the first Sunday sermon after the doctor announced that the ship was most likely free of the cholera scourge. It seemed every soul felt a form of gratitude at still being alive, even though many had bitterly condemned God during the outbreak.

Lady Farnsworth had made sure that they were on deck early, as she wanted to sit near the front. As she settled into her seat, she tapped Lauryn on the knee. "Did I tell you that Mr. McAlister is going to give the sermon today?" She patted her face nervously. "I do hope he's up to it so soon after his wife has died. She was such a dear sweet girl. I only met her a few times, but she was just charming."

Lauryn nodded in agreement but stayed silent. Lady Farnsworth had already informed her several times of the news that Ewen would be speaking, and she too was wondering how he would cope.

"Dr. Appleby said that he wasn't going to ask him, but he kept thinking it would be right, and Mr. McAlister said yes almost right away." Lady Farnsworth shook her head. "I do admire the man."

Just before eleven o'clock, Lauryn felt a hand on her shoulder and looked up to see Edward standing just behind her seat. He raised an eyebrow as he indicated the space beside her, and she nodded, her heart beating faster as she moved aside to make room for him on the bench.

"I was beginning to wonder if you were ill as well." She folded her hands in her lap. "How are you feeling?"

"Much better after a couple of days' sleep." Edward smiled. "I decided to let my body decide whether it should wake up in the morning, and it simply didn't."

"Many people were inquiring after you." Lauryn looked at him carefully. "I do wonder how you escaped sickness . . . both you and the doctor." She smiled. "Fiona told me that Connor said angels must be looking after you."

Edward looked up and glanced around the crowd before catching sight of the Irishman standing toward the back. "Then angels must have been looking after Connor as well. He worked as hard as anyone down in steerage, especially after Bess died." He nodded thoughtfully. "Have you been able to spend time with the children and Ewen at all?"

Lauryn nodded and had to bite at her lip to stop it from quivering. It was strange how even a mention of the family brought tears to her eyes.

"They stayed together for a while, in private, but then Fiona came back to me yesterday. She just wanted to talk about her mother." She swallowed. "I don't know how they can be so calm, and yet they are closer than ever and seem very . . . peaceful." She pointed to the front of the crowd, where Ewen had just arrived with the children beside him. "Did you know that Ewen is going to give the sermon today?"

"What?" Edward leaned forward in his seat and studied the Scotsman for a while, then he sat slowly back in his seat. "I shall look forward to this."

Only a few minutes lapsed before Dr. Appleby rose and held up his hand, and the crowd silenced quickly.

"Good morning, everyone. As we gather together this morning it is with mixed feelings. For many it is with relief that the sickness that was rife among us appears to have abated, while others come with heavy hearts for having lost loved ones." He hesitated as his face worked with emotion, then he looked carefully over the crowd. "I have spent time with many of you and have seen your distress and felt your sorrow. And I ask your forgiveness if I didn't serve you well enough." He bowed his head slightly. "I have come to realize, only too well, the limitations of my knowledge and ability. However,

I do believe I have seen the hand of God in many ways, and I have asked Mr. McAlister to elaborate on that, this morning." He turned to Ewen and held out his hand. "Ewen . . ."

There was a considerable murmur through the crowd as Ewen stood up, especially among the cabin-class passengers. It was unheard of for somebody from steerage to deliver a sermon.

"Excuse me, Dr. Appleby . . . I do not think this is appropriate." Mr. Pilcher stood up near the front, his thumbs tucked behind his jacket lapels. "The sermon should be given by someone who is . . . qualified to speak. Such as myself. As a long-standing member of the Church of England, it behooves me to object to this man speaking."

There was another murmur through the crowd, but Ewen stood still, his eyes fixed on a point halfway up the main mast as Dr. Appleby stood up slowly. He took his time before addressing the crowd.

"Mr. Pilcher . . . I do hear what you say, and I am in full agreement that this sermon should be preached only by someone who is qualified to speak." He fixed his gaze directly on the gentleman. "And from what I know of this man and his family, he is one of the most qualified on board the ship. The qualification to speak in the name of God lies with those who know God, and believe me, Mr. Pilcher, Mr. McAlister knows God in a way that you or I can't begin to comprehend." His voice was steady and deliberate as he finished. "We can wait a moment, however, if you would like to leave."

There was complete silence as the crowd waited, and Edward watched a range of emotions work over Mr. Pilcher's face as he slowly sat down—but not before he'd made a final comment.

"I shall remain only to ensure that the archbishop knows exactly what has happened here today."

Ewen was still standing without expression as Dr. Appleby gestured for him to begin. Then he nodded and smiled gently at the crowd.

"I appreciate the gentleman's concern, and because of that, I'd like to do what we usually do in our family." He paused and glanced back at his son, and there seemed to be a communication between them as Jimmy nodded very slightly. "I'd like to have a prayer before I begin, and I'd like my boy, Jimmy, to say it for us."

Another ripple ran through the crowd as Jimmy stood, but Mr. Pilcher was faster. "This is preposterous . . . a child cannot say a prayer!"

This time the crowd was visibly annoyed, and a number of passengers began yelling at him until his wife laid her hand on his arm and pulled him back to sit down.

Then it was Jimmy who stood quietly before the crowd, his arms folded in front of him as he waited for silence. He gave his father a quick look, then he bowed his head.

"Dear Father in Heaven . . . we are grateful for the chance to worship Thee today and . . . we know that Thou knows that we've been having lots of bad times with the cholera, but we want Thee to know that we love Thee, and today we need to know what we can do to be sure that we can be with our dads and . . ." His voice broke, and for a moment he struggled. "And with our mams and our wee brothers and sisters again . . . forever. Please let Thy Spirit be with us today." He closed the prayer.

A few people murmured amen after him, but many more simply stared as he silently sat down beside Fiona.

"Thank you, Jimmy," Ewen said quietly, then he bent down and picked up two books from off his seat. It was easy to see that both books were well used, and Ewen's fingers caressed the pages as he worked his way to a place in one of the books. He then closed the book around his finger while he looked out at the crowd.

"Twenty years ago I was a happy young lad living in the Highlands of Scotland—a tough life, but with a strong family. Then we were expelled in the clearances, and my father and brother were killed. A few years later, after Bess and I were married, we had a wee baby girl . . . but she died soon after she was born. A while later we had another girl, and she died too." He paused. "I think, then, that my belief in a God died as well, and I was bitter about what had happened to me . . . to my family." He smiled. "But my Bess . . . she never became bitter. In fact, she wanted to go to church more, but we were so poor that we weren't allowed to. That made me even more bitter, but it made her more determined until finally, as our circumstances changed, she was able to go, and she brought our children up to love the Bible and to love God." He stopped and took a deep breath.

"I still ignored God, but some time later a friend showed me that God hadn't forgotten me." He laid his hand on the cover of the book he was holding. "I will share with you what I believe is the word of God about death and about what happens to our dear ones when they die." He took his time opening the page, then he slowly and deliberately read the passage.

"'And now I would inquire what becometh of the souls of men from this time of death to the time appointed for the resurrection . . .'" He turned the page. "'There is a time appointed unto men that they shall rise from the dead . . . now, concerning the state of the soul between death and the resurrection—Behold, it has been made known unto me . . . that the spirits of all men, as soon as they are departed from this mortal body, yea, the spirits of all men, whether they be good or evil, are taken home to that God who gave them life.'"

There was an immediate splutter from Mr. Pilcher as he rose again. "Preposterous . . . evil men will go to hell, not to God! That's blasphemy!"

His wife pulled him down again while Ewen stood quietly. As soon as the murmuring settled, he continued.

"'And then shall it come to pass, that the spirits of those who are righteous . . .'" He paused after he emphasized the word *righteous.* "Are received into a state of happiness, which is called paradise, a state of rest, a state of peace, where they shall rest from all their troubles and from all care, and sorrow.'"

He smiled again. "It does go on to say what will happen to the wicked, but I'm more concerned about the righteous. I know . . . I know that my Bess was one of the most righteous women that ever lived, and it pleases me to know that she is happy now . . . in a state of peace and rest . . . with our daughters." He moved his finger to another passage and began to read carefully. "'The soul shall be restored to the body, and the body to the soul; yea, and every limb and joint shall be restored to its body; yea, even a hair of the head shall not be lost; but all things shall be restored to their proper and perfect frame.'"

He closed the book and looked straight ahead. "Jesus Christ died for us on the cross so that we might have that promise. He rose again so that we can rise again—and be together, as families, forever. His Atonement made that possible . . . if we are faithful to God." He opened the book again. "'I command you . . . in the fear of God . . . that ye turn to the Lord with all your mind, might, and strength . . . acknowledge your faults and that wrong which ye have done . . . seek not after riches nor the vain things of this world; for behold, ye cannot carry them with you.'" He looked up. "'Behold, I say unto you, is not a soul at this time as precious unto God as a soul will be at his coming?' I believe that my Bess and my girls are as precious to God as they are to me and to Jimmy and Fiona and that God wants us to be together forever . . . that we might have joy."

Ewen hesitated as if to think of anything else he wanted to say, then he nodded. "And I leave this testimony with you—that God lives and that Jesus Christ died for us that we might all live again—in the name of our Savior, Jesus Christ, amen."

Once more there was a murmur of assent as Ewen sat down, and then there was silence.

Dr. Appleby took his time standing up again, and then he stood quietly for a time before he nodded and smiled.

"Amen."

* * *

Mr. Pilcher was the only person to leave in a hurry, and in comparison with other services, the crowd took a long time to disperse. Lauryn could see many people nodding their heads as they talked amongst themselves, and she smiled as she saw Lady Farnsworth among them.

"So you agree with what Ewen was saying?"

"Oh my . . . it didn't last for long, but every word made sense." The lady folded her hands over the top of her bag. "The doctor was surely right about Mr. McAlister knowing God. I felt like I knew Him for the first time today as well, and I've been going to church for years."

Edward was still sitting silently as Lady Farnsworth leaned forward and tapped him on the arm.

"Wasn't that a wonderful sermon?"

"Indeed." Edward nodded thoughtfully. "And it does explain his family's attitude. I've been trying to describe how they have reacted, and it's as though they're at peace as well."

"They're still very sad . . . but yes, they're peaceful." Lauryn nodded. "That's what I've felt as I've been with them."

"Then they obviously do know something that the rest of us don't." Lady Farnsworth stood up and turned to Lauryn. "I'd like to talk with Ewen more, but not now. I'll wait until a better time." She hesitated and looked at Edward. "Do you happen to know what book he was quoting from?"

Edward opened his mouth, then he hesitated and shook his head. "You'll need to ask him that."

Lady Farnsworth stared at him, then she inclined her head and flicked her fan open. "I will do that. In fact, I shall discuss it with Jimmy and Ewen right after lunch. In the meantime, Lauryn, you do what you want for the rest of the day." She turned, and before she'd even taken a step, she had called out to Ewen and was soon engaged in conversation with him and the children.

Lauryn stood still beside Edward. Neither spoke.

"Are you . . ."

"Have you . . ."

They both spoke at once, then Lauryn shook her head and put her hand to her cheek. She felt apprehensive about being with him, and yet she wanted to be. She took a deep breath as Lady Farnsworth's voice seemed to whisper in her mind. *Just be a friend to everybody . . . let them enjoy your company.*

Lauryn looked up at Edward, tilting her head slightly. "Does the night we danced seem like a lifetime ago?"

Edward put his hands into his pockets and rocked on his heels. "Several lifetimes . . . about eleven of them, in fact." He squinted up at the sky as the sun began to shine down onto the ship. "One minute, dancing with you was all I could think about, and within such a short time . . . it was the last thing to think about." He looked down at her. "Not that I wanted it to be."

Lauryn felt the color rise in her cheeks, and she found herself wishing she had Lady Farnsworth's fan. The silence grew between them, but so did the comfort level.

"I did mean what I said that night." Edward cleared his throat. "About not wanting to lose you."

Lauryn tried to respond, but her throat felt tight and she could only nod.

"I . . . I lost my wife to cholera." Edward was looking straight at her, but she didn't feel to look at him. "I loved her very much, and it was a great blow to me. I believe she was also carrying our child at the time."

She could feel the pain in his voice, and she nodded as the tears stung her eyes.

"I hadn't thought to ever have feelings for a woman again, but . . . when everyone was getting so ill and I had the thought that I might lose you to the sickness, I felt . . ." Edward stopped, and she saw the muscle tighten in his jaw. "I believe I do have feelings for you, Lauryn, but I'm not sure what to make of them as yet."

She looked at him then, hoping he could read her emotions, because she felt incapable of putting anything into words. Instead, she responded by placing her hand gently on his arm. His hand immediately closed over hers. It was just a small movement, but a deep sense of acceptance filled her whole body.

"I understand." She barely murmured the words, but she felt his fingers tighten around hers.

"What I would like to say right now is—to put it in the words of Mr. Pilcher—'not appropriate in the middle of a deck full of people.'" Edward laughed as he put a little distance between them, then he bent his head slightly to look at her. "Would you like to take an appropriate walk along the decks with me, Miss Kelly . . . to discuss the school lessons for tomorrow?"

Lauryn laughed quietly as she felt a surge of happiness. "I would be delighted, Mr. Morgan."

They walked for a while, and the silence that had once stretched awkwardly between them now felt enjoyable. They were near the front of the boat when Lauryn finally spoke.

"I'm sorry I didn't tell you . . . about Connor."

"You didn't have to," Edward responded simply. "Although it might have been safer that way."

"Oh, I never felt as if I were in danger." Lauryn glanced at him quickly. "I was more concerned about him being in danger."

Edward smiled as he shook his head. "I think he enjoys taking risks. When he came 'round, he recognized my voice, apparently, and told me straightaway that he had killed eight rats that were trying to get into my merchandise."

"Eight!" Lauryn shivered. "Oh, imagine those running around you . . ."

"Not anymore." Edward hesitated. "Lauryn, when I found you . . . with him . . . you said you were of—"

"Lauryn! Lauryn!" Fiona ran up to them at that moment and took hold of her hand. Ewen and Jimmy were right behind, but she sensed Ewen's embarrassment as he looked at Edward then back at her. Fiona swung her hand again. "Lauryn, can we read some stories together . . . from your books?"

"I'm sorry. It's what . . ." Ewen shook his head. "It's what Bess used to do on Sunday afternoons. Fiona decided that you should do it today."

Lauryn looked at the man who had just been through so much, and her heart went out to him. "Then Fiona made a very good decision. I happen to have just the book we need . . . but it's in my cabin. Would you mind waiting while I go and get it?"

"I'll come with you." Fiona skipped ahead of her. "Then we can come back and read in the sunshine."

* * *

As they walked away, Ewen ran his hand through his hair. "Edward, I'm sorry if we interrupted anything. I'm just trying to keep the children occupied . . ."

"And we are happy to help." Edward rested his hand on Jimmy's shoulder. "You did a fine job of the prayer this morning, Jimmy. You certainly proved Mr. Pilcher wrong."

"I wasn't trying to prove anybody wrong." Jimmy frowned. "I just wanted the Spirit to be there . . . so Dad could talk properly."

Edward raised both eyebrows as he glanced at Ewen, then he nodded. "Well, you certainly did that too . . . and your dad did a fine job as well." He smiled. "Francis Farnsworth wanted to know what book you were quoting from."

"Aye, she talked to me about it." Ewen smiled. "She's a determined lady."

Edward nodded in agreement. "Actually, she asked me if I knew anything about the book."

"And what did you tell her?" Ewen watched Edward's face.

"I told her she needed to ask you. Knowing Francis, she'll want to read it cover to cover and interrogate you about it. I only know about Mormons—"

"Do you?" Jimmy asked quietly, and Edward looked at him for a moment then shrugged.

"Maybe I don't. Maybe I only know some Mormons . . . not about them," he amended and tilted his head as if to gain Jimmy's approval. Only then did the boy smile and give a brief nod, then he was serious again.

"We'll let you spend five minutes with Fiona, and she'll have us all summed up." Ewen smiled as Fiona came running to them, puffing as she held up a small red book. "Lauryn says we may read this one. Jimmy, do you want to read with us?"

She waited expectantly as Jimmy stared at the book then shook his head.

"No . . . I'm going to write in the journal Mam gave me," he answered briefly then looked up at his father. "I'll be in our bunks."

As he walked away, Ewen took a deep breath then rubbed his forehead. "He knows where his mam is, but he also knows where he'd rather have her be. I think he's scared that he'll forget her."

* * *

THE WIND PICKED UP IN the early afternoon, so Lauryn and Fiona went to Lauryn's cabin where the reading of one book soon turned into the reading of three. At the end of the third book, Lauryn looked down at Fiona, her head tucked comfortably against her shoulder as the child slept soundly. With as little movement as possible she laid the book down then sat with her back against the wall and eased Fiona's head onto her lap. Even the slight movement caused Fiona's eyelids to tremble, and she gazed sightlessly at Lauryn for an instant, then a tiny smile flitted over her lips.

"Mam."

Lauryn felt her heart miss a beat as she lifted her hand and let it gently rest against the little girl's forehead.

"Mam." She mouthed the word as she stroked Fiona's hair, fighting the tears that threatened as an image of Bess came clearly into her mind: Bess standing with Ewen and Fiona and Jimmy on the deck, the wind blowing her hair as she rested her hand on her stomach. Lauryn closed her eyes and the image changed. It was still Bess, but she was standing with two young women, one with long red hair like Fiona's, and the other with wavy brown hair. In Bess's arms was a young baby with curly blond hair. They were all smiling . . . and then they were gone.

"Your girls, Bess." Lauryn kept her eyes shut as if she could bring back the image. "You have your girls again."

This time her emotions ran unchecked as she rested her head back against the wall and sat for a long time, letting the tears fall. It was all so clear in her mind now. Bess had left one family, but she was with another, and Lauryn felt a growing sense of contentment as she remembered Fiona's words.

I'm sad Mam's gone, but she'll be happy that she's with my sisters.

"But how does she know?" Lauryn shook her head as the tears flowed again, this time as she thought about her own family. The short amount of time she had spent with Connor had brought back a flood of memories of Ireland and of her family. And the thought that had been playing over in her mind was the lingering fear that she would never see them again.

"But if Bess is with her girls, then I will see my family again. If not here then . . ." She stopped as the thought of where or when she might see them became too incomprehensible, and she opened her eyes.

Fiona was still fast asleep as Lauryn nodded slowly.

"We must be able to see them again. It wouldn't be right not to."

* * *

WHEN THE WIND INTENSIFIED, ALL hands were called to help with the rigging, and Edward was happy to be involved. The physical labor of hauling on the ropes and working in synchronized movement with the other sailors seemed to satisfy the lifelong yearning he'd had to be on the ocean. At such times, as the wind whipped against him and the thick, matted ropes ran through his hands, he would breathe in the smell of the salty wind and the tar and feel a sense of belonging.

"You've done this a few times." Connor swung up onto the deck beside him and began to pull on the rope. Edward nodded as they found the same rhythm and worked in silence for a few moments until the rope was gathered into a coiled mound on the deck. Another sailor waved and smiled above them, and they both turned and jumped down onto the main deck.

"I enjoy being on the ocean." Edward rubbed his hands together to get rid of the stickiness from the rope, then he nodded at Connor. "You seemed to have picked up the ways quickly as well."

"It's a case of having to prove myself quickly so I don't have to go back to swilling the privies." Connor grinned as he glanced up at the rigging. "But I confess I love being up there . . . the feeling of freedom."

"Especially after being in the hold, I imagine." Edward leaned back against the wooden base of the mast and folded his arms. "You know you nearly got Miss Kelly into a lot of trouble."

Connor continued to stare up at the rigging for a moment, then he shook his head slowly.

"I didn't mean to cause her harm, but I knew straightaway that I could trust her." He looked straight at Edward. "That I had to trust her."

"And fortunately for you, she responded." Edward's voice was flat as he raised one eyebrow. "She mentioned you were of . . . one heart."

Connor nodded as he studied Edward's face. "It did feel that way, and it's been a long time since I felt that connection." He hesitated. "I think we remind each other of the good things we left behind in Ireland."

"Not the bad things?"

"Those things a person tries to forget." Connor gave a tight smile, then he shrugged. "Lauryn said her father told her the same thing when she left Ireland . . . to remember that they were of one heart."

"And it struck a chord with her." Edward nodded. "It would have meant a great deal to her to hear that . . . especially with a strong Irish accent."

"Yes," Connor agreed, and a long silence ensued. Then he asked, "Have you known her long?"

"Ah . . . yes . . . in a way." Edward nodded slowly. "We met briefly some time ago but only renewed our acquaintance on board ship . . . primarily because I was asked to assist her with the school class." He hesitated. "But I admire her very much. She had quite an influence on me when I needed direction."

"And now you appear to be good friends," Connor responded with an easy smile. "I hope it will be the case with us as well."

"With Lauryn . . . or with me?" Edward returned the smile.

"Both," Connor responded quickly. "I would like to be friends with you, Edward Morgan, even though we got off to a very bad start." He paused. "I appreciate that you helped me even when I caused you grief."

Edward studied the Irishman and, almost against his will, he recognized that the man was genuine in what he was saying.

"You make it sound as if that grief is in the past." He attempted a smile and was not surprised when Connor grinned.

"She is a very fine woman." Connor put his hand in his pocket and pulled out the tin whistle. "And to be sure, she plays a grand whistle." He twirled the instrument between his fingertips then looked at it for a long moment before handing it to Edward. "It would please me if you would give this to her. Tell her it's for young Fiona if she wouldn't mind teaching the little girl some tunes."

Edward looked at the whistle then frowned. "You make it sound like a parting gift."

"I'd just call it a gift." Connor smiled as he proffered the whistle once more, and Edward took it slowly. "I prefer not to have farewells."

"She'll miss you."

"No . . . I'm confident you'll see she doesn't." Connor grinned as he held out his hand and waited until Edward took it. He pumped it once, firmly. "Though I do feel a certain brotherly interest in her welfare, and I would hate to ever hear that you did her wrong." He put his head to one side. "There's nothing quite so dangerous as an angry Irishman . . . especially where there's a lady concerned."

Edward responded to the handshake then held up the whistle. "When should I give it to her?" He waited as Connor stared up at the rigging then out toward the ocean.

"After the ship leaves Cape Town." He sunk his hands into his pockets. "I hear the crew will need help with picking up supplies."

Edward nodded as he followed Connor's gaze across the water. "I wish you well." He hesitated. "Would you like me to tell Lauryn anything else?"

Connor thought for a moment, then he nodded. "Tell her that Bess and Ewen . . . I listened a lot to them, and I believe they have many answers." He grinned. "Lauryn may not know she has the questions yet, but she will. Would you tell her . . . the Irishman thinks she would do well to listen to her heart?"

Chapter Twenty-Four

Cape of Good Hope, South Africa, 1849
The Antipodes

"It's HARD TO BELIEVE THAT our next stop will be New Zealand." Lauryn rested her elbows on the deck railing as she watched fresh supplies of food being loaded onto the boat from the port at Cape Town. Only the crew was allowed off the ship, since the New Zealand Company was enforcing a strict rule that no passengers disembark before reaching New Zealand.

"Indeed—and that we're now more than halfway there with the worst of the storms behind us." Lady Farnsworth rolled her eyes. "I'm most pleased about that part."

"Once we're on dry land again, how long do you think it will take us to lose our sea legs?" Lauryn smiled as she watched one of the sailors take a giant step to right himself as he carried a large box on board; then she recognized him as Connor. It seemed that Captain Bayliss had determined that the Irishman would continue to work his passage at this stop, and so he was now assisting the crew as they went backward and forward in a steady line from the boat to the carts full of produce that waited on the shore.

"And how long before we decide that ship's biscuits aren't the only food that tastes decent?" Edward joined in the discussion, but he too was watching as Connor dumped the crate then turned and made his way jauntily down the gangplank. "I thought they were the worst thing I'd ever tasted at the beginning, and now I look forward to them each day."

"That's only because our teeth have gotten used to them." Lady Farnsworth chuckled and held up one finger. "How long before our bodies realize that they can actually turn over in bed at night?" She nodded, but Lauryn and Edward were both watching the dock, so she smiled to herself. "Maybe I'm the only one with that problem." She followed their gaze as Connor moved toward the very last cart standing in the row on the dock. He appeared to be choosing which crate to lift but then he glanced up toward the boat several times and toward the end of the wharf.

"That young man has certainly proved helpful, hasn't he?" Lady Farnsworth looked at Edward. "He's almost given stowaways a good name."

"Yes." Edward nodded absently, but his eyes never left the wharf. There was a noticeable dwindling in the activity as it appeared the crew had loaded the last of the produce, but Connor was still by the last cart as the owner began to pack up.

Lauryn, too, was quiet as she watched Connor, but she could feel her heart beginning to beat more quickly. She glanced toward the gangplank where Mr. Frew was shouting orders to some of the crew, then she looked back to the wharf.

"Where . . . ?" She leaned forward slightly on the rail and looked quickly both ways.

"I believe he may have gone to look for more produce," Edward responded quietly.

"But . . ." Lauryn stared at the cart as it was driven off the wharf. "He'll—"

"He'll make his way as he did before." Lady Farnsworth had noticed the Irishman's movements, and she nodded approvingly. "I think he'll do just fine."

"So then . . . from the Cape of Good Hope, it's supposedly clear sailing to New Zealand." Lauryn forced herself to speak brightly as the tears gathered in her eyes. She could no longer see any sign of Connor. "And the first stop is Port Chalmers and then Lyttleton."

"And on to our new home in Canterbury." Lady Farnsworth glanced at Lauryn then covered her hand as it gripped the railing. "I do hope that nephew of mine has been keeping things in order. He never did very much in England, so I don't know why my brother expects much here. Still, people do change, and if you've survived one of these voyages you do tend to develop a different appreciation for life, I believe." She chattered on as she waved the fan at Edward and turned Lauryn away from the railing and the activity on the wharf. "And you, young man . . . are you still planning to stay on board and go on to Australia?"

Lauryn looked up quickly but not at Edward as she felt a sudden shiver work its way down her spine, despite the heat. Connor was gone. Edward would be gone once they reached New Zealand.

"I feel that I am bound to continue to Sydney." She heard him speak beside her. "I have cargo aboard that is promised there, and that was my original intention—to set up a store there and, depending on its success, then move to New Zealand in search of land to settle on." He hesitated. "At least, that was my intention."

"Well, plans do have a habit of going awry, but a gentleman needs to keep his word." Lady Farnsworth looked deliberately between him and Lauryn. "I hear that trade is doing very well in Australia, especially with word of the gold rush, so it would seem a likely place to make your fortune quickly." She gathered up her skirts to move away from the railing. "A gentleman I spoke with the other day is even wavering in his decision to settle in New Zealand. He is tempted to venture to Australia for a while to see what it holds. Perhaps we should all try." She glanced quickly at Lauryn then walked away, talking to herself. "Now, that could be an idea . . ."

For a time the only sounds came from the shouts of the crew as they loaded the produce into the hold. Lauryn pretended a fascination with the process until Edward finally spoke.

"I think I'm beginning to wish they had discovered gold in New Zealand instead of Australia." He turned and leaned back against the railing.

"It . . . it would have saved you a lot of extra travel." Lauryn nodded, but she was frowning, her mind elsewhere.

"Mmm." Edward nodded slowly as he watched the expression on her face. The tears had stopped, but she still had her head turned partly to the wharf. "Unfortunately, I am carrying goods for an agent that I have to deliver personally. He long ago stopped trusting the shipping line, and it meant an extra commission for me. I've just been down checking the goods this morning, and apart from some water damage to the containers, they seem to be in reasonable condition." He put his hands into his pockets as he suddenly seemed to run out of information.

"That must be pleasing." Lauryn nodded absently then strained her neck to see as Mr. Frew suddenly yelled an order and several of the crew raced back down the gangplank and began to run up and down the wharf.

"Yes . . . it is." Edward took a deep breath as he heard Connor's name being called. "I am bound to deliver these goods to Sydney . . ."

"Which, of course, you must do." Lauryn nodded as the first mate walked quickly down the gangplank and stood on the wharf with his hands on his hips. "How long will you stay . . . in Australia?"

"Ah, now that is a very good question." Edward pursed his lips as he watched the sailors returning to the first mate, shaking their heads and pointing in different directions. "My intention was to stay in Sydney and establish a store . . . either there or perhaps farther north. It seems logical to follow the gold rush, as miners tend to be men who take little thought as to how they spend." He paused as Mr. Frew swung his arm wide to indicate the crew should return aboard. "I want to earn enough to buy land in New Zealand and establish the farm I've always dreamed of owning." He drew a deep breath as the crew came back up the gangplank and Mr. Frew signaled for it to be raised.

"That is a worthy goal." Lauryn attempted a smile as she watched the stretch of water between the boat and the wharf widening. "You seem to have it well worked out."

"Indeed." Edward took a deep breath as the gangplank opening was sealed.

"It would be nice if everybody's plans went so smoothly." Her voice was quiet as she looked up at the sky.

"One can only make the plan and hope that Providence agrees with it." Edward watched her closely as he stood up, reached into his pocket, and very slowly drew out the tin whistle. He hesitated for a moment as she stared at it, then he held it out. "Connor said to tell you it's for young Fiona—if you wouldn't mind teaching her some tunes."

He waited as Lauryn continued to look at the whistle without speaking.

"He said he preferred not to have farewells."

"So you knew he wasn't coming back." She spoke quietly, and he nodded as she took a deep, quivering breath. "I will miss him . . . very much."

"I think he will miss you too." Edward's voice was gentle but level. "You appear to have become very close to Connor."

It was a statement, but Lauryn sensed the question behind Edward's words, and she took a moment to answer.

"Bess asked me what Connor meant to me." Lauryn stared down at the dock. "I told her that I felt no fear with Connor because he seemed to represent all my childhood memories rolled into one person—memories I want to remain loyal to."

"Memories of your family?" Edward asked quietly.

Lauryn nodded as she lifted her face to the light breeze. "I only had sisters, but it was like Connor was . . . my brother and . . ." She hesitated to swallow. "He sounded so much like my father. It was like, in a second, Connor was . . . Ireland to me."

She stood silently then, and Edward could see the battle as she fought to keep her emotions under control.

"I think Connor felt the same way." He finally spoke. "He warned me I had to look after you." He smiled as she glanced up at him then. "He also said to tell you that he listened a lot to Ewen and Bess and that he believes they have many answers." He held up his hand as she opened her mouth to say something. "He also said that 'Lauryn may not know she has the questions yet . . . but she will.'"

He watched as a smile spread across her face and she shook her head.

"A typical Irishman . . . thinks he knows everything." She took the whistle from his hand and studied it before she looked straight at him. "Was there anything else?"

Edward returned her gaze, and when Lauryn's didn't waver, he smiled. "He said that the Irishman thinks she would do well to listen to her heart."

* * *

"So DID YOU HAVE ANY idea Connor was going to jump ship?" Lady Farnsworth asked the question even before Lauryn had closed the door to the cabin. "I do like that expression . . . 'jump ship,'" she repeated as Lauryn sat down. "So . . . had he said anything?"

"Nothing at all." Lauryn shook her head. "I had no idea, but it appears that Edward was aware of his plans."

"Edward?" Lady Farnsworth looked genuinely surprised as she put her hands on her hips. "Well, that's a surprise. What brought that about, I wonder?"

"I don't know." Lauryn shrugged. "But they appear to have parted on good terms . . . with plenty of counsel for me thrown in."

"Counsel for you?" Lady Farnsworth raised both eyebrows. "What . . ."

"I am to teach Fiona to play the Irish whistle." Lauryn drew the whistle from her pocket and held it up. "I also need to think of some questions to which Ewen and Bess have answers, and . . ." She put her hand against her chest. "I am to listen to my heart."

"Well, my goodness. He certainly was thinking about you, wasn't he?" Lady Farnsworth sat down beside her. "And Edward told you all this?"

Lauryn nodded as she began to laugh quietly, her shoulders shaking as she suddenly thought about the two men together.

"I was so upset when I realized Connor had left the ship, but when Edward told me that they'd talked . . ." She stopped and took a deep breath. "It was so ridiculous it almost seemed normal."

"But you'll miss him." Lady Farnsworth wasn't smiling as she carefully watched Lauryn.

"I will." Lauryn didn't hesitate as she nodded slowly. "I'll miss him a lot . . . just as I miss my father and my mother and my sisters."

"Are you sure?" Lady Farnsworth spoke very quietly.

"I'm very sure." Lauryn smiled as she laid the tin whistle on her pillow.

* * *

APART FROM SOME ROUGHER SEAS during the night, the next few days passed uneventfully, and Lauryn felt her spirits lifting as each day brought hours of pleasant sunshine and light winds. The captain fretted that the sailing time would be longer as a result, but the passengers delighted in the mellow conditions.

Once, Lauryn invited Mr. Frew to tell the class some stories, and the children listened spellbound to his exuberant tales of giant squids and sea monsters.

"I believe Mr. Frew would have a future as a storyteller if he ever left the ship," Lauryn said as she walked beside Edward later that evening. "He even had me thinking that these monsters actually exist."

"Oh, they exist." Edward touched her forehead with his finger. "Up here, anyway."

Lauryn smiled as the touch of his hand against her head left a tingling sensation. She glanced up and saw that he was watching her, and once again she realized that she was enjoying his attention without reservation.

"Mam was saying that you mentioned a change of plans today." She clasped her hands in front of her as he walked with his arm brushing hers. "I thought you had everything worked out."

"Indeed . . . I have had it mostly worked out—since I met a bold young woman who suggested that I should resort to another option to emigrate rather than try to find a wife."

"Or a sister." The color rose in Lauryn's cheeks.

"Or a sister . . ." Edward shook his head. "How was I possibly to know that the very same young woman who set me on that plan would be the one person who would upset it?"

"But I . . ." Lauryn began to protest then stopped as he put a finger to her lips.

"Upset it . . . completely." Edward's voice softened as he drew her gently behind one of the small wooden boats. "I had dismissed the idea of a wife as being of no interest and certainly not part of the plan, but I keep finding myself wanting to reconsider the option." He reached out and placed a hand over hers. "What do think I should do, Lauryn Kelly? You had no hesitation telling me the first time."

Lauryn's thoughts suddenly backtracked to that day as she had stood outside the New Zealand Company office and the comment that had prompted her remark. There really had been no reason to be quite so tart in her response except the unusual feeling that she'd had when she'd looked at that face, those eyes—and felt a need to put him in his place.

"I think you should pursue the better option, of course," she answered primly, but a touch of a smile tugged at the corner of her mouth.

"And that is . . ."

"Well, of course you must go to Australia and fulfill your obligations, but I think you should also . . . take a wife." She lowered her lashes. "That would appear to be the better option . . . to me . . . but then, what if the wife has other obligations . . . in New Zealand?"

"Hmm . . . that does present a problem." Edward rubbed his chin. "Unless, of course, I meet my obligations while she meets hers, given a period of time and then . . ."

"Then . . . it could work very well."

He moved to stand behind her with his hands covering hers on the railing. She felt as if she were in a cocoon, safe from the world and everything in it as she dared to lean her head back against his chest.

"Can we make it work, Lauryn?" She felt the words whispered against her ear, and she nodded once as his arms closed around her waist and she turned to face him. He took his time studying her face as if trying to memorize every part of it, then he leaned his forehead against hers. "I did not think I could love again, but you must have worked an Irish spell."

She couldn't suppress the laugh that bubbled up as she lifted her head and he lowered his. They may have been in the middle of the ship for all to see, but Lauryn felt herself lifted as his lips pressed against hers and claimed her heart.

"Oh my . . ." she murmured against his cheek as they finally drew apart.

"Oh, my husband?" Edward gathered her closer again as he smiled broadly. "Is it possible, Lauryn?"

"Oh yes." She nodded against his chest then frowned. "But how long before you would come back?"

"As soon as possible . . . two years?" He glanced down expectantly, the hint of a smile on his lips.

"Two years!" Lauryn drew back then beat her fist against him as he laughed out loud.

"I'll give it six months, and then I will come to New Zealand regardless." He lifted her chin with his hand so that she was looking right at him, and then he was suddenly serious. "I would have you to be my wife, Lauryn . . . will you?"

"Oh yes, Edward." She felt no hesitation as she whispered his name, then he kissed her again.

The stares of some of the cabin-class passengers finally prompted them to move along the deck, but as they walked with Lauryn's hand in the crook of his arm, he rested his hand over hers then stopped. "I cannot even give you a ring . . . unless the captain has a stash somewhere beneath his whisky."

Lauryn laughed as she shook her head. "I have no need of a ring . . ." She stopped suddenly and held out her right hand. "I have my *máthair*'s *claddagh* ring."

"*Claddagh?*" Edward studied the small silver ring as she pointed to it.

"The Irish use this as a wedding ring but also to show they are betrothed." She paused as the tears welled in her eyes. "I remember when my *máthair* told me what the ring stood for. We were sitting in a tree at the bottom of our garden . . . a very big tree." She smiled as she caught his look. "And *Máthair* told me that the crown means I will be loyal to my husband forever, the heart means that I will love him forever, and the hands mean that we will be friends forever. Loyalty, love, and friendship. She said that is what marriage is about and what I must always strive to have when I meet my man someday."

Lauryn wrinkled up her nose as she touched the ring again. "I told her that I didn't think I wanted a ring . . . or a man . . . that I would rather have a horse like Finnbheara."

"Finn-var?" Edward smiled at her innocence.

"A horse belonging to the king of the Irish fairies . . ."

"The king's name wouldn't be Connor, would it?" Edward interrupted then smiled as she reached up to touch his cheek.

"Well, it just might be."

* * *

"So, WHEN ARE YOU GOING to tell me officially what is happening between you and Edward?" Lady Farnsworth didn't look at Lauryn as they readied for bed that night. "It's not hard to see that you're very comfortable with each other, and I think that, as your employer, I should be made aware of any . . . developments."

She pulled her nightdress over her head and chuckled at the size of it floating around her, then she looked at Lauryn. "Reason tells me that a girl your size should have faded away to nothing if I've lost all this weight. I needn't have bothered to bring most of my things with me. Thank goodness you can sew, and that delightful old dragon down the hall is an expert seamstress. I shall keep you both busy when we land." She fluffed the nightgown again. "And speaking of landing . . . where were we? Oh yes . . . what is happening with you and Edward?"

Lauryn smiled as she buttoned up the front of her own nightgown then straightened the long, gathered sleeves.

"I believe Edward is planning to talk to you himself in the morning." She glanced sideways. "While I'm teaching class."

"Oh." Lady Farnsworth closed her mouth then smiled knowingly. "So should I put the dear boy on tenterhooks?" She clasped her hands together. "I've never been in this situation before."

"Neither have I." Lauryn smiled and sat down on the bunk, resting her arms across her knees. "And I certainly never expected to be when I left England." She bit her lip. "So many things have happened that I must wonder if I'm dreaming. It wasn't long ago that we were terrified and so sad when Bess and the baby died, then so full of hope after hearing Ewen's talk. And then . . ." She stopped and blushed to the roots of her hair.

"And then?" Lady Farnsworth waited expectantly, but Lauryn shook her head.

"You must wait until tomorrow."

"Nonsense . . . I have to be prepared, girl." The lady tut-tutted for a moment then began to push her hair up into her gathered night bonnet as she regarded Lauryn carefully.

"Well, then . . . I need to know if you are happy—not just tingly happy, mind." She held up one finger then resumed putting on her bonnet. "I mean very happy. So much so that you can't think of anyone you would rather be with . . . ever." She paused and her voice softened. "As if being with him makes you feel complete."

Lauryn leaned her head back against the wall and thought for a while. Then she nodded. "I used to think that I felt happy with James, and I felt somehow content being with Connor, but . . . I realize that those feelings were nothing compared to what I feel with Edward." She rested her chin on her arms. "And now I can't imagine ever not feeling this way. Complete." She nodded. "That's how I feel . . . although it did come as a surprise at first. I almost resented him to begin with."

"Well, that was obvious." Lady Farnsworth puffed her cheeks. "Even I could see that you were meant for each other, but you looked like you were going to ruin everything for a while there. I'm glad I stepped in."

Lauryn stared at her employer with her mouth open then laughed and shook her head. "I almost wish I could be there tomorrow when Edward talks to you . . . to hear you tell him how you managed everything between us."

* * *

"YES, EDWARD—WHAT IS IT?" Lady Farnsworth paused by one of the small boats and sat down on the raised area beside it. As he had arranged at breakfast, they had left Lauryn teaching the morning class and walked along the deck together. "What's on your mind?"

Edward sat down beside her and took a minute to think before he looked straight at her. "Francis . . . you are aware of my feelings for Lauryn." He swallowed and she chuckled.

"I do think it's delightful that you should make that a statement and not a question, dear boy. It makes me feel very knowing . . . and yes, I am aware of your feelings . . . and Lauryn's." She smiled at the expression on his face. "I may be sixty, but I'm certainly not past remembering feelings, Edward . . . or recognizing them."

Edward nodded. He had been feeling uncharacteristically apprehensive about talking to Francis, but now he relaxed as he leaned back.

"Then you'll have recognized that I wish to have more than a simple friendship with Lauryn." He smiled. "That was a statement, not a question, as well."

Lady Farnsworth nodded. "I'm waiting for the question."

It was Edward's turn to nod, and he took a moment. "With your permission, as Lauryn's employer, I would like to ask you for her hand in marriage, Lady Farnsworth." He took a deep breath.

"And if I refuse?" She looked stern, but then she smiled. "Not that I intend to, but it is an interesting thought."

"Interesting, but not palatable." Edward frowned then he shrugged. "Then I would simply elope with her."

"Oh, good . . . that sounds like far more fun." Lady Farnsworth chuckled and patted his arm. "But this way makes me feel far more a part of it, Edward, and I appreciate that." She tilted her head. "Of course I give my permission, but when will you marry? Aren't you going on to Australia?"

Edward nodded. "That's the difficult part. I am bound to my contract, and Lauryn feels that she should stay with you in New Zealand, so we have decided that a six-month time frame will give us a chance to find out what the future holds. I will return in six months."

Lady Farnsworth nodded thoughtfully. "Again, I appreciate how you have considered me in your plans, Edward. I must confess I find it difficult to imagine what my life would be like without dear Lauryn, but things have a way of working themselves out, don't they?"

"Indeed, Francis, and we will only do what works for you as well as us." Edward made to stand up, but she put a hand on his arm to detain him.

"Edward . . . I do have a question. Please sit down for a moment."

She cleared her throat as he sat back beside her, then she clasped her hands in her lap. "Edward . . . you loved Lizzy." She smiled kindly. "That was a statement, not a question."

He smiled in response as he nodded. "I did . . . very much." He looked down at his hands. "So much that I didn't ever consider the possibility of loving someone else."

"But now you do, Edward . . . and that is wonderful." Lady Farnsworth looked into the distance. "My husband died in a dreadful horse-riding accident just eighteen months after we were married." Her lip trembled. "I've kept Charles and our love locked in my heart all these years. But they've been lonely years, Edward . . . and I don't think God meant for us to be lonely."

Edward reached out and covered her hand with his. "My sister tells me that God wants us to have joy. She told me not to lock anybody out."

"Then you have a very wise sister." Lady Farnsworth gave his hand a quick squeeze. "I think I would like her very much if she's anything like you."

Edward gave a short laugh and smiled. "We're very alike—we're twins—but she's the sensible one."

Lady Farnsworth smiled as she stood up. "The more I find out about you, Edward Morgan, the more I like, but there's just one thing. Once you do marry that girl, you realize you'll have to call me Mam as well."

Edward laughed as he took her arm. "Mam . . . Mam . . . I can get used to that."

* * *

"WELL, ONE COULD ALMOST BELIEVE the New Zealand Company brochure with weather like this." Lady Farnsworth spread her hands out as she looked up at the sky. "What did it say. . . something about looking forward to 'quite the summer cruise'?"

"Aye . . . that's what we read." Ewen nodded. "Bess was quite taken with it. She said that it would be best to come to New Zealand, since a ship builder would have more hope of finding a job on an island than in the middle of the desert."

"The middle of the desert?" Lady Farnsworth frowned. "What were you considering?"

Ewen glanced at Edward, then he looked down. They were all sitting on the deck as had become the habit in the last two weeks. Lauryn sat beside Edward with Fiona leaning against her. Jimmy sat beside his father, and they had been joined, as was increasingly the case, by Dr. Appleby.

"We were going to migrate to America, to join other Latter-day Saints and be a part of Zion there." Ewen stared into the sky. "But we decided to come to New Zealand first and make our way financially, then go in a few years."

There was silence for a while, then Lady Farnsworth cleared her throat. "So, this is what your Book of Mormon is about." She held up her hand as if anticipating his invitation. "I'm not saying I want to read it yet. Something tells me I might have to change my ways if I do . . . but tell me about . . . Zion."

Ewen took a deep breath, but it was Jimmy who spoke first. "Zion is where the pure in heart gather . . . to worship God as they want to and as He wants them to." He looked at his father then at Lady Farnsworth. "Where everybody is of one heart and one mind."

Lady Farnsworth's eyes grew wide, then she patted Jimmy on the knee and beamed at him. "Well, wouldn't that just be the loveliest place to live."

"My sister and brother tell me it is," Edward offered quietly, and Lauryn glanced at him. He had mentioned his family, but she had assumed they were still in England. What else didn't she know about this man? She kept looking at him as he shrugged.

"My sister is of the same faith as Ewen. She is a Latter-day Saint—a Mormon—and she and her husband and my brother migrated to Zion some four years ago." He nodded. "Her letters tell me of trials but also of the great blessings that they've experienced, and they love it there."

Ewen nodded. "One day we'll go there." He tousled Jimmy's hair. "Won't we, Jimmy?"

"Not without Mam." Jimmy spoke quietly but definitely, and once again the conversation stopped.

"Well . . . we'll just have to make New Zealand into a Zion, won't we then?" Lady Farnsworth refused to let her spirits be dampened as she clapped her hands. "And with only a few days to go on this ship, we need to be ready." She struggled to her feet, but Dr. Appleby was there to lend a hand before Lauryn could move. "I think I shall go and begin to pack my things."

Chapter Twenty-Five

Indian Ocean, 1849
Rogue Wave

ONE OF THE CABIN BOYS was the first to sight land off the main mast, and there was a rush onto the deck as everybody pushed to one side of the ship to try to catch a glimpse.

Lauryn was teaching a class when the cry rang out above their heads, and the children immediately looked at her hopefully. As most of their parents came past, she used both hands to shoo the children off and got up with Fiona to go and look as well.

Jimmy was already at the railing, straining his eyes to see anything that resembled land. "Nothing . . . we're too low down," he murmured as he narrowed his eyes then looked up the main mast to the crow's nest. "I wish I could climb up there and get a better view."

Lauryn glanced up at the mast and the huge sails flapping, and she put a hand on his shoulder. "I think it's a much better idea just to wait until we're closer."

"But some of the other boys have been up." Jimmy looked up again. "They only had to pay a wee amount to the sailors, and they got right to the top."

"And who was the boy who fell halfway and broke his arm?" Lauryn shook her head. "I really don't think your father would approve."

"Mam wouldn't either." Fiona kept her chin resting on the rail, then she suddenly pointed her finger and squealed. "Look, look, look . . . over there!"

They all stared hard, then Jimmy nudged his sister much harder than usual so that she fell against the side of the boat.

"'Tis only a whale." He sounded annoyed. "Can you not tell a whale from land?"

"Jimmy!" Lauryn spoke sharply as Fiona's bottom lip quivered. "There's no need to speak to your sister that way . . . or push her!"

Jimmy stared at Fiona, and Lauryn knew he was doing so to avoid looking at her.

"I think you should apologize." She kept her voice calm, as if she were teaching class. "Now." She spoke more firmly, but he scowled.

"I don't need to . . . you're not my mam." He looked straight at her then, and suddenly his voice cracked. "Don't you know it . . . you're not my mam!"

Then he was gone, running along the deck and down the stairwell, out of sight.

Fiona began crying softly as Lauryn knelt down and drew her in, holding her tightly. She had noticed an increasing sullenness about Jimmy in the last two weeks, but no one seemed to be able to get through to him except his father.

Lauryn crossed the deck to tell Ewen what had happened, thinking that Jimmy must have gone straight down to his bunk, but two hours later, Edward came and knocked on the door of her cabin.

"Ewen says he can't find Jimmy—do you have any idea where he might be?"

"No." Lauryn put her hand to her mouth. "I thought he'd be in his bunk." She drew back inside her cabin. "I'll just put my shoes on."

They found Ewen pacing near the stairwell. He stopped when they reached him, but he looked agitated.

"I have no idea where he's gone. I know I shouldn't worry because we're on a boat so he can't run away, but . . ."

"But it'd still be better to know where he is." Edward spoke calmly as he turned to Lauryn. "Has he ever mentioned anything to you about places he's been on the boat or people he's played with or talked to? Maybe he's made a new friend."

Ewen shook his head. "He's been staying close to me of late, hardly talking to anybody. It's actually been worrying me. It's been going on since his mam died . . . "

"And he's been missing her." Lauryn put her hand on Ewen's arm. "He just wants to be close . . ." She suddenly gasped. "The mast . . . he wanted to climb the mast."

Of one accord they moved to the middle of the deck and peered upward, but in the gathering dusk it was difficult to see clearly.

"Yes, there is someone there." Edward pointed to the crow's nest. "I just saw a head look over the top."

"But how do we get him down?" Lauryn hugged her shawl tightly around her shoulders. "It surely cannot hold two up there."

"Of course it can." Ewen was drawing off his jacket as he made his way to the mast. "Can you go to Fiona? She's asleep downstairs."

* * *

Ewen took no thought of how high he was climbing as he pulled himself toward the top of the mast, but near the crow's nest he could see Jimmy's face staring down at him, his cheeks stained with tears.

As he swung himself into the small, boxlike shelf, he had Jimmy in his arms in a second.

"I couldn't get down," Jimmy murmured against his father's shirt. "I was fine climbing up, but I couldn't get down."

"Its okay, Jimmy." Ewen soothed his son as he sat and eased his Jimmy down beside him. For a moment he simply sat with his arm around the boy while his breathing steadied, then Ewen leaned back and looked up at the very top of the mast. Close by they could see the tops of the riggings, but beyond that was a vast expanse of sky. "I can see why you wanted to come up." Ewen smiled. "It's glorious up here . . . like you're in heaven."

"Aye . . . it's the closest I could get to Mam." Jimmy spoke quietly. "Without dying myself."

They sat quietly for a while, then Ewen pointed out to the starboard side of the boat. "Have you seen that ship before?"

Jimmy squinted, then he shook his head. "I've seen others, but I don't think I've seen that one. They all look the same from a distance."

"Aye . . . but have you noticed how we've passed quite a few ships on this voyage? We're out here on this huge ocean, but there's always one close by." Ewen indicated the horizon. "I get the feeling that death is a bit like that. We say good-bye when someone dies, and they go away like a ship going over the horizon, but then . . . you catch glimpses of them sometimes . . . just to reassure you that they're still there."

"I do think Mam's near." Jimmy bit at his bottom lip. "But I still miss her."

"Oh, Jimmy . . ." Ewen laid his head against his son's. "I miss her too . . . so much." A few minutes later, he almost smiled as he gave his son a tight hug with one arm. "I wish we'd thought of coming up here sooner. It does feel like we're closer to her, doesn't it?"

"Mmm." Jimmy stared up at the sky. "I've been talking to her for a while." He ducked his head. "Nobody else can hear up here."

Ewen sat silently as the tears began to run down his own cheeks. He hadn't let anybody see him cry since Bess had passed, but now he let the tears flow as his chest heaved.

"Oh, Jimmy . . . do you think she hears you?"

Jimmy sat for a long time before he nodded. "Aye . . . I do."

They stayed for a while longer before Ewen moved to ease himself up. He smiled at his son.

"You know Fiona will be jealous when we tell her we were talking to Mam."

"No, she won't . . . she has Lauryn now," Jimmy answered immediately. "She's forgotten Mam already."

"Why do you say that?" Ewen frowned.

"She hardly talks about Mam at all anymore. She just wants to be with Lauryn."

Ewen rested his hand on his son's shoulder. "How do you know she doesn't talk to Lauryn about Mam?" He made Jimmy look at him. "Besides, people deal with things differently, and girls talk to girls and men talk to men." He smiled. "You know you can always talk to me, Jimmy, and if I'm not around then you can always talk to Heavenly Father."

"Aye . . ." Jimmy nodded. "I've not been doing that, but Mam says I should." He took a quick look down, then he stared up at the sky. "See you, Mam."

* * *

"WHY DO THEY CALL IT the crow's nest?" Fiona sat quietly on Lauryn's bunk the next evening while Lauryn gently stroked her long red hair, gradually easing the knots out. It was a routine they'd established since the little girl had been spending more and more time with Lauryn and Lady Farnsworth.

"I heard it had something to do with crows." Lady Farnsworth chuckled. "Apparently, crows hate water, so when the captain thought the ship might be near land, he'd let a crow go from up there and watch which direction it flew to get to the nearest land."

"But how would it know if it couldn't see it?" Fiona frowned. "That doesn't make sense."

"Lots of things don't make sense, but they work somehow." Lauryn smiled as she began to braid the long strands of hair again. "So, did your father tell you about our plans when we get to Lyttleton?"

"Yes . . . that we're going to stay there and that you and Francis are going to live close by for a while so we can visit." Fiona looked around. "He said that you are going to marry Edward soon, and then we might live really close by all the time."

Lauryn smiled as she nodded. "It won't be for a while, but would you like to have a new dress when we get married . . . and be my bridesmaid?"

"Oh yes." Fiona's eyes widened. "I will be very good."

"Of course you will, dear—" Lady Farnsworth suddenly fell to the floor as Lauryn and Fiona rolled sideways while the ship took a massive swing to the left.

"Oh no . . . not another storm!" Lauryn pulled Fiona against her and held to the side of the bunk.

"And where did it come from?" Lady Farnsworth pulled herself up and clung to the wooden edge of the bunk. "We were just rolling before."

She gasped as the ship shuddered then slammed down, causing all of the beams to groan and loose objects to fly across the cabin. Fiona screamed as she buried her face against Lauryn.

"Where's Daddy?" She kept her arms around Lauryn's waist. "He went upstairs with Jimmy."

Lauryn shook her head as she looked at Lady Farnsworth. Edward and Ewen had gone up to help fix some rigging more than an hour ago, and Jimmy had gone with them. Some of the crew had abandoned ship at Cape Town, so extra help was required from some of the passengers. It had been a routine job, but they hadn't expected any rough weather.

"Jimmy!" Lauryn reached out as Jimmy appeared in the doorway, clutching at both sides of the frame as the ship lifted again.

"It came out of nowhere . . ." His face was white as chalk. "A huge wave . . . Dad pushed me down the stairs to get out of the way." His voice came in a sob as he pushed himself over to the bunk and held on. "They have to get the sails down or everything will break."

Lauryn's eyes widened in horror as he spoke. At the same moment the prow pitched forward almost at a right angle, sending them all across the cabin and into a torrent as water crashed through an opening in the cabin walls.

In that moment all Lauryn could think of was Edward and Ewen.

"Rath de ort," she whispered against Fiona's forehead. "God be with them."

* * *

It had begun as a distinct sinking feeling as they were fixing the rigging and changing some sails. Edward had noticed it first as the ship began to dip very slowly. When he'd looked to the leeward side, the breath had stopped in his chest.

"Rogue wave!" The voice had been an absolute scream behind them as one of the crew pointed and began to run toward the cabins. "Rogue wave!"

"Down the sails! Down the sails!" the captain had cried with a scream-like urgency as he gestured furiously from the bridge.

"Down, Jimmy . . . get downstairs!" Ewen had said urgently. "Go to Fiona!"

"No, Dad!" Jimmy's voice had been frozen in fear as he looked behind his father at the gathering wall of water. "I want to stay with you!"

Ewen had used his strength to force his son down the stairs, then he had lurched his way back to Edward, joining three other crewmen as they hurriedly hauled on the ropes to pull down the sails.

The wave was almost upon them now, mounting as it moved toward them, and the ship seemed to suck downward, hard. Then an enormous, towering wall of water rose like a sheer, green cliff with a foam of white trembling along its crest.

"Don't look!" One of the crewmen yelled as he pulled frantically on the ropes. "Just hold onto the rigging!"

"We're going over!" Another crewman began to sob as the boat slowly listed onto its port side.

"It's coming." Edward pulled Ewen with him against the cabin and braced himself with the rope around his waist. Ewen did the same, and they had time for a quick glance before the wave struck.

The force was unimaginable, and Edward felt the ship shudder as if it would surely break apart. He heard the mast groan as it bowed beneath the sheer volume of water, and the remaining sails folded like a lace handkerchief around the rigging. Then the water was pinning him to the cabin side, exerting a pressure that seemed to be squeezing the very life out of his body. His fingers strained to keep their grip on the rope and on the edge of the door as the wave crashed into them and through them.

Out of the corner of his eye he saw Ewen gripping onto the edge of the small boat, his face white with effort as the torrent of water sucked around his body . . . and then he was gone.

"Ewen!" Edward's voice was a scream that hovered in the air as the wave surged past, leaving an unnatural silence in its wake.

* * *

"EWEN!" EDWARD EXERTED ALL HIS strength to move forward against the list of the ship, pulling himself against the cabin as he desperately searched for his friend. "Ewen!" He strained to see the railing, hoping that the wave had trapped Ewen against the side of the boat, but there was nothing except one crewman lying on the deck groaning and holding his leg.

"Dear God . . . why?" Edward sank to the deck as the ship slowly righted itself like a specter rising from the grave. The water flowed around him in a shallow river as it coursed over the deck, and he felt the agony rise in a sob from his stomach. "No!" He slammed his fist against the deck. "Not Ewen as well!"

He heard the cries of the passengers beginning to mount as the boat fully righted itself, and several people ventured up onto the deck, nervously looking around, but Edward lay where he was, numbed as he repeated his friend's name.

"'Twas a rogue wave . . . I've never seen the like of it before." The captain was speaking above his head to one of the passengers. "We're lucky to have made it through."

"Did we lose anyone?"

"I don't think so . . . I don't know, yet." The captain's voice was strained. "There were a number on deck."

"Will the doctor take a roll call, then?"

Edward seemed to hear the voices as if in a tunnel, and he tried to raise his hand, but nobody was listening. "Ewen's gone . . ." he tried to tell them, but nobody would hear.

* * *

"Edward . . . Edward . . . can you hear me?"

The voice was soft, like a breeze softly brushing over fields of flowers.

"Edward?"

He turned his head to the breeze and felt it rest against his cheek, cool and gentle.

"It may take a while for him to come around. And we don't know if he was actually hit by anything." The other voice was deep and mellow. "Or it may be shock."

"Do you think he knows . . . about Ewen?"

The breeze pressed against his cheek then, and he tried to get away from it.

"Edward . . . it's all right."

But it wasn't all right. He struggled to get away from the wave as it loomed overhead.

"Ewen!"

"Edward . . . it's gone now. The wave's gone. You're safe." The voice was soft but urgent.

"Ewen . . . no . . . not Ewen too."

Lauryn sat still with her hand on Edward's cheek as the sobs racked his body. She looked up at Dr. Appleby, and he nodded his head. Edward had been unconscious since they'd found him on deck and brought him to the infirmary, and Lauryn had stayed with him while a frantic search both on board and overboard had failed to find any sign of Ewen.

The captain had ordered Jimmy and Fiona to stay in the cabin with Lady Farnsworth, and now Lauryn stared at the doctor as the reality set in.

"Ewen's gone." Her face contorted as she pressed a hand to her forehead. "They're both gone. What are the children going to do?" She gently took Edward's limp hand in her own and laid her cheek against it. "Oh, Edward . . . please, come back soon."

* * *

"HE'S GONE." JIMMY SPOKE so quietly that Lady Farnsworth wasn't sure if he had said anything.

She stopped wringing the water out of a shawl and looked at him with a gentle smile. "We don't know what's happening up there, Jimmy. The captain just said to stay downstairs in case there was another wave." She gave the shawl a tight squeeze. "We'll know soon enough if it's safe."

She swallowed with difficulty as she deliberately lied. The captain had told her that there was no sign of Ewen, but they wanted time to do a full search overboard.

Fiona looked up from the book she was reading. "Dad will be helping. He's such a good helper, and if the boat is broken then they'll need him to fix it. He's a shipbuilder." She frowned as if they should have known this information and went back to the book.

Lady Farnsworth nodded at the child's ability to explain things away, but she knew from the look on Jimmy's face that he wasn't accepting this explanation.

"He's gone . . . in the wave." He pulled his knees up to his chest and wrapped his arms around his legs. "And probably Edward too."

"They'll both be helping, Jimmy. That's what they do," Fiona said as she continued reading. "You'll see."

Lady Farnsworth watched the boy's face and felt helpless as she realized, with a jolt, that the children were now orphans. She turned back and slowly placed the shawl on the bed then reached for a larger, sodden blanket.

"Jimmy, can you help me with this please?' She made as if the blanket was extra heavy. "We need to wring this out and get all the water into the basin." She indicated the tin basin on the floor. "You hold onto the other end, and we'll twist in opposite directions."

"I can do it." Fiona promptly put the book down, but Lady Farnsworth shook her head.

"I need a man's help with this, thank you, dear." She held the end of the blanket out to Jimmy, and he got up slowly from the bunk and took it in his hand.

"At the same time, dear. Twist it hard."

Jimmy's face furrowed in a deep frown as he began to turn the blanket in his hands. They kept turning in silence until the blanket tightened into a long twisted rope with the water streaming out of it. Just when Lady Farnsworth thought they'd done enough, she saw Jimmy's jaw set, and he began to twist the ends even harder, his fingers gripping the fabric and turning white with the effort. Suddenly the fabric wouldn't twist anymore, and he held it with clenched fists as long as he could then dropped it with a sob.

"Jimmy." Lady Farnsworth stepped to him and put her arms around him as he stood unresisting, his arms hanging at his sides.

"He is gone . . . and Mam. They're both gone now."

* * *

"WE WERE SO CLOSE TO New Zealand." Edward closed his eyes again and shifted his head restlessly on the pillow. "A few more days and he would have been safe."

Lauryn nodded silently. Edward had regained consciousness after two hours, but it had seemed like eternity as she sat and wondered what the future held. Now he was awake, and the horror of what had happened was renewed as she watched him relive it.

"I need to see the children." Edward struggled to get up but swayed as he sat upright.

"Just give it a minute, Edward." Dr. Appleby moved forward and put a hand on his shoulder. "The children are with Francis, and I'll send down for them shortly." He squeezed his shoulder briefly. "You need to be stable before you talk to them."

"Yes . . . yes," Edward murmured as he closed his eyes again and shook his head to clear it. "It was so quick . . . Jimmy was . . ." He stopped and looked at Lauryn. "Is Jimmy all right?"

Lauryn glanced at the doctor, then she nodded. "Jimmy is with Mam and Fiona. He got a fright, but he didn't get hurt."

"And now we have to tell him he has no parents." Edward's shoulders slumped. "He didn't want to leave his dad. He wanted to stay with him."

"And then they would have both been lost." Lauryn spoke quietly. "Ewen did the right thing. He saved his son."

Edward nodded, but Lauryn could see the pain in his face. He stared at the floor for a long time before finally looking up at the doctor.

"Can we see them now, Michael?"

* * *

EDWARD SLOWLY STOOD UP BEFORE the children arrived, then he leaned against the table as they walked in behind Dr. Appleby.

"The doctor says you have something to talk to us about." Jimmy looked directly at Edward as soon as he walked into the room. "But I already know."

Edward took a deep breath as he nodded. "I thought you might, Jimmy." He indicated toward Fiona, who had gone straight over to Lauryn. "Would you mind if I had a word with Fiona?"

Jimmy nodded, but he didn't watch as Edward went and knelt beside Fiona.

"Fiona . . . in the storm, your dad was doing a fine job helping with the sails, but that huge wave . . . it was bigger than we could cope with, and your dad . . ." His voice broke, but he quickly coughed and took hold of her hand. "Your dad couldn't hold on when the wave came, Fiona. He got carried away with it."

There was a long silence as Fiona stared at him, then she slowly withdrew her hand and wrapped her arms around Lauryn, burying her face against her dress. They couldn't hear her crying, but her body began to shudder as she clung to the dress.

"So what do we do now?" Jimmy's voice was a monotone as he looked squarely at Edward and Lauryn. "Now that we're orphans."

Lauryn suddenly knew what Edward was going to say as he turned to look at her, and there was no hesitation as she nodded. Then she felt a rush of relief as he said the very words she had prayed he would.

"You can stay with us, Jimmy." Edward didn't hesitate as he met Jimmy's gaze. "Lauryn and I are going to get married and we'd like to care for you and Fiona from now on." He gritted his jaw. "You had fine parents, Jimmy, and they were true friends. We'd be honored if you'd let us look after you and Fiona now."

Lauryn watched as the muscle in Jimmy's jaw worked hard, then he gave a slight nod, though he remained perfectly still, his hands at his side.

"We'll need to get our things packed, then." His face was absolutely calm as he turned to Fiona then walked to her and tapped her on the shoulder. Only then did she raise a tearstained face to look at him.

"Fiona . . . come and pack your things. We're going to stay with Lauryn and Edward now that Mam and Dad have gone."

There was something so mechanical about the way he spoke that Lauryn almost wanted to shake him, but she could see that he was handling things in his own way. Fiona, however, looked up at Lauryn, and she almost smiled.

"So you're going to be my mam?" She wiped her nose with her hand as she looked at Lauryn expectantly, but it was Jimmy who spoke first, his monotone replaced by a harshness beyond his years.

"She's not your mam, Fiona . . . and you mustn't ever forget that."

* * *

"I'm sorry I didn't ask you first, Lauryn." Edward put his hand over hers as they walked slowly along the deck late that night. It was hard to believe that the nearly silent ship could possibly be the same setting of such tragedy so short a time ago. Even the ocean was eerily still as the boat cleaved through the waves with a firm breeze behind it. The sky was clear, and countless stars shone above them.

Lauryn tightened her grip on his arm. "You asked me in your look, Edward." She nodded. "While you were unconscious I was hoping that we would be able to look after them, so when you said it, it was an answer to my prayers." She leaned against his arm. "What happened, Edward?"

"With Ewen?"

She nodded, and he took a deep breath.

"The wave was so . . . huge, and then it hit, and the pressure . . . I thought my body was going to collapse, and I was trying to hold on, and Ewen was . . . and then he was just . . . gone." His voice caught. "It happened so fast, Lauryn. I can only hope it was quick for him . . . that he didn't have time to think."

She stopped then and turned to face him, studying the grief reflected in his face.

"It's those that are left that will do the thinking." She gave a smile that wasn't meant to be happy. "Our job will be to help the children remember the joy and try to forget the pain."

Edward nodded as he drew her close and buried his face against her hair.

"I thought I had learned to do that, but now I feel like I'm starting all over again."

"But now we can learn together." She touched his face gently, and he looked up. "Together, Edward."

"Together." He nodded and bent his head to kiss her with a softness that sealed their promise.

Chapter Twenty-Six

Lyttleton Harbor, South Island, New Zealand, 1849
"See You, Jimmy."

FOR THE FINAL TWO NIGHTS of the voyage before they reached Lyttleton Harbor, Edward stayed down in steerage with Jimmy while Fiona stayed with Lauryn in Edward's cabin with its extra bunk.

No more mention was made about the tragedy as everyone became caught up in the frantic pace of packing up as the majority of passengers prepared to disembark. A small group had already left the boat farther south at Port Chalmers, but most were beginning their new life in Canterbury.

Lauryn stood with Fiona and Lady Farnsworth on the deck as the crew hauled large wooden and tin trunks out of the hold with a system of ropes, pulleys, and sheer strength.

"Oh, that's ours!" Fiona pointed to a large wooden trunk with the name E. J. McALISTER stenciled on the side and top. In the same instant, her face crumpled, and she leaned against Lauryn. "That's Daddy's name."

Lauryn swallowed hard as she looked at Lady Farnsworth. There would be another difficult time ahead when they had to unpack Ewen and Bess's belongings with the children.

"Yes, that is your dad's name, Fiona, and isn't it grand that you'll have that trunk to remember him by, for always."

Fiona nodded, but she put a handkerchief, which had become her constant companion, up to her face. It was a plain cotton lawn square that had her mother's initials carefully worked in lilac thread in the corner, and she seemed to find comfort in holding it close to her cheek.

"Where are Edward and Jimmy?" Lady Farnsworth was scrutinizing the movement of the trunks carefully, but she glanced at Lauryn. "I thought they were joining us on deck."

"They're meant to be." Lauryn nodded as she looked back to the stairwell, but there was no sign of either Edward or Jimmy. "I imagine it's bedlam downstairs, and they'll have to wait their turn, but handling Jimmy was proving a bit difficult."

"He really is taking it hard, isn't he?" Lady Farnsworth sighed. "Not that he's openly naughty, but he just seems to be closing us all out . . . except Edward."

"But even Edward is struggling." Lauryn shook her head. "He said that last night he heard Jimmy crying, but when Edward went to him, he simply wouldn't speak to him."

Lady Farnsworth nodded. "He is also twelve, and that's a difficult time for any boy . . . let alone the fact that he's lost his father and mother." She sighed. "I have no problem with looking after the children when we go to the homestead, but I do fear what Jimmy will do when Edward carries on to Sydney." She glanced at Lauryn. "You have told him that's what is happening?"

Lauryn nodded as she rested her hands on Fiona's shoulder.

"We told him last night, and he went even quieter than usual." She looked up at the sky. "Then he wanted to know why Edward was going and for how long and whether he was actually coming back."

"So the poor child is worried he's going to lose somebody else." Lady Farnsworth nodded. "That is understandable . . . but I'm not sure it'll help us cope here in New Zealand."

Lauryn stared into the distance. "Oh, Mam . . . this was going to be such an adventure for the two of us—going on a ship and moving to the other side of the world—and look at us now. I'm going to be married, and we have two children already and a series of tragedies and experiences that will stay with us for life."

"And we've only just begun." Lady Farnsworth nodded. "We're not even off the boat yet, so imagine what lies ahead."

"I really don't think I want to yet." Lauryn shook her head as she gazed toward the cluster of buildings that was the port of Lyttleton and then at the bush-covered hills that rose behind it like granite guardians to the land that lay beyond.

* * *

JIMMY WAS SITTING AT THE very back of the top wooden bunk when Edward found him, though in the darkness of the cabin it was almost impossible to make out his shape. A tin trunk sat open on the floor beside the bunks.

"What are you doing, Jimmy?" Edward asked quietly. "We need to get your things up on deck."

When there was no response, he placed his hands on the middle wooden beam and pulled himself up onto the bunk, ducking his head to fit into the narrow enclosure. As his eyes adjusted to the darkness he saw that Jimmy had a wooden box sitting beside him on the bed. The lid was open, and he was holding a long, slim dagger in his hand. A spot of blood was slowly forming a dark patch on a tartan blanket.

"Jimmy . . . what are you doing?" Edward felt his heart skip a beat as he edged closer. "What is that you've got?"

"'Tis *sgian dubh*." Jimmy spoke quietly. "It slipped when I was cutting." His hand tightened around the dagger. "My dad was going to teach me how to use it . . . when we got to New Zealand." He swallowed. "He said that every Highland boy needed to know how to use it so that he can protect his family and provide for them." His face crumpled. "But now he can't . . ."

Edward's throat tightened as he leaned toward Jimmy and touched the steel shaft of the dagger.

"It's a fine knife, Jimmy . . . and if you'll let me, I think I can teach you how to use it. My dad had one that he taught me how to use. It wasn't anywhere near as fine as this, but I learned to use it well." He didn't look at the boy. "Would you let me teach you, Jimmy?"

Jimmy didn't answer straightaway, but he lifted the tartan and used the knife to make a series of small cuts in the fabric. His hands were trembling, and Edward held his breath as he eased forward.

"Jimmy . . . can you show me what you're doing?" Edward asked quietly, but Jimmy kept his head down.

"'Tis my father's kilt." He bit at his lip. "I need to give half to Fiona."

"You need to . . . ?" Edward stopped as he tried to think what was going through the boy's head.

"She'll need to keep it . . . in case I don't come back."

"Come back?" Edward laid his hand on the knife to stop Jimmy from cutting. "Where are you going, Jimmy?"

"I'm coming with you." Jimmy still didn't look up. "I'm not staying here. My dad said that I should always stay with men who will make me be better . . . who I can trust." He finally looked up, straight at Edward. "You're the only one I know to trust, Edward. I have to come with you."

"Oh, Jimmy . . ." Edward couldn't speak as he watched the boy's eyes fill with tears.

"I'll help you, Edward. I can do a man's work . . . my dad would want me to do that . . . and my mam."

Edward nodded as he reached up and touched the boy's head with his hand.

"And you're right, Jimmy. I will need help . . . lots of help."

* * *

THE SECOND LOAD OF PASSENGERS had already pulled away in the longboat when Edward and Jimmy finally arrived on deck, and Lauryn watched them carefully as they walked toward her, Jimmy with a length of tartan fabric rolled up in his arms and another piece slung over his shoulder. He had nothing else in his hands.

"Jimmy, where are your things?" Fiona stared at her brother. "We need to be taking everything ashore now."

"I know . . . my things are in the cabin." Jimmy straightened his shoulders. "I'll be staying on board now . . . and going to Sydney with Edward."

There was a long silence as Lauryn looked quickly at Edward. He returned her look directly with a slight nod and the ghost of a smile.

"But Jimmy . . . you have to come with me and Lauryn." Fiona finally frowned as if she'd worked the whole situation out. "You cannot go to Sydney." She shrugged. "You just can't."

"Yes, I can, Fiona." Jimmy took a step toward her and held out the folded tartan. "You'll need to keep this with you. 'Tis half of our dad's kilt. I have the other half. This way we'll each always have a part of Mam and Dad."

"Oh, Jimmy." Fiona took the tartan and held it up to her cheek, and Lauryn watched the child relax as she closed her eyes. "I think I can smell them."

"Aye, Fiona . . . you can." Jimmy nodded as he adjusted the kilt on his shoulder then looked up at Edward. "Now, should we see them ashore?"

Once they had settled in the boat, Lady Farnsworth sat forward with Fiona and Jimmy, and Edward sat with Lauryn nearer the back. As the crew slowly dragged on the oars, Lauryn took one last look at the ship that had carried them so many miles and through so many events.

She had difficulty swallowing as she stared up at the full lengths of the mast and rigging. With the sails all furled as the ship lay at anchor, it reminded her of a skeleton compared with the majesty of the vessel under full sail. "I never imagined—"

"None of us did," Edward interrupted her quietly as her voice caught and he took her hand in his.

"Our lives are never going to be the same." Lauryn laid her head against his shoulder. "The joy of it is that I will be sharing it all with you."

"Mmm . . . the joy." Edward stared ahead to the cluster of buildings that were gradually gaining definition along the shoreline. "My sister wrote to me I was allowed to find joy."

"Allowed?" Lauryn asked, puzzled, as he moved his arm around her waist and drew her even closer.

"Meaning, that I needed to allow myself to find it." Edward rested his head against hers. "Now it's all I can think of or feel with you."

Lauryn sat very still, feeling his heartbeat against her arm and loving the security that it gave her.

"Please come back soon, Edward." She looked straight ahead, determined to be strong but at the same time feeling a palpable emptiness.

"I will, Lauryn." He nodded as he stared at Jimmy's back. "Soon we'll be together, and nothing will take us apart again. I promise."

* * *

"Well, that was a sudden change of plans." Lady Farnsworth settled down on one of the trunks that had just been brought ashore and folded her hands in her lap. "Do you think they'll be all right?"

She raised her hand to shade her eyes as the longboat cast off from the dock, Edward and Jimmy its only passengers.

"I think they'll be fine." Lauryn watched as the boat rowed away from the dock. Then as Edward sat down and put his arm around Jimmy's shoulders, she nodded. "I know they'll be fine."

It had been a surprise when Jimmy had announced that he would sail with Edward to Sydney, but at the same time she had felt a calmness that seemed to be threading itself through her life the more time she spent with Edward.

She wrapped her arms around her body, treasuring the last embrace they'd shared before he got back into the boat . . . and the tenderness and trust she'd felt in his kiss.

"It won't be long." Lady Farnsworth spoke gently beside her as she laid a hand on the small of Lauryn's back. "I don't think they'll last six months."

"I hope not." Lauryn tried to smile, but her eyes glistened. "Is it wrong to love somebody that much . . . to want to be with them all the time?"

"Oh no, dear." Lady Farnsworth smiled. "The world would be a very boring place without that sort of love." She patted Lauryn's arm. "Now, you're going to have plenty to do looking after an old lady and a wee lassie." She pointed to where Fiona was sitting quietly on her father's trunk, her hand running back and forth over his initials as she stared out over the water toward the boat.

"Look Lauryn . . . they're waving!" Fiona suddenly scrambled up to stand on the box, stumbling a little as she pulled the length of red-and-green tartan tightly around her shoulders and began to wave her arm in wide sweeps. "They're waving to us." She glanced at Lauryn as the tears flowed down her cheeks. She smiled then turned back and half raised her hand.

"See you soon, Jimmy."

Chapter Twenty-Seven

Lyttleton, New Zealand, 1849
Under Southern Stars

"I HONESTLY CANNOT BELIEVE THAT that good-for-nothing nephew of mine would desert us like this!" Lady Farnsworth stood up for the fourth time in the last five minutes and began to pace the same path between the bunks. "But then, what else should I have expected? The boy has never done anything responsible in his life. That's why they sent him here—to teach him . . . or to lose him!" She put a hand to her forehead and huffed. "I always accused my brother of being foolish to trust him, and now I've made exactly the same mistake! I'm the fool now!"

Fiona sat quietly on the narrow wooden bunk and rocked while she watched Lady Farnsworth pace. "Maybe . . . your nephew just got lost," she ventured quietly, frowning. They had anticipated the arrival of young Mr. Farnsworth for nearly eight days before repeated questioning of the locals in the small settlement of Lyttleton had revealed that no one knew of him or of any property that he supposedly owned.

"Goodness knows what the boy has done with his father's money or where he's disappeared to." Lady Farnsworth began to twist the handkerchief she held in her hand. "And goodness knows what we three ladies are going to do." Her voice dropped to a low whisper that was quite uncharacteristic. "We have nothing."

She sank slowly onto the edge of the bunk, and without hesitation Fiona moved close beside her, placing her small hand gently on Lady Farnsworth's arm.

"We'll be fine, Mam." Her fingers traced the pattern of the lace cuff on the older woman's dress. "You'll see . . . Edward and Jimmy will come back and help us."

Lady Farnsworth glanced at the jumble of red hair that was nearly resting on her shoulder, then she shook her head. Fiona seemed to have a simple belief that whatever she thought should happen, would.

"You know, my dear . . . as nice as that would be, I really don't think we'll be hearing from Edward and Jimmy for some time. Even if we wrote to them now, a letter would take weeks to catch up with them." She leaned back and took a deep breath then took a long look around the whitewashed walls of their accommodations. They had already overstayed their allotted time of five days in the barracks and had had to plead for an extra few days in the hope of the vanished nephew turning up. She shook her head and pursed her lips.

"No, Fiona, we shall simply have to do what all the other families are doing in this godforsaken place. We will get some help and construct our own makeshift dwelling until we find some way of making a living over in Christchurch." She nodded as if making the decision more conclusive. "I'm certain there will be a need for educators of some sort, with all of these children arriving. That will have to suffice until I can get things organized from England."

"Yes, Mam," Fiona responded almost absently as she glanced at the doorway again. Lauryn had gone down to the wharf, but she'd been gone a while. "Do you think Lauryn will have found some men to help us do the building? She's been gone a long time."

"Oh, she'll be back shortly." Lady Farnsworth stood up again and held out her hand. "Shall we go and meet her, Fiona? She should be on her way back by now."

They had barely made their way out onto the long veranda that ran the length of the immigration barracks when they noticed a small contingency of women and children gathering in a group near the bottom steps. As the crowd moved slightly, Lady Farnsworth glimpsed the slim figure of a Mrs. Charlotte Godley standing in the center of the group, slightly apart from the others. Wife of the Canterbury immigration agent, John Godley, she often came down from her large house to visit the new colonists in the barracks. Her finely featured face was inclined toward a woman who was speaking to her. Then Lady Farnsworth heard a soft laugh as Mrs. Godley nodded her head.

"Oh, dear me . . . I think no vessel has come here without some trouble about it."

"But what can we do?" Another woman held up her hand to speak. "Our men came thinking there would be jobs, and now we're expected to pay such a price for a small piece of land . . ."

"And move onto it without even a house or such to live in!" another woman said loudly.

"Aye, how can I look after five children in nothing more than a bush shelter?" The first woman shook her head. "It's criminal. We'd never have come if we'd known it would be like this."

Mrs. Godley put her hand out to placate them, then she nodded toward the barren brown hills that rose sharply behind the settlement. A growing cluster of V-shaped huts and small, round-roofed sod houses clung to the hillside and along the side of the rough path that snaked its way steeply to the summit of the hill.

"I do understand your feelings." She attempted a small smile and pointed to the top of the hill. "You must realize that once you go up over the bridle path and down into Christchurch there will be plenty of opportunities for you and your husbands. Lyttleton was never meant to be your last stop. It is just the doorway to Canterbury and plenty of land." She gestured behind her to the barracks. "The buildings simply can't cope with all of you here, and another three ships will be arriving soon. You have to move on," she finished quietly, but Lady Farnsworth detected a note of firmness in her tone.

"And we will move on, shan't we, Fiona?" She placed her arm around the child's shoulders and pulled her gently in the direction of the dock. "I refuse to be a burden to anyone . . . especially since I got you all into this situation."

* * *

Lauryn took care to lift the hem of her dress as she walked toward the dock. One of the curses of the Lyttleton settlement, she had discovered, was the endless dust that seemed to hover in the air and which turned to a sticky mud when it rained. She raised a hand to shield her eyes as she looked out toward the ocean then quickened her stride. Another ship had just come in, and she had learned that there was a reasonably large company of working-class men aboard.

She bit on her lip as she reached the wooden boards of the dock and looked for a likely person to talk to. There seemed to be an unspoken camaraderie amongst the new settlers that if you spoke to the right person, you could usually get the help you needed, especially if you were a woman, since the men outnumbered the women at least two to one.

"Watch out, miss!"

Lauryn jumped as a voice called out right behind her, and she swung to the side to avoid a man pushing a large wheelbarrow. He gave her the briefest nod as he maneuvered past with a load of goods that threatened to topple to the ground. Somehow, he managed to keep the wheelbarrow stable as it bumped across the uneven ground and through the crowd of people gathering on the dock. The new arrivals all had the look that she had quickly become familiar with—eyes wide, staring at the brown hills and looking around for the houses and hotels that they had expected to rest in after three months at sea.

"And some of you will want our rooms at the barracks," Lauryn murmured to herself as she moved past the large group of working-class people. She had learned that the wealthier immigrants usually alighted last.

"Did ye hear 'bout the one that went down off Port Nicholson t'other night? Bound for Sydney, it was." The words seemed to echo above the noise of the crowd, and she turned toward the speaker, a bearded sailor who was hauling a large wooden chest onto the dock.

"Aye . . . heard nobody much made it." The man he was working with nodded with a grunt as he pushed the trunk another few inches. "Lost everything on board, too, though I heard there was quite a bit o' produce washed ashore, and people were grabbing it quick as they could."

Lauryn moved almost automatically toward the two men.

"Poor sods . . . should've stayed here 'stead of tryin' for the gold stuff over there in Australia." The first man scratched his head. "I'd rather be doin' anythin' here than lyin' at the bottom of the Strait."

Lauryn felt her blood run cold, and she tightened her shawl around her shoulders as she approached the two men.

"Excuse me . . ." She coughed slightly as they turned and looked her up and down. "I heard you . . . what ship would you be talking about . . . that sank . . . off Port Nicholson?"

"Aye . . . that'd be the *Victory*." The second man nodded. "Did ye know it?"

Lauryn felt the ground shift beneath her as she barely nodded. She stared at the gray clouds moving restlessly above their heads for a moment, then she looked at the two men.

"And you say there was nothing . . ."

"Not that I know of, miss." The man seemed to sense her distress, and his voice softened. "Did you know of somebody, miss?"

Lauryn found it difficult to breathe as she nodded once then turned her face to the wind that suddenly whipped across the dock. Its fierceness only served to blow the tears that now coursed down her cheeks as she took slow strides along the dock.

The *Victory* . . . where she'd spent the last three months of her life. Where she'd pledged her love to Edward, and now . . . it was gone?

"Ed . . ." Her lips froze around his name, refusing to say it.

"No!" Her cry was shrill as it mingled with the wind. "No . . . no . . . no!"

* * *

FIONA SAW HER FIRST AS she and Lady Farnsworth reached the dock. She recognized the pale blue of Lauryn's dress as the crowd of people gathered around the spot where she'd collapsed. Fiona let go of Lady Farnsworth's hand and rushed into the group, pulling at their arms to get through.

"Lauryn! Lauryn!" She sank down beside Lauryn and took hold of her hand, patting it as if that would coax the color back into Lauryn's white cheeks. Lady Farnsworth was right behind her. She gave a brief glance of gratitude to the woman who was cradling Lauryn's head then quickly took her place. She looked up, and a man answered her unspoken question.

"We was talkin' about the wreck off Port Nicholson . . . the *Victory*." He swallowed hard. "She said she knew someone . . ." He stopped as Lady Farnsworth interrupted.

"The *Victory*?"

"Aye, ma'am." The man nodded. "We just heard of 'er goin' down off t' Heads a couple o' days ago. There wasn't much left of her, t' be sure."

Lady Farnsworth glanced at Fiona, but the child seemed to have frozen, her eyes fixed straight ahead, as Lauryn's eyes flickered open.

"Fiona?" Her name was soft on Lauryn's lips as she focused then looked up at Lady Farnsworth. Her lip quivered. "Jimmy . . . and Edward." His name was a quiet moan as she turned her face against Lady Farnsworth and her shoulders began to heave.

* * *

SOMEHOW THEY GOT BACK TO the barracks, but once there, Lauryn fell on her bed and was unable to make herself move. There was no distinction between day and night as she lay completely still, struggling to comprehend what had happened.

It had been difficult enough to bid farewell to Edward knowing he would return in six months, but to think that he would never return . . . Her whole body felt as if it were slowly being drained of life as this thought took hold. She found that if she closed her eyes she could conjure up his image in her mind, and occasionally, as she recalled tender moments, a wistful smile was a brief preface to more tears.

She was unaware that Lady Farnsworth was bargaining for them to stay more nights in the barracks or that Fiona lay on a blanket on the floor beside her because it was closer than her bunk. Sometimes she felt the girl's small hand slip around her own and hold it gently.

There was barely any light in the room when Lauryn finally drew a deep breath and fully opened her eyes, blinking to adjust to the darkness then finding comfort in it. She moved her legs to get off the bed but felt her foot touch something solid.

"Fiona," she whispered as her voice refused to cooperate. "I'm sorry."

She wasn't sure if she meant about Jimmy or about accidentally bumping the child with her foot, but it didn't matter as Fiona only smiled before she got up off her knees and came to stand near Lauryn's pillow.

"Are you really awake, Lauryn?" Fiona's voice trembled slightly. "I've been praying that you would wake soon."

Lauryn stared at the ceiling for a second, then she managed a tight smile.

"Maybe you should have just shaken me." She cleared her throat. "Where is Mam?"

"She's up talking with Mrs. Godley." Fiona nodded in the direction of the Godleys' house. "She's trying to pay for us to stay extra nights here."

"But we're already over our limit." Lauryn struggled to get up onto her elbow. "We'll have to move . . ."

"She said that you're not going anywhere for now," Fiona interrupted, her eyes wide. "She said that there's a time and a place to pull out the noble connections, and this is definitely one of them."

The little girl had Lady Farnsworth's tone and accent almost perfect except for a slight Scottish lilt, and Lauryn actually smiled.

"Then I'd say we'll be all right for a night or two, but we must still prepare ourselves." She slowly swung her legs over the side of the bunk, deliberately forcing thoughts of Edward into the back of her mind. Part of her desperately wanted to hold on to any recollection of him while part of her wanted to erase all feeling. She shook her head as if to clear it.

"Do you need help?" Fiona held out her hand, but instead of using it to stand up, Lauryn covered it with her own and lifted it to her cheek. For a moment she felt only the warmth of Fiona's hand against her skin, then she looked straight into the child's bright blue eyes.

"Fiona, I'm so sorry . . . about Jimmy." Her voice faltered, and she held a sob in her throat. "But I'm glad he and Edward were . . . together."

Fiona stood still for a moment then cupped Lauryn's cheek in her hand.

"They're all together, now." She looked upward. "Jimmy and Da . . . and Mam and baby Bessie and my sisters . . . and Edward." She withdrew her hand slowly. "Heavenly Father will look after them."

Fiona's simple expression of faith seemed to cause a physical reaction in Lauryn. It was as if a part of her heart had suddenly died. She stood up slowly, and her lips were tight as she reached for her shawl.

"You may choose to believe that, Fiona, but I find it hard to accept, since God clearly could not even look after them here—where they were needed more." She drew the shawl around her shoulders and folded her arms across her chest.

Fiona's fingers tightened on her arm, then her lips finally trembled and she turned her head away.

After a moment Lauryn moved to her and gathered her close. "I'm sorry, Fiona . . . it's just that . . ."

"You miss Edward." Fiona nodded then raised her face to Lauryn. The moonlight made silvery tracks of the tears on her cheeks. "But we will see them again, Lauryn. Mam and Da said so."

* * *

THE BRIDLE PATH BANKED STEEPLY from the end of Oxford Street, and Lauryn was breathless within five minutes as she made her way up the rough track on her own. Several times she stumbled as she forced herself to walk quickly; the heat made her lungs clamor for air the higher she got. It soon hurt to breathe, but the pain was almost welcome as she lifted her head to keep her eye on the summit.

Their four-day concession at the barracks was over and, rather than attempt to build a temporary hut in Lyttleton, Lady Farnsworth had bargained tirelessly to attach the three of them to a party that would traverse the hills on the bridle path the next morning. Their trunks and bags were packed and ready to be hauled on a dray up the steep path, and they had arranged for two men to assist them even though the men had demanded far more than expected for recompense. Despite Lady Farnsworth's ample funds, they were becoming seriously depleted with the extra costs they were incurring.

Sitting in the stifling barracks room just waiting for the afternoon to pass had proven too much for Lauryn, and she had announced her intention to acquaint herself with the pathway. Lady Farnsworth had merely nodded as she'd watched her young friend walk quickly out onto the veranda and up the dusty street.

Several sharp bends in the path created something of a resting place just as Lauryn felt her breath give out. She sank down onto a large rock that seemed to have been placed there for the sole purpose of providing rest, then she leaned forward and lay her head in her hands. Within seconds the tears were back, and she let them fall for a while, now used to their unpredicted flow. It seemed she could tell her mind not to fret, but her heart had a direct connection to her tears.

"'One day they'll stop.'" She repeated Lady Farnsworth's words quietly to herself. "But right now I don't believe you." She lifted her face to the sky and watched some fluffy clouds moving quickly across the relentlessly blue backdrop. "And I don't believe Fiona." She tightened her jaw. "I don't believe that a kind God would let so much suffering happen."

A sudden sequence of scenes began running through her mind: her mother and father kneeling in prayer; she and her sisters walking to church together. Then she could see herself talking with Megan after she'd had her accident and Megan wanting to know if Lauryn had seen God while she was unconscious. Then she saw a conversation with her mother while they sat up in the oak tree, talking about Lauryn's dream of heaven after her accident.

I didn't want to leave there . . . But I think you prayed me back . . .

Are you sad that I did?

Lauryn drew a deep breath. "Am I sad that she did?" She placed both hands beside her temples as she recalled that feeling from her childhood. "Am I sad that she prayed me back? Am I sad that I ever met Edward? Would he have been sad if I'd prayed him back?"

"Lauryn!"

She started as his voice came so clearly in her thoughts that she pressed her hand to her heart. Would she always be able to sense him so close? It was a comfort that also made her miss him desperately.

"Lauryn!"

Her eyes flew open as the voice came from below her and not from her mind.

"Edward." She could barely whisper as she stared down at the figure running up the final bend in the path below her. "But . . ."

He didn't pause or speak as he reached her, gathering her tightly to him, his chest rising and falling against her as he tried to regain his breath and kiss her at the same time.

Then they were laughing together, still holding one another tightly as Edward managed to draw a long, deep breath then claim her lips properly. She didn't know how long they stayed like that. She didn't care. Edward was back.

"What happened?" She finally managed to speak, but he managed another quick kiss before he drew her down to sit on the rock. "Why are you here? How . . . ?"

"It's all Jimmy's fault." Edward kept hold of her hand and put his other arm around her shoulder so she could lean against him. "We were only out of Lyttleton a few hours, and he asked if we really had to go to Australia. I thought he was homesick for you and Fiona already, so I explained why we were going. Then he asked if Wellington wouldn't be a better place for us . . . all."

"All of us?" Lauryn frowned. "Why would he say that? He knew we were planning on settling here."

Edward shrugged. "Exactly, but the next day he asked again, and then I got talking to one of the men who had got on board at Lyttleton, and he convinced me that Wellington was a very good place to be setting up my business. I explained that I was also delivering cargo, and he said he was going to the same place in Sydney and that he could deliver it for me." Edward shook his head. "He was a well-respected man . . . I checked with the captain. So I agreed."

"So he was on board?" Lauryn asked quietly, and Edward nodded.

"Yes . . . unfortunately." He tightened his grip around her. "I'll always be grateful to him, but it won't bring him back."

"But you came back." Lauryn lifted her face to look up at him. The sun seemed to illuminate his features—or was it her happiness? "I'll always be so very grateful for that."

Edward put his hand up and touched her cheek. "I hope so, my Lauryn." He kissed her forehead gently. "We've been given a second chance, and I'm never going to leave you again."

* * *

"My da once said that we would find a grand new life under the southern stars." Jimmy leaned out to wrap the plaid kilt around Fiona's shoulders. She had hardly left her brother's side since he and Edward had returned, and as the night sky darkened and a cool breeze off the sea blew across the veranda, she cuddled even more closely against him.

Lauryn nodded thoughtfully as she stared up at the brilliant specks of light that glimmered high above them. She could now easily identify the group of stars the colonists called the Southern Cross, and somehow, now, with Edward beside her, it seemed more welcoming.

"Your da was right, Jimmy." She rested her hand on his shoulder as he sat on the veranda step beneath her. "And it became grand as soon as we were together again." She hesitated. "And it's thanks to you."

"And Edward," Jimmy responded quietly. "He listened."

They all sat in silence, occupied with their own thoughts, until Fiona pointed upward.

"Do you think that if we sit and look up at the stars, then Mam and Da will be looking down at us?"

It was Lady Farnsworth who spoke first. "I really don't see why they wouldn't be."

"I think they are." Jimmy's response was immediate and emphatic.

"And I believe you, Jimmy." Edward briefly laid his hand on Jimmy's red curls. "And you can be sure that they're very proud of their youngsters."

"Aye." Jimmy's quiet answer was a simple statement of fact, and as Lauryn laid her head back against Edward's shoulder she got a sense of what it was going to be like being this boy's mother. He would never do anything that wouldn't make his parents proud.

"Edward . . ." Jimmy didn't turn his head. "Can we have prayers before we go to bed?"

"Aye." Fiona followed immediately. "We have so very much to be thankful for—even though I knew you and Jimmy would come back."

Lauryn felt her body tense as she waited for Edward's response. It was only yesterday that she had decided quite conclusively that God either didn't exist, or at least didn't care about them at all. She suddenly found it difficult to reconcile the simple faith of the children with her own feelings.

Edward glanced at Lauryn, then turned to Jimmy and nodded. "I think we should, Jimmy." He leaned his head against Lauryn's. "And I think you should say it for us . . . the first one for our new family."

"Um . . . can I just ask a question?" Lady Farnsworth cleared her throat as she took Fiona's hand and held it on her lap. Surprisingly, her voice had a slight tremble to it as she looked at them all. "Might I invite myself into your new family? I certainly have no one here, and I'm sure I could be quite a useful grandmother . . ." Her voice caught, and in an instant, Fiona's arms were wrapped tightly around her neck.

"Of course you will be." She settled herself on Lady Farnsworth's lap then nodded at her brother. "You can say the prayer now, Jimmy, and be sure and tell Heavenly Father that we're glad to be going to live in Wellington and that we're so happy to have Edward and Lauryn and Mam and . . ." She hesitated, and a tiny smile hovered on her lips as she folded her arms and lowered her head. "The new puppy that wants to join our New Zealand family too."

* * *

MAM TOOK THE CHILDREN INTO the barracks to settle for the night, so Edward took Lauryn by the hand and they began to walk slowly down to the dock, comfortable in the silence between them. When they reached the place where Lauryn had heard of the sinking of the *Victory*, she stopped and drew her shawl tightly around her shoulders as her whole body shuddered.

"This is where I thought I had lost you forever." She barely whispered the words so that Edward had to lean closer to hear. "When the man said the *Victory* had gone down . . ." She stopped and stared out at the black ocean. "I could not think of my life without you."

"But I did come back." Edward stood behind and wrapped his arms firmly around her.

Lauryn nodded slightly then rested her head back against his shoulder.

"I blamed God for taking you from me."

"I can imagine that." Edward responded quietly. "I've noticed you tell people what you think . . . so you probably wouldn't stop with God."

"You make me sound awful." Lauryn detected a lighter tone in his voice and she turned in the circle of his arms. "And maybe I really am."

"Awful?" Edward studied her face. "Headstrong . . . willful . . . determined . . ." He shook his head. "But never awful."

"But I blamed God. I may even have cursed Him." She frowned. "The thing that troubles me is that, for years, I have refused to acknowledge that God really exists because I have seen so much pain and suffering and it annoyed me that He wouldn't stop it."

"Many people feel that way." Edward was very still.

"But don't you see, I am actually acknowledging God exists when I tell Him off." Lauryn shook her head. "I don't want to be like that, especially when Jimmy and Fiona have such faith in . . . Him." She finished quietly then looked up at Edward. "What is it going to be like to rear the children when I don't feel the same way as they do? Will they end up disliking me?"

"They'll never dislike you, Lauryn." Edward gathered her tightly against him, sensing her real concern. "They'll just do what they do already . . . live what they believe and hope that we'll begin to believe as well." He paused. "Because I'm the same as you. I lost all faith that God existed when I thought my father was treating us badly and then when Lizzy and our child died, but I was still telling Him off like He was there . . . and listening to me."

Lauryn bit on her lip as she slowly nodded. "I wish I had my mother's faith. Nothing ever shook her from believing that God was there, and no matter what was wrong around her, the smallest thing made her grateful that He had remembered her." She managed a rueful smile. "It used to annoy me, and now I face the prospect of raising two children with the same strong belief."

They were both silent for a while, the only sound the waves lightly lapping against the wooden piles of the jetty, then Lauryn gave a short laugh.

"Actually, I can't be that bad because when you came back I did thank God for bringing you back to me."

Edward smiled. "And I did the same thing when I realized how Jimmy and I might have been drowned and that I would be with you again." He rested his head against Lauryn's. "So we do actually believe in God . . ."

"When it's convenient." Lauryn finished for him then smiled as he took her hand and led her down the jetty. "I think the children are going to have their hands full in rearing us."

"Well, they'll have help because Jimmy assures me he talks to God and his parents daily." Edward tightened his grip on her hand as he stared up at the sky. "He actually showed me some verses in that Book of Mormon of his the night before he convinced me to stay in Wellington. It said something like if we would only read about God then ask Him, sincerely and with faith, that He would manifest the truth to us." He hesitated. "By the power of the Holy Ghost."

"My *máthair* always said that." Lauryn tried to keep her tone light as she drew closer to him. "But I was never too ready to trust a ghost. It was easier to just trust my *máthair* and rely on her faith."

"Oh, my Lauryn." Edward chuckled slightly as he put his arm around her shoulders. "We're so much the same, and I almost hesitate to say this, but I think God did answer both our prayers."

"Because we're here . . . together?" She knew immediately what he meant.

Edward nodded before he pointed up to the star-ridden sky. "I find it really hard to comprehend a God that knows us . . . but the more I've thought about it, the more thoughts . . . dreams . . . I've had lately that make me think He does." He hesitated. "I had bad feelings about my father most of my grown-up life, but just the last few days I've been thinking about him and . . . it's hard to explain, but it's like I've softened . . . like

I understand what he went through now and I want him to know. I want him to feel the same about me." His voice caught with emotion. "Lauryn, I honestly have felt that if I tell God about how I feel then somehow my father will know."

"And forgive you?" Lauryn asked quietly then put her arm around his waist as he nodded.

"I can't deny the peace I feel with the children . . . because of their faith."

"I think I envy them," Lauryn added quietly.

"Maybe we can ask sincerely . . . together." Edward looked down at her.

"With faith." She searched his face, loving the features that had become so dear to her. "I never thought I'd say that, but it seems like my resolve has turned upside down just like my world has."

"We can both make a new start under the southern stars." Edward smiled.

He kissed her then, slowly and strongly, sealing his promise.

ABOUT THE AUTHOR

Grace Elliot is a native of Auckland, New Zealand, and resides there with her husband, Paul. They are the parents of five children. Grace graduated from Auckland University with a double major in English and Geography and also has a master's in Creative Writing. Teaching at BYU's Education Week and at other venues, she has lectured in personal and family history writing, family and marriage relations, religious philosophy, and fashion design. She has had several articles published in the *New Era, Friend,* and *Ensign,* and is the South Pacific editor for the *Ensign.* Grace has also written film scripts for the LDS audience, including an adaptation of the movie *Legacy.* All of her books are set against the scenic background of New Zealand and the expansive South Pacific.